The Sweetest Days

The Sweetest Days

John Hough Jr.

GALLERY BOOKS

New York   Toronto   London   Sydney   New Delhi

Gallery Books
An Imprint of Simon & Schuster, Inc.
1230 Avenue of the Americas
New York, NY 10020

First Gallery Books hardcover edition June 2021

GALLERY BOOKS and colophon are registered trademarks of Simon & Schuster, Inc.

For information about special discounts for bulk purchases, please contact Simon & Schuster Special Sales at 1-866-506-1949 or business@simonandschuster.com.

The Simon & Schuster Speakers Bureau can bring authors to your live event. For more information or to book an event, contact the Simon & Schuster Speakers Bureau at 1-866-248-3049 or visit our website at www.simonspeakers.com.

Interior design by Jaime Putorti

Manufactured in the United States of America

10 9 8 7 6 5 4 3 2 1

Library of Congress Cataloging-in-Publication Data is available.

ISBN 978-1-9821-5956-6
ISBN 978-1-9821-5958-0 (ebook)

For Marjorie Merklin and Bob Schwartz,
in equal measure

part one

one

We were waiting at the light by Bagel Heaven and the Shell self-serve when Jackie told me to stop at the liquor store up ahead, PJ's Wine & Spirits. There was a good bar in the motel and I didn't think we needed a bottle in our room, but then I wasn't the one who had cancer.

"Maker's," she said, "or Jim Beam Black."

"Which?" I said.

"Either. No: Maker's."

A Ford Bronco was parked in front of PJ's, its owner inside the store, a big swart guy in a Bruins hat. He'd lifted a case of Sam Adams onto the counter and was digging out his wallet. Saturday, midday, July still young. A radio in the back room was broadcasting the Red Sox pregame show. A kid in an apron was loading six-packs of beer into the cooler at the other end of the room. I pulled down a fifth of Maker's Mark. The customer lugged his beer out, shouldering through the glass double door, and the man at the register watched me come toward him with the Maker's. He was smiling.

"Pete Hatch," he said.

I stopped. It took a moment. "Well, damn," I said.

"You don't change, star," Walter Cummings said.

It happens every time I run into someone from high school: my heart catches, and I look for curiosity in back of the smile, a certain tilt of the head, a question forming. It's a reason I don't often go home, maybe *the* reason. But Walt Cummings's smile was unmitigated, his day merely brightened by my arrival, and I relaxed.

"You don't change, either," I said untruthfully.

"Like hell I don't. Too much beer. I shouldn't be working in a liquor store."

I set the bottle down, and we shook hands. Walt had been on the jayvee when I was a senior, a happy-go-lucky kid, skinny for football. But he hit hard and Coach Maguire had put him on the varsity kick-off team because he could fly downfield nearly as fast as the football, agile and slippery when they tried to block him. He'd also played some defense when the situation warranted a fleet safety. He'd gotten heavy—who would have thought?—but the bucktoothed grin was the old Walt, the bullet head and tight curls, gone gray now. He scanned the bottle of Maker's.

"I heard you were down in Washington," he said. "Working for Powell, I heard."

"I was," I said. "I'm out in western Mass now. Northampton."

A woman in dark glasses and a black two-piece bathing suit came in. A placard on the door said *Shoes and proper attire required,* and she could not have missed it. She was sun-browned and fleshy, scraping along in flip-flops. She looked pretty good, but ten or fifteen years ago she'd have caused traffic accidents in that bathing suit. She'd come from the beach, and her chestnut hair was damp and tangled, giving her a look of wantonness and abandon. You could imagine licking the salt off her skin.

She granted us a smile, appreciating the attention we were paying her, and went slowly down the nearest aisle with her purse hanging off her smooth bronze shoulder. The kid crouching in front of the cooler watched her as she stood pondering the vodkas. We all did.

Walt finally tore his gaze from her, gave me a wink and a smile, and reached below the counter for a paper bag.

"Why'd you leave Washington?" he said.

"I don't know," I said. "Tired of the life. I guess. What about you?"

"Never left town after the service. Dunstable's home, you know?"

I swiped my credit card and signed the slip. The woman had come back with a quart bottle of Absolut. She set the bottle on the counter. She looked at Walt, looked at me.

"What is this, old home week?" she said.

"High school buddies," Walt said. "We're catching up."

"How sweet."

"We were teammates," I said. "Football. Walt once intercepted a pass in the end zone, ran it back a hundred yards for a touchdown."

"I'm yawning," the woman said. "Tell me something interesting."

"I just did," I said.

"Tell her who you used to work for," Walt said.

"It won't impress her," I said.

"Probably not," she said.

"Senator Powell," Walt said.

The woman removed her dark glasses and considered me, wondering if it was true and deciding it was.

"Good for you," she said. "Brave new world. Black president, Black women in the House and Senate. Or do I say African American?"

"Senator Powell usually says Black," I said.

"She's a smart lady. Might be president herself someday. You should have stuck around, maybe get an office in the West Wing someday."

"A job came up, teaching," I said. "Seemed like a nice quiet change."

"Whereabouts?" Walt said.

"Smith College," I said.

"Yowza," said the woman. "My alma mater."

"Small world," I said.

"It's Pauline Powell's alma mater, come to think of it. She get you the job?"

"More or less."

The woman broke out a nice smile, my reward for being honest, then swung the smile to Walt. "Now, if you'll ring this bottle up, I've got a cookout to go to."

"BYOB?" Walt said.

"No, I just like to be prepared."

"*Semper paratus,*" I said.

"*In vino veritas.*" She began digging in her purse. She found her wallet. "What brings the prodigal home?"

Walt reached down for a bag. "Thirty-one eighty-nine," he said.

"Jesus," the woman said, "who sets these prices?"

"I'm giving a reading tonight," I said. "Signing books, I hope."

"Books?" Walt said.

"He's an author, apparently," the woman said.

"No shit," Walt said.

"A rookie author," I said. "A beginner."

"So was Faulkner, once," the woman said. She gave me another assessment. Nodded at what she saw. "Well, well. Come in to buy liquor, you never know what'll turn up. What did you say your name was?"

"I didn't."

"Pete Hatch," Walt said.

"The Village Bookstore, seven o'clock," I said. "I need all the help I can get."

"I'll try to get someone to cover for me," Walt said. "They got me scheduled till eleven tonight."

"I'll probably be three sheets to the wind by then," the woman said. "This book, you dishing the dirt on Pauline Powell?"

"There is no dirt on Pauline. It's a novel."

"A novel, then you ought to change your name. Or use a pen name. A novelist needs a name with two or three syllables. Updike. Dickens. Salinger. See what I mean?"

"What's she talking about?" Walt said.

"She's trying to prove she went to Smith," I said.

She smirked, fitted on her dark glasses, lifted the bottle in its bag and cradled it against an ample breast. She cast a farewell nod my way and moved with slow voluptuous dignity toward the door. She pushed through it sideways.

James Joyce, I thought, too late.

"She might actually come tonight," Walt said. "Your wife with you?"

"She's out in the car," I said.

"Uh-oh," Walt said. He looked out, squinting, found Jackie sitting there looking not too happy.

"I better go repair the damage," I said.

I was at the door when Walt said, "You married Jackie Lawrence, right?"

I stopped, turned, nodded.

"Yeah, I thought that was her. She looks good, Pete."

"I know," I said, and got out before Walt could ask any more questions.

"What was that all about?"

"You remember Walter Cummings, couple classes behind us? He's clerking in there."

"I have trouble remembering my own classmates, never mind sophomores. But that wasn't my question."

"I remember Walt from football."

I'd backed out and turned around and we waited now for a break in the traffic.

"What I was asking about was the sexpot in the bikini. Who can't read, by the way."

"Oh?"

"Proper attire? She walks in looking like a slut in a mafia movie."

"She can read," I said. "She went to Smith."

"Yeah, I bet. Majored in Russian literature."

"She was a character. Walt and I were having fun with her."

"I could see that."

A pickup truck stopped to let us out, and I waved thanks and swung out into the slow inbound parade of traffic, people pouring in to salvage what was left of the summer weekend.

"She could stand to lose a few pounds," Jackie said.

"A few," I said.

"God, Peter. She was a *tramp*."

"I told her and Walt about the reading."

Jackie was looking out the window. "That's all we need," she said, still looking away, quiet, as if to herself.

"We need everyone we can get," I said.

"I hope she puts some clothes on," Jackie said.

The dining room of the Holiday Inn in Dunstable is a high barnlike space with a mirror behind the bar, a fieldstone fireplace, and fake antique wagon wheels, yokes, branding irons, and spurs mounted on the plank walls. Dodge City on Cape Cod, something Disney would conjure. It was quiet now, the lunch crowd pretty well thinned out. The waitress put us by a window, and Jackie set her elbows on the table and looked out at the pond on the other side of the road. The biopsy had come back two days ago, and we'd driven into Boston, to Dana-Farber, and gotten the bad news, a 40 percent chance Jackie would survive this. That night, at home in bed, she'd wept on my chest, one of the few times I'd ever seen her cry. She could get plenty mad, but she wasn't a weeper.

"Might she really come tonight?" Jackie said.

"Who?"

"You know damn well who. I almost came in and pulled you out of there."

"She was on her way to a cookout with a bottle of vodka," I said. "She said she'll be smashed by seven o'clock."

"Too bad for you."

"I'm sorry, Jack."

"It's just—"

"I know."

Jackie turned again to stare out at the pond, which lay in a wide depression between two tree-clad hills, steel-blue in the glare of the sun.

"She was hot," she said. "I get that."

"You're hot too."

"You don't need to say that."

"I never needed to."

Jackie was a swimmer, we both were, and she'd stayed slender and leggy into her sixties. She colored her hair, which was still golden, and she had good posture and knew how to dress. White slacks, heels, a violet V-neck shirt on this hot day.

"Age doesn't make any difference, does it," she said. "Any hot young piece can turn an old guy like you on."

"She can make an old guy wistful for what he's lost."

Jackie took another long look out the window. "It's one loss after another, isn't it."

"Pretty much," I said.

"Until there's nothing left."

"If you live long enough," I said, and saw my mistake.

"One way to look at it," Jackie said.

"You're going to pull through this, Jack," I said.

"Maybe, maybe not."

The waitress arrived, smiling.

"I'm Tracey," she said. "I'll be your server." Her hair was an unnatural yellow, lemony, and she was deeply tanned. I wondered when waitresses had begun being called "servers."

"Something from the bar?"

"You're a mind reader," I said.

"Comes with the territory," the girl said.

Jackie stared out into the bright afternoon as if she hadn't heard. The girl was getting on her nerves, I could see that. She would lose a breast, radical mastectomy, then radiation, chemo. It would begin midweek, four days from now.

"Jack?" I said.

"A Manhattan, up," she said to the window.

"Sir?" said the waitress.

"Maker's Mark, on the rocks," I said.

"You got it," said Tracey, and left us.

"I still think Jennifer should be here," Jackie said.

"I didn't ask her to be."

"You shouldn't have to ask your own daughter. You've written a book, for Christ sake."

"If there's a signing in Washington, she said she'd take the train down from Philly."

"There damn well better be a signing in DC. If not there, where? Can't the senator do something?"

"I don't know. Maybe."

"Call your publisher and raise hell. Or I will."

"Figure out what you want to eat," I said.

"A salad, I guess," Jackie said.

The waitress arrived with our drinks. I watched her bend and set the glasses down, and when she straightened I asked her to bring us two chef's salads.

"You got it," she said, and gathered the menus and walked away, bare-legged in her short skirt.

"Don't strain your eyes," Jackie said.

"Cheers," I said, and raised my glass.

We sat awhile, Jackie drinking and gazing out at the pond. Slender fingers fondling the stem of her glass. Dark-red nail polish. The good bourbon I was drinking slid down smooth and sweet, and the air began to lighten around me.

"Walt Cummings might come," I said. "He didn't say he wouldn't."

"Him and bikini girl. Daisy Mae and Barney Fife. The bookstore could sell tickets."

"I just want a respectable turnout," I said. "I mean, what if no one shows up?"

"Jill should have given it a bigger writeup. She's your *sister*."

"She did what she could. If she runs too big a story, the bookstore doesn't advertise it."

The waitress was back with our salads. Jackie drained her glass and nodded at it as she handed it up to her, a silent request for another.

"I'll have another Maker's," I said.

"You got it."

I watched her go.

"She's starting to annoy me," Jackie said.

"I want you to eat," I said. "Keep your strength up."

"Don't nag."

But she shook out her napkin and placed it on her lap. Took up her fork and stabbed a cherry tomato.

"Linda Jean's at her wit's end about Daddy," she said. "She says he might not even know me."

"He's got to go to a nursing home," I said.

"Linda Jean says the home care ladies are managing all right. They're both Black, did I tell you?"

"You mentioned it."

"Daddy likes them."

"How broad-minded of him."

"I was thinking you might be a little nicer about him, now he's got . . . whatever it is."

"Alzheimer's."

"We don't know that."

The waitress broke it up, arriving with our drinks. I swigged the last of my bourbon and handed her my glass. She swung her smile from me to Jackie and back again.

"Anything else?" she said.

"Yeah," Jackie said. "Stop saying 'You got it.'"

The girl met Jackie's gaze and smiled.

"You got it," she said, and spun away, and I pictured her chuckling on her way back, then repeating it to the bartender.

"She gets a lousy tip," Jackie said.

"It was a pretty good answer," I said.

"My father's losing it and I'm about to have a boob chopped off. She should sense that."

We ate our salads and looked around the big, nearly empty room. Two men sat at the bar, nursing beers and watching the Red Sox game.

"I might take a swim before we go over there," I said.

"I might too," Jackie said.

"We take too long, Mike and Linda Jean'll wonder where we are," I said.

"You know how their minds work. They'll think we're getting it on in our room."

"Might be a good idea," I said.

"Don't make any rash promises."

"Maybe I can keep the promise."

"That never used to be a problem with us, did it," Jackie said.

The room was on the third floor and looked down on the parking lot, the rows of cars gleaming under the high white eye of the midsummer sun. The air conditioner blew, a steady insistent drone. Jackie chain-locked the door, went into the bathroom, and came out a few minutes later unbuttoning her blouse. I sat down on one of the queen-sized beds and watched her. The wide window was a pane of pure blue sky, the room daytime bright. Jackie tossed the blouse aside, sucked in her stomach, and unzipped her slacks. She stepped out of her heels and, after a couple of tries, wobbling maybe from the Manhattans, stepped out of the slacks. Time is unkind to all of us, but Jackie's swimmer's body wasn't so altered that you couldn't work with it, or with the memory of what it was not so long ago. She was a strong swimmer and did lap upon lap in the pool at Smith, not quite as fast as I swam, but she could swim for as long as I could. She shrugged her bra off and dropped it on the bed beside me. Her breasts would have been the pride of any woman her age. She sat down and slid off her underpants. Stood up and threw the blankets back, got in and covered herself. She lay on her side watching me, her eyes wide and sad. I laid a hand on her shoulder.

"You never think something like this is going to happen to you," she said. "Someone else, but not you."

"It's going to be all right," I said.

"Maybe."

"It is. I know it."

She looked past me, thinking. "How'd we get so old, Peter?"

"You don't see it coming, do you."

"And you don't remember when it *did* come. There's no bridge, like autumn bringing you to winter. Moving you into it a little at a time. You suddenly realize, I'm old. When did *that* happen?"

She thought awhile, staring past me. I caressed her bare shoulder.

"Peter?"

"What."

"Can you imagine dying?"

"I suppose it's like going to sleep. It *is* going to sleep."

"No. You vanish."

"You don't vanish. People remember you. I can see my mother and father. Their moods. Their smiles. I can *hear* them."

"You vanish from *yourself*," Jackie said, "and who can imagine that? No dreams. No memory. There's literally nothing, and time goes on without you, on and on. Millions of years. Billions."

"Maybe, maybe not."

"What else could it be?"

"I don't know."

"I don't know either."

"You aren't going to die, Jack," I said. "Not yet."

She smiled sadly, reached up with both hands and began unbuttoning my shirt. It was a blue cotton work shirt, Northampton attire. She tugged the shirt out and undid the final button. I stood up and went on undressing.

"You look good," Jackie said.

"Not anymore," I said.

"Bikini girl liked you."

"Not my looks. It impressed her that I worked for Pauline."

"Not that you'd written a book?"

"It got her attention, I guess. She was no dumbbell."

"If she comes tonight, you better behave yourself."

"She won't come."

"If she does . . ."

"I promise."

"Get in bed."

She drew the blankets back and made room for me. I could smell her perfume now, and vermouth-sweetened whiskey on her breath.

"We don't have to do anything," she said, "just be close."

"Be a waste of a good hotel room," I said, and got comfortable against her.

"When was the last time we did it? I can't even remember."

"The night after that reception for Rachel Maddow."

"Lesbo Rachel. I wonder if she'd like Jennifer."

"Probably."

"And Jen would like her, I imagine."

"She does like her," I said.

"You know what I mean."

"Rachel's a good-looking woman."

"Think so?"

"Yeah."

"I got plastered at the reception."

"You got amorous."

She rolled away from me, lay on her back, eyes open. "Sex. It's what kept us together, isn't it."

"You know that isn't true."

"It's all right, Peter. What the hell. It's as good a thing as any."

"Thirty-four years. Takes more than sex."

"Well, Jennifer."

"It takes more than sex and a daughter."

"You should have married an English major. Sophisticated little Smithie with a Ph.D."

"Don't start that."

"Just hold me, okay?"

"I'll do more than that," I said.

"You sure?"

"Can't you tell?"

I was above her now, moving a hand down her hip, her thigh. I kissed her.

"Nice and slow," she whispered.

"I know," I said.

"Gentle," she said. "Gentle, gentle."

Two

Jennifer was twenty-nine and had been in Philadelphia a couple of years when the revelation transpired in a routine phone conversation. Jen knew her own mind and never acted precipitously, and I took the news as final, a fact of our lives now, and anyway nothing we should worry about. Jackie had no moral objection: it was as if Jennifer had become a vegan or Christian Scientist. It was okay, but why complicate your life like that?

"How come Jennifer never goes out?" Jackie had asked me.

"She goes out," I said.

"With who?"

"Friends."

"What friends?"

"I don't know. Other lawyers. Lots of people."

"Peter. I'm talking about men. She lives in Philadelphia, which is an hour from New York. How could she not have a boyfriend?"

"Maybe she has one. Why don't you ask her?"

When Jennifer called a few days later, Jackie did, point-blank, and Jennifer said, "Wake up, Mom."

"I'm awake," Jackie said, "and I'm asking you if you have a boyfriend."

"I have a girlfriend."

Jackie took this in and revolved it in her mind while Jen waited. "A girlfriend," she said, "as in a sexual way?"

"I'm gay, Mom. I thought you might have figured that out by now."

"I guess I'm slow," Jackie said.

"Does it bother you?"

"I'm surprised. Who wouldn't be?"

"It bothers you," Jen said.

"Surprise and bother are two different things," Jackie said. "As you should know."

I got on the phone and couldn't think beyond clichés. "We just want you to be happy."

"Christ, Dad. Why wouldn't I be?"

"No reason," I said.

After I'd hung up, Jackie said, "Daddy'll have a fit."

"He doesn't have to know," I said.

"Knowing Jen, she'll find a way to tell him. He'll say something, and Jen'll answer him back, and we're off to the races."

"I'll talk to her," I said.

"A lesbian," Jackie said. "What a waste of a good body."

A few months later Jennifer moved in with a fellow lawyer named Allison, a Philadelphia Main Line society girl who'd gone left-wing and true to herself sexually. Jen brought her home a couple of times, and Jackie didn't much like her, and I could see why. There was a coolness about her, something guarded and calculating. You felt she knew more about you, or thought she did, than she was letting on. "There won't be any kids," Jackie said, after their second visit.

"So what?" I said.

"It would be good for her. Make her more patient. And that bitch Allison would have to think of someone besides herself."

"She thinks of Jen."

"That's not enough."

"They could adopt a kid," I said.

"Or do in vitro," Jackie said. "That's the big thing now. Wouldn't you like to be a grandfather?"

"I never thought about it," I said.

"I'm going to suggest in vitro to Jen."

"I'd stay out of it, if I were you."

"I'm her mother, Peter."

"Exactly," I said.

Jackie felt good under the sheet on this lazy summer afternoon, and afterward I shifted onto my back and pulled her in, cradling her, and stared at the white ceiling, listening to the breathing of the AC.

"You got cheated," I said.

"It was still nice," she said.

I rose on an elbow and looked at the bedside clock. Three-thirty and change; there wouldn't be any swimming. The sun had moved over toward the trees curtaining the parking lot, but it was still very bright in the room. I thought again about the book signing and wondered how many people would come, and who they'd be. There'd been the notice Jill had run in the *Inquirer*, and the bookstore had taken out an ad, eight column inches. I wondered yet again if any of our classmates would show up, then told myself— again—not to worry, this was a public forum, no opportunity for personal questions, for digging up old memories. I sank back, and Jackie moved over and lay huddled against me. Her perfume had lost its freshness, its tang. Car doors slammed below our window. A woman's voice rose in the stillness. A man called a brief answer from nearer the motel.

"Peter."

"What."

"If I get better, I want to get out of Northampton. I want to come home."

"It isn't home anymore," I said.

"Call it what you want. Daddy's here, for a while, anyway. Linda Jean and Mike. Margie and Wayne over in Yarmouth. The nieces and nephews. Not to mention your own sister."

"I can't take too much of Mike. Linda Jean, either."

"I can't, either, and we won't have to. We've always lived where you wanted to."

"Where my work was."

"What about my work? I didn't want to leave Hale and Dorr. They loved me there."

"They loved you in McDermott's office."

"I hated DC. I didn't like the Hill, either."

"And we left."

"To a new job for *you*."

"And you. I'd have stayed with Pauline if you'd been happy down there. I'd still be with her. You know that."

She'd moved away from me, and now she rolled onto her back, gazing not at the ceiling but through it, to days gone, some season of her life that seemed unblemished now, bright with contentment and promise.

"I still miss Boston. I miss Hale and Dorr. The guys there didn't take themselves so seriously, like they do in Washington. We laughed. We had fun."

"You said they were cheap."

"They were, but we had fun, and they didn't hit on me."

"You survived the Hill."

"I got tired of it. 'Buy you a drink before you head home?' How many times did I hear that one? I got tired of telling grown men to behave themselves."

"Which they always did."

"They had no choice."

"I know."

"Good. Now go down the hall and get me some ice."

"Maybe you ought to slack off now."

"I get a little squiffed, what does it matter?"

"It doesn't, I guess."

She got up, padded naked to the bathroom while I pulled on my pants and shirt. The carpeted hallway was empty, rooms all silent behind their locked doors. Everyone at the beach, on charter fishing boats, playing miniature golf, strolling the aquarium at Quick's Hole with their kids. The machine coughed its avalanche of cubes into the plastic bucket. Jackie had gotten back into bed and was sitting with the sheet drawn up to her waist, bare-breasted and oddly regal in her composure. I had less than three hours to get us to her father's house, maybe eat something, and present myself and my wife at the bookstore sober.

"There are glasses in the bathroom," she said.

I brought one out and filled it with ice cubes. I'd zipped the bagged bottle of bourbon into my suitcase. I broke the wax seal and poured. I handed the drink to Jackie and sat down on the bed. She watched me.

"Take a good look," she said, nodding at her left breast. "Only a few more chances."

I leaned forward and placed my palm over it. It filled my hand, so soft. Warm. Almost liquid. Jackie closed her eyes, opened them. She smiled a slant half smile, wry and sad, and lifted the glass and drank.

"How will it be, making love to a woman with one boob?"

"It'll be fun."

"Maybe you won't want to."

"Maybe I will. It might be sexy."

"Well aren't you sweet." She placed a hand on my arm.

"What's your problem with Northampton?" I said.

"I'm lonely."

"You've got friends."

"Julie Palmer. Peggy Whitmore. Secretaries, like me. Not your friends."

"Sure they are."

"Not like your professor friends."

"They're *our* professor friends. They all love you."

"They think I'm a character, that's all. They wouldn't pay me any attention if I weren't your wife."

"Oh yes they would. They'd pay more. The men sure would."

"Not the kind I want."

"Everyone loves you, Jack. What's the matter with you?"

"You could write here in Dunstable. We'll get a house someplace quiet, you'll have a study. You'll write another book."

"Maybe."

"You want to, don't you?"

"If I can."

"Of course you can."

"Maybe, maybe not. You know what Sandra said?"

"Your brilliant editor. I think she has a crush on you."

"I wish," I said.

"I bet you do."

"She said writing a second or third novel is like inventing the wheel all over again. No matter how many times you do it."

"So invent another wheel."

She raised her glass, half full now, and took a thoughtful sip. A car door slammed in the parking lot. The air conditioner groaned and began to blow. The digital clock told me four-oh-six. There would be cheese and crackers at the bookstore, I remembered.

"No one's ever going to confuse me with William Styron," I said.

"You're just beginning. You don't know that."

"I don't have time to become William Styron."

"Forget William Styron, okay? You're Peter Thomas Hatch. And it's a good book, by the way."

"It's pretty light fare."

"So is Robert Parker—you like him, don't you?"

"He's good at what he does."

"So are you."

She brought the glass up, drank, tilting it till she'd finished. I was afraid she'd ask for another, but she did not. I took the glass from her and set it on the bedside table.

"We'd better go," I said.

"I want you to get back in bed."

"Jack . . ."

"Please, Peter. I need a little more time."

So I took off my shirt and crawled in with her again. She shifted to face me, huddling against me as before.

"I just don't *feel* sick," she said. "I feel like I'm in my forties."

"You look like it," I said.

She laughed then—it had pleased her. We lay awhile, Jackie clinging to me childlike with an arm circling my waist, and still that mingled smell of bourbon and stale perfume, and the smell too of Jackie herself, a fragrant woman smell as old and familiar as the touch of her hand.

"I'm going to take a little nap," she said.

She rolled onto her side and lay, fetal, with her back to me. I still liked her back, and I kissed her now between her shoulder blades.

"Linda Jean's going to think we're having an orgy."

"My sister has sex on the brain. Wake me in ten minutes."

three

I was a city reporter for the *Boston Globe*, had won a Pulitzer, and
written some speeches for our former governor when Pauline Powell
hired me. Pauline was a congresswoman then, with ambitions and
some national visibility. The governor had spoken to her and sent her
a couple of my speeches, and Pauline had liked some reporting I'd
done on a county training school scandal. Her appointment secretary
called me, said the congresswoman would like to talk to me, and it
wouldn't cost me anything but the airfare. Jackie was against it from
the start, but I was restless, tired of being a newspaper reporter, the
sameness of it, the writing too easy now, ledes composing themselves
before you got back to your desk. I would be an editor one day if I
stayed with it, or a columnist, but here was a chance at distinction of
a rarer sort. Pauline was a rising star, and she had, as I said, ambitions.

She favored blood-red lipstick, a brash hue that gave her face a
striking Technicolor aspect. She was a handsome woman, tall and
big-boned, with a dignity that seemed earned as well as natural, as if
white people had worn themselves out trying to belittle and hold her
back, and here she was, stronger and wiser for it, and here we were,
powerless to trouble her anymore.

"I want to be a voice, not just in the House, but in the country," she said.

She was behind her big desk in the Rayburn Building, sitting back with her chin in her hand, studying me. Thinking about the Senate, as I soon learned.

"Yes, ma'am," I said.

She smiled. "You can call me Pauline."

"I'll try."

Another smile. Then, "Whatever you think of Reagan, he's a voice. The country listens to him, you know what I'm saying?"

"I think so."

"You think so. You have to do better than that."

"A wide constituency," I said. "You want to speak for certain people everywhere."

"To them and for them."

"Like Bobby Kennedy," I said.

"Or Nixon," Pauline said.

"Hitler," I said, "when you get right down to it."

"And Dr. King. Maybe I should rephrase it: a moral voice."

"I take your point."

"I know you do. And I know you'll give me speeches that'll raise the temperature in a room. You want the job?"

She had to go over to the Floor, and she left me in her office with permission to use her desk phone to call my wife.

"She's going to start me at forty thousand," I said.

"You already said yes?"

"It's the chance of a lifetime, Jack."

"I thought you were going to come home, we were going to talk about it."

"Did you hear me say forty thousand?"

"So I quit my job and we sell the house."

"We were going to sell the house, anyway."

"And move to a nicer one. We were talking about Concord, remember?"

"I have to do this, Jack."

"All right, fuck it. Go ahead."

"What's your problem?"

"Nothing."

"Something."

"Did you hear me? Nothing."

"It isn't because she's Black, is it?"

Silence on the other end. Then, slowly: "What are you saying, exactly?"

"I'm just trying to think why you'd hesitate at this."

There was an even longer silence. The ceilings in the Rayburn Building are very high, and Pauline's private office was elegantly furnished and august-feeling. On the walls were photos of her and various Black celebrities: Jesse Jackson, Coretta Scott King, Muhammad Ali. There were pictures, too, of Pauline and Hubert Humphrey, Pauline and Jimmy Carter.

"You son of a bitch," Jackie said.

"Excuse me?"

"I said you son of a bitch."

"You're right. It was a dumb thing to say. How's Jen? She have a good day today?"

Jackie snorted a laugh of pure contempt and hung up.

I'd driven myself to Logan Airport, and I bought flowers on the way home the next day and left them on the dining table with a note. Jackie came home from work, read the note, asked Jennifer where I was, and found me upstairs, waiting for her.

"Jack . . ." I said.

"It's okay," she said, and kissed me, and it was over, leaving one more scar.

*   *   *

We found a three-bedroom apartment in Fairlington, a good place for Jennifer, the neighborhood safe, populated by young families, bus stop at the end of the block. Jackie spent a couple of days traipsing around the Hill, dropping off her résumé, and Pauline, without telling us, called Hale and Dorr and got Alan Keating on the phone and asked him about Jackie. Pauline told me about it afterward. She told Keating he could speak frankly, neither Jackie nor I needed to hear what he said.

"They can hear it," Keating said. "Jacqueline Hatch is the best secretary we ever had. She knows how to keep her mouth shut and she's smart as a whip."

Pauline called Congressman Eddie McDermott, and McDermott told Pauline to send her over.

four

I shook her gently, and she rolled over and found me sleepily and smiled.

"I was dreaming," she said. "You were running for the Senate and you wanted me to be your press secretary. I said I couldn't, I had to take care of Daddy, and you said maybe Linda Jean would take the job. Linda Jean's too young, I said."

"Linda Jean's too dumb," I said.

"She seemed smart in the dream."

"She is, in a way. She's smarter than her husband, I'll say that."

"A doorknob's smarter than her husband."

Jackie threw the sheet back, swung her legs off the bed, sat up, yawned.

"I better shower," she said. "Brush my teeth. I smell like a distillery."

I looked at the bottle on the vanity and thought about it. I hadn't been in Clayton Lawrence's house for nearly a year, and a drink would ease the reentry. Mr. Lawrence broken and pitiable, and then Linda Jean's husband, who had been Special Forces in Vietnam at the tail end of the war and took every opportunity to mention "Nam," and

being "in country," and the murderous ingenuity of the North Viet-
namese. Mike Ballard's way of rubbing it in: I'd been deferred, working with troubled kids in a middle school in Detroit, and then my
lottery number wasn't drawn. I'd demonstrated against the war, but I
didn't tell Ballard that.

Jackie, at the bathroom door, turned and saw me eyeing the
Maker's, saw me thinking about it. "Wait till after the reading," she
said. "We'll come back here and toast your big success."

"I'll settle for a small success," I said.

I opened my suitcase and took out my novel and stood with it
by the window, in the golden wash of the westering sun. I'd written
a book, a novel, and here it was. You could hold it, you could open
it. *The Minutes of This Night* was the title, from *Hamlet*, bestowed,
finally, by my editor. I was dubious; it seemed in no way descriptive
of the novel, but I'd ransacked *Bartlett's Familiar Quotations*, Ecclesiastes, the *Fireside Book of Folk Songs*, and the novel itself, and found
nothing right, and time had run out. On the dust jacket was some
scrabbling artist's rendering of the U.S. Capitol with a chessboard
spread in front of it, a dozen or so scattered pieces, and, about in the
middle of the board, a man in a coat and tie, lying on his stomach,
unmistakably dead. That would be Senator Thomas Abernathy, presidential hopeful, age sixty-five, who is found slumped over his desk
one morning, dead of an apparent heart attack, a day after a secret
meeting with senatorial candidate and former Navy SEAL Lincoln
Beard.

On the back cover, *Advance Praise for* The Minutes of This
Night*:*

*"A gripping tale of conspiracy and intrigue that shows that things
are not always what they seem in the nation's capital."* —Tom Daschle,
Former United States Senator and Majority Leader

"Elmore Leonard meets John Grisham in this DC thriller." —Maureen Dowd, New York Times *Columnist*

"The best political thriller I have ever read."—William Cohen, Former United States Senator and Secretary of Defense

"I had a terrifying thought while reading this splendid first novel—this could really happen."—United States Senator Pauline Powell

I doubted any of them except Pauline had read the book, but she had given them her guarantee. Pauline with her degree from Smith, a double major, history and English, an acquaintance of Toni Morrison, occasional guest of Mr. and Mrs. William Styron on Martha's Vineyard. *Her* guarantee.

"I loved it," Pauline said. "It has panache."

This was two months ago. Pauline had come to Smith to give the commencement address, which I'd written for her as a favor, and we were having a late breakfast at the Haymarket Cafe. Here and there kids sat grouped over coffee or smoothies, occasionally glancing our way as they talked.

"How's Jackie?" Pauline said.

I looked out at the traffic moving slowly in the sunlight on Main Street. "She's fine," I said, and believed it. The lump had appeared, but Jackie was ignoring it, as if it would disappear if left to itself—as if treating it as inconsequential would make it so. I found this out later, when she admitted to herself, and to me, that she was in trouble.

"I like Jackie," Pauline said.

"I know you do."

"I like her spunk."

Pauline looked at her watch. The two of us were speaking at a colloquium at eleven, then moving on to lunch at the college president's home.

"You won't take money for the speech," she said.

"We've been through that," I said. "You know what I want."

"I'll start with Maureen Dowd. She owes me. And Tom Daschle. He's got time to read these days."

"And you'll say something."

"You want to write it?"

It made me laugh. Students looked over.

"That might not be ethical," I said.

"Probably not," Pauline said, smiling. "You want to do it anyway?"

"Pauline . . ."

"Just kidding," she said.

five

She wore a raspberry silk blouse, navy slacks, heels, and pendant earrings, and now had the look of a dolled-up beauty of a certain age,
faded but still in the game, heading out for a dinner party, maybe a
play at the Cape Playhouse. She seemed steady on her feet, and the
clarity had come back into her sea-blue eyes. She'd always been able
to hold her liquor. We went out through the flagstone lobby, Jackie
on my arm, my book in my other hand, into the golden early evening. High summer, my father used to say. The air thick with fragrant
growth and bloom.

I unlocked the Subaru and opened the passenger door for Jackie.
I wondered how many times I'd pulled a car door open for her, how
many journeys, minutes or hours long, we'd made together. I turned
left out of the parking lot and drove to the traffic light a quarter of
a mile on. Cars were backed up at the light in four directions: summertime, people flooding the roads on their way to the restaurants
and bars, to parties, the theater. I remembered the woman in the
liquor store and wondered if she was at her cookout still, and in what
condition. She'd be a sloppy drunk, loud and profane.

"Peter."

"What."

I'd stopped for the red light, several cars in line ahead of us.

"Did you ever have sex with the senator?"

She was looking away from me, out her window. Waiting.

"What a question," I said.

"Did you?"

The light went green, and we crept forward and turned left, and I pulled into the empty parking lot of the Methodist church. I cut the engine. Jackie folded her arms and looked out at the redbrick church.

"I'm wondering," I said, "why you're asking."

"I'm asking because I want to know."

"All right."

"All right what?"

"I didn't."

Jackie thought awhile, and I stayed silent.

"See, I always wondered about all those long hours you worked. Home at seven, eight."

"It's like that on the Hill. You're at your boss's beck and call. You know that."

"Not so much for secretaries. Good thing: what would Jennifer have done if I'd worked your hours?"

"She'd have been fine."

"Not at first."

"We'd have hired somebody to look in on her, cook dinner."

"I pictured you and the senator alone in her office, everyone's gone home. Big sofa, which I've seen. The senator isn't married."

"But I was."

"That's why I'm asking."

"What brought this on?"

"When you might be dying, you want to clear things up. Answer old questions."

"You aren't dying."

"I don't like the odds."

"You aren't dying."

I unbuckled my seatbelt, leaned and kissed her. She'd brushed her teeth and her breath tasted clean and minty. After a moment she woke to the kiss, returned it. Then she leaned back, resettled herself, fluffed her hair.

"Did we put that to rest?" I said.

"I think so," Jackie said.

"You *think* so."

"It's over. Buried. Okay?"

"Okay," I said.

I buckled myself back in and started the car.

"By the way," I said, "I think Pauline swings the other way."

Jackie looked at me. "Lesbian?"

"I think so."

"Does Jen know?"

"Probably."

"Will wonders never cease," Jackie said.

Clayton Lawrence sat like a collapsed marionette in the stuffed chair he'd occupied when I'd come calling on his daughter as a high school senior, Mr. Lawrence discoursing on this or that while I sat on the sofa in my letter jacket and Jackie finished primping for our date. He was bone-thin now, shrunken, and his face was haggard and colorless, his skin almost transparent. Jackie stopped just inside the door, caught her breath. It had been two months since she'd seen him, and those months had evidently been pitiless. I hadn't seen the old man since Thanksgiving.

He studied his daughter from across the room, squinting, trying to make out who this was.

"What did you do, get stuck in traffic?" Linda Jean said, rising from the sofa.

Mike Ballard, seated beside her, in a skintight Black Sabbath T-shirt and Patriots hat, lifted a bottle of Rolling Rock by the neck, toasted us by way of a greeting, and took a swig. Ballard pumped iron, and it showed. He belted home runs in an over-fifty softball league.

"I took a nap at the motel," Jackie said.

Mr. Lawrence still squinted, his wondering gaze moving from person to person.

"A nap, huh?" Ballard said.

Linda Jean was grinning. "A little afternoon delight, maybe?"

She'd held on to her good looks, like her older sister, but what Linda Jean offered was a lanky rawboned sexiness I'd seen taking shape when she was fifteen.

"Hey, sis," she said, and wrapped Jackie in an embrace.

"Hey yourself," Jackie said.

Jackie released her and handed me her purse without looking at me.

"Daddy," she said.

"Jacqueline?" he said.

"Yes, Daddy, it's me."

She went to him, leaned over and put her lips to Mr. Lawrence's papery cheek. She straightened, smiling, and he looked up at her through his glasses, squinching, regarding his oldest daughter curiously, as if still trying to place her.

"It's me, Daddy. Jackie."

"Jacqueline. Ah."

She bent down, kissed him again, and he found her hand and clasped it. Jackie sat down on the chair arm, perching, still with her hand in her father's tight claw. The lines of puzzlement had been smoothed from his face, and he was smiling a euphoric smile that struck me as both beatific and imbecilic. Jackie lifted his hand and kissed it. Her eyes had filled.

"I knew you'd come," her father said.

"Daddy, of *course*," she said.

It was my turn. Linda Jean had sat down beside her husband. I set Jackie's purse on the coffee table.

"Good to see you, Mr. Lawrence," I said.

The watery gaze rose, considered me with bland interest and then a troubled curiosity.

"It's Pete, Daddy. My husband."

"Yes," he said. "Pete Hatch. The football player."

"Yes, sir."

"Been a long time."

"Too long."

"How's your father?"

I looked at Jackie. "Play along," she whispered.

"He's fine, Mr. Lawrence," I said.

"He always liked Grace."

"Did he."

"Then he went away to school, I believe. Took himself out of the running."

"Supper's ready, if you guys want to eat before you go," Linda Jean said.

"I have to talk to you first," Jackie said.

"About what?"

"Let's go into the kitchen."

"Bernice is out there."

"The back porch, then," Jackie said.

Jackie lifted her father's hand and kissed it again. She slid down off the arm of the chair, and gestured Linda Jean toward the kitchen, which opened onto the deck, with a sideways duck of her head. Linda Jean stood up and followed her. Ballard watched them go. He watched Jackie. I sat down in the chair that had been Mrs. Lawrence's. Mr. Lawrence was gazing into space as if deep in thought.

"Is it about the you-know-what?" Ballard said. He raised the bottle and drank.

"Linda Jean'll tell you," I said.

"Okay, fuck it. Don't tell me."

Mr. Lawrence heard it and turned, smiling slyly.

"Fuck it," he said. "Fuck it, fuck it, fuck it."

"You tell 'em, Mr. Lawrence," Ballard said.

"I'd better eat something, if you'll excuse me," I said.

"Yeah, you're excused," Ballard said.

Jackie and Linda Jean had gone out onto the deck and closed the glass slider. They were sitting on plastic lawn chairs looking out across the backyard to the sun-splashed pewter-gray trunks of a rank of locust trees that stood along the edge of the property. The daytime aide was washing dishes.

"I'm Bernice," she said. "Lenny Gomes was my aunt's brother. He'd have been my uncle."

Lenny had been in Jackie's and my class. A football player, a lean, mean defensive end.

"I'm sorry about Lenny," I said.

"Well, that damn Vietnam," Bernice said.

"Don't say that around Mike," I said.

"I hear you. Get you some silverware and sit down. Got a nice chicken curry for you."

Jackie and Linda Jean were still talking, or Jackie was. Linda Jean sat very still, looking out at the trees. I sat down at the varnished kitchen table and Bernice got busy dishing rice and curry, pulling out serving spoons. She set the plate down in front of me.

"How long has Mr. Lawrence been this bad?" I said.

"A month, maybe," Bernice said. "Anita and I have to dress him, undress him. Help him do his business in the bathroom."

"Is he okay with that?"

"Meek as a lamb."

"Great curry," I said.

"Mr. Lawrence still does enjoy his food," Bernice said.

Ballard came in, bringing his empty. He placed it on the counter for Bernice to rinse and dispose of, opened the refrigerator, and found another green bottle.

"Hey," he said, "sorry we're not coming to your thing tonight."

"It's fine," I said. "You'd be bored."

"Linda Jean made this plan with some friends. I'd come without her, but my truck's in the garage. Transmission's shot to hell."

"It's fine," I said again.

"What's your book about, anyway?" he said.

"You wrote a book?" Bernice said over her shoulder.

Ballard pried the cap off the bottle and dropped the opener back in its drawer. "He's a famous author," he said, "didn't you know that?"

"Well, I should," Bernice said.

"I'm not famous," I said.

"Okay, not a famous author *yet*," Mike said. "But a famous speechwriter, at least."

"My boss was famous, I wasn't."

"What boss was this?" Bernice said.

"Powell," Ballard said.

Bernice looked at him. "*Senator* Powell?"

"He was her right-hand man. Her consigliere."

"Mike, enough, okay?" I said.

"I love Senator Powell," Bernice said.

"I don't," Ballard said, and took a swig of beer and turned to regard Jackie and his wife, sitting in the shade of the house with their backs to him. I wondered how many beers he'd had.

"What the hell are they talking about?" he said.

"Mr. Ballard, why don't you go sit with Mr. Lawrence," Bernice said, "not leave him all by his lonesome."

"Your turn, Pete," Ballard said. "I've kind of run out of conversation."

But then Jackie stood up. Linda Jean looked up at her sister and spoke, and Jackie answered. Linda Jean shrugged, got up, moved in front of Jackie, and heaved the slider open. Jackie followed her in.

"What the hell's going on?" Ballard said.

Jackie opened a cupboard and pulled down a plate. She didn't look at me, didn't look at anybody. Her face set, unreadable.

"Sit down, Mrs. Hatch," Bernice said, and took the plate from her.

"Is anyone going to tell me, or do I have to read it in the paper tomorrow?" Ballard said.

"Jackie got some bad news about the cancer," Linda Jean said.

"How bad?"

"Just bad."

"*Just bad* is not a fucking answer, Linda Jean."

"Oh, screw yourself, Mike," said Linda Jean.

Bernice glanced at them, and I saw a smile as she went back to washing dishes.

"Not *that* bad," I said. "She hasn't even had surgery yet."

Jackie was eating. She went about it slowly, thoughtfully, as if the conversation around her were of no import.

"Will someone tell me what the hell's going on?" Ballard said. Ballard in his dark-blue Patriots hat, clamped tight on his head. He stood with his beer bottle, looking at his wife, at Jackie, who woke now, set her fork down and met his gaze, locked on it.

"The odds aren't so hot," she said. "Sixty-forty I don't make it."

He looked down, and I saw him swallow. Silence, everyone looking at him. "Well, shit," he said, very quietly, and went into the other room carrying his beer.

Linda Jean and Ballard had disappeared, and Mr. Lawrence sat alone, gazing absently into space. Jackie sat down on the arm of his chair again and put her arm around him.

"Daddy, Peter's written a book," she said.

Mr. Lawrence studied her. "A book," he said.

"Yeah, about a plot to take over the government. Sort of like Hitler did, step by step."

Mr. Lawrence seemed to be thinking this over. Jackie looked up at me and shrugged. I turned, looked out the picture window at our car at the foot of the flagstone walk. Where I'd parked my father's Ford Falcon Friday and Saturday nights, Sunday afternoons, and come sauntering up the walk in my letter jacket. I could see it, the cheap tinny car, my younger self in the maroon suede jacket with the white D over my heart.

"The good guys win in the end," Jackie said.

"Where's your daughter?" Mr. Lawrence said.

"She's in Philadelphia, Daddy. She lives down there, remember?"

"Margie does?"

"No, Daddy. Jennifer. Margie's in Yarmouth. Mike and Linda Jean are here."

I turned, tapped my watch.

"We have to go, Daddy," Jackie said. "We'll come see you again tomorrow."

"Tomorrow," Mr. Lawrence said.

"That's right. You be a good boy meantime. Do what Bernice says."

She kissed him and slipped down off the chair arm.

"Good night, Mr. Lawrence," I said.

"Your son-in-law's an author, Daddy," Jackie said. "Isn't that great?"

Mr. Lawrence looked up at her. "What is?" he said.

"Love you, Daddy," she said.

six

"God," Jackie said in the car.

"I know," I said.

"It'll only get worse, won't it."

"I don't know."

"Yes you do."

"All right, I do," I said. "What was wrong with Linda Jean?"

"She was ticked off that I told Margie about the diagnosis and not her."

"Why didn't you?"

"I'd rather say it in person if I can. I *had* to call Margie, I wasn't going to see her today. With Linda Jean it's all about when I tell her, not that I might be dying."

"Maybe that was her way of coping."

"She's a little bitch and you know it."

"Ballard was upset," I said.

"Mike likes me."

"I'll say."

"Not *that* way. As a friend."

We passed the school tennis courts, and I remembered Jackie and me stopping here to kiss as I walked her home on Thanksgiving Day senior year, after the football game. We were flush with victory, and with our own youth and vitality, and awed, too, by the utter stillness, as if the town were under a spell. I wondered now if I'd ever felt more alive than in that moment before I'd kissed Jackie's cool, sweet lips.

"Anyway," she said, "this is your night, I don't want to spoil it feeling sorry for myself. Just tell me to shut up."

"Okay. Shut up."

It made her smile. "In all our years, I don't ever remember you telling me to shut up," she said.

"Jennifer says it all the time."

"Naturally."

"Your manners are pretty good," I said. "Except for the cussing."

"I only cuss in front of certain people."

"Me. Who else?"

"Certain women. Friends, but only certain ones."

"Did you cuss in McDermott's office?"

"The congressman loved my manners."

"Your manners and your legs," I said.

"He ought to, he looked at them enough."

"Who could blame him?"

Jackie looked at me. A half smile. "You're on your game tonight," she said.

"Trying," I said.

"Keep it up," she said.

Cars were parked along both sides of Main Street in front of the bookstore, so we drove on and tried the big lot in front of Town Hall, and I finally found a space. I locked the car, so no one would steal our phones and CDs, straightened and took a deep breath of the exhaust-scented downtown summer air.

"Nervous?" Jackie said.

"A little."

"Pretend you're at Smith, teaching your class. Piece of cake."

"This is different. Talking about something *I* wrote, not Jon Meacham or Elizabeth Drew. I feel like a huckster. Selling something I invented at home."

"Which you did."

"I would have thought the publisher would take over, do the selling."

"Not anymore. I was talking to Julie Palmer, she said you have to promote yourself. Facebook, social media, all that crap."

"Facebook. I don't think so."

"You want to be like Don Quixote, living in the wrong century?"

"I want to live in Paris in the 1920s," I said.

"That's just what I'm talking about," Jackie said. She took my hand, and we started walking. I carried the book in my other hand, displaying the title in case anyone's eye happened down that far.

"Do I look okay?" I said.

"Handsome. Bikini girl'll love you."

"She's not going to be there."

"I have a feeling she will. Don't flirt too hard, if you know what's good for you."

"I'll only have eyes for you."

The sidewalk was alive with families, couples, gaggles of teenagers. They wandered in and out of the shops, looked in display windows, perused the menus by restaurant doors. A chalkboard on the sidewalk in front of the bookstore announced me in a looping, overwrought scrawl: *Peter Hatch discusses and signs copies of his novel,* <u>*The Minutes of This Night*</u>, *7 P.M.* Under it, "*Elmore Leonard meets John Grisham in this DC thriller." —Maureen Dowd.*

"Are you going to talk about the FBI woman?" Jackie said.

Pauline had made a call to the Bureau, and the director had let Special Agent Constance Dryer discuss Bureau policy and criminal investigation with me over a cup of coffee.

"Not by name," I said. "Just that she helped me, and how I used it in the book."

Jackie still held my hand, hers warm and weightless and perfect in mine, as we stood contemplating the chalkboard.

"Was she as hot as she is in the book?"

"Not hot at all. She looks like a fussy biology professor."

"She'll be flattered, then."

"I hope so. Sandra sent her a copy of the book. Hoped she'd say something they could put on the jacket."

"FBI, are you kidding?"

"I told Sandra that."

A man and woman stopped to study the chalkboard. The woman took his arm.

"Never heard of the guy," she said.

"Me neither. Probably a local guy. A townie."

"Shall we go in?" the woman said.

"Nah."

They strolled on, the woman still on his arm.

"Well, fuck them," Jackie said, and tugged me toward the door.

It was quarter to seven, and the bookstore was empty but for the owner, her young assistant, and my brother-in-law and sister, editor and publisher of the *Dunstable Inquirer*, as our father had been before her, and our grandfather before him. Jill and Joe sat in the front row of a tight little gallery of folding metal chairs facing a podium at the front of the store. Off to the side stood a folding table with two stacks of my novel rising like pillars at either end. The room was long and narrow. A second folding table had been set up behind the chairs, and on it were platters of cheese and crackers and grapes and a big bottle of red wine and one of white.

"Ah," said Carol Littlefield, coming forward and offering her hand. She wore a lavender summer dress, a trim, nice-looking divorcée with gray-streaked hair.

"Sorry I'm late," I said.

"You're right on time," Carol said.

The assistant was a college girl named Erica, a summer hire. Jill and Joe had risen. They embraced Jackie tentatively, gently, as if the cancer had rendered her breakable.

"You look great," Jill said.

"I wish," Jackie said.

"No, really," Jill said.

"Why wouldn't she?" Carol said.

"She would," Jill said. "She always does."

"Doesn't look like much of a crowd," I said.

"You never know," Carol said. "Could be five, could be thirty."

"Five," I said. "Good God."

"It can happen," Carol said. "It doesn't reflect on you."

"What *does* it reflect on?" I said.

"Who sees the ad. Who's busy. Who buys the book on Amazon."

"We're buying books for the kids," Jill said, "and one for ourselves, of course."

"There's three right there," Jackie said. "You're off and running."

"Between ten and twenty books sold is a good night," Carol said.

The clock above the counter said ten to seven, and the rows of empty chairs were taking on a forlorn and futile look, as if they'd been set out in a moment of harebrained optimism.

"Glass of wine?" Carol said.

"I'd better keep my wits about me," I said.

"Jackie?"

Jackie eyed the table in back, the two big bottles, then smiled and shook her head.

"Maybe afterwards," she said.

Time inched along toward five of. Jill and Joe sat down, and I saw Jill glance at the clock, thinking the same thing I was. Jackie gave me a quick good-luck kiss and sat down beside Jill. I moved to the podium and laid the book on it and opened to the first scene, the one I'd chosen to read. Speak for ten minutes, read for ten, ten minutes of questions, Carol had said. I wondered what she'd do with the piles of books if no one came, and if it had ever happened before. There was a bottle of Poland Spring on the shelf under the podium, and I uncapped it and drank.

The door opened, a teenage girl holding it with her arm outstretched for an old woman laboring forward on a walker. The old woman was short and stout and wore a sweater on this warm evening. The girl took her arm, guided her to a front-row seat, and sat down beside her.

A sloe-eyed young woman wearing faded jeans and a black scoop-neck T-shirt slouched in. She was lissome and gypsy-dark, with raven hair tumbling to her shoulders. She stopped to look me over, and I gave her what I hoped was a winning nod and smile. She returned the nod briefly and noncommittally and went on and sat down behind the old woman.

I looked at Jackie, and she met my eye and winked, telling me it was going to be all right, which it clearly was not. She sat straight, as always, looking very poised, and I imagined leaving with her, walking out on this burgeoning disaster and taking refuge in the quiet soft-lit restaurant at the Holiday Inn. A candle in a hurricane glass on the table, Jackie in its dusky light across from me. Drink some Maker's, quell the false idea that I was a writer, and plan some other future for myself, go back to speechwriting or stay on at Smith, which I might do commuting from Dunstable, where we could own that house

Jackie dreamed of. I looked down, scanned the first page of *The Min-utes of This Night.* I'd liked the opening, had thought it established my voice right off the bat as possessing something of the stripped-down poetry of Hemingway or Kent Haruf, but this was an illusion, I saw now. My prose seemed jerry-rigged and stumbling, Hemingway on gin and Percocet. I couldn't read these opening pages aloud—to any-body. I flipped pages, looking for the scene in which Abernathy's secretary walks in and finds him dead.

And then at seven, the woman from the liquor store came in on the arm of a bronze, somewhat younger man who looked as if he'd come straight from a tennis court—white shorts, white polo shirt, white Nikes. The woman wore a fuchsia T-shirt, pink shorts, and the flip-flops she'd worn in PJ's Wine & Spirits. Her chestnut hair looked blow-dried and waved.

"I was afraid we'd be late," she said, addressing the room, as if we'd all be waiting for her.

"We're about to begin," Carol said.

The woman considered my audience of five. "You think people got the time wrong?" she said.

"I'm sure not," Carol said. "Why don't you take a seat."

"You heard her, Craig," the woman said, and the two of them sat down in the front row, the woman a seat away from Jackie. The two of them eyed each other. Jackie nodded.

"I'm Rita Clare," the woman said.

Jackie said, "I'm Peter's wife."

"Aren't you lucky," Rita Clare said.

"Very," Jackie said.

Rita's tennis player sat forward with his elbows resting on his knees, head lowered, thoughtful, perhaps oblivious to this bookstore and the people around him. The old woman looked at her watch. The gypsy girl looked at hers.

"We'll wait a few more minutes," Carol said.

I found the scene I'd been looking for, the discovery of Abernathy's body. The secretary freezes, drops her papers, backs out of the room. The prose seemed as clumsy and self-conscious as those opening sentences, and I wondered if I should read the first scene, after all. I looked at Jackie, sitting squarely in front of me, and shook my head, and she answered with a very slight shrug, as if to say, *Hey, who cares?* My mouth had gone ash dry, and I felt for the bottle of water and realized my hands were shaking. I uncapped the bottle and raised it, and that is when Adrian Denton walked in, and the night went haywire.

part two

Seven

"Dance?"

Spoken suavely and with no doubt of the answer, this was my maiden utterance to Jacqueline Lawrence. She was new in town that fall, and it had quickly become known around the senior class that her father had been in the Coast Guard, a peripatetic profession, and that the family had resided most recently in Houston, Texas, where—and this was the interesting part—Jacqueline had been a cheerleader.

A cheerleader in Texas! Texas, the Lone Star State, that faraway, outsized state of bronco busters, Winchester-toting lawmen, football All-Americans, and the beauty queens who were their natural accessories. And the big Texas sun did seem to shine on Jacqueline Lawrence as she walked the hallways of parochial Dunstable High with her schoolbooks clasped to her perfect, sweater-draped breasts. She was as yet unattached, ripe and available, biding her time, and it was I who won the prize.

These were the glory days of football, the season still young, and had I not played football—had I been just another smart boy in the crowd, tall and reasonably good-looking but no Adonis—I wouldn't have had the nerve to ask a Texas cheerleader to dance with me. I think about this sometimes, think about all that football led to.

Because I'd never really liked the game, had even considered not playing that year. Baseball was my chosen sport, the game to which I am temperamentally suited. No other game can equal the balletic beauty of a big-league outfielder gliding to a fly ball, a shortstop darting and scooping and throwing in one lovely fluid sequence. I love the timelessness of baseball, no clock governing it, and the hitter's lonely stroll to the plate, two out, ninth inning, tying run out there on second base. I loved playing this unhurried, nuanced game in the sweet soft air of a spring afternoon.

I had never become inured to the violence of football and had only played out of a desire to stand out, to excel where others feared to tread. Let's face it: girls go for football players—or they did, in 1963. We had an advantage over everyone else, including stars of other team sports and the standouts in track and field. Even so, I thought seriously about quitting football, but I did go out for it, finally—that preening desire winning out—girls!—and in this new season a miracle took hold. Suddenly I was ten pounds stronger and as quick as my former, slenderer self. And now the fear that had turned my insides watery in the long hushed hour before kickoff— the team sitting hunched on the benches in front of our lockers, heads bowed in meditation, the coaches talking quietly in the next room, the distant, muffled off-key bleating of the bands—had hardened to an edgy atavistic desire to go out into the electric sunshine, the combustive noise, and prove myself in physical conflict. Hadn't Coach Maguire named me a starter, offense and defense? Football is a game of will and self-belief, and I possessed both now, in equal measure.

Jacqueline Lawrence had come to the annual Harvest Dance— Dunstable is a resort town, there is no fall harvest, just strawberries and cranberries in the spring—and was sitting with another pretty girl named Bonnie Williams, waiting for something to happen, as it surely would. I didn't have any classes with Jacqueline and had never spoken to her, but I'd had my eye on her—what guy in the senior class hadn't?—passing her in the hallways, sitting several tables over in the cafeteria.

We'd won that afternoon, and I was swaggering around with a beautiful pink abrasion on my forehead where a lineman's elbow had caught me. I'd come to the dance stag and was watching Jacqueline Lawrence across the blue-lit gym as I talked with Jimmy Soares, who also had his eye on her, and Tom DeMello, our quarterback, who was on his feet showing Jimmy and me how to do the monkey. The DJ finally cued a slow song, and I got up with purposive deliberation, like Alan Ladd unlimbering in *Shane*, and was on my way across the parquet one crucial step ahead of all others with the same idea.

"Dance?" Succinct, offhand, as if I were largely indifferent but just thought I'd ask.

Jacqueline looked at Bonnie Williams, smiled as if I'd delivered some mildly amusing witticism, and rose from her folding chair. She was wearing a hip-clinging ebony dress and still had a nice summer tan. The song was "Mr. Blue," by the Fleetwoods. I wrapped my right arm around the firm incurve of her back, and she rose against me on her toes, and now I was breathing the perfume on her neck.

"I'm Pete," I said.

"Peter Hatch, I know. Everyone does. Big football hero."

"You're Jacqueline."

"Jackie. Like Jackie Kennedy?"

There was no Texas drawl to her pert voice, or any accent I could discern, but I thought little of this at the time.

"People are talking about you," I said.

"New girl. They'll lose interest."

"I doubt it."

"Yeah?"

"I think you're going to have a busy year."

"Good."

She snuggled in a little tighter, a little more contentedly. We danced awhile, then she arched back and looked at me.

"How'd you get that strawberry?" she said.

"An illegal elbow," I said. "The guy should have been penalized."

"Twenty-four to nothing," Jackie said, citing the final score. "I'd say he was penalized plenty."

"Good point," I said.

We danced to the Fleetwoods' wistful lament, enjoying being locked together, the sensual feel of it, and then, as if it had just occurred to me, "How are you getting home?"

Jackie leaned back once more, looked me in the eye. "Any suggestions?" she said.

It made me laugh.

"Well, yeah," I said.

My father's Ford Falcon was one of the cheapest cars on the planet. As editor of the *Dunstable Inquirer*, Dad was one of the town's most eminent citizens, but Grandpa Hatch was still publisher, and he kept a tight rein on the payroll, even when it came to his son. Not that Dad minded; he loved his work and wasn't in it for the money. He didn't care about cars, either, and was content with the Falcon's performance and indifferent, if not oblivious, to its status alongside a Pontiac, say, or a Buick. It had come with a radio, thank God, which Dad hadn't wanted and of which he often complained.

Jackie and I left the dance before eleven, and I drove her to the beach parking lot off Shore Road, where teenagers had been necking since the invention of the automobile. There were two other cars, one at either end of the lot, and I parked midway between them. A half-moon dangled high above the sound. I peeled off my jacket and tossed it onto the back seat. I loosened my tie.

"What's Texas like," I said, "a lot of cowboy hats and six-shooters?"

"Lots of hats, which look great, by the way. Girls wear them, too."

"I never saw one except in the movies."

"You'd look good in one. Did you ever ride a horse?"

"Just a bicycle."

"Just a bicycle. Cute. You're going to have to try harder than that."

I smiled. "What's so great about riding a horse?" I said. "I never had the urge."

"It's a feeling of freedom. You can move so far, so fast. It makes you understand why they hung horse thieves in the old days. You stole a man's horse, you took away his freedom. You left him help-less."

"That's because everyone else had a horse. But if they didn't . . ."

"I'm talking about the *feeling*. You asked me what it *felt* like to ride a horse."

"Freedom."

"You're free as the wind when you're on a horse."

"I guess you'll miss it."

"Some. I didn't ride that often. A woman who owned horses let me and a couple of girlfriends ride, in exchange for mucking out stalls. I won't miss that."

"But you'll miss Texas."

She looked at me quietly, sagely. "Maybe."

"No Stetsons. No horses. Why'd you move here?"

"You don't know?"

"If I knew I wouldn't have asked, would I?"

"Why don't you skip the sarcasm."

"Sorry."

"My parents grew up here. Daddy wanted to come home when he left the Coast Guard. He wasn't crazy about Texas."

This was an utter surprise, and good news. The Lawrences had lived different places in their Coast Guard odyssey, but Texas had taken over my imagination, and I'd assembled Jackie's mother in my mind's eye as an unsettlingly shapely, long-legged woman who spoke with a smoky drawl and whose slate-blue gaze saw through teen-age posturing. Her husband would be rawboned and leathery, with a friendly smile and iron grip who would be inclined to think of New England boys, even football players, as soft.

"Both my parents went to school with your father," Jackie said, another surprise. "Daddy talks about him when he reads the news-paper. 'What's Ed Hatch up to now, I wonder? What's Ed Hatch saying about such-and-such?'"

I took a long look at the water, silk-smooth tonight and glazed with starlight and the half-moon's broken silvery veneer. This was going to be easier than I'd thought.

"A penny for your thoughts," Jackie said.

"Just thinking how pretty you are."

"That's the best you can do? Pretty?"

"Gorgeous," I said.

"Better."

"And modest," I said.

"Modesty is overrated."

The car at the end of the lot to our left started, coughing white exhaust into the darkness. The driver backed out, turned, and drove away on Shore Road. Jackie was watching me, waiting. Her gaze was bright and utterly serene. The moonlight distilled itself in her golden hair. It softened her perfect face.

"God you're beautiful," I said.

"Gorgeous. Beautiful. You've got my attention, Peter Hatch. Was that so hard?"

I kissed her then, and again, and after perhaps a minute we were deep kissing, and a little later Jackie swung herself around and slung her right leg over my lap. Her dress had hiked up, and I put my hand on a nylon-stockinged thigh, and she went on kissing me as if she'd expected this, and now I understood that the coming year would eclipse all my previous experiences with the opposite sex.

I drove her home at midnight, the two of us quiet now, but comfortable. I'd gone so far as to move my hand up her leg to the flesh above her stocking, anatomical terra incognita until this moment, and I wondered what other delights were in store. She turned the radio on, found a late-night show playing Frank Sinatra's "Witchcraft," and rested her head on my shoulder.

She lived in a smallish Cape-style house on a quiet street off the main road into town. Brick stoop, picture window to the right of the front door, bouquet of Indian corn tied to the brass knocker. The porch light was on, but the house was dark. We kissed good night on the stoop.

"Can I see you Friday?" I said.

"My number's in the book," she said.

"It wouldn't be," I said. "You've only just arrived."

"Guess you'll have to call information," she said, and winked and opened the door.

The porch light went off when I was halfway to the car.

eight

"Lovey Lawrence's daughter," my father said.

"Be nice, Ed," my mother said.

"I give up," I said. "Why Lovey Lawrence?"

"He used to chase the girls around the playground and try to kiss them," my father said.

"And you didn't?" my mother said.

"Not in fifth grade. He was sweet on the teachers, too. They were always women in those days. Lovey was always the teacher's pet."

"Don't listen to him," my mother told me.

"Married Grace Peck," my father said. "I always liked Grace. She wasn't bad looking. I always wondered why she married Lovey."

"He was a technician in the Coast Guard," I said. "He must be pretty smart."

"Oh he's smart, all right. Early retirement from the Coast Guard with a pension, and now he's on the payroll doing something or other at the Sea View."

"Accountant," I said. "Jackie said he's good with numbers."

"I'll say," my father said.

"Stop it," said my mother.

"By the way," my father said, "he's a John Bircher."

"You don't know that," my mother said.

"Yes I do," Dad said. "Oh yes I do."

I kept quiet after that, but the damage was done. Lovey Law-rence, as I now thought of him, opened the door on Friday night and introduced himself as *Clayton* Lawrence, then settled back down in his soft chair and crossed his bony legs. He had a gray pallor, graying hair, and wore thick glasses, which flashed when the light caught them just right. He'd been reading the *Inquirer*, which came out on Friday. There was no sign of Jackie, so I sat down on the sofa in my letter jacket, maroon suede with the big white D over my heart. *Lovey*, I thought. *Yeah.* He regarded me cordially through his glasses.

"Your father and I go way back," he said.

"He mentioned that," I said.

"Before he went away to private school, that is. How your grand-parents came up with the money for that during the Depression, I'll never know."

I wondered if Lovey was suggesting some sort of impropriety and remembered what my father had said about his Coast Guard pension and job at the Sea View, which seemed ethically dubious to my father—and to me, as I thought about it. Double-dipping, Dad called it. Lovey was pulling a fast one.

"They sent my uncle away too," I said. "Uncle James liked private school, but my father didn't. He hated it, in fact. He wishes he'd stayed here."

"I bet he does. He had a crush on Grace in seventh grade, did he tell you that?"

"He told me she was pretty," I said.

"She was indeed. He went away to school, so it didn't go any-where. I could be wrong, but I don't think Grace was terribly keen on him."

Grace came in from the kitchen—waddled in, smiling, broad and shapeless, looking like a stout European peasant in a black house dress and slippers. I popped up.

"You must be Pete," she said. "I'm pleased to meet you."

"Likewise," I said.

"Sit, sit, sit," said Mrs. Lawrence.

I sat back down. The house was one story; I knew Jackie had two sisters, and I wondered where they all slept.

"I was telling Pete how Ed Hatch used to be sweet on you," Lovey said.

"Oh he was *not*," Mrs. Lawrence said with a wide smile, sinking heavily into another chair. Jack Sprat's wife. Her hair was dark, and I wondered where Jackie had gotten her lustrous mane.

"How do you like being back in town?" I said.

"I could do without some of the changes," Lovey said.

"He doesn't like the shopping plaza," Mrs. Lawrence said.

"I used to hunt rabbits in those fields," Lovey said.

"Shoot them, you mean."

"Sure. Twenty-gauge shotgun. I had it when I was twelve."

I tried to picture this thin, squinting, bespectacled man kicking through high grass with a shotgun resting in the crook of his arm, and could not.

"Did you eat them?" I said.

"During the Depression? You bet we did."

Then Jackie appeared from the hall doorway with her sisters spilling into the room behind her. The sisters looked to be about eleven and fourteen or fifteen. I stood up. Jackie wore a Scotch plaid skirt that came short of her knees, and a white blouse.

"This is Margie," she said, "and Linda Jean."

The girls smiled. It wasn't clear to me who was Margie and who was Linda Jean. Jackie opened the closet and pulled down her coat. Her sisters were looking me over, smirking slyly. The younger one—

Margie, I would learn—was a little kid, blond like Jackie, gap-toothed and freckled. Linda Jean was as tall as Jackie but gangly, not yet pretty, but you knew she would be. I took Jackie's coat and held it for her.

"I'll be home early," she said. "Game tomorrow. Pete's got curfew."

"Sounds familiar," Lovey said.

"Jackie goes for football players," said the older sister, Linda Jean, still hanging with Margie in the doorway.

"Or the other way around," Jackie said.

"Last year's edition was the team quarterback," Lovey said. "A lineman's kind of a step down, Jacqueline."

"Linemen are tougher than quarterbacks," Jackie said.

"Yeah," said Linda Jean.

"Yeah," said Margie.

Lovey glanced at them, and his smile died away. "Say hello to your dad," he said, and I met his gray gaze and smiled and said I would, thinking *Lovey Lawrence*, and Lovey read something in my face, and I knew then that the man knew what my father thought of him, and that it went all the way back to grade school.

We drove to the new A&W Root Beer drive-in out on Route 26, and while we were waiting for our order Jackie asked me what I had in mind for tomorrow night, if anything. I said I didn't know, there was no dance, and no party that I knew of. My curfew tonight was eight thirty, so we'd eat and talk awhile, and I'd take Jackie home. Tomorrow night was ours.

"We'll go to the parsonage," she said.

It was an old word, quaint. I thought of Trollope and George Eliot. "Parsonage?" I said.

"At our church," Jackie said. "The Congregational. It's a kind of hangout for the CYF, the Christian Youth Fellowship. It's open all weekend."

"Wait a minute," I said.

"What's the problem?"

The girl brought our order, cheeseburgers and root beer floats. It was a summery September night, and the car windows were open. The girl attached the trays to our window ledges, and I paid and tipped her a dollar. Jackie tore into her cheeseburger, and I wondered how she could eat like that and stay looking like a centerfold.

"I'm not a Congregationalist," I said.

"It doesn't matter, you can come as my guest. I want you to meet Martin and Sonya—Martin and Sonya Gibson. Martin's our supervisor. They're both real smart. You'll like them."

Martin Gibson, Jackie went on to explain, was a seminarian at Harvard Divinity School, and overseeing and advising the Christian Youth Fellowship was somehow ancillary to his studies. He kept open house at the parsonage—a hangout, as Jackie said—assisted the Reverend Broadbent in the Sunday services, and taught the Bible to CYF members in the church basement on Sunday night. Then he and Sonya drove back to Cambridge for the week.

"Religion isn't my thing, to be honest," I said.

"Don't tell me you're an atheist."

"An agnostic."

"What's the difference? I never quite got that."

"The atheist denies that God exists, the agnostic doesn't know."

"I don't see how you can deny God exists. I mean, you can't *know* he doesn't."

"You can't know he *does*."

She thought about this, looking through the glass wall into the small neon-lit room of the A&W.

"Seems to me being an agnostic is the easy way out," she said.

"Out of what?" I said.

"Believing."

"Believing what?"

"Anything. It takes courage to believe. Anyone can say *I don't know.*"

"Atheists have courage?"

"More than you. They take a stand, don't they?"

"My stand is, I don't know."

"Some stand," Jackie said. "Did you ever go to church?"

"St. Andrew's when I was younger."

"So you're Episcopalian."

"I'm an agnostic."

"Well, the good news is, it doesn't matter what you believe or don't believe. Martin and Sonya are very broad-minded. Atheists, agnostics, whatever. You could be a communist, they wouldn't care."

"We just drop in tomorrow night, stay an hour and leave?"

"Leave sooner if you want to. Then we'll go park somewhere."

"All right, then."

"You'll especially like Sonya, by the way. She's got a body that doesn't quit."

"Oh?"

"I thought that would get you," Jackie said.

nine

The two churches, Episcopal and Congregational, regard each other across the Village Green—mutually aloof, I've always thought, as if disdainful of each other's notions of doctrine and worship. St. Andrew's is much the younger, built in the 1880s. It sits on a low but conspicuous rise, back from the street, a somber brownstone, medieval-looking with its Romanesque arches and buttresses, its keep-like steeple tower. My grandmother Hatch, who taught Sunday school in the rectory and served on the Altar Guild, loved its stained-glass windows, which depict scenes from the New Testament, and her praise of them convinced me at an early age that they were an aesthetic wonder. They are, at any rate, my only fond memory of the place, their blues, clarets, ochres, and jewel-greens luminous even on a gray day in March, as if they captured sunlight and held it as collateral to be dispensed on bleaker days.

As a boy I went to Sunday services sporadically to please Grandma Hatch, and her beloved stained-glass windows both literally and figuratively brightened the drear monotony of the service, in which God never spoke to me, and no apprehension of Him ever kindled. I would sit there daydreaming and eyeing one window or another, finding comfort in those prismatic colors while Mr. Wallace's service floated out over my head. Grandma Hatch retired as a parishioner in her late sixties for reasons known only to herself, enabling me to do the same at about the time I entered high school.

The First Congregational Church, a graceful building of chalk-white clapboard, is by far the prettier of the two. It seems to float, weightless, tending heavenward. Its narrow steeple shoots up gleaming white, visible in the summertime above the trees. Its bell was cast by Paul Revere some years before his storied midnight ride and bears this unhelpful description, which amused my sardonic father:

> *The living to the church I call,*
> *And to the grave I summon all.*

The parsonage is a small neat ancient house, also of white clapboard, with a Greek Revival front façade and a balustraded widow's walk, where wives could pace, in pre-parsonage days, scanning the horizon for a sail. Its rooms, when I knew it, held the pleasant, peaceful smell particular to very old houses, at once musty and dry, which I've always thought of as the smell of time itself. These rooms were small and boxy, the ceilings low, the floors random-width planks painted pea green.

Jackie led me in the back way that first night, through a mudroom and kitchen and what would have been the dining room when ministers and their families lived here, and where now a couple of sophomores, Billy Day and Ernie Holcomb, were slapping a ping-pong ball back and forth. I could hear a TV going in another room. I followed Jackie upstairs and down a hallway to a relatively spacious back room, where people sat around talking and a hi-fi played "The End of the World," that song of heartbreak by Skeeter Davis.

Martin Gibson was sitting on the floor with his arms wrapping his knees, Sonya was enthroned in an upholstered chair behind him.

Martin was square-jawed and broad-shouldered, with horn-rimmed glasses like Buddy Holly's, the glasses giving him a gentle look, a look of diffidence and sweetness. Sonya was a honey blonde with blue Nordic eyes and wonderful long legs. Later I thought of something Dorothy Parker is supposed to have said of the young Scott and Zelda, that they looked as if they'd just stepped out of the sun.

Adrian Denton, a sophomore that year, was draped in another cloth chair with a leg thrown over the arm—an attitude of haughty indolence and boredom. I was surprised to see Denton here. He was known in school to be a misfit, an adolescent version of his father, Nate, writer of splenetic letters to the *Inquirer*, pest at selectmen's meetings, perennial dissident and filibusterer at Town Meeting. On a sofa sat Skip Gladding, our backup center, and his girlfriend, Donna Murray. Skip lived down the road from me; we'd grown up together and been in the same homeroom since seventh grade. He was a second-rate comedian and an academic mediocrity, and I could not have imagined him and Denton in the same room and scarcely believed it now. I'd seen Skip a short time ago, in the quiet postgame locker room, where the team had undressed and showered sullenly, contemplating our first loss of the season and our own contributions to it, if any. Skip had contributed signally.

"Look what the cat dragged in," Skip said.

"Hi, sweetie," Donna said, meaning Jackie.

"What are you doing here, Hatch?" Denton said.

"He's my guest, that's what he's doing here," Jackie said. She took my hand. "This is Peter," she told Martin and Sonya. "Peter Hatch."

"Son of the local yellow journalist?" Martin said.

"Guilty," I said.

"Yellow?" Jackie said.

"It's an expression," I said. "I don't think it applies."

Martin pivoted on one arm and rose, strapping, to grip my hand.

"It was a bad joke," he said. "We love the *Inquirer*, pick it up every week on our way into town. Your dad's editorials are spot-on."

Now Sonya extended her hand, crooking her wrist as if offering it to be kissed. She wore a short skirt, black tights, and ballet slippers. I took the hand and met the pale-blue gaze and felt its cool burn.

"Join us," she said. "We're having a stimulating conversation about the Beatles."

Skip and Donna made room on the sofa, and Jackie and I snuggled down and Jackie took my arm. Martin lowered himself to the floor.

"Adrian doesn't like them," he said.

"They're con artists," Denton said. "They can't sing, they can't play."

"They look like freaks," Skip said. "You could turn them upside down and mop floors with them."

"You guys are jealous," Jackie said.

"Of those twerps?" Skip said.

Sonya looked from speaker to speaker with a charitable smile. Martin listened gravely, as if these inanities were grist for his studies at Harvard Divinity.

"I happen to think they're super talented," Donna Murray said.

Then Glenda Jane Perkins came in. Poor gangly Glenda Jane, with her buckteeth and round astonished eyes. She saw me and stopped.

"Why, Pete," she said, "what are you doing here?"

"I'm Jackie's guest," I said.

"And ours," Sonya said.

Glenda Jane sat down and smoothed her ill-fitting pink dress over her knees.

"Do you like the Beatles, Glenda Jane?" Martin said.

"Well . . ." Her hand went to her flat chest and she looked at me and blinked. "I *sort* of like them," she said.

"I know what you mean," Sonya said. "They're *okay*, but let's wait and see."

"Precisely," said Martin.

The 45s kept dropping. The Beach Boys, the Four Seasons, Lesley Gore. The last record ended, and Adrian Denton got up. There was a stack of LPs on the low table beside the record player. Denton removed the 45s from the spindle and unsheathed an LP. In a moment the record dropped, the Ronettes singing "Be My Baby." Denton sat down, and we were silent, listening. It was good stuff, the girls' voices smooth and caressing, but with a supple, sassy lilt.

"Here's some *music*," Denton said.

"Colored music," Skip said.

I saw Martin glance over his shoulder at Sonya.

"And just what is that supposed to mean?" Denton said.

Skip said, "Well . . ."

"We had a Negro band at our prom last year," Jackie said. "They rocked the place, let me tell you."

"They can sing," Skip said.

"Who's *they*?" Denton said.

"Colored people," Skip said.

I kept quiet. I was a guest, and anyway Skip didn't know any better.

"No race can sing better than any other," Martin said, "but if there *is* such a thing as Negro music, it's spirituals and blues. And think about where that music came from. The pain of slavery. Segregation. Jim Crow laws."

The Ronettes were singing "Be My Baby."

"This don't sound too painful," said Skip.

And Denton: "You know what, Gladding? You're an idiot."

But before Skip could muster a clever rejoinder, no easy thing for him, Sonya leaned forward and placed a hand on his arm while she sent Denton a lovely smile, stripping the scowl from his soft young face.

"We don't allow idiots in here," she said. "Jackie, by any chance is this guy Hatch an idiot?"

"Not that I've noticed," Jackie said.

"Then I guess he can stay."

Smiles, the tension broken.

"Too bad about the game," Donna said.

"Will you shut up about the game?" Skip said.

"I'm talking to Pete, not you," Donna said.

We'd been hopelessly behind in the fourth quarter, and the coach had sent Skip into the game at center, to give him some exercise. Second play from scrimmage, shotgun formation, Skip had sailed the football over the quarterback's head, gifting Somerset with another touchdown.

"I didn't go to the game," Glenda Jane said, eyeing the floor. Speaking to herself, I think.

"Win some, lose some," I said.

"Brilliant observation," Denton said.

Jackie shot him a look.

"Did you ever play football, Martin?" asked Glenda Jane.

I'd been wondering the same thing. The shoulders, the legs. A center, maybe. A middle linebacker.

"Some," Martin said.

"Some?" Sonya said. "He was a Little All-American."

"Where?" I said.

"Grinnell?"

"Sure," I said, "Harry Hopkins's alma mater."

Everyone looked at me, Skip and Donna and maybe Jackie thinking, *Show-off*. Denton wondering how the hell I knew *that*, and Glenda Jane not thinking much of anything. Sonya came to my rescue with a smile.

"An Easterner who's heard of Grinnell," she said.

"I guess that proves he's not an idiot," Jackie said.

"*Quel* relief," Sonya said.

"Who's Harry Hoskins?" Skip said.

"What's with Adrian Denton?" Jackie said, twisting the radio dial, searching.

"Who knows?" I said.

She found "In Dreams," Roy Orbison, and quit looking.

"How come he doesn't like you?" she said.

"I don't know."

"Did you do something to him?"

"Of course not."

"Well, he's jealous, then. That's all it can be."

"Of what?"

"Me. Football. All your friends. Losers hate winners."

"Glenda Jane's a loser, poor kid. Denton isn't."

"He thinks he is," Jackie said, "and I agree with him."

"He's smart," I said. "He'll go to a good school. Get a good job."

"It won't change him," Jackie said. "He can't escape it. He's going to carry it around all his life. A chip on his shoulder."

"We'll never know, will we."

"I hope not," Jackie said.

There's a little headland on the bay side of Dunstable called the Devil's Foot, maybe because of the dangerous offshore rocks, some of them hidden, others bulging out of the water, craggy and kelp-shaggy and crusted with barnacles. I'd been out here a few times with my spinning rod in the early spring, when the stripers and bluefish start running, and I'd never seen anyone after dark but a fisherman or two. It was at the end of a long dirt road that emptied into a sandy clearing large enough for four or five cars.

It was my inspiration to bring Jackie to the Devil's Foot after we left the parsonage that first night. Sure enough, we had the place to ourselves. The night was clear, the stars swarmed down over the water, and a half-moon was up. I parked and left the radio on softly. I slid out from behind the wheel and Jackie swung her right leg over and sat straddling my lap, as she had a week ago. A long kiss, my hand venturing higher and higher up her leg, then she broke back, stopping the proceedings, and looked at me in the soft interior darkness with her arms resting on my shoulders. Her face pale, vivid, lovely, inches from mine.

"I've been thinking," she said.

"Thinking," I said. "Why don't you do that later?"

"Be quiet and listen to me. I think you should join the Fellowship."

"No thanks."

"Why not?"

"I'll come to the parsonage anytime," I said.

"That would be cheating. You can't just do the light, fun part."

"I thought that was the idea."

"Once or twice, but not every week."

"I'm not going to church. Forget that."

"I'm not asking you to. But you can come to Bible study."

"No thanks."

"Have you read the Bible?"

"Not much."

"Not at all, you mean."

"I guess not."

"And you call yourself educated."

"Well, yeah."

"You know who Harry Hopkins was and that he went to Grin-nell College, but you've never read the Gospels. I'd call that a gap that needs filling."

She had a point.

"I'll think about it," I said.

"You'll do more than think about it if you're smart," Jackie said, and straightened and began, slowly, unbuttoning her blouse.

Ten

I had to borrow a Bible from Grandma Hatch, who let me know what she thought about an educated family not owning one. I told her we probably did own one; I just couldn't find it. She gave me a leatherbound King James and told me to read no other version.

The class met in the warm, wax-smelling church basement. We sat on folding chairs, a dozen or so of us, with Martin presiding, perched on a varnished church-supper table with his big legs dangling. Sonya sat behind him and didn't say much. They were working their way through Paul's Letter to the Romans when I arrived. Martin would ask for a volunteer, who would read a verse or two aloud, and then we'd parse it, with Martin's guidance. Mine was the only King James Bible in the room, and when called upon to read I would do so from Jackie's New Oxford Annotated Bible, less beautifully archaic of course but more accessible to my classmates.

Martin, as I expected, was a wise and patient teacher. His choice of texts seemed random; we would hopscotch around as the year went along: Genesis, First Isaiah, Corinthians, the Gospels of Mark and John, and this erratic tour of the Bible has stood me in good stead ever since. I like knowing what Corinthians is when someone reads from it at a wedding, and where the words of "The Messiah" come from. I like knowing that the birth narrative we hear at Christmas is only one man's version of that long-ago event.

There was always the question whether to read the Gospels literally—the miracle of the loaves and fishes, say—or as embellishments of Jesus's ministry, true stories turned into tall tales for impact and entertainment value. Martin always left it up to us. He believed in Jesus's divinity—there were witnesses to the Resurrection, he said—and in the greatness of Jesus the man, walking the cobbled streets of those ancient bustling cities, speaking to a yearning in people, haranguing malefactors and scoffers.

Sunday night, so I would drive Jackie straight home afterward. The Lawrences' living room was dark behind the picture window and you could hear the murmur of the TV, the family gathered around *The Ed Sullivan Show*. Jackie would give me a kiss and vanish inside in time for *Bonanza*, which came on at nine and was as much a ritual of the Lawrence family Sabbath as church and Sunday dinner.

My parents found this new involvement of mine highly amusing. A Youth Fellowship at St. Andrew's would have been one thing, but in their view the local Congregationalists were illiberal and hidebound—a sort of ecclesiastical branch of the DAR. Their amusement, I understood, had a mordant cast; it was as if Jackie had bewitched me into joining a whites-only country club.

"Martin and Sonya aren't like that," I said. "They went to Grinnell. They're big fans of Harry Hopkins and FDR."

My father was sitting to the left of the hearth fire with his *New York Times*, his necktie loosened after his work day, his sleeves rolled up his thin pale arms.

"What I'm saying is, they're broad-minded," I said.

"That's a relief, in practicing Christians," my father said.

"I'm serious," I said.

"I am too," he said. "How does the Reverend Mr. Broadbent feel about him?"

"He likes him, I assume."

"Well, I hope your Gibsons don't get themselves in trouble."

"In trouble with who?"

"*Whom.* The righteous. Does Clay Lawrence like them?"

"Everyone likes them," I said, and I think everyone did at that point, even Lovey Lawrence.

But what did I care about the Congregationalists' politics, or Lovey Lawrence's, or even Jackie's, if she had any? To everything there is a season, as it says in Ecclesiastes, and in this season of love at the Devil's Foot, Jackie was stripping to the waist, unpeeling my madras shirts, unbuckling my belt, and affording me pleasures I'd never imagined, stopping always just short of the ultimate and—to me—unimaginable act of intercourse itself. Saturdays, if there was no dance or party, we'd spend an hour or two at the parsonage or take in the early show at the Empire, then adjourn to the Devil's Foot, where we never encountered a soul.

Then, on a Saturday night in late October, we were sitting in a booth at the Howard Johnson's at the end of Main Street when Jackie polished off her sundae and licked the spoon, eyeing me in a way both sly and speculative. Something was up, I was pretty sure. We'd been to a party in Jimmy Ferreira's basement; we'd slow-danced in the near-dark, and she'd fingered the back of my neck in a suggestive way that had both pleased and puzzled me.

"I have to go to the drugstore," she said.

"It's eleven o'clock," I said.

"CVS is open till midnight."

"What do you need?"

"Never mind."

The CVS was in the new shopping plaza, once a field where Lovey Lawrence stalked rabbits with a shotgun. It lay just beyond Howard Johnson's, where Main Street curved east and became Route 26. I sat in the car while Jackie went into the big, brightly lit drugstore. I figured she needed aspirin or Tums, or maybe some unmentionable female item. The radio was going, the Beatles singing "Words of Love," the old Buddy Holly song. I thought Buddy did it better and wondered if Adrian Denton could be right about the Beatles. Jackie came out of the big drugstore. She jackknifed into the car and dropped a small white paper bag in my lap.

"After this," she said, "you're on your own."

I dug the little box out of the bag and held it up to the plaza lamplight: Trojan Pleasure Pack. The Four Seasons were singing "Candy Girl." I stared at the bright little box, trying to think what to say. Jackie reached out, touched the back of my neck under my jacket collar.

"We're a team," she said. "I knew you'd be shy about it."

"I guess you know I'm a virgin," I said.

"I guess you know I'm not."

"I wasn't sure," I said.

Jackie smiled. "Really?"

"Really."

I started the car, and we swung out of the plaza lot, west on Main, in the direction of the Devil's Foot.

"We're going to my house," Jackie said.

I looked at her. "You aren't serious."

"The basement. No one'll bother us down there, it's kind of a house rule."

"No one'll bother us at the Devil's Foot," I said.

"Doing it in a car is kind of awkward," she said. "You can't really stretch out."

"What if your parents wake up?"

"They'll think we're making out, if they *do* hear us, which they won't."

"I'll be too nervous."

"Want to bet?"

"Jack . . ."

"Trust me."

The house was dark, the outdoor light burning over the brick stoop. We crept up the flagstone walk. Jackie swung the front door open gently. I followed her in. She put her purse down on the coffee table and removed her jacket, and I took off mine. We stole through the dining room and into the kitchen. Jackie draped a dish towel on the knob of the cellar door, a signal for Linda Jean, who she thought might still be out. She turned on the cellar light. I went down ahead of her. She closed the door behind us.

The basement was paneled, with a partitioned room for the furnace. There was an old sofa, a bookshelf containing a stack of LPs and several board games, and a record player on a four-legged stand. Next to the sofa stood a lamp with a red bulb, and Jackie lit it, then went back to the foot of the stairs and killed the overhead.

I dug the Trojans out of my pocket and fell into the sag of the sofa. I could not imagine the next ten minutes of my life. Jackie fitted an LP onto the spindle and came over, dyed a soft rose by the red bulb, as the record dropped. The Lettermen commenced to croon on low volume. Jackie sat down and took my hand.

"You won't talk about this, will you?" she said.

"With whom?"

"Anybody. Guys like to brag."

"Some guys, maybe."

"Another thing. I may be fast, but I don't run around. It's just going to be you."

"Same here."

"You remember that."

A car stopped out front. The door slammed.

"Linda Jean," Jackie said.

Linda Jean came into the house, and we heard her footsteps thump across the living room overhead and on into the kitchen. Jackie and I sat still. Linda Jean opened the cellar door.

"Having fun down there?" she said.

Jackie smiled.

Linda Jean said, "Hah," and closed the door. She moved around the kitchen, then her footsteps retreated to the other end of the house, fading into silence. Jackie let go of my hand, put her arms around my shoulders, and looked me in the eye.

"What we're about to do, Peter. It's all about trust."

Her face was inches from mine. I could smell her perfume. Smiling now, she moved in and kissed me, and that's how it began—with a kiss, like any other, but a prelude this time, the key to a kingdom.

Jackie didn't think teenage sex, so long as it wasn't promiscuous, was at odds with Christian piety. She was clear on this, as she was about everything—profanity, for instance. She could swear with the best of them, unlike most girls in those days, but profanity, she said, was like sex, so long as you were discreet about it, a matter of indifference to God, who had greater things on His mind.

"Who are we hurting?" she asked rhetorically.

"Nobody," I said.

"It's not like we're cheating on somebody, or committing adultery, which I will never do."

I knew she meant it. Falsehood and deception were foreign to her nature, as remote from her dealings with the world as languages she didn't speak.

"I'm easy, but I'm not," she said, and I think that captured it.

She was a considerate and generous lover, and in later years with other women I understood how considerate and how generous. She let me watch her undress because she knew I liked to, facing me, in the rosy lamplight. She was patient and innovative at the same time, encouraging me to be the same, and I began to see what she meant about trusting each other. And so our Saturday nights ended here in the basement instead of the Devil's Foot—on the musty sofa, in that gentle tinctured light, with the Lettermen or the Drifters accompanying us half-heard.

One midnight as we were getting started footsteps crossed the floor above us and went on into the kitchen. A pause, perhaps at the refrigerator, then Lovey opened the cellar door.

"Jacqueline?"

"Hi, Daddy."

"What are you doing down there?"

I untangled our legs and struggled to sit up, looking for my clothes, but Jackie gripped my arm and pulled me back down beside her. She put her finger to her lips, then spoke across the room, toward the stairs running up to the open door, where I pictured Lovey standing in his pajamas.

"We're making out, Daddy. It's what kids do. Go back to bed."

Silence, as Lovey ruminated on this. I lay there with Jackie's arm around me and a warm firm leg between my two, praying. Jackie stroked my cheek.

"Well," Lovey said finally. "Okay, I guess." The door closed gently, and we heard him traipse back to his bedroom.

"What would he do if he knew?" I whispered.

"Nothing, but it would hurt him."

"He'd blame me."

"Probably, but I don't want to hurt him, either way." She turned, slid herself on top of me, smiling.

"Now where were we?" she said.

*   *   *

I was now a frequent customer at the CVS, where no one knew me. I'd been going into the Rexall on West Main since I was a kid, stopping in for baseball cards or to order a cherry Coke at the lunch counter. There was also Appel's Pharmacy halfway down Main, but we'd always gotten our prescriptions there, and Mr. Appel knew my parents. Everyone working at the CVS was a stranger—new in town, like the store itself, or maybe commuting to the job. I would walk in, affecting nonchalance, and ask for a couple of "Pleasure Packs," as casually as if I were buying cigarettes or chewing gum. The clerks were young men, hardly older than I, and they would serve me with faint, superior smirks, as if they saw the embarrassment beneath my act and pictured me getting it on guiltily and in secret with the class tramp, some poor skinny unloved girl. I would keep my gaze down, pay, and get out of there.

"They're condescending," I said. "They treat me like a kid."

"You *are* a kid," Jackie said, "and what do you care what they think?"

"Come in with me sometime," I said.

"What for?"

"Wipe the smiles off their faces."

We were lying naked, Jackie warm against me, in the musty embrace of the basement sofa. It was where we did most of our talking.

"Show me off, you mean," she said.

"Why not?"

"Because I'm not a trophy, that's why not." Then she shifted onto her side and brought a hand to my chin and made me look at her in the soft lamplight. "You aren't a trophy, either," she said. "Neither of us is. That's not what this is about anymore."

"Anymore?" I said.

"You heard me."

She'd released my chin. I rose above her on my elbow.

"But I want to know what you mean, *anymore*," I said.

"Anymore means anymore. Just say okay, Peter."

I lay back and thought a moment, wondering what had changed, and when it had happened.

"Okay," I said.

eleven

John Fitzgerald Kennedy was killed on a mellow Indian summer afternoon, the Friday before Thanksgiving. It was Coach Maguire who announced his death to me and my teammates, and because I was a stranger to sorrow, I'd been certain, as the news from Dallas had flooded the airwaves, that our young president would not die, could not die. A bulletin would come any minute saying he was out of danger. The world would spin on, and we could get back to our lives—football, school, Jackie—while JFK returned to his work, standing up to Khrushchev, building up the Peace Corps, pushing civil rights, bantering with reporters—that Irish wit!—on national TV.

Until that moment we knew only that the president had been shot and taken to a hospital, and we were suiting up for practice in a preternatural silence, avoiding eye contact with one another, keeping our emotions to ourselves, whatever they might be. There was a radio in the coaches' room, we could hear its nervous staccato chatter, and then the door opened and Coach Maguire came in. He crossed the gray-painted cleat-pocked cement floor halfway and stopped. He wore his gray hooded sweatshirt, a maroon baseball hat clamped tight on his close-cropped head.

"Boys," he said, "the president is dead."

I remember the yellow sunshine in the high frosted windows, and the smell of sweat and Bengay. I remember the silence. I remember Coach Maguire's pained squint, the grim set of his broad ruddy Irish face. He spoke that one sentence, then turned and walked out, leaving his words etched in the close, stale, liniment-smelling air, and in my memory forever.

My father ran a banner across the top of the front page that afternoon, lines from Katharine Lee Bates's poem, *When Lincoln Died*:

> *And not one angel to catch the bullet!*
> *What had become of God?*

This *cri de coeur* offended numerous townspeople, including Lovey Lawrence, as I discovered that evening, when I called for Jackie. I sat down on the sofa to wait for her, as usual, and Lovey crossed his legs and regarded me through his glasses, sizing me up as if for the first time. Today's *Inquirer* lay on the coffee table.

He and I had gotten along all right since that first unpromising encounter. You only have to keep quiet, listen, and pretend to agree with people like Lovey Lawrence, and they will like you. *Approve* of you, in Lovey's parlance. I understood that he regarded my father as a misguided but essentially harmless left-winger, and in deference to me he stayed away from politics on the national level, keeping instead to Town Hall matters, selectmen's decrees and budget proposals, which I feigned interest in. He also liked to talk about Dunstable "in the old days," which was mildly entertaining and sometimes informative. Lovey liked an audience, and listening to him and nodding thoughtfully were a small price to pay for the favors of his daughter.

"Jackie tells me you're an agnostic," Lovey began on that evening of national sorrow.

I knew immediately what this was about. My father had gotten the first phone call shortly before dinner, this one from a dim-brained Rotarian who'd accused Dad of blasphemy. Dad had come back to the table muttering *Goddamn fool* and shaking his head. There'd been two more calls.

"It isn't that I don't want to believe," I told Lovey.

I looked into the little dining room, and the lighted kitchen beyond. Mrs. Lawrence was out there washing the dishes.

"And your father," Lovey said. "He must be an agnostic, too."

"I don't know," I said. "Maybe." Dad, in fact, was a thorough-going atheist.

Lovey leaned forward, picked up the *Inquirer* and shook it at me, like a fussy schoolmaster out of Hawthorne or Washington Irving.

"What was the idea of this business about God not stopping bullets?" he said.

"It's just a . . ."

"Just a what?"

Lovey dropped the newspaper and sat back. He recrossed his legs and watched me form an explanation.

"She was so upset," I said, meaning Katharine Lee Bates, "that she lashed out at God. Blaming Him, because she didn't know who else to blame."

I looked away, at the silent TV, wondering what was taking Jackie so long, wishing, at least, that one of her sisters would appear.

"God has reasons that we can't see," Lovey said. "He works in His own mysterious ways, and it's an insult to Him to blame Him for what He has wrought."

But I'd already seen the mistake in Miss Bates's plaint, if it *was* a mistake and not a poetical construct. God—anybody's God, whatever He was—or It, or She—was no intercessor. He didn't save

Lincoln, He didn't interfere at Auschwitz, He didn't push aside that bomb drifting down over Hiroshima. To expect Him to intercede, in mysterious ways or otherwise, was childish. Whatever He was, God wasn't a manipulator.

"It was tasteless," Lovey said, summing up.

Mrs. Lawrence came in, drying her puffy hands on her apron. She sank into her chair.

"What an awful, awful day," she said.

"I was telling Pete that we disapprove of his father's headline."

"Banner," I said.

"Banner?" Lovey said.

"It's called a banner," I said.

"We know he didn't mean anything by it," Mrs. Lawrence said.

Lovey tried a smile. "Your dad was always a little impulsive," he said. "It's why we liked him, isn't it, Grace."

I stood up and looked out the picture window with my back to them. The Falcon sat at the edge of the little lawn in the dark. Lights were on in the houses up and down the street, and they seemed muted, sad. Jackie came in while I was standing there, and I turned and helped her into her coat. Her face was quiet, expressionless, with a pallor as of sleeplessness. I opened the door for her.

"Cheer him up, Jacqueline," Lovey called after us.

Jackie pulled the car door shut with both hands and settled herself. We left the radio off; I didn't want to hear any more news, and music, if there was any, would be out of place.

"Was Daddy being a jerk about the poem?" Jackie said.

"A bit of one."

"He's an old crank. Don't listen to him. I told him it was just a poem, and not to get all bent out of shape about it.

"He didn't like Kennedy, I assume."

"He's a Republican, what do you think?"

"I think he'd be happy living in czarist Russia."

Jackie looked at me, and I knew I'd gone too far.

"Why not say Nazi Germany, go all the way?" she said.

"I'm upset, Jack."

"We all are."

"I never knew how you felt about the president," I said.

"I don't argue with Daddy, if that's what you mean."

"But do you agree with him?"

"Not much."

"Some?"

"Maybe. Now and then. No one's perfect, Peter. Not even President Kennedy."

The parsonage was dark, the parking lot empty, and there was a handwritten note signed by Martin taped to the mudroom door, legible by the floodlight on the white church on the other side of the driveway. Martin's cursive was spirited—shapely loops, a slanted, eager forward motion. *We've been called back to Cambridge for a convocation. We're so sorry we can't be with you on this night. Remember that God loves us and that we draw strength from that love. Blessings.*

We got back in the car.

"Now what?" I said.

There was no game until next week, Thanksgiving Day, and Saturday practice had been called off. Jackie and I had all night.

"I don't know," she said.

A car stopped at the end of the driveway and someone got out and closed the door. The car waited, idling, and Glenda Jane Perkins came up the driveway, casting puzzled looks at the darkened parsonage windows. I rolled down my window.

"Hi, Glenda Jane," I said.

"Where is everybody?" she said.

I told her.

"Geez," she said. "I didn't want to be alone tonight."

"Maybe your mother doesn't, either," I said.

"Yeah, that's probably true," Glenda Jane said.

Her mother, a widow or divorcée, I never knew which, was a fleshier, lipsticked version of Glenda Jane, and Glenda Jane's driver tonight. I could make her out now, watching us. Glenda Jane leaned, found Jackie in the passenger seat.

"Hi, Jackie."

"Hi."

"Sad day, huh?" Glenda Jean said.

"A bitch," Jackie said.

"Well. I guess I'll go home. 'Night, you two."

"'Night, Glenda Jane," I said.

She turned and went slowly down the driveway in her winter coat.

"You're so nice to her," Jackie said.

"Why not?"

"You should be. I should be nicer. I'm selfish, aren't I."

"You know what you want."

"Everybody does, but I'm more determined about it."

"Clarity and determination aren't selfishness."

Jackie looked out at the darkened house, thinking about this. She shrugged, buying my absolution or not buying it, I couldn't tell. She looked at me.

"What do you want to do?"

"I don't know. Maybe we should just go home."

"I don't like that idea."

"I guess I don't, either."

"Want to go to the Devil's Foot?"

"Or we could wait till your parents go to bed," I said.

"That'll be a couple of hours," Jackie said. Then: "Wait a minute."

She was out of the car. A glance down the driveway, then she went quickly to the mudroom door. She opened the storm door, tried the inside door, and it swung in with a creak. I got out of the car.

"Park somewhere else," Jackie said. "I'll meet you upstairs."

"Don't turn on any lights," I said.

"No kidding," Jackie said.

Martin and Sonya had neglected to turn the heat down, as well as lock the door, and Jackie and I needed no blanket on the big comfortable sofa upstairs. We undressed by the chalky light of the church floodlight and lay down, and for the first time I had no answer to Jackie's caresses and the feel of her against me. Puzzled, I kissed her and ran my hand around and moved against her, but the harder I tried, the more useless it seemed, and after a while I fell back defeated and stared at the plaster ceiling. Jackie shifted around, laid her palm on my chest.

"I don't understand it," I said.

"It happens to everybody," Jackie said. "You're just sad, that's all."

"It happens to *everybody*?" I wondered how she knew this.

"Sure," she said. "For all kinds of reasons. Sometimes no reason at all. We can just lie here. It's nice, don't you think?"

A car came up the driveway and stopped, and people got out, and Jackie and I lay still, and I could hear myself breathing. Voices down below, several guys, they'd read Martin's note and were discussing it. The car doors opened and closed, and the car started and muttered away down the driveway.

I tried again, moved my hand over her hip and leg, pressed myself against her, but it was still no good.

"I'm sorry, Jack," I said.

"Hon, it doesn't *matter*."

She moved again, lay now with her head over my heart, her soft sweet-smelling hair bunched under my chin.

"I remember his inaugural address," I said. "I remember listening to it on the radio."

It had snowed off and on through the morning of the inaugural: heavy soggy snow, reducing to gray slush where you stepped in it. I came in through the kitchen door and found my parents standing by the Zenith tube radio with their heads bowed, listening to the new president. They nodded to me and went on listening. I put my schoolbooks down. I'd heard Eisenhower on the radio, and he'd sounded toneless and studied and didactic, like some well-meaning but tiresome uncle. This was different. John Kennedy was young, I knew that, and now his voice, with its salty New England elongation of vowels, its tonal rise and fall, its sheer vibrancy, woke something in me. This was my president, mine, and there in our warm kitchen with the wet snow outside and the sky a dingy sodden gray in the windows, I knew I would grow to love him.

"It had snowed," I said. "I remember the snow, and the steam radiator hissing."

And then I was weeping. I had not, all day.

"Oh, hon," Jackie said.

Her hand came up and found my wet cheek. She caressed it, smoothing away the tears. She kissed me lightly.

"Hey," she said.

And rose, swung a leg over and straddled me. She bent down and kissed me, kissed me again.

Boys, the president is dead . . .

Jackie, rising over me with her hair dropping forward in the semi-darkness, rocking gently, touching me, whispering, *Where are those things?*

"Here. On the floor."

"Get them."

The president is . . .

"Good, Peter. Wait now."

"Okay?"

"Yes yes . . ."

"Oh Jack . . ."

"Isn't this better isn't it?"

"Yes it is yes yes"

Then I drifted into half sleep with Jackie's arm and leg slung around me. She gave me ten minutes, then touched my cheek, waking me.

"Hey there."

"Hey," I said.

"I'm going to start being nice to Glenda Jane Perkins," Jackie said. "I'm going to say hello to her. I'm going to go out of my way."

She lay watching me, awaiting my answer. I smiled.

"It isn't so hard," I said.

"That's the thing," she said. "It's so damn easy, but hardly anyone does it."

A car passed out front, and another. We could hear them faintly.

"Maybe we'd better get out of here," I said.

"Not yet," she said.

I would remember this in days to come, sitting on this sofa in the lamplight, talking music or movies or maybe religion with Martin and Sonya, and with Denton and others, the room, the sofa, now in possession of a secret unimaginable even to Martin and Sonya. I thought of it then as a sort of joke we'd played, a wild prank, forgetting my own initial difficulty, and only years later saw it for what it really was: an act of pure love on Jackie's part, her gift to me in the first hour of sorrow I'd ever known.

Twelve

Thanksgiving Day broke cold and bright, and on that vivid morning of blue sky and brass bands and football, grief recused itself, went on holiday. We beat archrival Dover at home by two points, the game in doubt till the final play. I made that play: their quarterback dropped back to throw a pass that could win the game, I broke through, grazed a halfback who made a flat-footed attempt to block me, and leapt at the startled QB, who'd cocked his arm to throw. We went down hard, him on top of me somehow, and I blacked out. When I came to, I was on my feet, the game was over, and we were swarming exultantly off the field.

We moved to the gap in the snow fence, where girlfriends waited, a few fathers, a gaggle of worshipful little boys. I'd assumed Jackie would go straight home to her Thanksgiving dinner, but there she was, rosy-cheeked from the cold air, her hair wind-mussed and golden. She wore her maroon school sweater with the big white D on front, the pleated gray skirt, white tennis shoes, and she still held her pom-pom.

I tugged my helmet off and pulled her against my dirt- and grass-stained jersey, and we climbed the hill with my arm around

her, not speaking till we reached the whitewashed cinderblock
locker room.

"Wait for me," I said.

She was alone when I came out, and the day was eerily transformed,
the sky low and overcast, the air thin and lightless and much warmer.
The field was deserted, the hillside, the bleachers; we had the world
to ourselves. We strolled down Main, Jackie on my arm, carrying her
pom-pom, the street and sidewalks empty, silent. Even the Mobil
station was closed, and the 7-Eleven. A car came by, and the driver
saw Jackie's pom-pom and blared his horn. She raised and shook it,
smiling back at the man.

"Now what?" she said. "You don't look like a basketball player."

"Baseball," I said.

"I guess the yearbook'll keep you busy for a while."

"That, and I'll do some running to stay in shape."

"Editor of the yearbook. Maybe you'll be a great writer someday."

We turned by the brick telephone office, kicked through drifted
leaves past houses whose lights were on in the gray afternoon, and I
pictured the gathered families, the laden tables, the conviviality.

"Peter?"

"What."

"Your father doesn't like me."

"Sure he does."

*But she knows better. She has been to the house a few times, briefly.
She stands uneasily in the living room while Peter goes upstairs to get
something he's forgotten—a sweater, money—erect posture, as always,
shoulders squared, her hands down in front of her one over the other, as if
she were undergoing an inspection.*

How are you today, young lady?

Good.

She knows it's the wrong answer, grammatically suspect and all but meaningless, but something about this avid little owl of a man in his wrinkled ink-stained white shirts confuses her, turns her speechless. He dislikes her father, she is sure of that, sees him as smug and slightly ridiculous. But then, so does Peter, though he has never said as much.

"He's short with me," she said. "He thinks I'm dumb."

"He's short with everybody, and no one thinks you're dumb."

"I'm not as smart as you. I get that."

"You're smart in a different way."

"Which is a polite way of saying I'm dumb."

"Would I be with you if you were dumb?"

"As long I was putting out for you."

I laughed and gave her a squeeze.

"I was with you before that, remember?" I said. "And I didn't know you were going to put out for me."

"You didn't?"

"Not for a while."

We walked on, past the sleeping high school, the empty tennis courts.

"Peter?"

She stopped, stopping me, and turned to face me.

"I've fallen for you," she said. She closed her eyes, opened them. "I'm in love with you. I always will be, I think."

No girl had ever said it, and it struck deep, thrilling, but in some vague way disconcerting, like thunder off in the distance. I searched for an answer and couldn't find one, except to take her in my arms and kiss her. There was the apple taste of fall on her cool lips. She stepped back and studied me, smiling uncertainly, and I embraced her again, kissed her harder, longer. Again she stepped back and looked up at me.

"I can't help it," she said, and I thought, *You have to. You have to say it.*

"I'm in love with you, too. Hell, I fell for you weeks ago."

"Yeah?" Eyeing me.

"Of course."

"Well, good," she said, and took my arm again, and we walked on.

We'd just turned onto her street when my father found us. The Falcon approached from the opposite direction, and Dad saw us and came on slowly. Jackie released my arm, as if she'd been caught in some impropriety. My father pulled over across the street from us. He was smiling in that dry, almost mordant way he had, half annoyed and half amused. His window was closed. Jackie waved to him, and Dad nodded.

"He likes you fine," I said.

"No he doesn't."

"Jackie . . ."

"It's okay, hon. You go on."

I crossed the street and got in the car. Dad was still smiling that smile. He turned the car around, and we drove home in the premature twilight, the stillness of this day of respite and thanksgiving.

Thirteen

People wondered for a long time why I married Jackie: I could see it in the way their eyes shifted when I mentioned her, and in the careful way they chose their words when talking about her, uttering bland generic compliments and observations that stopped short of any deep truth. They may still be wondering, though it's hard to tell anymore, and I've long ceased caring what they think.

I married her impulsively, it's true, but that was later, more than a decade after high school. We never spoke of marriage that school year; Jackie knew better than to rush things and seemed content to let the future bring whatever it would. I let her think we'd stay pledged to each other in some fashion come fall, planning secretly to leave her then for good. Which meant I was leading a double life— living a lie, as they say.

The certainty that Jackie simply wouldn't do, over the long haul, had its genesis on a Friday night in March, when I came home late and found my father alone at the dining table hunched over a book and drinking beer out of the bottle. The house was dark and silent around him, my mother and Jill fast asleep. Dad had put the paper out today, and now came the respite of the weekend, a half day of light work tomorrow, then Sunday off. His eyelids were heavy. His sleeves were rolled to his pale knobby elbows, his tie loosened. I could tell he'd drunk quite a bit, and that his mood was mellow, kindly disposed.

"Have a beer," he said.

I brought one to the table and sat down.

"What did you do tonight?" Dad said.

"There was a hootenanny at the Armory," I said. "A group from Providence, copying the Kingston Trio. They even sang the same songs."

Dad nodded, half-listening. He'd asked just to be polite, but I was glad he did. He was reading *Custer's Luck*. He had a shelf of histories of George Armstrong Custer and the battle at the Little Bighorn River, and I'd read all of them at an early age—*Custer's Luck*, *Bugles in the Afternoon*, *I Fought With Custer*, *The Custer Myth*, *Boots and Saddles*. The story lived vividly in my imagination—Custer on that dusty hill, arrows raining down, men dying around him, horses, smoke, dust, screaming. His scouts had told him there were more Sioux and Cheyenne in the valley than he could handle, but he went, anyway. I understood *hubris* before I knew the word.

"Are we ever going to go out there?" I said.

"One of these years."

"You keep saying that."

"We'll go."

"When?"

"We'll go," he said.

He took a pull at his bottle and looked past me, into the night beyond the mullioned window, seeing something far away. There was something on his mind, something he wanted to say, but I knew I couldn't rush it.

"I put out a good paper today," he said.

"You always do."

"Not always. But I did today. Peabody's speech at the Sea View, a big fight at the selectmen's meeting, and Wayne Lopes scored forty points last night against Chatham. Hell of a front page." He lifted his bottle, saw that it was empty, and put it down. "Tomorrow they'll be wrapping garbage in it."

"They'll be wrapping garbage in the *New York Times*," I said.

"They'll also be handing out Pulitzers at the end of the year."

He closed *Custer's Luck*, pushed the book aside. He'd been a young reporter covering the courthouse and city hall for the *Philadelphia Bulletin*, on a trajectory, no one doubted, to New York or Washington or a bureau overseas. Then his father asked him to come home to work for him at the *Inquirer*. Dad's older brother, my uncle James, had been the heir designate since birth, but Uncle James had suddenly, on a whim or perhaps in an act of rebellion, bought a weekly newspaper in Wisconsin, spurning his father and his inheritance. So Grandpa Hatch had turned to his second son, take it or leave it, I'll find somebody else if you're not interested. *Give me a few days*, Dad said. And he'd read his own heart and seen the orneriness in it, the pleasure it took in doing battle with fools, hypocrites, and bigots. He'd understood the constraints he'd be under to be judicious in his views and temperate in expressing himself, no matter how high he rose, at the *New York Times* or the *Paris Herald Tribune*. At the *Dunstable Inquirer* he could be his own man, he could raise all the hell he wanted. He came home.

"You didn't want that, Dad," I said.

"I think about it sometimes."

"But you didn't want it."

"No, but you might. You might not want to publish the *Inquirer*."

"Why wouldn't I?" I said.

"The petty crap. Merchants pulling ads because they don't like an editorial. The police chief refusing to talk to your reporter because of some story he didn't like, so you have to call the son of a bitch and flatter him. Selectmen calling you at home at night to complain about your coverage. And then there are the hotheads who work for you. They're always in the back shop, I don't know why. There's something about machinists, maybe, makes them temperamental. Red Cowan threw a lead slug at Walter Tuttle the other day. Last Friday Bob Geggatt quit halfway through the press run, then came back on Monday wanting his job back. I have to cajole these guys, threaten them, fire them if it comes to that. Your grandfather was good at it and so am I, but I don't know that you would be."

"I haven't thought about it," I said.

"I have."

"What about the *Inquirer*? Who'd take it over if I didn't?"

"Jill, maybe. There's no law says a woman can't publish a newspaper. If not Jill, I guess you two aren't the only smart young people in the world."

"Grandpa Hatch might not like it."

"So go out in the world and spread your wings. Make him proud."

"Doing what?"

"I think you'd make a hell of a sports writer."

A car went by the house, a low rumble in the night, quickly dying away. I lifted my bottle, drank, and thought about covering big-league baseball. I imagined sitting ringside at the Clay–Liston fight last month.

"You could be the next Jimmy Cannon," my father said. "The next Red Smith. Why not?"

"I don't know."

"I don't, either."

And so a dream would take shape in the coming days and weeks of a life lived in the glamorous cities of major-league football and baseball, the remote and colorful venues of heavyweight championship bouts. Wimbledon. The Olympics. I knew that Red Smith was regarded as supremely literary, and that Jimmy Cannon had been a pal of Hemingway and Damon Runyon, and I began to descry writerly gatherings in little bars in Greenwich Village, cocktail parties on Martha's Vineyard, where the John Herseys and Thornton Wilders owned summer homes.

And I would see Jackie's incompatibility with this future. I would conjure another girl, Radcliffe instead of Framingham State, where Jackie was bound next year on her way to becoming a schoolteacher. The girl of my imagination had been to Europe, had read *Crime and Punishment*, and knew who Henry Wallace and Harry Hopkins were. Still later I would suspect that my father saw it too, saw the Radcliffe girl, even down to Wallace and Hopkins, and that she was on his mind when he urged me to spread my wings.

I swallowed the last of my beer. It had gotten warm, flat.

"You want another one?" my father said.

"I think I'll head up," I said, and stood up.

"You'll think about what I said."

"I already am," I said.

He pulled *Custer's Luck* over in front of him and opened it, rubbed his eyes and bent to it, thin in his white shirt, slumped, weary, and in that moment I knew we wouldn't get to the Little Bighorn, knew that time would run out on my father before we could.

fourteen

April arrived, and baseball, and on a Sunday evening with twilight lingering at the high basement windows, Martin Gibson left his Bible on the table beside him, folded his arms, and smiled his gentle smile. "Sonya and I need your help," he said. He removed his glasses, rubbed his eyes with the flat of his hand, and put the glasses back on.

"That's wrong," he said. "Some *people* need your help. Poor people, mostly, in a tough spot."

And he told us about the town of Waynesboro, North Carolina, and the dilemma of Waynesboro's Negro population. It was a small town with two grocery stores; a white man owned the store in the Negro section, and he was setting prices his customers couldn't afford. Fleecing them, Martin said. A neighborhood delegation had sat down with the man, to no avail. The Negroes weren't welcome at the town's second grocery—several had been warned off, and a young man beaten with a two-by-four.

The Student Nonviolent Coordinating Committee—"SNICK" to me later; I'd never heard of it then—was organizing a boycott of the grocery store. An appeal had gone north, and people were donating food to sustain the boycott, which was where we came in. Next

Saturday, Martin explained, we would go out into the town in teams of two, knocking on doors and soliciting donations of canned food. Martin and Sonya would transport the food in a U-Haul trailer to Boston, where, in two days, they would join a convoy of food-laden vehicles bound for North Carolina.

"We'll need cars," Martin said. "I assume most of you can borrow your parents'?"

Now people stirred, looked at each other, shrugged. Some few nodded slowly. Jackie turned and looked at me, but I couldn't read what she was thinking.

"We'll need everybody," Martin said. "You've got all week, so talk to everyone who isn't here tonight. Questions?"

Dennis Metcalf, a bookish senior with blond cowlicks, raised his hand. Metcalf always looked as if he'd just gotten out of bed: sleepy, irritable, those cowlicks standing up. "Maybe the grocer has a legitimate reason for charging what he does," he said. "Overhead, say."

Martin turned and looked at Sonya. Sonya smiled thinly. Martin turned back to Metcalf.

"He says his insurance is high," he said. "He says people steal from him, and he has to cover the losses."

"Which is baloney," Sonya said.

"How do you know?" Metcalf said.

"God, Metcalf," said Adrian Denton. "Don't you know what it's like down there?"

"SNICK looked into it," Martin said. "His insurance is only marginally higher than the grocer's across town, and there's no evidence of a high theft rate. Even the police admit that."

"I'll help," said Glenda Jane Perkins.

Billy Day and Ernie Holcomb shrugged, said they guessed they'd come.

"Can you get your father's car?" Donna asked Skip.

"I think so," Skip said.

"Any more questions?" Martin said.

"What do we say when we knock on people's doors?" asked Laura Hampton, a rosy-cheeked junior.

Martin smiled. "You tell them what I just told you."

"I might mess it up," Laura said.

"I doubt it. We can rehearse it Saturday morning if you'd like." He swept us with his mild gaze. "More questions?"

There weren't, but I could sense an unease in the room, a brittle quiet taking hold. Some furtive glances, friend to friend. A look, a shrug. Jackie was watching Martin, and I still couldn't read her mind. Martin reached beside him for his Bible, oblivious of the mood shift. It was the moment I realized what an innocent he was, and wondered, for the first time, how a man so gentle and trusting could excel at the crushing game of football.

"I thought," he said, "we'd go back to our old friend Paul of Tarsus, tonight."

"Daddy's going to have a cow," Jackie said.

"So what else is new?" I said.

"A boycott, Jesus. Sit-ins, boycotts, he hates all that stuff."

"I guess he wouldn't want to loan us the station wagon," I said.

"Yeah, right. Maybe he'll help Martin and Sonya drive the food down to North Carolina."

We drove through the intersection, past Dyer's Gulf, which was still open, the kid inside the little office watching a TV with rabbit ears.

"Pete?" Jackie said.

"What."

"I wonder why we haven't heard about this."

"Heard about what?"

"This boycott."

"Why should we?"

"You'd think it would be in the news."

"Jack, stuff like this goes on all the time. This is small. Negroes get lynched down there and we don't hear about it."

We were on her street now, the snug ranch and Capes, the occasional streetlamp.

"I thought you had baseball practice on Saturday," she said.

"I can skip it," I said. "It's not like football, where you're practically in the military."

"What'll you tell the coach?"

"I'll tell him I have a church obligation. He's a Catholic, he'll understand."

The Indian corn still hung from the Lawrences' front door knocker, a relic of football days. The picture window was dark. They were in there watching *Ed Sullivan*.

"It'll be fun," I said. "An adventure."

"'Night, hon," Jackie said, and kissed me quickly, lightly, and went inside to watch *Bonanza*.

She put off telling her father till Thursday, postponing it the way you do any unpleasantness that can wait another day. She told me about it at lunch the next day, sitting with Skip and Donna under the cafeteria skylight, a bright oblong of spring sky.

"He says it's communism," Jackie said. "I gave up arguing with him."

She bit into her sandwich and looked away, avoiding my eye. Skip and Donna continued eating, thinking about this.

"You know what that sounds like?" I said. "You guys know the song 'The John Birch Society,' by the Chad Mitchell Trio?"

"Who's the Chad Mitchell Trio?" Donna said.

"A folk group, like the Kingston Trio, the Limeliters. 'The John Birch Society' is about these right-wing crackpots who think there are communists everywhere."

"Crackpots," Jackie said. "Back off."

"Jack, it's crazy," I said. "Who are the communists here? Martin and Sonya?"

"You better lay off," Donna said.

"Maybe," Skip said, "there's communists down *there*, trying to take advantage of the situation."

"Take advantage of the situation to do what?" I said.

"Shit, I don't know. Whatever they do."

"They start revolutions in Cuba and Southeast Asia," I said, "they don't boycott grocery stores."

"Maybe it *is* a kind of revolution down there," Donna said.

"It's a revolution for civil rights," I said.

"It seems to me," Donna said, "we don't know much about it."

"Are you coming tomorrow or not?" I said.

Skip and Donna looked at each other.

"We'll be there," Skip said.

"Just get off your high horse, okay?" Donna said.

"I'm off it," I said.

The bell rang.

"See you tonight," I told Jackie, rising with my tray in one hand, my books under the other arm.

"Yeah," she said, busy pushing her wax paper, her orange peels, into her lunch bag.

Skip and Donna got up and headed with their trays toward the counter.

"You okay, Jack?" I said.

"Just fine," she said, still gathering her trash, still not looking at me.

She called at five and said it was best we didn't see each other tonight, and that I should pull up in front of her house and wait for her in the car tomorrow.

"Is he that bent out of shape?" I said.

"Do what I ask you, Peter."

"Quarter of nine, then. Be ready, okay?"

I hadn't stayed home on a Friday night since September, and I lingered over dinner with the family, then adjourned with them to sit around the fire with our books in our laps, talking at intervals. We didn't own a TV; my father wouldn't consider it, maybe because he knew there would be no evenings like this one, the fire quietly sibilant, the dog snoozing with her pink belly to its warmth, Jill on the floor, stroking her as she read *Charlotte's Web*. I went to bed at nine and fell asleep listening to the Red Sox game on my transistor radio. No score in the eighth, and then Mickey Mantle unloaded with two on, lifting one over the left field wall and the screen above it, the last thing I remembered.

Saturday unfolded as one of those warm gray spring days with the lawns a hard green in the overcast, daffodils nodding along front walks, lemony forsythia erupting. I made a U-turn so that the passenger door would face the house and stopped with the motor idling. I tapped the horn, and again.

The front door opened and Jackie came out in a skirt and blouse, no jacket. Her arms were folded. She came up the flagstone walk, slow, and stopped at the passenger door. I leaned and pushed the door open. Jackie stood with her arms still folded, looking down the street.

"I'm not coming," she said.

"Get in the car," I said, "we'll talk about it."

"I can't, Peter. Do you understand?"

"I guess your father got to you," I said.

"Don't do this. Just please don't do this."

She turned, walked slowly back, still with her arms folded. I killed the engine and got out of the car and went after her. She glanced over her shoulder and went on, nodding, as if she'd expected this. I followed her into the house, the living room, where Lovey Lawrence sat in his upholstered chair with his bony legs crossed.

"Have a seat, Pete," he said.

"No thanks," I said. I stood just inside the door with my hands stuffed in the pockets of my letter jacket.

"Jacqueline, why don't you go on, let us two talk," he said.

But Jackie sat down on the sofa. She crossed her legs and sat back, looking at neither her father nor me. The house was quiet, and I wondered where Mrs. Lawrence and the girls were, Linda Jean and Margie.

"This is America, Pete," Lovey said. "A man owns a store, he can set his own prices. You can't do that in Russia, but this is a free country."

"That's right," I said, "and if people want to boycott the store, they can, which they can't in Russia."

"There's a lot of things you can't do in Russia. Whose idea was it, this boycott?"

"Theirs, I imagine. The customers."

Jackie sat very still, looking straight ahead.

"I don't think so," Lovey said. "I think communistic types got them all stirred up. People up North, who know nothing about the Negro problem. If you keep stirring the Negroes up, God help this country."

I realized something then, knew it without knowing how I knew. Mrs. Lawrence and the two girls were listening to this. They were in the dining room or around the corner in the hallway, heads cocked.

"Anyway," Lovey said, "I'll not have my daughter be a part of it."

"Why don't you let her decide," I said.

"I think she already has," Lovey said.

"Jack?" I said.

It was the first time I saw her weep. Hot tears, angry ones. They broke loose, slid cleanly down. She wouldn't look at me.

"Jack," I said again.

"I'm not coming," she said.

I smiled, but it was the sour smile of chagrin, of defeat, and I knew it. I turned and opened the door, and when I looked again Jackie was sitting as before, eyes front, arms folded, legs crossed, immovable.

fifteen

Besides Martin and Sonya's VW bug, there was one car in the parsonage lot, an old red Ford Galaxie I'd never seen. Martin and Sonya were sitting at the kitchen table drinking coffee with Adrian Denton and a girl with creamy skin and hair so deeply red-blond it looked incandescent. She wore a black leather jacket, a blue denim skirt that stopped above her knees. There was an ashtray on the table, and an open pack of Camels, and the various coffee cups.

"Where *is* everybody?" I said, trying not to look at the girl.

"Where do you think?" Denton said.

The redhead had finished looking me over and was staring out the window.

"Where's Jackie?" Martin said.

"She isn't feeling well," I said. "She's got a bad cold."

"There's a lot of sickness going around today," Denton said.

"Sit down, Pete," Martin said. "Coffee?"

I said no and pulled a chair and sat down across from Denton and the girl. I'd kept my letter jacket on, collar up, on account of the girl. A ready, virile look, you think, when you're eighteen.

"This is Corinna Devlin," Martin said. "Adrian's cousin. Pete Hatch, Corinna."

Corinna Devlin eyed me. Nodded. She wore coral-pink lipstick. Her eyes were jade green. A little constellation of champagne-gold freckles spilled away from the straight bridge of her nose. My eye kept seeking her, and I would catch myself and look quickly someplace else. Sonya reached for the cigarettes and plucked one out. She lit it and shook out the match. I'd never seen her smoke.

"Glenda Jane called in tears," Martin said. "Her mother won't let her come."

"Who else called?" I said.

"No one."

"What are we going to do?" Sonya said.

"We're going to wait," Martin said.

"No one else is coming," Denton said.

"It's early," Martin said.

"It's nine-fifteen," Sonya said.

It was very quiet in the house—so unlike nighttime, with the music going, the TV, the smack of the ping-pong ball, voices upstairs and down.

"Where are you from?" I asked Denton's cousin Corinna.

"Saugus," she said. She looked at Sonya. "May I bum a cigarette?"

Sonya pushed the Camels toward her. Corinna shook one out and lit it expertly.

"Saugus," I said. "That's near Boston, right?"

"Don't get any ideas, Hatch," Denton said. "She's got a boyfriend. And her father's a policeman."

"I didn't propose to her, I asked her where she lived," I said.

Sonya smiled and tapped ash from her cigarette.

"Why do you call him Hatch?" Corinna said.

"It's his name," Denton said.

"We don't like each other," I said.

"I can see that," she said. "Maybe today you could give it a rest."

"It's okay," I said. "I don't listen to him."

Corinna smiled at this, then blew smoke down past her shoulder.

"Adrian's right," Sonya said. "No one else is coming."

"Are the three of you still game?" Martin said.

Corinna leaned forward and rubbed out her cigarette. "Sure."

"Hell, yes," Denton said.

"Pete?" Sonya said.

"Of course," I said.

Sonya looked across the table at her husband. "Sweetheart, you'd better stay here."

"Not on your life," he said.

"Someone has to, and it'll give you some immunity if there's trouble about this. I think there might be."

"I didn't sense any last week," Martin said. "Pete, have you heard anything?"

I gave it a moment. Jackie had removed herself from the day's considerations, and fate had placed a beautiful girl across the table from me. I felt suddenly unbound, venturesome, and charitable.

"Just some dumb talk from Skip," I said. "But that was just Skip. He said he was coming. So did Donna."

"No one is," Denton said. "Let's face it."

"All the more reason I should help," Martin said.

"You're staying," Sonya said.

"Sweetheart . . ."

"End of discussion," Sonya said. She looked at Corrina. "How do you feel about me driving your car?"

"Sure," Corinna said.

"What's going on?" Denton said.

"Mix and match," Sonya said. "You and I are partners."

"Corinna goes with *Hatch?*"

"Why not?" Sonya said.

"They don't know each other," Denton said.

"I guess they can remedy that."

"She's my *cousin*," Denton said.

"You don't want to go with me, Adrian? I'm hurt."

I looked away and kept quiet, praying this would come out the way it was headed and wondering what Sonya was up to. Corinna watched the two of them neutrally.

"I didn't say that," Denton said.

"Well, then," Sonya said.

"Can we just settle it?" Corinna said.

"Sonya would enjoy your company, Adrian," Martin said.

Denton looked at him, then at Sonya, who was training her comeliest smile on him. He woke to the smile, smiled faintly himself, seeing finally that a day alone with Sonya was no small consolation.

"Fine," he said.

At my suggestion we divided the town in half, east and west of Main Street and Route 26, Corinna and I taking the eastern half, which took in my neighborhood.

"Let's rock and roll," Sonya said, rising.

"The key's in the car," Corinna said.

"Hatch has a girlfriend, Corinna," Denton said.

"Apparently," Corinna said.

"Just don't let him snow you."

"I'll be on my guard," she said.

We left Martin washing breakfast dishes—he would spend the day writing a paper on Martin Luther and watching an NBA playoff game—and spilled out into the gray morning. I opened the passenger door of the Falcon for Corinna Devlin. Her legs were bare, and she swung them into the car and tossed her purse onto the back seat.

I shut the door and went around to the other side and saw Sonya watching me from the driver's seat of the Galaxie. I'd been wondering why she was doing this, consigning herself to a day of listening to Denton's sophomoric spiels, and as I slid in beside Corinna I saw Sonya smile, and knew she knew Jackie wasn't sick today.

"Why'd your girlfriend bail out?" Corinna said. She was looking out the window, at the houses on Carriage Street, old ones built by China traders and sea captains. White picket fences, towering ancient shade trees canopying front lawns.

"I believe I explained that," I said.

"Not very convincingly."

"Her father wouldn't let her come."

Corinna looked at me. I could feel her jade eyes, their cool light. "What's wrong with him?" she said.

"Let's just say he doesn't approve of what we're doing."

"Because?"

I smiled. "He says it's communistic."

"You're joking, right?"

"Who could make that up?"

"What is he, a moron?"

"In some ways," I said.

"Great town you got here," Corinna said. "No wonder Adrian hates it."

"He'd hate wherever he was," I said.

"How would you know that?"

"He's a misfit," I said. "He's unhappy."

"How come he doesn't like you?"

"Who knows?"

"You don't pick on him?"

"All the time. Can't you tell?"

Corinna smiled. "Adrian's not a bad kid," she said. "He tries to emulate his father—the cynic, the gadfly. I gather Uncle Nate makes a spectacle of himself at Town Meeting."

"He's famous," I said.

"I think it embarrasses Adrian, and he deals with it by taking on the same role. Make sense?"

"No," I said.

I'd made her smile again. "It's subconscious," she said. "He can't change his father or get rid of him, so he emulates him. Accepts his behavior as normal and right."

"Still doesn't make sense."

"It's the best I can do."

"You're doing pretty well," I said.

She glanced at me and smiled, but the smile was for herself, not me.

We bumped across the railroad tracks and turned onto Elm Road, named for the trees growing out of the warping asphalt sidewalk and sprawling their limbs overhead. We passed several houses and turned onto our gravel driveway, which sloped gently down past the granite foundation of a barn that had stood in the long ago, lost now to memory.

We got out of the car and Corinna stopped halfway to the kitchen door with her hands in the pockets of her leather jacket, considering the tall weathered-shingle house. My mother threw the kitchen door open and looked at her and then at me, wondering who this was, and where Jackie was. I introduced Corinna and said Jackie was sick and that Corinna had come with me instead. My mother was eyeing me, wondering what was really going on. I followed Corinna up the brick steps and into the cluttered, ripe-fruit-smelling kitchen. Two grocery bags, staggering with their load of cans, stood on the Formica table. My mother had nearly filled a shopping cart at the A&P: peas, corn, spaghetti, ravioli, corned beef hash, fruit cocktail, peaches, string beans.

"I've added a few things," she said. "Coffee, for instance. People might not think of that."

Our dog, an aged white bull terrier, shambled stiffly in to see who was here, and Corinna knelt and rubbed her head.

"That's Roxie," my mother said.

"Hi, Roxie," Corinna said. "Hi, you beautiful dog."

"Beautiful?" I said.

"I hope Jackie isn't *too* sick," my mother said, watching Corinna.

"Just a cold," I said.

Jill appeared in the doorway. She was twelve that year. She studied Corinna. Corinna rose smoothly from her crouch.

"This is Corinna Devlin, Jill," I said.

"Hello, Jill."

"Are you a motorcycle rider?" Jill said. She'd been eyeing the leather jacket.

"Just a rebel," Corinna said.

"Against what?"

Corinna smiled. "What have you got?"

I picked up a bag. "Marlon Brando," I said, "*The Wild One*."

Corinna looked at me. "Your son knows his movies, Mrs. Hatch."

"I'm lost," Jill said.

"Brando's the leader of a motorcycle gang," I said. "He says he's a rebel, and a girl asks him what he's rebelling against. 'What have you got?' he says."

Corinna hoisted the second bag. "I'm being a wise guy, Jill. Just like Brando in the movie."

"I don't mind a rebel," Jill said.

"Good for you," Corinna said.

"You're in the Fellowship?" my mother said. "Pete never mentioned you."

"She's down from Saugus," I said. "She's Adrian Denton's cousin."

"Nate's son?"

"My famous uncle," Corinna said.

"How good of you to come, Corinna," my mother said.

"Not really," Corinna said. "Thank you for the food, Mrs. Hatch."

"I'm sorry Jackie couldn't come," my mother said, maybe the only lie she ever told me.

We drove back to the foot of the road, just this side of the railroad tracks. The first house was a small, paint-peeling yellow clapboard with a flat tar roof. A short dirt driveway cut in beside it. Billy and Johnny Dumont's rusted basketball hoop, the net long gone, hung askew above the garage door. Billy and Johnny had both graduated— barely—and moved on.

"Mr. Dumont's a widower," I said. "He may be a little cranky."

I knocked on the door. You could hear the TV going inside. The door opened, and Mr. Dumont squinted out at me. The TV was blaring an old Western.

"What's up?" Mr. Dumont said.

"We're helping the Youth Fellowship of the Congregational Church collect food for some people down in North Carolina," I said. "Town called Waynesboro. They can't afford to buy groceries, because . . ."

"Who's this?" Mr. Dumont said.

Corinna gave him a smile. "I'm Corinna Devlin, Mr. Dumont, and if you donate just one can of food, you'll be doing your part."

Mr. Dumont brought up a gnarled hand and massaged the back of his neck. Gunshots broke out on the TV.

"One can, you say."

"Of anything," Corinna said.

Mr. Dumont gestured us in with a toss of his head and went padding back to the kitchen in his stocking feet. The television was showing a rerun of *Wagon Train*. There was no rug on the floor, and the TV voices, the clatter of hooves, caromed off the bare hard-wood.

"Keep it simple," Corinna whispered.

"I am."

"No you're not."

I wanted to ask her what the hell she was talking about, but Mr. Dumont was back already, with a can in each hand. He presented both to Corinna: Franco-American Spaghetti, Campbell's Chicken Noodle Soup.

"You're a true hero," Corinna said.

"One can, two, it don't matter. Who's this for again?"

"Some people down South," Corinna said. "Ignorant little hick town in North Carolina. Guy owns the grocery store is cheating them. It's pure greed, and they don't have any other place to go."

"Tell 'em to burn the goddamn store down," Mr. Dumont said.

"That'll be the next step," Corinna said.

We moved to the door.

"I talk to Johnny, I'll tell him you come by," Mr. Dumont said.

"How's he doing?" I said.

"Well, he ain't in jail. Listen, they burn that store down, lemme know."

"You'll be the first," Corinna said.

I pulled away from Mr. Dumont's and stopped a hundred yards or so on, letting the car idle. There were woods on either side of this stretch of the road, and the lofty old sidewalk elms.

"I don't think we should be talking about burning the store down," I said.

"That was Mr. Dumont's idea."

"You said it was the next step. That was *your* idea."

"He liked it."

She was half-turned toward me now, with her legs crossed. Denim skirt climbing above the top knee, a black flat cupping her suspended porcelain foot. She had terrific ankles.

"We don't need to be talking about burning buildings down," I said. "Martin and Sonya might be in trouble over this as it is."

"Yeah. Collecting food for Black people getting the shaft from a white guy. Major felony."

"That's another thing. We didn't tell Mr. Dumont the people are Negroes."

"Black."

"What?"

"You don't say Negro, you say Black. Negro is the white man's term. We call ourselves white people, don't we?"

"Is this what you learn in the big city?"

"It's what you learn in the *world*. From which this town seems to be a little remote."

"You think my mother's remote?"

"Your mother's lovely. And we don't need to say it's Black people we're collecting food for unless it helps us. The point is to get the food, right?"

"I think we should say it. Let people know what's happening."

"Oh Jesus. Put the car in gear, Hatch. We're wasting time."

Next stop was the Harwoods' ranch-style house with its mint-green vinyl siding. Mr. Harwood taught English over at the community college. They had two kids, a daughter off in nursing school and a son, George, a year behind me at Dunstable High. I parked along the road, and Corinna and I went up the driveway, where the Harwoods' two Chevy compacts stood side by side.

Mrs. Harwood opened the door and smiled a greeting. She wore a dress, a necklace.

"George is still asleep," she said.

"I'm not looking for him, Mrs. Harwood."

"Oh?" She stood aside and we stepped into her small tidy kitchen.

"We're collecting food for some people down in Waynesboro, North Carolina," I said. "The grocery store is overcharging them. There's a boycott. We're collecting food to keep it going."

"The Congregational Church, that is," Corinna said.

Mr. Harwood materialized in the doorway, tall and gaunt-looking in a blue bathrobe and bedroom slippers. He was smoking a pipe.

"What's this?" he said.

"They're collecting food for a boycott down South," Mrs. Harwood said. "The Congregational Church."

"Did you secede from St. Andrew's, Pete?" Mr. Harwood said.

"Corinna and I are just helping out," I said. "Freelancing."

Mr. Harwood removed the pipe from his mouth and looked it over. "You know where the word 'boycott' comes from?" he said.

"Not offhand," I said.

"Wasn't he some English lord or something?" Corinna said. "Something to do with Ireland."

"Very good," Mr. Harwood said. "Captain Boycott was an English land owner. He evicted his tenants, and got shunned for it. Stores wouldn't sell to him, laborers wouldn't work for him. Fixed him good."

"Well, we want to fix this store owner," Corinna said. "He's gouging people."

"Are these people Negroes?" Mrs. Harwood said.

"Of course they are," Mr. Harwood said. "And the scoundrel who's squeezing them is white. Give them some food, Betty, before we end up in one of Ed Hatch's editorials."

Mrs. Harwood turned and opened a cupboard and peered around inside it. She pulled down a can of tuna. Mr. Harwood drew on his pipe, watching.

"Give them that big can of baked beans," Mr. Harwood said. "Then I won't have to eat them."

Mrs. Harwood brought the can down with both hands.

Corinna and I gathered up the two cans. Mrs. Harwood opened the door for us.

"I like your coat, young lady," Mr. Harwood said.

"It's my Marlon Brando jacket," Corinna said.

"Tell George I came by," I said.

"He'll be sorry he missed Marlon Brando, here," Mr. Harwood said.

"The Congregational Church?" I said.

"Isn't it?" Corinna said.

"It's the Fellowship."

"What's the difference?"

"The difference, as you well know, is that you and I aren't members of the Congregational Church."

"And your church is what?" Corinna said.

"Episcopal."

"Figures."

"Why?"

"You're so Waspy, that's why."

"Waspy?"

"Never mind."

"Well, I haven't been to church in years, so it's irrelevant."

"A lapsed Episcopalian and a lapsed Catholic," Corinna said. "We're freelancing, as you said. We can say anything we want."

"I'm thinking of Martin and Sonya," I said.

"I'm thinking of hungry families in North Carolina. Start the car."

"That one looks promising," she said.

Skip Gladding's Tudor stucco on its rise, creosoted railroad tie steps ascending to it. Skip's father owned a construction company and made good money.

"No," I said, "kid who lives there's in the Fellowship. I imagine he's asleep."

"There must be someone awake."

"I don't want to see him. He said he was coming today. I don't want to see any of them."

"You going to quit the Fellowship?"

"I would, except for Martin and Sonya."

"That'll be Adrian's position."

"Me and Adrian. Misery makes strange bedfellows."

"So do principles," Corinna said. "He has them, you know."

"I never said he didn't."

"Keep it in mind, okay?"

"Always," I said.

My grandmother Hatch was a small woman beginning to hunch and shrink, but her opal-blue eyes and satiny skin evoked the charmer she'd once been. I introduced Corinna and told Grandma Hatch how she'd come down from Saugus to help us. My grandmother took Corinna's hand in both of hers and looked her up and down.

"I don't think much of your jacket," she said.

"Your grandson doesn't, either," Corinna said.

"I don't?" I said.

Grandma Hatch led us in, hunched with her arms folded. Grandpa Hatch was sitting in his big soft chair in the sunny alcove off the living room, semi-recumbent with his feet on the matching stool, the *New York Times* blanketing his lap. On the other side of the picture window blue jays and chickadees were fluttering in and out of the trees to the feeder.

"My colleague, Corinna Devlin," I told my grandfather.

Corinna gave me a look of faux puzzlement—*colleague?*—and stepped forward and offered the old man her hand. Grandpa Hatch raised a fleshy paw and took it, and I saw his watery gaze hold on her face then travel down the length of her.

"Begging food, are you," said my grandfather.

"On our knees," Corinna said, "and I *know* you'll come through."

"Doris emptied the damn cupboard," Grandpa Hatch said.

She'd set two bags of groceries on the dining table, and Corinna and I each lifted one and went back out through the alcove. A couple of jays now were squabbling on the bird feeder, flapping and darting at each other.

"You're a hero, Mr. Hatch," Corinna said.

"Doris, not me," Grandpa Hatch said.

"George, you know that's not true," Grandma Hatch said.

"We all know it," Corinna said.

We followed Grandma Hatch to the door.

"You'd be quite pretty if you dressed like a lady," she said.

"You were a rebel, Grandma," I said. "You bobbed your hair. You smoked. You still curse."

"I didn't dress like a thug," Grandma Hatch said.

"I'm beginning to think this jacket is more trouble than it's worth," Corinna said.

"I shouldn't wonder," my grandmother said.

"Thanks again, Mrs. Hatch," Corinna said.

We lugged the bags down the brick front walk, dropped them in the back seat of the Falcon, and got in. The neighborhood seemed still asleep in the gray breathless morning.

"They liked you," I said.

"If they liked me any more they'd set the dogs on me."

"*Oklahoma!*," I said.

Corinna turned, eyed me. "You're scaring me, Hatch."

"I grew up on musicals," I said. "The Music Circus, in Dover. Theater in the round."

"Lucky you."

"I remember the line, and the laugh it got. I must have been thirteen or fourteen. I've seen the show since, of course."

"I saw the movie version on TV. Gordon MacRae and Shirley Jones. When I was a kid, I'd stay up Saturday night, watch the late movies. I saw everything. *Double Indemnity. High Noon.* Musicals— *Show Boat, Brigadoon,* with Gene Kelly."

"*Casablanca?*"

"Here's lookin' at you, kid."

"We'll always have Paris," I said.

"Play it, Sam. Play 'As Time Goes By.'"

I started the car then turned to look at her, the sprinkle of freckles, the drape of her hair. She did not sit up straight, as Jackie did, but folded herself forward, a languorous, sexy slouch. The distance between Jackie and me now felt spatial, as if an ocean lay between us, a continent. I pushed the stick into gear and we went on.

We'd gone to two more places, and I'd stopped in front of Mrs. Wright's house.

"Adrian said your father owns the newspaper," Corinna said.

"My grandfather. Dad'll be editor *and* publisher when Grandpa dies."

"Then you? The next William Allen White?"

"The next Red Smith. I'm going to get out of here, be a sports writer."

"The next Ring Lardner. Shoot high."

"Red Smith's pretty high."

"He never wrote fiction. Lardner did. Some of it very good."

"'Haircut,'" I said.

"'Comb it wet or dry?'" Corinna said, the ironic last line of Lardner's indelible short story. She looked at me. "Impressed?"

"Surprised," I said.

"Which means impressed."

"Okay. Impressed."

"I read it in English class freshman year, in an anthology. Write a story like 'Haircut,' Hatch, and you'll live forever."

I pictured Mrs. Wright peering out her kitchen window, wondering what was going on. *Let her wonder,* I thought.

"What are you going to do while I'm becoming the next Ring Lardner?" I said.

"Practice law, I hope."

"Really."

"*Really?* I'm a girl, I'm not supposed to be a lawyer?"

"I didn't say that."

"You thought it."

"I thought the opposite. You'll make a great lawyer. You'll wear people out arguing with them. They'll be staggering around the courtroom. We give up, Your Honor."

"I hope so," Corinna said.

"Next year Radcliffe," I said. "Or Smith. Barnard. Vassar, maybe."

"Bryn Mawr," she said.

I was surprised, yet not surprised. The day was taking on an impregnable logic. A fatedness.

"It's a small school down near Philadelphia," Corinna said.

"I know," I said. "I'm going to Haverford."

Corinna Devlin closed her eyes, opened them. A faint smile. She shook her head. "You're hard to get rid of," she said, and swung the car door open before I had a smart answer.

*   *   *

We went door to door to the end of the road, and everyone gave us a can of food, if only to get rid of us. Tomato soup. Peas. Creamed corn. Then we worked our way along the winding back road to the seaside enclave called Quick's Hole.

"Mentioning the Congregational Church will get us nowhere over here," I said.

"Except to embarrass the church, which is a priority."

"Forget it. The church'll go up in their esteem. They'll admire it. Tell them we're working with SNICK, they'll love that even more. Quick's Hole is a world unto itself."

"I can't wait," Corinna said.

We came in past the Coast Guard Base onto Water Street, whined across the drawbridge, where the sound gushes into the tranquil mud-redolent inlet and small-craft anchorage known as the Oyster Pond. Then on past the Topside Bar, the auxiliary fire station, the enormous redbrick Marine Laboratory. We could see the sound now, and the small, low-lying islands that comprise the archipelago known prettily as the Queens, which are inhabited only by small game and spindly deer, with the exception of Shawmut, lying about a mile out and owned by the wealthy Elliot family of Boston. We went on, past Jaskin's Market, an art gallery, and a couple of souvenir shops, which hadn't opened yet for summer, and cut back inland, into the concentrated residential section, squeezed between the bay and the sound.

The streets here are narrow, short, with cars bunched along either side. The houses stand close to each other, clapboard and weathered shingle, and back then they had a comfortable, cluttered, rundown feel—the homes of freethinking marine biologists, weavers, folk singers, fishermen with degrees from Marlboro and Goddard. "Bug hunters and hippies," according to the youth of every other village and neighborhood in Dunstable, and the Student Nonviolent Coordinating Committee was music to their ears. They all but emptied their cupboards to us. They gave us jars of peanut butter, a tin of ham, a tin of corned beef, cans of roast beef hash. They gave us juices. They gave us minced clams and pineapple chunks, a can of beef stew, soups of all kinds, vegetables. By two o'clock we'd filled the trunk of the Falcon and buried the back seat.

"There's hope for you yet, Hatch," Corinna said. "*And* your town."

"Hungry?"

"Starved."

I took the main road back toward town, breezing along in the light Saturday traffic, and got my second lesson in the culture of race in the world beyond Dunstable. Corinna had turned on the radio, first time all day. She spun the dial and found the Righteous Brothers, "You've Lost That Lovin' Feelin'."

"Good choice," I said.

"Blue-eyed soul," she said.

I nodded in sage agreement with this inscrutable observation, but Corinna wasn't fooled.

"Soul music, Hatch. Please tell me you know what soul music is."

"Sorry."

"Blues, rock and roll. Add a touch of gospel, or more than a touch. And then that indefinable thing—emotion. Soul. The Impressions. Smokey Robinson. James Brown."

"Black singers," I said.

"Except for the Righteous Brothers. Some people think Elvis Presley sings soul. There's some disagreement about that."

"The Ronettes," I said.

"Slinky soul."

"Fats Domino. Jackie Wilson."

"Love Jackie Wilson."

The Righteous Brothers harmonized in elegant alignment, silk smooth, their voices rising, choir-like, ecstatic, then dropping for an interval of ache and meditation. Soulful.

"I thought you didn't like Adrian calling me 'Hatch,'" I said.

"It's different with him. He calls you 'Hatch' because he doesn't like you."

"And you do," I said.

"So far," she said.

We drove past the Village Green and the parsonage, where I pictured Martin working on his Martin Luther paper at the kitchen table, books and papers spread out in front of him, and drove the length of Main Street, past the Rec Building with the football field nestled down behind it, to the asphalt sprawl of the shopping plaza. I parked in front of Friendly's, which was a couple of doors down from the CVS, where I bought my condoms. I thought about this, and wondered what sex with Corinna Devlin would be like, and whether it was different with each new girl, and thought it must be, just as kissing was.

A woman was getting into the car next to us, and she saw the back seat of the Falcon.

"You guys taking a trip?" she said.

"It's for our bomb shelter," Corinna said.

The woman smiled.

"We're collecting food for some people down South," I said. "They're staging a boycott. We're with the Congregational Church."

Corinna looked at me.

"A boycott, huh," the woman said.

"Black people," I said. "They're being gouged by a white grocery store owner. Waynesboro, North Carolina. You could donate."

"I think I'll pass," the woman said, and got into her car and shut the door.

We walked toward the restaurant, Corinna close beside me. "We're with the Congregational Church?" she said.

"You're a bad influence," I said.

"I think you scared her."

"I hope so," I said.

"My, my," Corinna said.

The lunch crowd was gone, the big room nearly empty, the girl at the register staring out the window. The hostess led us to a booth and laid two menus down. We asked her for coffee. Corinna slid in and placed her purse on the seat beside her. She removed her jacket. She was wearing a pale-green cashmere sweater, and her eyes seemed to draw light from the sweater's soft, glossy green. I shrugged out of my jacket.

Corinna took up a menu, considered it briefly. We looked around: an elderly couple, glumly stirring their coffee and not talking, a young couple with their little girl, eating dishes of ice cream. At the counter a little way down from us sat Cookie Trevino, who'd graduated a couple of years ago and now drove a truck for Gladding Construction, Skip's old man's company. He was smoking and drinking coffee. He turned on his stool and took a long look at Corinna, then gave me a curt nod and went back to his coffee.

"Is your father really a cop?" I said.

"Is that so strange?"

"I wouldn't have guessed it, is all."

The waitress arrived with the coffee and a bowl of plastic containers of half-and-half.

"You kids know what you want?" she said.

I ordered a cheeseburger, Corinna a grilled chicken Caesar salad. The waitress wrote it down and gathered up our menus, and Corinna got up and headed for the ladies' room. Cookie Trevino turned and watched her, and I did too—her smooth white legs, her hips in the grip of the denim skirt. We watched her come back.

"That guy at the counter's got eye trouble," she said, and slid in across from me.

"Just enjoying the scenery," I said. "How long has your father been a policeman?"

"Since I was born. He's a sergeant now. What's your problem with my father? You have something against cops?"

"I was just wondering how he felt about our food drive."

"He doesn't know about it. I didn't know about it myself till I got here yesterday. Adrian asked me to help, and of course I said yes."

"You came down to visit."

"Sure. What's with all the questions?"

"I don't know."

"My aunt Mary is very cool. My mother's sister. She and I are close."

"How about Adrian?"

"Adrian again. If you and I are going to be friends, you're going to have to get used to him, if not actually like him. You know that, right?"

"I'll work on it," I said.

"He's mixed up. Have some compassion."

The waitress arrived with our order. She set the plates down, asked us if we needed anything else, and took off. Corinna took up her fork and began to eat, very dainty about it, deliberate and lady-like. She sat with that languorous slouch, which now seemed feline to me, relaxed yet watchful, her gaze missing nothing.

"Can I ask you something?" I said.

She smiled. "It always makes me laugh when people say 'Can I ask you something?' Of course you can *ask* me something. Ask me what time it is. Ask me if I've heard a weather report. What they mean is, 'Can I ask you something *personal*.'"

"Right."

"Go ahead."

"Do you have a boyfriend?"

"Sure. Just like you have a girlfriend."

"Not anymore."

"Don't be hasty. She'll think it over, realize her father's a little nutty."

"You called him a moron."

"I *asked* if he was a moron. And it doesn't mean his daughter's one."

"It's over," I said. "Jackie and I are different. Is it serious with your boyfriend?"

"We've been going out since last summer. I guess that's serious."

"Want to tell me about him?"

Corinna swallowed, patted her mouth with her napkin. "Captain of the football team. He's going to Dartmouth next year on a scholarship. He's a good Catholic. John O'Brien. We'll go our separate ways in the fall."

"I don't mean to pry," I said.

She'd grown thoughtful. "You're allowed," she said.

Then Cookie Trevino let himself down off his stool, blatantly eyeing Corinna, and sauntered toward the door.

"Charmer," she said.

"You wear that skirt, what do you expect?"

"I expect to be looked at, what do you think?"

"Then don't complain."

"I was *observing*. Ask the waitress for more coffee."

"You ask her," I said.

Corinna looked at me. She smiled. "Good, Hatch. Don't let me push you around."

"I actually like your skirt, by the way," I said.

"I know you do," she said.

sixteen

We worked the neighborhoods between Route 26 and the shore, burying the back seat deeper in jars and cans. Fruit cocktail. Wax beans. Franco-American spaghetti. The clouds were beginning to scramble apart, uncovering some soft springtime sky.

"Where do the rich people live?" Corinna said. "The millionaires."

It was four o'clock; we were expected at the parsonage in an hour.

"A place called Gosnold Point, most of them," I said. "It runs out from Quick's Hole, across an isthmus. Why?"

"Let's go there."

"They probably won't let us in," I said. "There's a gatehouse."

"I bet we can talk our way in."

"You bet *you* can."

"You're my straight man. Just play along."

"All right, but take the jacket off."

"What the hell for?"

"What's wrong with looking like a lady?"

"You sound like your grandmother."

"Take it off," I said.

She gave me a look, a smirk that seemed to distill in itself both mockery and reluctant agreement, and leaned forward and shucked the leather jacket. I watched her fold it and stuff it down on the floor.

"Nice sweater," I said.

"A gift from my boyfriend," she said.

"Expensive. Are you in love with him?"

"I told you I wasn't."

"You did?"

"Pay attention, Hatch."

The gatehouse was a white shed with a peaked roof, a front window, black door, and black shutters. It looked like a rich child's playhouse. I stopped, and the door opened and the guard came out. He was wearing a white shirt and narrow black knit tie. He stared at our back-seat cargo. I rolled the window down.

"We're with the Congregational Church," I said, "collecting food for some poor people down South."

Corinna leaned in front of me and spoke through the window. "It's in conjunction with UNICEF," she said.

I cut her a look—*Say what?*—but she slipped it, smiling up at the guard. He looked her over—her face, then her breasts in the sweater.

"Got some ID?" he said.

Corinna reached down for her purse. I dug out my wallet. The guard looked at our licenses and handed them back.

"UNICEF, and what church was it?" he said.

"Congregational," Corinna said. "People all over town have been incredibly generous, as you can see."

"Let me make a call," the guard said. He went back into the gate-house, and we could see him lift a phone.

"UNICEF?" I said.

"It worked, didn't it?"

"The guy's a dope, or it wouldn't have. Do you know what UNI-CEF is?"

"Please, Hatch. Even you know that."

The guard came back and leaned down where he could see Corinna. "You should have something from the church, a letter or something," he said, "but Mr. Tilden said you can come on in. He's the association president, is why I called him, and kind of broad-minded, you might say. I think he'll help you out, but I don't know about others that live here. Second house on the left."

"You're a sweetheart," Corinna said.

"Yeah, I know. Good luck."

"Whitney Tilden," I said, as we drove on, "is more or less famous in town. My father talks about him. Rich as Croesus, doesn't have to work. Married, but he likes the girls, as Dad puts it. Dad kind of likes him. 'Whit's okay,' he says, 'he just never grew up.'"

"He likes the girls, I might have to flirt with him," Corinna said.

"You might get more than you bargained for," I said.

"Whatever works, remember? Anyhow, I'll have you there to protect me."

The house was a weathered-shingle chateau with gambrel roofs, a turret, and tall narrow windows that gave the illusion the building was surging skyward. Tilden opened the door, his agate gaze shift-ing from Corinna to me and back to Corinna. He looked to be in his early thirties, lean and blond with a drooping golden mustache that called to mind a Western gunslinger. He wore a white cashmere turtleneck, gray slacks, tasseled loafers.

"Mr. Hatch," he said.

"Yes, sir," I said.

"And Miss . . . ?"

"Devlin," Corinna said.

"Let's talk," he said, and turned and led us down a spacious cen-tral hallway past an antique highboy, a carved oak bench that the

Medicis might have lounged on, and some wingback chairs. Chandeliers glittered, and the white walls were hung with expressionist oils.

We turned into a living room, white, like the hall, with a fieldstone fireplace and glass sliders giving onto a screened porch with a lawn beyond, and down beyond that, the sound, smooth and gun-blue with its low, greening islands strung out to the southwest.

"Sit," said our host.

Corinna and I traded glances, wondering already what we'd gotten ourselves into, and sat down on the white sofa. Above the mantel shelf hung an oil painting of an oarsman pulling his dory up the steep slope of a heaving, foaming wave.

"Winslow Homer," Tilden said. "It was my father's. Tea? Coffee?"

We said no thank you.

"Something stronger, then. You old enough to drink?"

"Depends what you mean by 'old enough,'" Corinna said.

Tilden eyed her. He grinned under the sickle of his mustache. "Legally," he said.

"Legally, no," Corinna said.

"Want an illegal drink, then?"

"Better not, but thanks for the thought."

Still smiling, Tilden turned, put his hands in his pockets and looked out over the water. "Your old man runs the *Inquirer*," he said.

"Yes, sir."

"He does a good job."

"Thank you."

"Thank *him*, not me," Tilden said.

He turned abruptly, moved to a white stuffed chair, and sat nimbly down.

"Okay," he said, "what's this shit about UNICEF?"

"Shit?" Corinna said.

"Yeah, shit. How stupid do you think I am?"

Corinna smiled an easy, unflustered smile. "We were improvising," she said. "We just wanted to get in, so we could make our case."

"Who are you with, and no bullshit this time," Tilden said.

"The Congregational Church," I said.

"You don't act like Congregationalists, telling lies. I like your skirt, by the way."

"It's the skirt of a lapsed Roman Catholic," Corinna said. "I have a black leather jacket to go with it, but Hatch made me take it off. He thought it might offend some people out here."

"It might, but you're pretty safe in this house."

"I'm not so sure," Corinna said.

Tilden grinned. "I'm not either," he said.

Then a woman came in, and everything stopped. She wore white slacks, black spike heels, and a peach angora sweater. Her hair was jet black and fell in waves to her shoulders. She wore bright-red lipstick.

"My wife, Angela," Tilden said.

I stood up.

Angela dropped me a smile, considered Corinna a moment, seemed to approve, and fell into a second soft chair. She crossed her legs, showing slices of tan ankle, and looked around at the three of us with her eyebrows cocked, as if waiting to be entertained. Beside me Corinna shifted and recrossed *her* legs, letting her skirt ride higher, accepting the challenge. My gaze kept moving, I couldn't settle on anything. It was hard to look at Angela, and hard not to.

"Young Hatch here is Ed Hatch's son," Tilden said.

"Whit loves the *Inquirer*," Angela said.

"Thank you," I said.

"He keeps thanking me," Tilden said.

"I believe he was thanking *me*," Angela said, "and I don't mind a bit."

"Then I'll thank you again," I said.

Angela awarded me another smile. "Nicely done," she said. "Girls must like you."

"He thinks so," Corinna said.

"He could be right. Will someone tell me what's going on?"

"Some bullshit story about collecting food for poor people," Tilden said.

"It isn't bullshit," Corinna said. "We have a carload of food out front if you want to have a look."

"Of course we believe you," Angela said. "Whit, don't be an asshole."

"They're boycotting a grocery store down in North Carolina," I said. "The people are being overcharged, and they have no place else to go."

"These are Negroes, I'm guessing," Tilden said.

"Black people," Corinna said.

"And the guy owns the store is white, I also assume," Tilden said, missing the correction. "He's screwing them over and no one gives a shit."

"That's about it," I said.

"In a nutshell," Corinna said.

"This shit goes on all the time," Angela said. "Give them some money, Whit."

"We're collecting food," I said. "A couple of cans would be great."

"We don't go in much for canned food," Angela said.

"Well, money buys food, doesn't it," I said.

The afternoon had cleared, not a cloud remaining, and the sun hung above the rim of the bay. I'd never heard adults swear so often and easily, but Whitney Tilden, as my father had said, had never grown up. Neither, it seemed, had Angela.

"You kids want a drink?" she said.

She was breathtaking, but there was something unsettling about her, an audacity that seemed not just reckless but designed to stir

136 JOHN HOUGH JR.

things up, and an indifference to the consequences, as long as there *were* consequences.

"I offered, and they said no," Tilden said.

"We have to get back to the church," I said.

"Ah, shit, have a drink," Angela said.

She was watching me, red lips limning the ghost of a smile, and I tried to think of something smart to say. Tilden got up in the silence, sat down on the arm of her chair, and looped an arm around her.

"Some other time," Corinna said.

"How about tonight?" Angela said. "Come on back. We could have some fun."

"It's been a long day," Corinna said.

"We'll think about it," I said.

Corinna looked at me. "We will?"

"Sure you will," Angela said. "Meanwhile, I have a present for you."

She rose, leaving Tilden on the chair arm, and left the room, switching in her snug white slacks.

"She likes you," Tilden said. "She isn't usually so friendly."

"Glad to hear it," Corinna said.

"A couple of Jehovah's Witnesses knocked on the door the other day," Tilden said. "Got past the gatehouse somehow. Angela almost decapitated them."

"You ought to put a sign out front," Corinna said. "Beware of dog."

Tilden's mustache-hooded smile rebrightened. "She's high maintenance," he said. "But worth it, of course."

"Of course," Corinna said.

Angela was back, bringing a bottle. She crossed the room, the white carpet, and leaned, bending gracefully from the waist, presenting the bottle for my inspection like a sommelier, and presenting also a view down her sweater. There was liquor on her breath, a yeasty tang, and I understood finally that she was slightly lit.

"Merry Christmas," she said.

The bottle was scotch, Glenfiddich, and I knew it was pricey stuff.

"I'm not sure we can take this," I said.

Angela straightened, regarded me with a feigned, comical puzzlement. "You're starting to disappoint me," she said.

"Legally, I mean."

"Sweetheart, not everything illegal is wrong."

I looked at Corinna.

She shrugged, and I knew she wanted to get out of here, whatever it took.

"Thanks," I said, and accepted the bottle.

Corinna stood up, and I did. Tilden came up off the chair arm and dug a roll of bills from his pocket. "Which one of you is the treasurer?" he said.

"He is," Corinna said.

Tilden unpeeled a bill and handed it to me.

"Good God," I said.

A one-hundred-dollar bill, the first I'd ever seen.

"Give him another one, Whit," Angela said.

Tilden peeled off another hundred.

"Maybe just the one," I said.

"Take it," Corinna said.

"How are we going to spend it all before five o'clock?"

"Take it."

I did, and shoved the bills into the front pocket of my jeans. We moved out into the baronial hallway and on to the big front door. I held the bottle cradled in the crook of my arm, like a football. Tilden opened the door, and we stepped out under the portico. In the doorway, Angela took her husband's arm.

"We'll tell the gatehouse to let you in tonight, in case you change your mind," Angela said.

"Don't wait up," Corinna said.

"Oh, we'll be up," Angela said.

"Thanks for your contribution," I said.

"Sippin' whiskey," Tilden said. "Enjoy it."

"That and the money," I said.

"Money, scotch—our pleasure," Tilden said.

"Tell those Negroes to burn the fucking store down," Angela called after us.

seventeen

"We'll *think* about it?" Corinna said. "We'll think about having group sex with them?"

"Group sex?" I said.

The sky was still clear and pastel blue; we were on daylight savings now, and I knew it wouldn't be dark for a good while. Corinna had put her jacket back on. The bottle of scotch rested on the floor beside her purse.

"What did you think she meant?" she said. Barbara Lewis was singing "Hello Stranger," and Corinna turned the radio off.

"Have some drinks," I said. "Talk."

"You can't be that dense."

"Group sex," I said. "How does that work?"

"Use your imagination."

"I'm trying," I said.

"You must really want to screw Angela, is all I can say."

"Jealous?" I said. "No. You couldn't be."

"I'm just worried about your standards."

"You didn't think she was gorgeous?"

"If you like nymphomaniacs. Plus she was drunk. You got that, I hope."

"A little high, maybe. So what?"

"So maybe it affected her judgment."

"You *are* jealous."

"Hah."

We were crossing the isthmus, reentering Quick's Hole and the real world. Corinna had turned back to the window. We passed the aquarium, and the one-engine fire station. The lobby of the Marine Lab was dark, but several upper-story rooms were lighted, and I pictured scientists in lab coats dissecting horseshoe crabs or studying plankton under microscopes, forgetting it was time to go home for what was left of the weekend.

"She was just talking," I said. "I didn't take her too seriously."

"You took her seriously."

"Do I need to remind you we came away with two hundred dollars?"

"I need to talk to you about that."

"We aren't going to give it back, if that's what you're thinking."

"I don't want to give it back. You need to stop the car. Find us a place where we can talk."

"We should get back to the parsonage."

"We're going to talk first. Please."

I looked at her. *Please?*

"As long as you want," I said.

I took the back road to town, winding among low wooded hills past the occasional house nestled in a swale or astride a ridge, where the owners might have a view of the sound. These woods were disappearing, like so many others around the town, but the destruction had only just begun. We came downhill into the open, the sound off to our right, and I turned onto a dirt road that skirted a salt marsh, circling toward the water. There was a little gravel parking area where you could leave your car and walk the short distance to the beach, or you could sit in the car and watch the sun go down over the water. I pulled onto this patch of gravel and killed the engine.

Corinna sat awhile and I was quiet while she looked out over the pale marsh grasses to the steel-blue sound and collected herself for whatever was coming. She drew a deep breath.

"I've decided to tell you something," she said. "If you don't want to hear it, I'll understand. We can drive back to the parsonage and forget it."

"How can I not want to hear it if I don't know what it is?"

"It's pretty serious."

"I want to hear it."

"If you don't want to deal with it, that's fine. End of discussion."

"I'll deal with it."

"You ready?"

"I hope so."

She drew another breath. "I hope so, too. I'm pregnant."

Her gaze was far away now, rueful with its knowledge. "It's why I came down here," she said. "To see a doctor and take the test."

I felt disoriented, confused. *Pregnant.* I couldn't make it fit Corinna Devlin, or the day we'd just spent together. It was as if she'd told me she had a fatal disease or a criminal record. It was too fantastic.

"I didn't want our family doctor to know," she said. "Nobody knows, not my parents, not John. They all think I came to see Aunt Mary, walk on the beach, get some fresh air. Everyone thinks that."

"I'm not getting this," I said, and knew how stupid it sounded.

"What aren't you getting?"

"Maybe you aren't. I mean, are you sure?"

"Are you listening to me? I was tested."

"All right. You're pregnant. Now what?"

"An abortion."

Here was another anomaly in my experience, an event that occurred by arcane and clandestine arrangement abroad, or in the anonymity of New York City.

"I'm a sinner," Corinna said. "Or I will be."

She glanced at me, then away again, waiting for me to declare where I stood.

But I knew that now. It wasn't theoretical anymore, but a hard choice that would make all the difference to both of us. I didn't grapple with the morality of abortion, there was no time and I didn't care; I only knew that if Corinna Devlin had her baby, she'd be lost to me.

"It isn't a sin," I said.

"My boyfriend would disagree. My father. I'd have to marry John if I had this baby. No college. No law school. John would want another kid. And another. He already talks about it."

"But you don't love him."

"Not enough for that."

She pushed her hands into the pockets of her leather jacket and again looked out over the marsh.

"Do you love him at all?"

"He's a sweet boy. He deserves the best. Someone better than me."

It was ripe for a compliment, a gallantry, but this wasn't the moment, and she knew it as well as I did. "How does it work, getting an abortion?" I said. "Where do you go?"

"I had no idea, starting out. Turns out there's a network of doctors who will do them or set them up. Gynecologists *and* GPs. I was lucky. I started with a GP out of the Dunstable phone book, chose him at random. James Norton. Do you know him?"

"I know *of* him. He's well regarded."

"Pure blind luck. When I tested positive, I asked him if I could speak confidentially to him and he said yes. I'm sure he guessed what I wanted. I told him, and he asked me some questions, pressed me a little bit, then said he'd make a call for me. Said he knows a doctor who does this, a GP, and that I'd be in good hands, as he put it. I'm supposed to call Norton tonight. He said to call him after six. If it's a go, he'll put me in touch with the guy."

She reached down and felt for the scotch. I watched her strip the seal and work the cap off.

"Liquid courage," she said. She took a drink and offered me the bottle.

I shook my head.

"I asked Dr. Norton how much it would cost." She took another pull at the scotch. "You sure you don't want a swig? It's good whiskey."

"How much?" I said.

She replaced the cap and slapped it home with the flat of her hand.

"Two hundred dollars."

The disc of the sun was a fierce molten pink still high above the darkening water. I would remember that for the rest of my life. I would remember Corinna sitting statue-still with the bottle in her lap, eyes front, giving me whatever time I needed to make this next irrevocable choice. But it, too, was easy.

"The Lord provides," I said.

"I could pay for it. I've got a few hundred dollars in the bank, but it's all I've got to get me through the school year. And if I ask my parents for money they're going to want to know why."

"Take the two hundred," I said.

"It would buy a ton of food."

"Look in the back seat," I said. "We've done our part."

"If I can pay it back, I will. If the boycott's over, I'll send two hundred dollars to SNICK."

"Forget it. You earned that money. We both did. Angela would say the same thing. She'd approve."

It got a thin smile. "What *wouldn't* she approve of?"

"Did Norton say where this doctor is?"

"He said it wasn't far from here. I'm thinking maybe I could get it done this weekend."

"On a Sunday? I don't know."

"I don't, either. Maybe. But it's okay about the two hundred dollars?"

"Stop worrying about it."

"I can't help it."

"Put the bottle down."

She placed it on the floor. I slid over, and she turned and shaped herself against me. She was encased in the leather jacket, but I could feel or imagine the flesh inside it, the smooth firm back and softness above her hips, and the kiss was slow and probing and piquant with the taste of scotch whiskey. We sat back finally and looked at each other. Her green eyes had softened, they'd brightened, and she was lovely.

"I don't want to get you into any trouble over this," she said.

"Too late," I said.

"There's one other thing—if you're still game."

"I'm in all the way," I said.

"I have to ditch Adrian long enough to make the phone call."

"We'll find a way," I said.

eighteen

A police cruiser was parked beside Corinna's Galaxie in the parsonage lot, and Corinna thought immediately of the abortion, the doctor a snitch in her careering imagination, an informant, dropping a dime on abortion seekers.

"Do you know how far-fetched that is?" I said.

"What else could it be?"

"It's nothing. Relax."

We were out of the car now, moving toward the back door. The Galaxie was about as full of comestibles as our Falcon.

"I wonder if Adrian did something foolish," Corinna said.

"Sonya wouldn't let him," I said.

Two young patrolmen, Ray Fish and George Crocker, were sitting at the kitchen table with Martin, Sonya, and Denton. The cops turned to regard us as we came in through the mudroom. I didn't know Crocker personally, but I knew Ray Fish. We'd been Little League teammates when I was ten and he twelve. He'd graduated from Dunstable High a couple of years ago and had been the victim, his senior year, of a famous practical joke. He had gone drinking with several buddies on a warm December night and had passed out in the back seat of Franklin Jonas's car. The night waned, the sun rose, and people going to work noticed an addition to the Christmas display on the Village Green: Ray Fish in the back of Santa's sleigh, asleep with his head pillowed on the sack of toys.

"Hey, Ray," I said.

"'Lo, Pete."

He and Crocker were looking Corinna over.

"Are we interrupting something?" she said.

"We're about done," Crocker said. "What do you folks want to do?"

"Can you give us a few minutes?" Martin said.

"Sure."

Sonya's eyes were a bitter, arctic blue. Denton glared out the window.

Crocker stood up. "Officer Fish and I'll step outside. You folks take your time."

Fish rose, his gaze wandering one more time to Corinna. Girls had liked him, which I could never figure out. A cop had shaken him awake in the sleigh and driven him home. He told everybody he was as surprised as the cop was to find himself there. He and Crocker shuffled out through the mudroom. Corinna and I watched them go, then took their chairs.

"Bastards," Denton said.

"It's my fault," Martin said.

"Stop *saying* that," Sonya said.

"Are we getting arrested?" Corinna said.

"We're getting screwed," Denton said.

"We needed a soliciting permit," Martin said. "I never thought of it. I should have. *God* I should have."

"Someone should have told us," Sonya said.

"Who?" Martin said.

"The organizers. SNICK. *Somebody.*"

"So they didn't," Corinna said. "Now what?"

"We have to return the food or give it to charity," Martin said.

"Return the food," Corinna said. "They're kidding, right?"

"No."

"What the hell happened?" I said.

"Someone called Broadbent," Sonya said, "and he called one of the selectmen. Or someone did."

"I think it was a parent," Martin said.

"Or several," Sonya said.

"Your girlfriend's father, for a guess," Denton said.

"Adrian, shut up," Corinna said.

"Well, he's a well-known right-wing nut," Adrian said.

"Shut *up*."

Denton fell back in his chair. "God, Corinna, cool out, okay?"

"*You* cool out," she said.

The back door opened and Crocker and Fish came in and stood over us with their hands in their jacket pockets.

"What did you folks decide?" said George Crocker.

"We haven't," Sonya said.

"What if we lock the cars and refuse to give over the food?" Martin said.

The two cops looked at each other. Fish smiled. Crocker shrugged.

"It's pretty simple," he said. "We impound the cars. Have them towed. You guys pay the tow fee, which is twenty-five dollars. Then ten bucks a day storage fee till you decide you want your cars back." He rubbed the back of his neck, as if massaging a crick. "When the amount you owe exceeds the value of the cars, we sell the cars," he said. "Give the food to charity."

"Take the food," Sonya said, "but we're not helping. You want to give it away, you can unload it."

Crocker and Fish looked at each other. Fish was smiling again. "Call Eddie Bernard," Crocker said. "Tell him we need a couple of tow trucks over here."

"You only need one," Corinna said.

"You don't need any," I said.

Sonya closed her eyes, fighting tears. Martin took her hand. Denton squinted out the window. Corinna eyed me, the two hundred dollars on both our minds, and I gave my head a short quick shake. The money was ours.

Returning the food to its donors was out of the question, so the cops gave us a choice of three charities: the Poorhouse, which was twenty miles away; the Society of St. Vincent de Paul at the Catholic Church; or the Food Pantry at St. Andrew's. Geography made it an easy call, and I imagined the stolid brownstone, with its treasure of stained glass, enjoying this Congregationalist snafu from its elevation across the Village Green.

"We needn't all go," Sonya said.

We were still at the wooden table. Fish and Crocker were lolling against their cruiser, watching the traffic go by.

"Hatch and I'll go," Corinna said.

I saw it now, a beat behind the two women: Martin surrendering the food, traipsing back and forth with armloads of cans and jars like a schoolboy undoing an act of mischief or vandalism, being taught a lesson, while the cops looked on, making sure. I couldn't tell if Martin had thought of it yet—he was such an innocent—but I knew he would, soon enough.

"We insist," I said.

"No," Martin said. "I'm the one who got us into this mess."

"Let them, sweetheart," Sonya said, and put a hand on his arm.

"It wouldn't be right."

"Let them."

"End of discussion," Corinna said.

"I guess it won't kill me to help you," Denton said.

"It won't kill you to stay here," Corinna said.

"Let Hatch stay here," Denton said.

"I don't want you sassing the cops. Or the minister."

"I won't sass the minister."

"Do what I say, Adrian. Please?"

He looked at her, puzzled, and saw something in her eyes that stripped the obstinacy from his soft pale face. He shrugged.

"Don't take all night," he said.

The two cops had gone ahead of us, and Corinna followed me in the Galaxie around the apex of the Green and down the driveway to the brownstone parish hall behind St. Andrew's. Fish and Crocker were waiting for us by the front door with the minister, Mr. Crowell, who was wearing his collar. He'd taken over at St. Andrew's after I'd slipped away from the congregation and into agnosticism, but my parents knew him from a couple of cocktail parties and by reputation, and he was the only local clergyman my father had any respect for. Dick Crowell and his wife had taken part in the March on Washington the previous summer, riding down in a chartered bus, which alone would have endeared him to my parents.

"I'm very sorry," he said. "The law's being hard on you, in my opinion."

"The law's the law, sir," Crocker said. "Let's get this stuff unloaded and we can all go home."

There were cartons of Food Pantry donations in the basement; we had to empty them, take them up the stairs and out to the cars, fill them with our own jars and cans, and carry the boxes back to the basement. Fish and Crocker helped us, and so did Mr. Crowell, and in twenty minutes it was done.

"Sorry it had to be this way," Crocker said.

"Not as sorry as we are," Corinna said.

"Win some, lose some," Fish said, and cast a final wolfish grin at her.

We watched them get in their cruiser and roll away down the long driveway.

"Jerk," Corinna said.

"He likes the girls," I said. "He always has."

"He needs a lesson in professionalism, and I don't want to hear a crack about my skirt."

Crowell glanced down at the skirt and smiled. "Tell me about your food collection," he said.

He listened with his head bowed and his hands clasped behind him, nodding occasionally, as if at something he'd heard before, or had suspected. Then he looked down the driveway to the slow, thin parade of traffic on Main Street.

"I think that food should go where it was meant to," he said. "How do you feel about lugging it back up the stairs?"

Corinna and I looked at each other.

"I don't mean right away," the minister said. "Tonight. I'll leave the back door open."

"Are you sure about this?" I said.

"Very."

"We wouldn't want to get you in trouble," I said.

"I'll risk it. Don't come till full dark. I'll leave a light on for you."

"We're grateful," Corinna said.

"Truly," I said.

"Just doing my job," said the minister.

nineteen

She made the call from the phone booth at the Gulf station. I watched from the car as she shut herself in and dialed Dr. Norton at home, reading his number from a pocket notebook. A car drove in for gas, and the kid came out and looked over at us as he pumped it. Corinna listened awhile, then lodged the phone against her shoulder and took down a number. She spoke briefly and hung up.

She looked out at me and nodded—so far, so good. She placed the open notebook on the metal shelf, reached for the receiver, and hesitated, as if some new and sobering thought had come to her. Her head was bowed, and in the thin sour light of the phone booth her face looked suddenly blood-drained and penitent, and I understood that the truth of it was hitting her now, and how enormous that truth was.

I leaned and found the bottle on the floor. Liquid courage. I uncapped the bottle, smelled its raw bouquet. Corinna had inserted her dime and was dialing now—briskly, no more hesitation. The call went through and she turned her back to me. I'd never drunk hard liquor, only beer, and the whiskey's burn flared on my tongue and down my throat. I tried to decide if I liked it, then took another, more cautious taste. The burn wasn't quite so sharp this time. Corinna was feeding another coin into the slot. She waited for it to register, then bent over the notebook with her ballpoint. She nodded, wrote, nodded, wrote again, then listened for a long time. She nodded finally, said something, and very slowly replaced the receiver. I capped the scotch. Corinna gathered up the notebook and pen and let herself out through the folding door with her purse strapped to her shoulder. She came around the front of the Falcon and got in.

"He wants to do it tonight," she said. "I said yes."

I'd placed the bottle on the seat beside me, and Corinna took it up now, but did not open it.

"Here?" I said.

"Dover?"

"Sure. It's a half hour away."

"He said to come at ten."

"I'll drive you," I said.

She pulled a deep breath and did not answer. Another car had come in for gas, and the young attendant regarded us again as he fed the tank, wondering what was going on.

"You don't want to do this alone," I said.

"I don't want to do it at all."

"You could still change your mind."

"No," she said. "No, I can't."

She looked down at the bottle, which she'd been holding carelessly in her lap, and after a moment opened it, lifted it by the neck, and swallowed. She offered it to me and this time I accepted. I drank again and passed the bottle to Corinna. She took a pull and capped it.

"You don't have to come in with me," she said. "You can drop me off, take a walk, go have something to eat. You won't even have to see the doctor."

"You know I'm not going to do that."

She looked over at the service station, the dark cave of the bay. "He'll think you're the father."

"Okay by me," I said. "What are we going to do about Adrian?"

"You and I have a date tonight."

"He won't like it."

"I'll make it up to him," Corinna said.

"An Episcopalian," Sonya said. "Who'd have thought?"

"No one," Corinna said.

"I'd better walk over and thank him," Martin said.

"We'll thank him for you," I said. "Best to keep this simple."

"Agree," Sonya said.

She was drinking red wine from a tumbler, and smoking. The wine jug squatted on the counter, a cheap Chianti my parents sometimes bought. Martin was drinking Piels from the bottle, and Denton ginger ale from a can. He watched us deliver our news, took a long pull of ginger ale, and looked out the window with a studied disinterest. Corinna and I took our jackets off and sat down. I'd begun to feel a pleasant floaty high from the three swigs of scotch.

"Our news isn't as good," Sonya said.

Martin smiled his sweet pastoral smile. "Reverend Broadbent called. I've been suspended," he said.

"Fired," Sonya said.

"We don't know that," Martin said.

"Yes we do," Sonya said. "Broadbent was too chickenshit to say it. You'll get a letter." She lit another cigarette, shook out the match.

"It's a deliverance," Corinna said. "You don't need to waste your time with these idiots."

"Corinna," Denton said, "Mom called. She wants to know when we're coming home for dinner."

"Adrian, listen to me. Pete and I are going out to dinner."

Denton looked at her, searched her face as if for clarification. As if there had to be something more to it.

"Going out where?" he said.

"A restaurant, where do you think? To celebrate."

"You came down here to see *us*," Denton said, "not this guy you never met."

"Come outside with me," Corinna said, rising.

"What for?" Denton said.

"Just come, okay?"

Denton lifted the soda can. He drained it, shook it to see that it was empty.

"Adrian," Corinna said.

"Coming," Denton said.

We watched them go out through the mudroom, Denton following. He was no taller than his cousin, maybe an inch shorter. *He's going to be pudgy*, I thought. *Soft and pudgy.*

"Poor Adrian," Sonya said.

"Poor Adrian is a pain in the neck," I said. "The kid's never happy."

"He's jealous of you," Sonya said. "You don't see that?"

He's jealous. Jackie had said it in the long-ago fall, under the stars at the Devil's Foot.

"I can't help that," I said.

"You can be sensitive to it. Respect it, even. He's in love with her."

"In *love*? Come on, Sonya."

"He talked about her all day. How smart she is. How she got into Bryn Mawr early admission. How she dresses the way she wants to and defies conventions."

"She's right, Pete," Martin said.

"He's her cousin," I said.

"It happens. Don't you read Jane Austen?"

And I saw it now, Denton glancing her way time after time. The glances seeking, hopeful. *Are you watching me? I'm a player, here, do you see? Look at me!*

"I'm in love with her myself," I said.

"We know that," Sonya said, "and she might be with you. You can afford to cut Adrian some slack."

The outer door opened and closed, and Corinna came in alone. We heard Denton start the Galaxie.

"He's going home," Corinna said. "In my car. Which he doesn't know how to drive."

"Is he okay?" Sonya said.

"Not really."

Corinna pulled the chair across from me and fell into it. She looked out the window as her car floated past, slow, its headlights blazing. We heard it pause at the end of the driveway.

"I gave him a hug, told him I loved him," Corinna said. "I told him to trust me. I'm going to take him to breakfast tomorrow."

Denton stepped too hard on the pedal, and the car screeched into the street, and screeched to a stop.

"He's going to ruin the transmission," Corinna said.

The Galaxie began moving again, but cautiously. It purred away and was gone.

"Pete's going to start being nicer to him," Sonya said.

"I am too," Corinna said.

She called before Denton could get there and told her aunt the story of our celebratory restaurant dinner, and I called my mother and told it to her. Martin and Sonya heard us, so the lie was to them, too, which I would regret for a long time.

We went for the food a little after eight, Corinna following me in the Gibsons' bug, driving very slowly around the tip of the Green and down the driveway to the parish hall. The back door was open, as Crowell had promised, and a light on in the basement. I found a light switch by the door, and we crossed the big hall, where I'd seen magic acts, Punch and Judy shows, and our local ventriloquist, a janitor at the high school named Wilbur Peck, and his dummy pal Butch. Butch and his dummy Wilbur, the wags said, and at a young age I thought that was very funny. Our cartons of food were stacked against the wall in the basement, as we'd left them. The basement air was warm and dry, and the silence seemed thick, something you could compress between your hands.

"Corinna," I said, and put my hand on her arm and turned her.

She looked up, studying me, it seemed, and I saw for the first time that she was half a head shorter than I. The leather jacket was open, and I slid my hands inside it and around the small of her back, which was warm and beautifully concave beneath the soft cashmere of her sweater. She did the same, wrapping her arms around me under my open jacket, her face uptilted, studying me again.

"Corinna . . ."

"Don't talk, Hatch. There's no need."

She closed her eyes and I kissed her, broke the kiss and kissed her again, moving against her, our breaths coming faster. She dropped back finally and laid her head against my chest and tightened her arms around me, surprisingly strong, and I sensed she was thinking about her boyfriend John and what lay ahead tonight, and her return home, but it would be all right, I knew that, and thought she did too.

She leaned back, still holding me, and we looked at each other and smiled.

"You're beautiful," I said.

"You aren't bad yourself."

"I'm not in your league," I said.

"You'd be surprised. Should we get to work?"

"Not yet."

I had my hand inside her sweater, her back so smooth, so firm, when a door opened upstairs, closed with a bump.

Corinna swore softly, let go of me and stepped back.

"Hello," called the minister.

His footsteps moved across the floor above us. Corinna hastily smoothed some hair back from her face, tugged her sweater down. Crowell came down the stairs, smiling, pleased with the conspiracy he'd set in motion. He was wearing khaki slacks and a nylon jacket, which gave him a youthful look.

"How are we coming along?" he said.

His gaze went to the boxes of food, nothing moved yet.

"We got talking," I said. "We didn't think there was any hurry."

"There isn't."

The door opened again.

"My wife," Crowell said. "She wants to help."

She was a small, spare woman in blue jeans, and she looked older than her husband, an air about her of sagacity and mordant humor. Her name was Ginny. She had a sharp chiseled face and her hair was cut short as a boy's, which was unusual in those days.

"Maybe you two joined the wrong Youth Fellowship," she said. "From a Christian point of view, that is."

"I'm just a ringer," Corinna said. "A hired gun. You couldn't pay me to join."

"It was kind of a social thing for me," I said.

"His girlfriend's a member," Corinna said.

"Looks like he's moved on," Ginny Crowell said.

"He's been auditioning," Corinna said.

"Successfully?"

"I have pretty high standards," Corinna said.

"I suggest we get started," said the minister.

Mrs. Crowell was wiry and seemed indefatigable, and her husband was stronger than he looked, so it didn't take us long to get the boxes up the stairs and into the two cars, stacking the back seat of the VW above the rear window. Crowell doused the cellar light and locked the back door, and the four of us spilled out into the cooling spring night.

"Suppose the cops come back tomorrow to check," I said.

"Why would they?" Crowell said.

"I'm being paranoid," I said.

"After you brought it, the food belonged to us. We could do with it what we thought best, and we did."

"He's got a point," Corinna said.

"Will you let us know if you get news of the boycott?" Crowell said.

"We'll call on you, tell you in person," Corinna said.

"Come for tea," said Ginny Crowell.

"Or something stronger," said her husband.

"Tell your father to keep up the good work," Mrs. Crowell said.

"He feels the same about you," I said.

"God bless you," the minister said.

"And you," Corinna said. "Both of you."

There was a garden shed in back of the parsonage, and moving the cartons to it was easy enough, though I was tired of lugging boxes and thought Corinna must be, too. When we were done, the little shed was full, the boxes stacked chest high. Martin closed the door and fastened the hasp.

"Have some supper with us?" he said. "We'd like the company."

"They have a date, remember?" Sonya said.

A warm wind had come up out of the southwest, chasing scraps of cloud past the quarter moon. The kitchen light ran out across the little parking lot. It fell on the Falcon and VW with a faint buttery sheen.

"Will you need help tomorrow?" I said.

"We'll be fine," Martin said. "Hertz opens at eight. We'll load up and be gone before the nine-thirty service."

"We'll take a rain check on dinner," Corinna said, "meet you in Cambridge sometime. We'll look back on this and laugh."

"I'm laughing already," Sonya said. "The food's going to Waynesboro."

"Think that little bug'll make it, pulling a trailer?" Corinna said.

"God willing," Martin said.

"Do you expect trouble when you get there?"

"It's possible," Martin said.

"Be careful, then," Corinna said. "Leave the food and get the hell out of there."

"You sound like my wife," Martin said.

"Sensible, you mean," Corinna said.

"Bossy," Martin said, and hooked his arm around Sonya's slim waist and pulled her in close. A cloud blew past the moon, dragging its shadow over us. The time had come, and we all knew it.

"Call us when you get back north," I said. "Or write me, care of the *Inquirer.*"

"We'll worry till we hear," Corinna said.

"Don't," Martin said. "God'll have his eye on us."

"Good-bye, you two," Sonya said, and the next thing I knew her arms were wrapping me, clinging, as if she might cry on my shoulder. I could smell her hair, and her warm clean skin. She broke back, weeping, and embraced Corinna in a gentle sisterly fashion.

"Godspeed," I said.

Sonya wiped her eyes with the back of her wrist. "Damn," she said.

"So long," Martin said, and thrust out his big hand.

I gripped it, held on a moment. Then he turned to Corinna and offered his hand, but she stepped past it and hugged him.

"Au revoir," she said.

"I hope so," Sonya said.

"Bless you both," Martin said.

I held the car door for Corinna. Martin's arm still encircled Sonya's waist and they stood like that, softly moonlit, and watched us back out and roll away. Last I saw, they were walking slowly to the parsonage, Martin with his arm around her still.

twenty

Route 26 wound out of town past the A&W Root Beer, the East Dunstable Elementary School, a junkyard, the drive-in movie theater, and a cranberry bog, with Cape-style and smallish vinyl-sided houses crouched here and there on treeless quarter acre lots. Traffic was light the night we drove it, as it was almost any night in those days, and we made good time. A few miles from Dover I pulled into the small front lot of a diner called the Sea Breeze, which I'd passed dozens of times but never patronized.

"Can we do this later?" Corinna said.

"I can't. I'm a growing boy."

"Shouldn't we get over there? What if we get lost?"

"We've got an hour," I said. "I know Dover. I know the street. We're golden."

She nodded doubtfully and pushed her door open.

The diner was very bright, with stainless-steel stools along a counter, booths along the opposite wall with window views of Route 26. Two of the booths were crammed with teenagers I didn't know, kids from Dover. Several men in work clothes sat along the counter. We chose the far booth and peeled off our jackets. The waitress came over and put two laminated menus down. Corinna propped her chin on her hand and stared out the window. An antique shop loomed on the other side of the road, an old gray-clapboard house with dormers peeping from its third floor. I scanned the menu while Corinna studied the darkened, slumberous one-time domicile, which would sleep on till Memorial Day.

"Steak and eggs, that's what you need," I said.

"Jesus, Hatch. I'll puke."

"You've got to eat."

"All right, but not that."

"BLT?"

"I guess so."

She looked down at her pale almond-shaped hands, now folded on the table. Her hair fell forward, red-gold in this sheer light.

"Tell me I'm doing the right thing," she said.

"I can tell you you're not committing a sin, I don't care what the Catholic Church says."

"It isn't just the Catholic Church."

"Sure, evangelicals down South, where Black people are being waylaid at night and murdered. Life is sacred unless you're Black."

Again she looked down, regarded her folded hands. "You wonder what they're going to suck out of you. The person those cells might have become. A dancer. A great lawyer. Someone beautiful."

"It isn't too late," I said.

"Yes it is. I'm just talking. Feeling sorry for myself. I won't look back when it's over."

The kids three booths away, boys and girls, erupted in laughter. *I'm serious*, a girl said, and the laughter broke out all over again. The waitress stood over us, smirking and shaking her head.

"I don't know what the heck's so funny," she said. "What can I get you?"

"A BLT for the lady," I said, " steak and eggs for me. Two coffees."

"Lady?" Corinna said.

"Don't complain when they're polite," the waitress told her, and left, still smiling.

The kids were laughing again. Corinna turned, watched them.

"I played football against one of them," I said. "The tall blond guy. Name is Tulis. He was all-conference."

Corinna smiled wryly and shook her head. "Football," she said. "It follows me around. My father played, my two brothers. John. I don't even like the game."

"It sounds like you like it and don't know it."

"Tell me, Hatch. How is it possible to like something and not know it?"

"You repress it."

"You don't know what you're talking about, do you."

"No."

It sparked a brief smile. "But I'm glad you like baseball," she said.

The waitress set down a pitcher of cream and our mugs of coffee, watching Corinna as she did but not speaking.

"What position does John play?" I said.

"Center."

"So he's good. Scholarship to Dartmouth."

"They sent someone down to look at him. He's good, all right." Her gaze fell again to her hands. "I think he's counting on marrying me. Even if I weren't pregnant, I mean."

"And you didn't discourage him."

"I've been thinking all along that the separation next year'll take care of it. Bryn Mawr's a long way from New Hampshire."

"That's what I thought with Jackie. It won't matter now."

"Tell me about Jackie. Good-looking, I imagine."

"She was a cheerleader in Texas last year."

"Say no more."

"She's not a dumbbell."

"I didn't say she was."

"She's just not . . ."

"Not what?"

"Intellectual, I guess."

"And that worried you."

"It worried my family."

"And therefore you."

"I guess it did."

"Think for yourself, Hatch. Whether it's Jackie, whether it's me. You're the one who knows."

The waitress was back with our order. Corinna's BLT came with a pile of potato chips, my steak and eggs with fried potatoes and buttered toast. The waitress refilled our coffee mugs. The noisy group of teenagers rose, moved slowly to the door, and spilled out into the night.

"Eat," I said.

"Oh shut up," Corinna said.

But she lifted a severed half of her sandwich and bit into it. I broke the yolks of my eggs and cut into my steak.

"What happens now," I said, "with you and John?"

Corinna looked out the window, chewing very slowly. She put her sandwich down and patted her mouth with her paper napkin.

"I tell him I've met somebody."

"Met somebody. It's a funny way to break the news."

"It's the gentle way."

"Not very."

"No, not very."

"He'll want to beat the hell out of me."

"He isn't like that. He's sweet, I told you that. I wish he weren't."

"I guess I do too," I said.

We ate, drank our coffee. The steak was tough but delicious, aswim in juice and yolk. Corinna finished half of her BLT, lifted the second half and dropped it on the plate.

"I'm done," she said.

She sipped her coffee, cradling the mug in both hands, watching me eat. One of the workmen at the counter got down from his stool and sauntered toward the door, picking his teeth. He took a look at Corinna, opened the door, looked again, and went out.

"Could you eat some ice cream?" I said.

Corinna smiled. "Maybe afterwards. Ice cream and scotch, to celebrate. We can't keep slugging it out of the bottle, though. We'll need to find an ice machine and some cups."

"There's a 7-Eleven on Main Street," I said.

The waitress brought the check, and Corinna snatched it up.

"Hey," I said.

"I owe you."

"I can't let you pay," I said.

"Because I'm a girl."

"Well, yeah."

"You're smarter than that."

"Old habits die hard."

"That's where intelligence comes in. You recognize the errors in those old habits. The illogic."

Her purse was on the seat beside her, and I watched her lift it to her lap and dig out her wallet. I loved watching her: the sure, unhurried way she moved, her self-command. She studied the check, and I looked away as she chose bills from her wallet. She laid the bills on the check and pushed it to the edge of the table.

"Time," she said, and slid out of the booth, pulling on her jacket.

I followed her past the register, where the waitress was chatting with the cashier, a heavy woman with dyed-orange hair. The remaining group of teenagers stopped talking and watched us go by, noting my Dunstable letter jacket. I held the door for Corinna, and we went out into the faintly illumined darkness, the softening springtime air. A sweet earth smell coming from somewhere, the sky moon-blued and sprinkled with stars. I got into the car beside Corinna, and when I reached for the ignition, she put her hand on my arm, stopping me.

"Listen," she said, "if something goes wrong . . ."

"Nothing will. Norton wouldn't send you to a quack."

"I know that, but I want to thank you before it happens. I haven't yet."

"Sure you have."

"No. I'm not good at saying thank you."

"Except when you're asking for food for poor people."

"Yeah, I'm hell at that."

"Because it's more important."

"No, Hatch. No it isn't."

I reached for the ignition, and again she stopped me.

"Do you think the doctor will mind if I have alcohol on my breath?"

"I don't think it's any of his business."

"I don't, either." She groped for the bottle. She opened it and drank. She drank again and capped it.

"Come here," she said, turning and sliding closer to me.

The leather jacket was still open, and I worked my hands inside it while I kissed her. Again there was the taste of good whiskey on her lips and tongue, and the leather smell of the jacket and the rinsed fresh smell of her hair. But she broke the kiss after a moment and drew back.

"Not now," she said. "Later, okay?"

"Sure."

She laid a palm like a petal on my cheek. "But I appreciate the thought," she said.

The doctor's office stood between a rustic-looking greengrocer's and an auto repair called Autoeuropa, where it seemed you could bring your Porsche, your Mercedes, your Audi, but not your Ford or Chevy.

The building was a weathered-shingle former residence, and the sign, HENRY SUTTON, M.D., pointed you up a short rising driveway to a small dirt lot in back. The lot was deep in tree shade and invisible from the road. A shiny sedan—a Buick, maybe—was parked with its nose to a board fence, the lone car. The downstairs lights were on in the office, but the porch light, conspicuously, was not.

Corinna took my hand as we approached the homey-looking building and mounted the wooden porch steps. WALK IN, said the sign, and we did, into a carpeted waiting room with upholstered chairs, a loveseat, coffee table strewn with magazines, the room discreetly lamp-lit and empty, like a stage set waiting for the play to begin. A gray metal receptionist's desk, vinyl-shrouded electric typewriter.

Corinna's hand was cool and dry in mine, which I took to be a good sign. We looked at each other.

"Don't you wish you were home listening to the Red Sox game?" she said.

"In September," I said, "we'll go see the Phillies play. We'll see Willie Mays when the Giants come in."

She squeezed my hand, and there was surprising strength in hers. "I've always wanted to see Mays," she said. "The Say Hey Kid."

His office door opened and the doctor came in. He wore a lab coat and was smiling. His hair was thick and white, and a hairbrush-like mustache, as white as his hair, crowded his upper lip. The mustache looked tenuously and hastily affixed, it looked fake.

"Dr. Sutton," he said, extending his hand to Corinna.

"Corinna," she said.

He shook mine. "Pete," I said.

"You're the father, Pete."

"Yes, sir."

"And you two have talked about this."

"Of course," I said.

"And you're sure."

"We are," I said.

"Corinna?" Sutton was still smiling. His eyes were pale blue and very bright, twinkly.

"Very sure," she said.

"Does either of you have any questions?"

Corinna and I looked at each other.

"No questions," Corinna said.

"Good. Take her coat, Pete."

Corinna turned, and I peeled the leather jacket from her shoulders and tossed it on a chair. Sutton turned toward his office, then stopped as though he'd just thought of something. "If you don't mind," he said, still with that smile, "I customarily ask for payment in advance of the procedure."

"We have the money, if that's what you're worried about," I said. I was beginning not to like this. The relentless avuncular smile. The calcified twinkle.

"Oh, I don't doubt that," he said.

"Pay him," Corinna said.

Whitney Tilden's two C-notes were still snugged in the right front pocket of my blue jeans. I dug for them. Sutton took them, smiling, and deposited them in the deep side pocket of his lab coat. He gestured Corinna toward the open door. She gave me a brave smile, blew me a kiss, and Sutton followed her into his office and closed the white door.

I took off my jacket and sat down and looked out at the darkness hugging the window. I looked at my watch: ten thirty. I inspected the magazines: *Sports Illustrated, Redbook, Town & Country*. I picked up *SI*, Sandy Koufax on the cover, photographed in midstride, left arm in motion, flexed whiplike in the split second before snapping the fastball that even Mantle couldn't hit. *We can see him pitch. She and I can ride the train into Philadelphia and see the great Koufax, and on another day the great Willie Mays. We'll see movies and plays and I'll bring her to dinner in Founders Hall one night and the place will go quiet, even seniors staring, and she'll take my arm and ignore the stares, the sudden cessation of voices, and she'll say something to me and smile, and they'll all go back to eating, shaking their heads at the luck of this mere freshman.*

I looked at the white door and wondered what was happening in the sterile room beyond. I had no idea: the procedure was as occult to me as splitting the atom or playing the stock market. I tossed the magazine down and went out jacketless onto the little back porch and sat down in the dark. A breeze rustled in the tall old oaks, and far away a police siren whooped. I thought of all that had happened today and wondered at it, and knew my life had changed forever.

It was over in less than fifteen minutes. I heard the white door open and was up and through the screen door as Sutton was closing it. He wore his smile, and his bright little eyes were fixed on me, shrewd now and knowing, and I wondered if he'd divined our secret, or if Corinna had confessed it in the fog of whatever anesthesia she'd received.

"Everything's fine," the doctor said.

I sat down heavily.

"She's getting dressed," the doctor said. "I'm going to talk to her, then you can see her. I'll keep her here awhile, to make sure everything's all right."

"You said it *was* all right."

"So far. It's a normal precaution. Stop worrying."

He took his smile back into his office and closed the door, and I fell back in the chair and closed my eyes. I wanted to see her, to speak with her. I wanted to hold her hand. The lamplight was whiskey blond through my eyelids. Dr. Sutton was talking to Corinna now beyond the white door; I could hear nothing, but I knew it. Instructing her, I supposed, on hygiene and precautions to be taken. I knew nothing of the inside of a woman, had never bothered or cared to inform myself. The vagina a recondite mystery to me, the uterus.

The white door opened again, and she stood in the doorway hesitant and blinking, as if she'd stepped out of a pitch-dark cellar. She was ghost pale. I stood up, and she came across the carpet and stepped into my arms. She laid her head against my chest. Dr. Sutton watched, smiling, from the doorway.

"I'll be back in a few minutes," he said. "You two make yourselves comfortable."

Corinna took my hand and we sat down shoulder to shoulder on the loveseat. She slumped forward, exhausted.

"Don't ask me if I'm okay," she said.

"Are you okay?"

"No, goddamn it. *Yes.* Yes, I'm okay."

Sutton had left his door ajar, and there was music in his room now, soft and discreet, from the classical station up in Boston. A Haydn symphony, I would discover, hearing it years later.

"Does it hurt?" I said.

"Like a bastard, but he gave me something for it. Ergo-something. And Tylenol for later."

I turned, kissed the silken fall of her hair.

"I think he knows I'm not the father," I said.

"How could he?"

"I don't know. It was the way he looked at me when he came out."

"Well, who cares? It's done."

I'd kept her hand, and I lifted it now and kissed it.

"What are you going to tell the Dentons?"

"I'm out late. So what? They'll all be in bed, anyway."

"Adrian won't be. He'll wait up for you."

"I suppose he will."

THE SWEETEST DAYS   *171*

"Sonya says he's in love with you."

Corinna set her chin on her hand and looked across the room, thinking this over.

"Something like that," she said.

"Sonya's right," I said. "I see it now."

"He'll get over it."

"She wants me to be nice to him."

"I do too."

"Then I will. Is the pain any better?"

"A little, I guess. Hard to tell."

We sat holding hands, listening to the music. A pause, then a new movement began, this one measured, stately.

"I wonder if it was a boy or a girl," Corinna said.

"It was just some cells," I said.

"I never wondered till now. I wouldn't let myself."

"Don't think about it."

"I won't. I can't."

Sutton came out, bringing a blood pressure cuff. I stood up, and he sat down beside Corinna and wrapped her arm with the cuff, no longer smiling, and inflated it. He watched the dial.

"One twenty-four over eighty-two," he said. "Excellent."

He unwrapped the cuff, put it aside, helped himself to Corinna's wrist, and found the pulse with his thumb. He watched his wrist-watch, counting silently. Corinna looked up at me, and I winked at her, the wink implying some knowledge between us of which Sutton had no inkling, some binding secret. Corinna understood it and smiled through the pain. The Haydn played on, sluicing through the open door. Sutton placed Corinna's wrist on her lap, restoring it like something borrowed, and his smile rekindled and took hold again.

"Excellent," he said, and got up.

"It still hurts a little," Corinna said.

"It will for a while. Talk to her, Pete. Distract her."

He left us, and I sat down again and reclaimed Corinna's hand.

"You're doing beautifully," I said.

"Distract me," she said.

"Trivia?"

"Perfect."

The symphony ended, and the public radio DJ spoke in that precise unhurried way they have, the dispassionate voice of culture.

"Who'd Maris hit his sixty-first home run off of?" I said.

"Tracy Stallard."

"MVP of the 'fifty-eight Series."

"Bullet Bob Turley."

"The final out in Larsen's perfect game."

"Dale Mitchell. Ask me something hard."

"Something hard, let's see . . . Who's the only guy in history who was thrown out of a big-league baseball game but never played in one?"

"Nobody. You made that one up."

"I didn't. Hint: he also played for the Celtics. One of their greats."

"I don't follow basketball."

"So you give up."

"Just tell me, Hatch."

"Bill Sharman."

"Never heard of him."

"He came up with the Dodgers, briefly. Never got in a game, but he was yelling at the umpire from the dugout one time and the umpire threw him out."

"I hope he was a good basketball player."

"He was."

"Ask me another one."

"Are you feeling better?"

"Not much," she said.

"Maybe we should tell Sutton."

"I did tell him."

"Tell me about your family," I said. "Your brothers. Your father the cop."

Corinna, her hand still in mine, sat back and stared at something I couldn't see. Music commenced again on Sutton's FM radio, a violin concerto packing more brio than the Haydn but still mellifluous and palliative.

"I'm the youngest," Corinna said, "and my father dotes on me. Daddy's little girl. He spoiled the hell out of me. My brothers spoil me too. Baby sister. Woe to anybody who picked on me in grade school. They're all out of school now. Hard workers, too. Kevin climbs poles for the phone company. Michael's a fisherman out of Gloucester. Patrick and Christopher have a drywall business together."

"And now a Bryn Mawr girl in the family."

"They're all proud of me."

"Expensive," I said.

"Daddy would have mortgaged the house to pay for it, but I'm getting a lot of financial aid. Bryn Mawr loves the idea of a cop's daughter, blue-collar family. And my SATs were through the roof."

"You waltzed in," I said.

"And you waltzed into Haverford."

"Yeah, but not like you. My father went there. That's pretty much a guarantee at Haverford, unless you're demonstrably a moron."

The white door swung in.

"How are we doing?" Dr. Sutton said.

"It still hurts," Corinna said.

"Any bleeding?"

"I don't think so. Maybe a little."

"Give it time. Take a Tylenol in an hour or so."

I got up, and he sat down and took Corinna's blood pressure. He took her pulse.

"You're doing just fine," he said. "Another twenty minutes, and you'll walk out of here and begin the rest of your life."

twenty-one

Whitney Tilden may have put up the money for purchase of the fifty acres of ridgetop woodlands for our hospital by then, but construction was some years off and wouldn't be completed until after Tilden mashed his Aston Martin against a telephone pole on this same Route 26, ending his short happy life. And so the only hospital this side of the two bridges was in the town of Hyannis, which lies west of Dover on the Nantucket Sound.

Another difference between today and that night in April, 1964: Route 26, between the outskirts of Dunstable and Dover, wasn't much more than a country road. Scrub woods walled it in on either side, with here and there a filling station, a package store, the Sea Breeze Diner, McNally's Seafood Restaurant, a country church or two. Drive this road now and you pass malls, warehouses, pillared entrances to gated communities. You hit traffic lights, some within a few miles of each other. The traffic is steady, even late at night, and keeps you honest at forty, forty-five. But in those days, except in the summertime and often even then, cars were few and far between after ten o'clock, the roadway unspooling in darkness, empty and lonesome feeling. If you were in a hurry, or just felt like it, there wasn't much impediment to speeding, as Whitney Tilden so fatally demonstrated.

We passed the great orange-and-yellow tent of the Music Circus just outside Dover, and I spoke of the musicals I'd seen here, my parents driving me over a couple of times a summer, with Jill when she was old enough, and how strange I thought it was that my irascible father enjoyed not just the sly wit and blunt comedy of Broadway shows, but their romance and sweet sorrow as well.

"Me, I'm a sucker for the leading ladies," I said. "Marian the librarian. Miss Sarah Brown, the Salvation Army girl. They're always beautiful, these actresses, and they have beautiful soprano voices, and I fall in love with them."

I looked at Corinna. She nodded, smiled slightly, but the strain still showed in her lovely ashen face, her worried eyes. I was trying to distract her, as she and the doctor had urged, with this vapid monologue.

"Dad likes the women who get billing under the leading ladies, the ones that are there for comic effect. Adelaide in *Guys and Dolls*. That little tart, Ado Annie, in *Oklahoma!* They're the ones with the pizzazz, he says."

I looked at her again. "Are you okay?"

"I think so."

"Take the Tylenol."

"It hasn't been an hour."

"It almost has. Take it."

She found her purse, fished around for the plastic vial Sutton had given her. She uncapped it.

"He should have given you something to drink," I said.

"I don't mind," she said.

She tilted her head back, showing her soft white throat, and tossed a pill into her mouth. She bowed her head, swallowed, and made a face.

"Take another," I said.

"Why?"

"You always take two."

"He didn't say that."

"He thought you knew. Go ahead."

Corinna swallowed another pill. We were in the country now, the road empty, our headlights scraping the low woods to our right.

"Can you hide the pain from the Dentons?" I said.

"If I'm uncomfortable, I'll tell Aunt Mary I'm having menstrual cramps. I can tell my parents I'm sick if I have to. Sutton told me to take my temperature once a day for a week or so, and watch for bleeding. I'm supposed to call him if there's a problem."

"You'll call me tomorrow?"

"When I get on the road. I'll stop somewhere."

"Maybe you shouldn't drive tomorrow."

"I'll be all right," she said.

"You'll come visit?" I said.

"That might be a little hard on Jackie."

"She'll find someone else. Guys'll be lining up."

"In that case, I might."

"My parents'll love you. My mother already does."

Corinna turned the radio on, and we drove a while, listening to Motown and British Invasion music on WABC, coming up over the water from New York. We passed the Sea Breeze Diner, still open and bright within, several cars parked out front. The Righteous Brothers sang "You've Lost That Lovin Feeling," and I smiled.

"Blue-eyed soul," I said.

But she didn't hear me.

"Corinna?"

"Uh-oh," she said. "Oh God."

"What is it?"

"I'm bleeding."

"Bad?"

"Pretty bad."

"It hurts?"

"Yeah."

"Bad?"

"Yeah. Just suddenly."

"Hold on," I said.

"I will, but . . . Oh God."

I drove on, trying to think. Maybe our family doctor, George Langdon, would see her, Dad could roust him out of bed. Or Dr. Norton, who bore some responsibility, we could pound on his door.

"Let's stop and call Sutton," Corinna said.

"He's home by now."

"His answering service. He gave me the number."

"How bad is it, Corinna?"

"Bad."

I stepped hard on the brake, spun the wheel, and the Falcon looped back toward Dover in a tight U-turn, skidding sideways, throwing its weight on the two right wheels, then catching itself, gripping the road again as I shifted down and floored it.

"What are we . . . ?"

"The hospital," I said.

I was hoping she'd refuse and tell me to slow the hell down, tell me the pain was bad but not *that* bad, but she only nodded, not just acquiescing but in full agreement, a hospital now the only answer.

I turned the radio off, the DJ, Bruce Morrow, doing an ad for Gillette Blue Blades. Corinna sat back and closed her eyes. She'd broken a sweat. I kept the pedal down and the Falcon roused slowly, surged to sixty, sixty-five, seventy. At seventy-five the steering wheel began to judder and the car to slew back and forth as if on ice, and I thought, *You'll kill us both* and slowed to sixty-five and kept it there.

"We'll get stopped for speeding," Corrina said with her eyes still closed.

"The cop would help us," I said.

"What would we tell him?"

"It's an emergency, we wouldn't have to tell him anything."

"Yes we would."

"I'm not worried about it. Hide the scotch."

She opened her eyes, leaned and pushed the bottle under the seat.

There was a car in front of us now, a VW bug like Martin and Sonya's. The road here was winding, no passing, and I got on the tail of the VW and blew the horn. It was poking along at thirty-five, the driver lost, perhaps, searching ahead for a crossroad, an open filling station. He seemed to be thinking it over, whether to comply with my harassment or ignore it. I honked again, leaning on it, and the VW's turn signal blinked on and it wandered over onto the shoulder, and we took off again. Corinna sat forward, hugging herself.

"It hurts," she said. "Jesus it hurts."

"We'll be there soon."

"Sutton said everything was okay."

"It will be."

"You don't know that."

"I do. I *do.*"

She grimaced, gasped a breath. "Oh Hatch. Oh Jesus."

"Hang on, Corinna. Just hang on."

I looked at her, placed my hand on her leg. She wasn't wearing the jacket, and the pale-green sweater is aglow in my memory, iridescent, and Corinna is smiling through the pain, her hand going to mine, grasping it as if in desperate appeal, a fatal second lost, two seconds maybe, the Falcon flying along at sixty-five, nearly on top of the shadowy abandoned car by the time I looked, a broad sedan hunkering on two blown tires, more in the road than off it, Florida plates,

I saw it all in the glare of the Falcon's headlights a second before I veered too late and we hit it.

Slow motion, the final seconds unfolding as if in a dream, the front end of the Falcon collapsing back on itself with a sound that seemed far away, half-heard, which I would remember as the savage clank of a sledgehammer flattening metal as darkness rolled over me, and the thought that death had come.

I was thrown from the car but have no memory of it. Headlights woke me, brilliant, blinding. I was in the middle of Route 26, struggling to a sitting position, half-conscious, groping for some understanding of what had happened. A woman was running toward me out of the headlights' fierce brightness. I turned and looked at the Falcon, which had sent the stalled car ten yards on and which sat broken and grotesque with its front half squashed, the hood sprung open crazily. The driver's door was swung open on one hinge and Corinna Devlin sat in the front seat half-turned toward the passenger door, her head tucked down to the open window, her red hair curtaining her face. Her left arm was bent behind her, the pale hand resting on the seat, palm up and lifeless.

The woman knelt beside me as I stared, as the understanding broke over me.

"Lie down," she said. "Lie *down*."

I slumped forward, hugging myself, and bowed my head. "No," I said, rocking, rocking. "*No*." Telling God He'd made a mistake, it couldn't end this way, rewind and get it right.

"Oh Lord," the woman said. She'd seen Corinna. She stood up.

Another car had arrived, this one behind me. Its headlights washed the woman, and I saw that she wore a cardinal-red Dover High School letter jacket. Someone had gotten out of the second car.

"Go for a phone," the woman shouted. "*Go*, goddamn it."

"Oh God," I said.

The woman knelt again. "Lie down," she said, and put an arm around me and cradled me as I sank back onto the warm asphalt. I heard the other car start and drive away. The woman found a Kleenex in her jacket pocket and pressed it to my forehead, which was cut, I realized, bloody.

"Oh I know this is hard, oh God I know," she said.

A sob broke from me, wrenching; the woman held me gently down. Another sob, convulsive, like vomiting. Surrendering to it, letting myself sob, bawl, some faint brief allayment in it.

"I know," the woman said. "I know, I know."

And I remember, sometime later, the long, shrill, otherworldly cry of the sirens.

twenty-two

Not long after World War II, my aunt Jessica, my mother's youngest sister, was drinking champagne in a nightclub in Geneva, Switzerland, with her traveling companion, Betty Kesey, when Aunt Jess felt something catch in her eye. Both young women were fresh out of college and both good-looking, especially Aunt Jessica, who had a broad infectious smile. Tears welled in the eye, and she rubbed at it and blinked, while Betty leaned in, peering, trying to locate the thing.

A man at a nearby table, apparently alone, had been observing them—observing Aunt Jessica, especially—and he got up now and came rapidly to their table, his face knitted with what looked like alarm.

"Excuse me," he said in French-accented English, "I am a doctor. You must not rub the eye. Please."

"Why not?" said Betty Kesey.

The doctor shook his head, as if the question did not merit an answer. He pulled a chair, sat down, put his hand gently to Aunt Jessica's cheek and left it there while he studied the reddened tear-swollen eye. Aunt Jessica watched him with the other eye, thinking how competent and gentle he was. He nodded, *Just as I thought,* turned, and found a clean linen napkin. He dipped the napkin in Aunt Jessica's water glass, leaned in again, and very gently dabbed the eye with the wet cool cloth. When he withdrew the napkin, the particle was gone from Aunt Jessica's cornea. She smiled her smile.

"How'd you do that?" she said.

"Do not move," said the doctor.

He turned, wetted the napkin again, and this time dabbed the bottom of the eye.

"*Voila,*" he said, and sat back and showed them the miniscule black speck on the napkin.

This was my uncle Maurice.

"It was like a magic trick," Aunt Jess said. A suspicion had been forming. "Are you really a doctor?"

"Please. Permit me to buy you a drink."

"What, both of us?" Betty said.

"But of course."

"Are you an eye doctor?" Aunt Jess said.

"Not exactly."

"Maybe," Aunt Jess said, "you aren't a doctor at all."

"I don't think he is," Betty said.

Uncle Maurice smiled, showing a snaggletooth. He had brown hair, a cowlick on his crown, and kindly gray eyes. "Say I am not. Would you refuse a drink?"

"I never refuse a drink," said Aunt Jess.

"What are you, really?" said Betty.

He was an accountant at a department store with a high school education who had taught himself English, Spanish, and Italian. He and Aunt Jessica were married a year later at my grandparents' house outside Philadelphia, then Uncle Maurice took Aunt Jess back to Switzerland, to the tiny village of Chanvry-Sur-Rhône, some fif-

teen miles southwest of beautiful Geneva, where their love story had
begun.

It was here my parents sent me in the spring of Corinna Devlin's death, when they saw that I couldn't or wouldn't go to school,
even to play baseball; refused to take phone calls and wouldn't
leave the house except in the dark of night, alone, to walk on the
beach or take long runs, my parents worrying every minute I was
gone that I might step in front of a moving automobile or drown
myself in the sound. Sleep wouldn't come till one or two in the
morning, deep and mercifully dreamless, and I would drowse on
until eleven or even noon. *He should see a psychiatrist*, my mother
said, but my father thought shrinks were "frauds" and "leeches"
who prolonged depression rather than cured it, and proposed
instead my escape to Switzerland. It was accomplished within
the week, a disappearance as sudden and nearly clandestine as
if I were the cause of some tawdry family embarrassment, being
spirited out of the country.

Chanvry-Sur-Rhône huddled timelessly beside the broad, swirling, aqua-green river. On the other side of the Rhône lay France,
rolling west to the distant smoke-blue silhouette of the Jura. My
aunt and uncle's house was milk-white stucco with green shutters
and a red tile roof. It sat back from the village and the river at the
end of a looping dirt driveway. Behind it were deep woods where an
icy stream coursed into a small shallow swimming hole. There was a
ramshackle stable and a rickety corral where two donkeys, Pablo and
Nanette, lived the carefree life of family pets, braying for their hay at
suppertime. There was a small black dog named Missy, and a flock of
feral cats that Aunt Jessica fed on the front stoop.

She kept a huge vegetable garden on a flat quarter acre owned
by the neighbors, Monsieur and Madame Gardi, and her hands
were sunned to a nut brown and ribbed with strong veins, like
a man's. In the grassy backyard stood a candelabra cherry tree,

which my cousin Charles, who was ten or so, would climb of an afternoon, disappearing up there and gorging himself on cherries. I spoke French to Charles, and to Belle and Julia, his older sisters, and when they laughed at my syntax or pronunciation Aunt Jess stepped in, sarcastic, *"Et j'imagine que votre Anglais est parfait, non?"* The girls smirked, said their English *was* perfect, and went on teasing me.

Uncle Maurice had his own business now, assembling and calibrating wristwatches. He had an office in Geneva on the Rue du Rhône and worked there alone. He sold his watches to retailers as "Prely" watches, the name of his "company." He worked long days, returning in his sporty Citroën when the sun was lowering, by which time Aunt Jess had bathed, made herself up, and put on a dress, heels, and earrings, a vivid fragrant presence in the summer twilight. We would sit down on the back terrace then for *aperitifs*, vermouth and sometimes scotch whiskey, and talk about my family, or politics in America, which greatly interested Uncle Maurice, who brought me the *International Herald Tribune* from Geneva each day and read it himself when I'd finished. Aunt Jess would gossip about people in the village, especially the "vamp," a term new to me, Mademoiselle Chenet, proprietress of the little *magasin* near the bridge, and about the gullible rustics whom she used and discarded as it pleased her. Aunt Jess found humor in the vamp's machinations, her conquests. She had a laugh that pitched her head forward, a laugh of enjoyment, not derision. She liked humankind, found its follies, delusions, and vanities more endearing than not.

The guest bedroom was on the first floor at the end of the house. A hill, shaggy with summer grasses, rose steeply just outside my windows, and I would wake at sunrise to the lazy intermittent *plink* of cowbells—Monsieur Gardi's two milk cows, grazing the hillside. My aunt and uncle had a sizable library of American titles, and I read the mornings away on the shaded back terrace while Aunt Jessica cooked and tended her garden. Afternoons, she and I went down the footpath through the woods with the dog, Missy, to the little swimming hole, where the sun shone bright and hot on a narrow *plage* of smooth pale stones that spilled down into the streambed and up the other side. The stream scurried along over the stones, gathered dark blue in the swimming hole, then swept on into the woods, a stream again. We sat on towels and talked and finally dove into the bowl of water, so cold it flashed to your bones. We would thrash our way across it, about thirty feet, and quickly back again, and come out into the baking heat of the high sun.

Sometimes we walked in France, crossing the girder bridge over the wide luminous river, stepping across the railroad tracks that led west to Paris, stopping at the little stucco customs house, where I would show the man my passport. He would nod and gesture us on with a toss of his head. We walked for miles. The countryside was open and grazed, with clumps of dark-green firs and an occasional barn. The roads were little driven and forked off and wound here and there, and we would go different ways and come sooner or later to a village. The villages were very much alike: an ancient peach-blond stucco church, a shaded churchyard, a few stores, maybe a gas station, and, always, a cafe.

The cafes were low, dim, smoky, and amutter with men's voices. The men would look at Aunt Jessica with keen but polite interest, then go back to their conversations. The waiter, sometimes a waitress, would come and stand before us expressionless, and we would order snifters of pear brandy, *eau de vie de poire,* so dulcet in French, the most exquisite beverage I'd ever tasted—the very essence of ripe sweet pear, distilled to a sharp and lovely redoubling of itself. The snifters came on saucers with lumps of sugar, and you dipped the cube in the brandy, steeped it, then let it melt on your tongue. "*Santé,*" Aunt Jess would say, and lift her glass. She was beautiful in a stark way, her face sculpted in flat planes, her mouth generous and expressive, as if her creator had dispensed with nuance and subtlety, and I think I was a little in love with her.

And I told her everything. It felt good, as if I could talk Corinna alive and defer the moment I rear-ended the stalled car in the dark on Route 26. Aunt Jessica said little about the abortion—to spare me, I knew—but it was plain she considered the disaster the fault of an antiquated religion-based law that forced girls and women to put their lives in danger. She said the accident, on the other hand, was an act of God, and that I mustn't blame myself.

"God didn't kill her, Aunt Jess," I said. "I did."

"A car was in the road where it shouldn't have been. Would Corinna say you killed her?"

"She would think it," I said.

"Not if she loved you."

"But that wouldn't absolve me," I said.

"Then you must absolve yourself."

"Forgive myself. I can't."

"She would want you to. Just remember that, okay?"

Uncle Maurice's counsel was more practical and cosmopolitan. He said I shouldn't let myself get attached to any one girl for a while, but should sleep with as many girls as I could—stay busy, and forget, as it were. I liked the idea, but it seemed distinctly European to me, and I knew it wouldn't work out that way—for me, at least—in the States.

Time seemed to stand still, or maybe I had the illusion that I was living outside of it, in an enchantment, as if Chanvry-sur-Rhône were something conjured out of the air, a storybook village with its chromatic swirling river, the Jura rising soft blue and mystical in the distance. The woods, the icy stream, the cherry tree. On Sunday Aunt Jess made ice cream. Strawberry, blueberry. Uncle Maurice grilled trout from the Rhône in the backyard, where there was a picnic table. I went every day to Mademoiselle Chenet's little store by the bridge, where I bought postcards and chocolate and green quart bottles of German beer. Mademoiselle Chenet had dark pageboy hair and the lithe leggy build of a dancer, and between customers she would sit behind the counter with her legs crossed reading the Geneva newspaper, waiting for the next man to come along.

"*Bonjour, madame.*"

"*Bonjour, monsieur.*" Smiling, laying down her newspaper. "*Ça va?*"

"*Oui, ça va bien.*"

"*Vous parlez tres bien maintenant.*"

"*Pas encore, mais j'essaie.*"

My French did improve, and I told my cousins about American football, Lizzie Borden, the gunfight at the O.K. Corral, and swimming in the ocean. I taught Charles to say, in English, *You're a moron, Give me a double bourbon*, and *Bring on the dancing girls.* I taught Belle and Julia the first five lines of "The Highwayman."

Then one evening we were sitting around the backyard after dinner, the dog and the three kids lolling in the long silken grass, talking lazily and intermittently in both French and English, when it struck me that it was nearly full dark already. Crickets chirred on the hillside where Monsieur Gardi's milk cows browsed, the hill a looming shadow against the gun-blue sky, where now the soft stars were winking out. I looked at my new Prely watch: eight o'clock. Dark at eight o'clock! When had that happened? It was the moment I understood that I was going home.

"Don't expect to be happy all the time," Aunt Jess said, as time ran out, a valedictory summation.

"You can *hope* to be," I said.

We were taking our *aperitifs* on the terrace. The sun was already behind Gardi's hill. I was leaving in three days, Geneva to Boston, Swissair. Aunt Jess had gotten herself up in a kelly-green dress, black heels. Because Uncle Maurice loved seeing her that way. I did, too.

"People talk about a happy life," she said, "but there is no such thing. Who can be happy all the time? There are only happy moments. It's enough."

"You two are happy," I said.

"We have loads of happy moments," Aunt Jess said. "Some not so happy, right, sweetie?"

Uncle Maurice smiled a grim slant smile and sipped his vermouth. "Jessica becomes homesick sometimes. Sometimes I think I should not have brought her here."

"I get sad," Aunt Jess said. "I get weepy."

Music commenced inside, Johnny Hallyday moaning a love song on vinyl. Julia and Belle had told me all about Johnny, and about Sylvie Vartan, his sultry platinum-blond paramour. *"Quel beau couple!"* Okay, there are only happy moments, but couldn't you contrive a steady run of them, a life of them? *Corinna*, I thought. *Oh, Corinna.* I drew a deep breath of the country air just for the pleasure of it. It was the sweetest air I'd ever known and perhaps ever would. I looked down at the poured cement terrace floor and felt tears coming. I put my drink down.

"I don't want to go home," I said.

"It is okay," said Uncle Maurice. "We would be insulted if you were not sad. *We* will be sad."

"But you're ready," Aunt Jess said. "I know you are, even if you don't."

"As ready as I'll ever be," I said, and knew it was true.

I wiped my eyes with the back of my wrist and took up my drink. Johnny Hallyday had stopped singing. The crickets were noisy in the tall grasses of Monsieur Gardi's hill, and somewhere in the village a dog barked.

"Partir, c'est mourir un peu," said Aunt Jess.

Uncle Maurice looked at me. *"Tu comprends?"*

"I think so," I said. "To part . . ."

"To part is to die a little," Aunt Jess said.

"But you will come back," Uncle Maurice said.

"And then I'll leave, and we'll die a little. It'll keep happening."

"C'est la vie," said my uncle.

"One small death after another," I said.

"C'est la vie."

twenty-three

After three days she knows he won't be back, divines it as by ESP, Peter confirming the rupture as final by telephathy, making sure she knows. His one last favor to her, if you want to look at it that way. She may never see him again. She probably will not. Private school, she thinks. His father made a phone call, spun a story, sent a check, and Peter is reading Latin and Shakespeare at some hundred-year-old boys' prep school up north somewhere, Vermont or New Hampshire, wearing a coat and tie to musty classrooms where the sons of diplomats and governors have matriculated down the changeless years of the place. The privilege of being a Hatch, of having a clever father who knows how the game is played. Peter has left it all behind—the questions, the gossip, the wrath of the Dentons, the blood on his hands, his betrayal of her.

Betrayal.

She passes the first week in a daze—she will remember it only in fragments—but already she can feel a strength accruing at her center, a resilience born of the pride that has always stiffened her, and that stiffens her now beyond all previous experience, a refusal to pity herself or countenance pity in others. And so she withdraws, isolates herself, goes her own way.

It is all over the school by Tuesday: the accident, the girl's death, and how they had been illegally soliciting food for an insurrectionary crowd of Negroes down South who were up to something or other, the food confiscated by the cops, the student minister and his wife who started all the trouble sent packing. And where, exactly, were Pete and the girl going, heading east on Route 26 at midnight?

"I don't know where they were going, but I know what they were going to do when they got there," says Skip Gladding, hunched over his slab of meatloaf and gravy, his carton of milk, his Jell-O.

Donna Murray turns, fixes him with a stare.

"Hey," she says.

Jackie, across from them, looks away, chewing her sandwich. Juniors and seniors are arrayed up and down the long tables, bent over their lunch trays. She wonders if they are all talking about it.

"I'm just stating the obvious," Skip says.

"Well, keep it to yourself," Donna says.

"It's okay," Jackie says. She hears them as if from a distance. They don't matter anymore. No one in this building does.

"You live with your mistakes, right?" she says, and lets them make of that what they will.

Her father adopts the mien of an undertaker. Melancholy shadows his colorless face, and he moves deliberately about the house, creeping, as if not to stir the air. He says nothing to her about the accident, about Peter, about Martin and Sonya and the fiasco of the food collection. Her mother and sisters are silent also, perhaps in deference to him. They would all like her to open up to them, to spill her wronged and broken heart, to weep, to seek their love; she can see it in the furtive hopeful way they look at her, but she will not, because their pity only hardens her. *I've grown up*, she thinks. *I'm not a girl anymore.*

She will remember certain moments.

At dinner Linda Jean says, "Today in Ancient History Mr. Roberts asked what was Rome's greatest invention."

"You mean *ancient* Rome," her father says.

"Right. Ancient Rome. And Russell Leighton raises his hand and says the wheel."

Linda Jean looks around the table. "That's funny, guys," she says.

"Why?" says little Marjorie.

"Because the wheel goes way back," her father says. "No one knows who invented the wheel."

"Anyways," Linda Jean says, "and here's the real funny part, Mr. Roberts hears that, he gets up from his desk and goes over and bangs his head against the blackboard."

They do smile now, even Marjorie. Her mother laughs, showing her teeth, and sneaks a glance at Jackie.

"I'm trying to cheer you up, sis," Linda Jean says.

"You did," Jackie says.

"You don't act like it."

Peter would know. Peter would know what ancient Rome's greatest invention was.

"What was the answer?" Marjorie says.

"Aqueducts," her father says.

"Not *aqueducts*, Daddy," says Linda Jean. "Something about the law. The main thing I remember is Mr. Roberts banging his head against the blackboard."

"Aqueducts too," her father says.

"Didn't the cavemen invent the wheel?" her mother says.

"I would imagine so," her father says.

"Homework time," Jackie says. "May I be excused?"

"There's dessert," her mother says.

"No thanks," Jackie says, rising.

*   *   *

One evening after dinner her father taps on her bedroom door and comes in carrying a broad flat box in a white CVS bag. Jackie turns in her desk chair.

"I don't want you to share this with anybody," he says, and hands her the box, presenting it horizontally with both hands. An offering.

She knows already what it is, a pricey box of chocolates. She slides it from the bag. Whitman's Sampler, the old-timey yellow box decorated with faux needlework.

"Sweets for the sweet," her father says.

He stands there, Jackie still sitting. His smile is incredibly tender. It is hopeful, pleading, lorn.

"Oh, Daddy," she says, and lays the big box down and rises.

He smells of cloves. How thin he is, how pliant. He returns her hug, squeezing her.

"I'm sorry, Jacqueline," he says.

"I know you are."

"I feel like it's all my fault somehow," he says.

"You did what you thought was right," she says.

He steps back, wipes his eyes with the back of his hand.

"It's all we can do, Daddy," she says.

Her father nods, smiles sadly. It's as much as she will give him, and he knows it.

"Want a chocolate?" she says.

"I told you: they're all for you."

Freshman and sophomore classrooms are in the other wing, and Jackie can reasonably hope she won't run into Adrian Denton in school, or ever again. But then she comes out of the office of the guidance counselor, Mr. Tassinari, middle of third period, the hallway empty, and sees Adrian coming toward her. He is wearing a madras shirt, and she is struck by how pale and fleshy he looks, and how small. Those eyes, though: dark, lit with malevolence when he sees her. *He hates me,* she thinks dispassionately.

He stops ten feet from her. In his hand a wooden hall pass. Jackie stops, too. She will not run, she will not be bullied. It is quiet, the classroom doors all shut. There's the distant clacking of a typewriter in the office, a ringing phone.

"Where's your boyfriend?" says Adrian.

"What boyfriend?" Jackie says.

"Your boyfriend who killed my cousin."

"If he killed her, he'd be in jail, wouldn't he."

"Where is he?"

"I wouldn't know," Jackie says.

"When you see him . . ."

"I won't see him."

Adrian turns. Looks far down the hallway. One hand in a trouser pocket. He faces her again.

"She was better than either of you will ever be," he says.

Jackie takes her time answering. Eyeing him, deadpan, till she has it just right.

"You know what, Adrian? You don't know a goddamn thing about me."

She smiles, gives her head a toss, and walks on, leaving him behind, she thinks, forever.

twenty-four

Her boyfriend junior year at Lamar High in Houston, Sonny Jenerette, had scholarship offers from Baylor, SMU, and Stanford, which was either desperate for a quarterback or didn't know how dumb Sonny was underneath all that smooth talk and the level way he looked you in the eye, like he knew things you never would. Not *dumb*, maybe, but not as smart as he thought he was, which is a kind of stupidity in itself—maybe the worst kind. Sonny was gorgeous—dark, with a chiseled chin and a quick tight smile, and he could spiral a football fifty yards with dead-on accuracy. Lamar's best QB in decades, maybe ever, said the Football Boosters Club.

Sonny Jenerette was the most coveted boy in the entire school, and Jackie, a year younger than he, resolved to capture him in the middle of the summer, when he broke up with Sue May Britton. (Jackie had the advantage of being a cheerleader, always helpful in entrapping a boy, any boy.) Later she read the famous mountain climber's answer to why he would want to climb Mount Everest: because it's there. Sonny Jenerette was *there*, the Mount Everest of Lamar High School, rising kingly and beautiful in the middle distance, impossible to ignore.

Jackie had been going with Bobby Hotchkiss, but dumping Bobby was ethical because she hadn't gone to bed with him and had made him no promises. He cried when she told him she'd fallen for someone else, a two-hundred-pound crewcut offensive tackle slicking his round sun-browned face with tears and nose leak. Jackie's heart went out to him, the two of them sitting in the dark in Bobby's convertible behind J. C. Penney. Bobby, when you got right down to it, was a lot nicer than Sonny Jenerette.

She sprang the trap at a party in Joanie Roper's paneled basement, which had an actual bar with barstools. She positioned herself on a stool with her back to the bar and watched Sonny across the room as he drank Lone Star and chatted and joked with his football buddies. She let him see her giving him the eye, and pretty soon over he came, bringing his beer, walking slow and cocky, like John Wayne. Wrangler jeans, black penny loafers, a white shirt that gave off a neon-like glow in the dim, red-lit basement. He popped lightly up onto the barstool beside her.

"Hey, Jackie."

"Hey," she said.

"Nice party."

"It's okay, if you like the Beach Boys." ("Surfin' Safari" playing on the hi-fi in the corner for the zillionth time.)

"Yeah," Sonny said, "I'm a little tired of this surfer shit myself. California, sun and surf. The mythology, you know?"

Jackie leaned back, looked at him. His olive face was dead serious, as if he'd just come up with some weighty and learned opinion. Jackie smiled.

Catching the smile, Sonny smiled too. "How you getting home?" he said.

"Any suggestions?" Jackie said.

*   *   *

She never told Peter of Sonny's football prowess, or how good-looking he was; never held Sonny over him, like a lot of girls would have, to tease him, make him jealous, keep him from getting too full of himself. She never told him, riding in his father's clunky Ford Falcon, that Sonny drove his own Buick Riviera. She never told him, either, how cheesy Cape Cod football was alongside the game in Texas. How Lamar High, with its massive linemen, cat-quick running backs, and depth at every position, would have annihilated Dunstable. Peter would not, she was pretty sure, have been a starter, defense or offense, at Lamar.

It was all out of kindness, and Jackie had never been particularly kind to boys. But Peter was different from all the boys she'd known, except for his football swagger. Sonny talked just to be talking, like so many of them, equating talk with intelligence and a knowledge beyond yours, while Peter talked to *her*, his mind on her and not himself. Even when he was preaching to her—about civil rights, about those three boys who were murdered in Mississippi the previous summer—it was she he was thinking of, maybe wanting to change her but wanting it because he cared. He knew how to care, knew what caring was. Conversing with him—driving somewhere in his father's junk heap, necking at the Devil's Foot, lying naked after sex on the sofa in her basement—you forgot he was a football player. And really, it didn't matter, not anymore. He could have run cross-country. He could have played dominoes after school. She wanted to tell him this, but she never did, out of kindness. Because the idea had taken root in him, thanks to her and hundreds of other dopes like her, that football set him apart, made him some kind of hero. Like he'd fought at D-Day, or the Battle of Gettysburg. She had believed it herself, as she had believed that cheerleaders were a kind of royalty, the rightful queens of any high school. But she had seen the light, the elevation of cheerleading a delusion based on tits and ass and choreography that any sixth grader could learn in ten minutes; football was all but beside the point in the boy you loved, the very least of who he was.

She didn't have the heart to take the belief away from Peter.

So much kindness.

And her love, which she'd confessed.

And what had they gotten her?

A week passes, and another, and the phone calls begin. Sandy Slater, captain of the golf team. Rob Pendergast, who sits behind her in chem class and doesn't play sports. Chip Carroll, the quick backcourt man on the basketball team. She tells them she's busy whichever night they propose, a lie she knows is obvious to them. No football player calls, and she wonders if it is out of loyalty to Peter. She finally stops answering the phone and tells whoever does answer to say she's not home.

"Sis, I got to talk to you," Linda Jean says one evening, and flops onto Jackie's bed on her back and crosses her ankles.

"I'm busy," Jackie says.

"You sure are. You're turning into a grind, you know that?"

In four years of high school Jackie has never earned an A in a major subject, and has never cared. She doesn't care now, really, but she has taken a vow, in this final quarter, to get A's in French II, World History, and Senior English, and at least a B in Chemistry. The honor roll is published every quarter in the *Inquirer*, and if Peter doesn't see it, his father will.

"What do you want, Linda Jean?" She has gone back to her homework, translating a sentence into French.

"How come you won't go out with anybody?"

"I don't feel like it."

"I know you don't *feel* like it. *Why* don't you feel like it?"

Jackie puts down her pencil. She gets up, turns her chair, and sits facing her sister.

"You know why they want to go out with me?" she says.

"Sure. Why they always want to go out with you. I wonder what happened to Sonny Jenerette, by the way."

"They want to get in my pants," Jackie says, "and they think I'm going to be easy after what happened."

"So?"

"It would mean it was okay, what Peter did. He moves on, I move on. It would be just what he wants."

"You have to move on, sis."

"Not yet."

"When?"

"When I get away to school next year."

"All summer you don't go out on a date?"

"Watch me."

Linda Jean has to think about this, her dark liquid eyes focused on the ceiling. She is boy crazy herself at sixteen, alighting on one poor sucker after another, the suckers never wising up to what is going to happen to them inevitably, sooner or later. Jackie doesn't know if Linda Jean has had sex with any of them, but nothing would surprise her.

"What'll you do when Pete comes back?" Linda Jean says.

"He isn't coming back."

"How do you know?"

"I just do."

"Is he at home?"

"I don't know," Jackie says. "I don't think anyone does."

"Sooner or later you'll see him."

"I hope not," Jackie says, and knows already that it is both true and untrue, knows how closely related, how conjoined, dread and hope can be.

*   *   *

By mid-May the freshwater ponds are warm enough for swimming. Her mother tells her it's dangerous to swim alone, there's no telling what might happen to you in the water, a cramp, or you hit your head on a rock, but solitude is requisite for this, a remaking of herself in secret. She asks around and learns that the Punchbowl is about a half-mile wide, and she drives up there every day after her father brings the station wagon home from work. She parks in the clearing and swims across the pond, stopping to rest twice, resting again on the far shore before swimming back. The pond nestles in woods up beyond the Briarwood Theater, where they put on musicals in the summer and which doesn't open till June, and it is deserted this time of year, silent, pristine, as if she were miles from civilization. The water is cold, but it is a thin cold, its grip is light, and she can bear it. After some days she can swim across without resting, and by graduation the water is tea warm, and she can swim the mile without stopping. She will, before the summer ends and she departs for Framingham State, swim over and back twice, without stopping.

She gets three As and a B-plus in Chemistry, and thinks of Peter. Honor roll, her name in the *Inquirer*.

She wonders what he would say.

Tells herself it doesn't matter.

She waitresses evenings at the Shady Nook that summer and makes good money. She swims her daily two miles in the Punchbowl, preferring it to the ocean, the public beaches, with their crowds, their sun-bronzed men and boys on the make. At the Punchbowl young mothers sit pondside on towels and blankets, gossiping or reading paperback books while their toddlers totter in and out of the warm water with their buckets, their shovels. Jackie in her two-piece suit elicits only mild curiosity from these mothers. They grow used to her smooth tireless trips across the pond and back, they smile and say hello when she arrives with her towel. Afterward she dries herself and departs before they can draw her into conversation. They never even learn her name.

On her nights off from waitressing she watches TV or reads books from the library, improving her mind. *Catcher in the Rye, Exodus, The Old Man and the Sea, Hawaii, To Kill a Mockingbird.* Linda Jean smiles, rolls her eyes, shakes her head at all this reading, these summer nights passed at home.

"Promise me you'll start dating when you get to college," she says.

"Don't worry about me, okay?" Jackie says.

twenty-five

My dreams of literary renown fell quietly away during my employment at the *Globe*. I'd put in a two-year apprenticeship, covering minor-league baseball and high school football and basketball for the *Berkshire Eagle*, when I sought an interview at the *Globe*, presenting myself as a sports writer. They were impressed enough to hire me, but as their State House reporter, their need at the time. This was my job—not ringside at an Ali bout, but not a bad gig, either, and who knew where it would lead?—when I ran into Jackie, eleven years after I'd last seen her. I'd expected never to see her again and had not thought about her for some time.

She was coming out of the shadowy carport of the State House on Mount Vernon Street, a stranger in the middle distance, a young woman with golden hair and golden-brown legs carrying a leather portfolio under her arm. Then: *Jackie*. She looked both ways, then crossed Mount Vernon and headed down Hancock Street, declining to return the look I was giving her, as no doubt was her habit with men on the street, or she'd be locking eyes sooner or later with every male in Boston.

"Hey," I said.

She stopped, found me in front of the brick townhouse near the corner, squinted in the bright midmorning sunlight of May. I was moving now, across the narrow street, Jackie waiting. I stood in front of her and we looked at each other, assessing these older versions of each other. Her face seemed thinner, more sharply defined—stripped down to a more permanent and womanly essence. She seemed taller, bustier, but she hadn't put on weight that you could see. I checked: no wedding ring.

"I figured this would happen sooner or later," she said.

"You did?"

"I read the *Globe*, believe it or not."

"I believe it. What are you doing in Boston?"

She looked away, down Hancock, cars parked tightly along both sides. As if debating whether to tell me. "I'm a secretary," she said. "Hale and Dorr."

"Good for you," I said. "Best law firm in Boston."

"I suppose."

"I know Alan Keating. Mark Lowenstein. Several others. They do some great pro bono work."

She looked away again, silent, declining to help me keep this going.

"How have you been?" I said.

"Peter, what do you want?"

I didn't know, exactly. I wasn't seeing anybody just then, but I'm not sure that would have changed anything. I looked at my watch. Ten-fifteen. I was on my way to the governor's office to see Barney Stahl, his AA, but Barney had said I could stop by anytime this morning.

"Buy you a coffee?" I said.

Again she looked down Hancock, thinking. She shrugged. "All right."

We cut through the State House, in by the back door and out the front, past the equestrian statue of General Hooker on the landing, down the marble steps to Beacon Street. Jackie in a white blouse, white skirt, heels.

"I don't see a wedding ring," I said.

"I don't see one on you, either. So what?"

"It's just interesting," I said.

"Is it."

"Well, yeah."

I paid for the coffees, takeout, at the Dunkin' Donuts on Park Street, and we found a park bench on the Common. Jackie placed the portfolio in her lap and crossed her legs. We sipped our coffee, watching the passersby.

"I thought you were going to be a schoolteacher," I said.

"I was. Third grade, down in Plymouth. There was a guy down there I was living with, but we broke up and I got out of there, away from him."

She sipped her coffee. Looked at me.

"Why am I telling you this?"

"Because I want to know," I said.

She sipped again, staring out ahead, thinking.

"Teaching bored me," she said. "I don't have the patience. I enrolled in Katie Gibbs, got my secretarial degree. I thought a big law firm would be exciting, and the pay would be good. It was one out of two. They're nice guys, but they're cheap bastards, except when it comes to themselves."

"I like Keating and Lowenstein," I said. "Alan does most of their pro bono work."

"Yeah. Represents a guy in solitary out at Walpole. He's suing the whole Department of Corrections. Right up your alley."

"But not yours," I said.

"I've changed, Peter. I voted for McGovern. And don't start in on me."

"McGovern?"

"I said don't start."

"I'm not," I said. "But McGovern . . ."

"Big surprise. Maybe it shouldn't be."

We drank our coffee. I could enjoy Jackie's legs without turning my head.

"Are you seeing anyone?" I said.

"Maybe."

"*Maybe*'s a little hard to interpret," I said.

"Like I said, let's cut through the crap and you tell me what you want."

So here it was, one of those turning points, no going back, though I didn't see it then. You almost never do. I only wanted what was in front of me on this perfect spring day, the sportive girl who had leaned over me in red lamplight, the poised woman she had become.

"I guess I want to buy you dinner," I said.

"You guess."

"I mean I *do* want to."

She looked down at her slender hands, nails glossed with silver polish. "You broke my heart," she said.

"If you'd come with me, none of it would have happened."

"So it's my fault."

"In a way."

"I was in the middle. You made me choose between you and Daddy."

"He did too."

"So what? You wanted me to break *his* heart. You wanted me to walk away from him. Reject him. Jesus, it was one *day*, Peter. I loved you. You knew that."

"We can't undo it, Jack."

"He was scared. That's all it was. People are afraid of what they don't understand."

"Afraid of Black people," I said.

"Black people. Communists. Hippies. Can you not understand that?"

"It's still ignorance. You could have talked to him. Educated him a little."

"Oh, go to hell," Jackie said.

I looked at her, and saw it now. Saw it for the first time. My father was as intractable in his way as Lovey Lawrence, and could I have chosen against him, walked out on him in defiance of his convictions?

"I'm sorry," I said.

She cut me a look, then sipped some coffee. She glanced at her watch, sipped again, draining the paper cup.

"Suppose I *had* come with you," she said. "Would you have ignored the girl? Not looked at her?"

"I'd have looked at her, but that's all," I said, which may or may not have been true. I'd worked the question a million times.

"So what really happened?"

"You know what happened. Everybody does."

"Not all of it. Did you screw her?"

"Jack . . ."

"Did you?"

"No."

"Everyone thought so. Or that you were going to."

"Everyone was wrong."

"Where were you going?"

"Nowhere. Just driving around."

"Looking for a place to have sex."

"Just driving around. We never had sex."

"How'd they let you into college, when you didn't finish high school? Because you're so smart? I've always wondered about that."

"They were understanding. They made an exception."

"What did they understand?"

"Isn't it obvious?"

"There was a rumor you were in a mental hospital."

I looked down, smiled, shook my head. "Not quite."

"Guys on the baseball team were saying it."

"Coach Wilson called, and my father talked to him. Wilson wanted to know if I was coming back. I don't know what Dad told him, but he didn't tell him that."

"Girls pitied me. Guys hounded me to go out with them, thought I'd be easy, on the rebound. I said no to every one of them. I didn't go to the prom."

"It was no picnic for me, either," I said.

"Where were you, if you weren't in a loony bin?"

"I was home, for a while. Then I went away. Have dinner with me."

"Away to where?"

"Switzerland," I said.

"Switzerland. Am I supposed to believe that?"

"I have family over there. I'll tell you all about them. Have dinner with me."

She took a long time, sitting motionless with the portfolio now hugged against her, looking out over the elm-shaded Common past the people going by, college kids, men in suits, a woman pushing a baby carriage, a shuffling, hollow-eyed wino.

"Sure, what the hell," she said.

We were married three months later.

twenty-six

My apartment that summer was on the first floor of a large old house on Inman Street in Cambridge. Trees grew up out of the brick sidewalk, and it was shaded in summer and quiet at all times of day. I had a sofa bed that I opened when Jackie came over, and we made love on top of the sheets with an electric fan blowing warm air over us. I would leave the Red Sox game going on my transistor radio, and there was the intermittent groan of traffic over on Mass Avenue, the occasional gripe of a car horn.

Her apartment was high up in the Prudential Tower, a corner apartment, spacious and air-conditioned. She had sublet it, cheap, from a Hale and Dorr lawyer who'd been suddenly lured away to a job in Chicago with six months on his lease. I would get up after we made love and walk out into the darkened, air-cooled living room and look southward at the city lights glittering myriad to the horizon, or west, down into the illumined canyon of Fenway Park. Jackie would come out in the ambient city light and stand with me and maybe take my arm, maybe turn me toward her for a kiss, and pretty soon we'd move to the sofa, which was very soft and gave under us, and we remembered the sofa in her parents' basement and laughed.

It was a good summer for me at the *Globe*, enlivened by regard for my work from Beacon Hill and the admiration of reformers for my coverage of riots at Walpole prison, and of the subsequent stand-off between the cons and the administration.

"The do-good attorneys at Hale and Dorr love you," Jackie said. "The pro bono guys. They say you've got balls."

"What do you say to that?" I asked her.

"I tell them to watch their mouths."

"Right. Miss Priss."

We were sipping preprandial Manhattans at Dini's Sea Grill, sitting by the window watching the people go by on Tremont Street. Across Tremont, the Granary Burying Ground was shadow-steeped, drawing darkness in ahead of the rest of the city, it seemed. John Hancock over there beneath his leaning, weather-worn headstone, asleep down through time. Paul Revere, Samuel Adams.

"Jerry Williams called me today," I said. I'd been saving this.

"No way," Jackie said.

"He wants me to be on his show tomorrow night. Me and Sam Tyler, guy who runs the Mass Council on Crime and Correction."

"I guess I'll have to tune in," Jackie said.

"Come with me," I said. "Sit in the studio and watch."

"I can do that?"

"Sure. Williams'll love it."

"Yeah?"

"So will Sam, and every other guy in the studio."

Jackie looked down at her slender, sun-tanned hands, long silvered nails. I sipped my sweet, strong drink. She looked up and met my gaze. Sea-blue eyes questioning, sensing something. *She's beautiful*, I thought. Thought *I never knew how beautiful*. Her eyes now locked on mine, anxious but patient, too, as if she knew what was coming and would give me all the time I needed.

"Jack?" I said.

"Say it," she said.

"Let's get married."

She looked out at the Burying Ground. Then again at me.

"Why not?" I said.

Her gaze fell. She smiled a half smile, as at some droll witticism. The smile's import, its meaning, a mystery to me to this day.

"Why not," she said.

Neither of our parents were thrilled, no surprise there, and on the Sunday night of the weekend on which we told them, Jackie and I drove back to Boston and ate fish and chips, late, at Charlie's Seafood on Central Square in Cambridge. The big room was windowless, the lighting a thin sherry yellow that gave it a perpetual feeling of two a.m. It smelled pleasantly of its wood floor, its deep-stained plank walls. The question was the venue.

"Not the Congregational Church," I said.

"Not St. Andrew's," Jackie said.

"Agreed," I said.

"Where, then?"

"We could get married on a beach," I said.

"Like hippies. Daddy'll love it."

We weren't married on a beach, after all, but in my parents' living room, on a cool, bright fall day, Jackie newly pregnant with Jennifer. A small gathering, family, a few friends of mine from the *Globe*, five or six of Jackie's coworkers, including Alan Keating. The officiant, a concession to Lovey Lawrence, was the young Congregational minister, Mr. Doane, who had no memory of Martin and Sonya Gibson.

Lovey didn't give his daughter away; no one did. She descended the narrow stairwell trailed by her sisters and a young woman named Kathleen Sweeney from Hale and Dorr. My bride wore a knee-length white cotton dress with a yellow sash, white high heels, and her legs were bare, and you could hear a collective intake of breath when she appeared. I watched her come toward me and the minister carrying a bouquet of yellow roses, her gaze demurely lowered. She was perfectly lovely, but something was wrong, it had happened all too quickly, two months since my proposal in Dini's Sea Grill, three since our chance encounter on Mount Vernon Street, and by the time Jackie had handed the roses off to Kathleen Sweeney and come beside me and raised her eyes to the smiling face of Mr. Doane, I'd seen the years raveling out ahead of us, on and on toward the distant twilight of old age, and I knew I was making a mistake.

part three

twenty-seven

I recognized Adrian Denton the moment he walked into the bookstore, though the years had broadened him and blanched his thick hair pure white. He'd been soft then and was softer now, pale, the dark eyes lit with the old disdain and cynicism and with, now, a new and sharper glint of pure malice. Adrian Denton in his late middle age, in a black Elton John T-shirt, baggy black jeans—a sprite, an avatar. Jackie stared at him, knew him finally, and her hand went to her mouth as if to stop herself from speaking out.

Silence. Trouble had shown up, and everyone sensed it as Denton stood there, just inside the door, not quite smiling but almost, looking first at me, then at Jackie, and on around the room at Carol Littlefield, the tiny audience, young Erica behind the counter.

"Well," I said.

Denton drew himself up and regarded me with that contemptuous almost-smile.

"Well?" he said. "That's what you say to me, *well?*"

"Come in, then," I said. "Make yourself comfortable."

"Mr. Hatch is about to give a reading," Carol said, "and we'd like to get started."

Again Denton surveyed the room. Everyone silent, waiting.

"I thought there'd be more people," he said. "I guess you're not much of a writer, Hatch."

"I think maybe you ought to leave," Carol said.

"No, I think I'll come in," Denton said. "Listen to what the great man has to say."

I closed *The Minutes of This Night.* "This isn't going to work," I said.

"Of course it's going to work," Carol said.

"Go ahead, Hatch," Denton said. "Give us some wisdom out of your great novel."

"It was a long time ago, Adrian," I said. "I'm sorry. I'm sorrier than you know."

Adrian. My sister darted me a look, remembering the name, Adrian Denton, cousin of the dead girl.

"You're sorry," Denton said. "You killed her, Hatch. Then you took off. You disappeared. You killed her and ran away, and now you're sorry."

I looked at him, fleshy moon face, snow-white thatch, a tired old man except for those bright black eyes. "I couldn't run away from it," I said. "I loved her."

"Bullshit," Denton said.

"I did, I loved her," I said. "God, Adrian, didn't you see that?"

"Bull*shit.*"

"Here," Carol said, "enough of this. Erica, call the police."

"Craig," said Rita Clare to her companion, "are you going to throw this little fucker out, or do I have to?"

"I'd be glad to," Craig said.

But then Jackie stood up, flushed, eyes ablaze, and Craig sat back and Erica paused with the phone halfway to her ear, and that dead flat silence fell again, all eyes on my wife.

"Get out of here," Jackie said. "Get the hell out *now.*"

Denton eyed her, still with that maddening ghost of a smile, then swung his gaze back to me.

"How does it feel to be married to a racist, Hatch?" he said.

"Erica," Carol said, "call them."

"Don't bother," Denton said. He turned, pulled the door open, looked at me over his shoulder in a mild almost friendly way, as if we'd settled something between us, had even conspired together, and strolled out into the summer twilight.

"Good heavens," said the old woman.

"Yowza," said Rita Clare.

Jackie had sat down again. She was staring out the display window. She'd gone pale and was sitting very still.

"Pete?" Carol said. "Would you like to read?"

"Jesus," Rita said, "would *you*?"

"Pete?" Carol said.

"I don't think so," I said.

Jill stood up and turned to the benumbed little audience. "Pete didn't kill anybody," she said.

"Of course he didn't," Carol said.

"He was in an auto accident years ago," Jill said. "He was in *high* school."

Another silence, and I wondered if Jill had only made things worse. I moved past her and sat down between the old woman and Craig. I slumped forward and set my arms on my knees. I did not look at Jackie, but I knew she hadn't moved. I thought about leaving, making for the door and not looking back. Jackie would follow me. She'd have to.

"I think we could all use some wine," Carol Littlefield said.

"Capital idea," the old woman said, and lurched to her feet.

The gypsy girl stood up, Rita rose and took Craig's hand and drew him up. "Wine, Craigie," she said. "Wake up."

Joe had gotten up, and now he and Jill sat down on either side of me while the others all moved toward the wine.

"Are you okay?" Jill said.

"I guess so," I said.

"You don't look okay."

"I'll be fine. Go get yourself some wine."

I was alone with Jackie now, and I moved over beside her and took her hand. It was limp, dead to me.

"You're not a racist, Jack. You never were."

"Do you think I care about that?" she said.

"He never liked me," I said. "Or you. He was an angry kid, now he's an angry old man."

"I wonder why."

"He loved his cousin. He was *in* love with her."

"So were you, apparently."

"It was almost fifty years ago. One day."

"It was enough, wasn't it. And you still love her. I could see it in your face."

"That's crazy. How could I?"

"It's quite common, actually."

"What is?"

"What happened that day? What *really* happened?"

"You know what happened. She died."

"You're going to tell me, Peter. You're going to fucking tell me before you ever touch me again."

She rose and went for the wine.

Maybe it was the calming influence of the wine, though she hadn't drunk much, or maybe a mastery of herself that I'd seen before: Jackie stood composed, chatting quietly with Jill and Joe while I inscribed books for the old woman, whose name was Adelaide Tapper, her aide—"Just Robin's okay"—the gypsy girl, Cassandra Smith, and Rita Clare and her friend, Craig Smythe, who paid for his and hers. *For Adelaide Tapper, with best wishes, Peter Hatch.* It sounded glib, artificial, patronizing—best wishes for what, and what were my best wishes worth, anyway? *For Cassandra Smith, cheers.* I was sitting behind the side table with the piles of books on either side of me, like a merchant awaiting business at a trade show or street fair.

"Something inspirational," Rita said, sliding the book toward me. She was drinking merlot out of a plastic cup. "Write me a sonnet."

"I don't think I'm up to it," I said.

"What was it all about, anyway?" she said.

"A long story," I said.

"Obviously."

I glanced at Jackie, still conversing with Jill and Joe. Craig Smythe stood beside Rita with my book under his arm, a cup of white wine in the other hand, looking around the room as if he'd only just arrived. Rita, I guessed, had picked him up at the barbeque, a stranger. I wondered where she was from, and whether he lived in Dunstable.

For Rita Clare, Thank you for coming to my non-reading, and for your moral support. I'm glad the cookout was a bust. What happened to the Absolut?

She took it up, read it, and smiled.

"Not bad," she said.

For Craig Smythe, Salud!

"Maybe you should write about it," Rita said, "whatever it was."

"I don't think he wants to talk about it," said Craig Smythe.

"I said *write* about it, are you deaf?"

"Maybe someday," I said.

There was no more business—I'd signed the three books for Jill and Joe—just this quiet room, Erica now folding the chairs and stacking them against the wall.

"Cheer up," Carol said. She was nursing a plastic cup of the merlot. "Last year Ward Just was here, and seven people showed up."

"But no enemy from out of his past," I said.

"It was a hiccup," Carol said. "No harm done, except we all missed hearing you read."

"Such an odd little man," said Adelaide Tapper. "He seemed slightly touched."

Adelaide was halfway through her second cup of white wine. Robin had sat down in the front row and had opened my novel and was leafing through it in a mildly curious sort of way. Adelaide had paid for her copy.

"Do you have time to sign the rest of the books?" Carol said.

"All of them?" I said.

"Sure."

"What if you don't sell them?"

"Let me worry about that."

Cassandra Smith was across the narrow room looking over the modern fiction shelves, a cup of wine in one hand, my book in the other. She turned now, strolled past Erica, and placed her empty cup on my table as if she expected me to dispose of it for her.

"I ought to attend more book signings," she said. "I didn't know they were so exciting."

"I hope you enjoy the book," I said.

"Oh, I will," she said. "I can't wait."

We watched her trail out, tall and willowy, unhurried.

"Mrs. Tapper, we should get going," Robin said.

"Coming, dear."

Jackie had moved to the window and stood with her arms folded in that graceful way she had, looking out. The sun was lowering, and Main Street was blurred in a deepening twilight.

"Split time, Craig," Rita said.

"I'm ready," Craig said.

"You've been ready since we got here."

Adelaide Tapper set her cup down, pivoted on her walker, and swung herself toward the door. Robin pushed the door open for her and followed her out without looking back.

"It's been swell," Rita said.

"Thanks for coming," I said.

"Are you kidding? It was a hoot. Too bad your buddy in the liquor store didn't make it."

"Just as well," I said.

Walt Cummings and Adrian Denton—I thought of it only now—had been classmates.

"Ciao," Rita said. "Keep that chin up. Write another book."

I watched her walk away, her bronze legs, her hips in those tight candy-pink shorts, and felt the pang of some irretrievable loss I couldn't identify. Craig followed her out, and the door bumped shut, locking us in the drear silence that lingers over a battlefield, a smoking ruin. All I wanted was to get out of there.

"Last call for wine,'" Carol said.

Joe looked at his watch. "We have a dinner reservation," he said.

"Erica, you go on home," Carol said. "I'll close up."

"Join us, Pete?" Joe said. "I'm buying."

I looked at Jackie. Everyone did. She stood as before, alone by the big window.

"Jack?" I said.

"It's up to you," she said to the window.

"We're pretty tired," I told Joe.

"Rain check, then," he said.

"What about the food, Mrs. Littlefield?" Erica said.

"I'll take care of it," Carol said.

"Night, Jackie," Joe said.

She turned with her arms still folded. "See you, Joe," she said, but sadly, as if she doubted it.

*   *   *

I autographed the title pages of Carol Littlefield's twenty remaining copies of *The Minutes of This Night* while she and Jackie boxed the cheese and crackers and grapes and whatever else there was of that pointless collation and put it all away somewhere out back. The lights were on now, bright in the empty room. I signed a final book and stacked it.

"Do you honestly think you'll sell these?" I said.

"Oh for God's sake," said Carol Littlefield. "You just published a novel. Go out and celebrate."

"There are a lot of lousy novels," I said.

"I don't stock lousy novels," Carol said. "Jackie, take him out and cheer him up."

I stood up and looked around for my copy of the book. I'd left it on the podium. The cover seemed to mock me, a joke somebody had played on me in my inexperience—the ghostly Capitol in the background, the chess board with its scattered pieces, erect and toppled, and the dead man asprawl in his own blood. I wondered who had been commissioned to produce this eyesore, which my editor had extolled as "wonderfully creepy." Those writers' conclaves in Greenwich Village bars, the cocktail parties at the John Herseys', had been cruel jokes played on my imagination.

"Anything else we can do for you?" Jackie said.

"I just told you," Carol said, "go out and enjoy yourselves."

I opened the door and turned. "Carol . . ."

"Beat it," she said, smiling, pretty in her summer dress, philosophical, amenable even, to the waste of this summer evening.

twenty-eight

There was a new Italian restaurant across the street, sidewalk tables with candles, couples bent toward each other in the candles' soft aureoles.

"Want to go have some pasta?" I said. "Some Chianti?"

"I want to talk," Jackie said, and kept walking.

"I'm too tired to talk," I said.

"You think I'm not tired?"

We turned into the Town Hall lot, which was still full, and I unlocked the car by remote and opened the passenger door for Jackie. She did not look at me as she jackknifed in. I got in and shut the door, snuffing the overhead light. I retrieved our phones from the glove box. A voice message on mine from Jennifer. *How did it go? Call me, Dad, ASAP.*

"She can wait," Jackie said. "Or do you want to tell her how Adrian Denton crashed your party?"

"Jack, listen to me."

"I'm listening. You bet I'm listening."

"I sold seven goddamn books, three of them bought by my sister and Joe. It was a fucking nightmare."

"It was a fucking nightmare when Adrian Denton showed up, that was the nightmare. What does he know that I don't?"

"Nothing."

"Bullshit."

"It's true. He was in love with her, is his problem. I guess he still is."

"So are you. She must have been something."

"I spent one day with her."

"The day she died," Jackie said. "Start the car. I want to look at the water. I haven't seen it in a while."

"The water," I said.

"I miss it. It's one reason I want to come back here."

"The water. Jesus."

"Start the damn car, Peter."

We drove east on Main, past the Rug Barn, which had been the Empire Theater, where I'd seen Audie Murphy and Jane Russell in Saturday matinees for a quarter. Past the library and the World War II monument, past Liam Mahoney's Irish Pub. The pub door was propped open and we could hear an all-male trio chorusing "Roddy McCorley" over a clamor of guitars and a banjo. I turned right, toward the water.

"I'm not a writer," I said. "I don't know why I thought I was."

"What was her name?" Jackie said. "I've forgotten."

"You know what the difference is between me and a real writer?"

"What was her name?"

"Corinna."

"Corinna. She was very intellectual, I imagine."

"Can I tell you this? This difference? Or are you not interested?"

"Sure, tell it."

"You open *The Confessions of Nat Turner*, *Fair and Tender Ladies*, anything by Dickens, and you enter a heightened, exciting world. It's the way it happens in a theater when the house lights go down and the stage is lit in that brilliant milky light, and everything looks shiny and brand-new. They're ordinary objects—a fire hydrant, a table, window drapes—but they look so different, so perfect, it's like you've never seen them before. Then the actors come on, the beautiful actresses, the men with their chiseled faces, and they seem so *alive*. They seem to . . . to exude emotion and humanity. You open a great novel, or even a good one, and that's what happens."

Jackie was looking out the window. Arms folded.

"Open my novel," I said, "and it's a stage in daylight, plain and ordinary. Ever see a rehearsal that wasn't a dress rehearsal? Guys in blue jeans, women in slacks and sweatshirts. They're acting, but something's missing. The beautiful illusion. The magic. A second-rate novel is like that."

Jackie watched Faye Driscoll's house go by, Faye our other senior-class beauty, blond like Jackie but smaller, more compactly curvaceous. Faye's father, dead now, had been an optometrist, Dr. Driscoll, a sweet shy bespectacled man from whom Faye had not gotten her looks.

"Did you hear anything I said, Jack?"

"I heard it. It was beautiful."

"It isn't beautiful, it's sad."

"Don't you wish you had someone who could say wise beautiful things like that?"

"I'm not going to answer that."

I can tell you every World Series starting with the Whiz Kids in 'fifty, she said.

I doubt it, I said.

Go ahead. Ask me. Dare you.

'Fifty-four.

Indians-Giants, Giants sweep. Willie Mays makes his famous catch.

Off the bat of . . . . ?

Vic Wertz.

How the hell do you know so much?

I was right. You hate it when a girl knows as much as you do.

Only when they're obnoxious about it, I said.

We were in the Falcon, on our way to Quick's Hole.

"I can't do this, Jack. I can't keep telling you I love you. I married you, didn't I?"

"People fall into marriages. It seems like a good idea at the time."

"Is that what you think happened?"

"I don't know, Peter. It was hasty, I know that."

The road curved west, becoming Shore Road, broad and sun-whitened in the headlights. I drove into the public beach parking lot where I'd brought Jackie in my father's Ford Falcon the night of the Harvest Dance, the first time I'd ever put my hand on a woman's thigh. I wondered if she was remembering that night, and in what spirit. There were four cars in the lot, parked at generous intervals facing the sound, and rap or hip-hop, I've never known the difference, thundered in all four, reverberating from car to car.

"No," Jackie said. "Christ."

I swung the car around in a broad U and continued west on Shore Drive.

"They're out early, those kids," I said.

"They're probably all stoned," Jackie said.

"Something like that," I said. "I wonder how their eardrums stand it."

"They're going deaf. A whole generation."

"Jen thinks rap music's misogynistic."

"She thinks everything is. Turn right on Walker Street."

"Where are we going?" I said.

"The Devil's Foot," Jackie said.

"Good idea," I said.

"Are you going to call Jennifer?" Jackie said.

"I'm driving."

"It's you she wants to talk to."

"Call her," I said. "Tell her it went fine, and we're out for a romantic drive and I'll talk to her tomorrow. She'll start to worry and keep calling if you don't."

"A romantic drive, I'm supposed to tell her?" Jackie said, and took up her own phone.

"If she thinks we're fighting, she'll want to know what's going on," I said.

"It's none of her business."

Jennifer picked up.

"Hi, hon," Jackie said. "Your father's driving, he asked me to call you. It went great . . . Really . . . *Nothing's* wrong . . . Well, there isn't. I'm just tired. I have cancer, remember? . . . I don't know, maybe ten, twelve people. But he signed about thirty books, so . . . We're driving out to the Devil's Foot to look at the water, which I miss . . . Yeah, the Devil's Foot, why not? . . . Yeah . . . I'll tell him, hon . . . Yeah . . . Love you too."

Jackie dropped the phone into her purse.

"That girl wears me out," she said.

twenty-nine

There were six or seven driveways off the long dirt road to the Devil's Foot now, with residents' names painted attractively on signposts—Comiskey, Hubbard, Goldstein—narrow dirt roads disappearing into the woods toward unseen houses, but no house had risen on the headland itself. We came out onto the flat sandy clearing with the bay spread before us and the plump moon hung halfway down the sky. Neither of us had been here since high school. I parked at the edge of the clearing, where we could see the waves tumbling onshore, and a moment later there was the smooth potent rumble of a truck's diesel engine behind us.

"Now what?" I said.

"Wait and see," Jackie said.

I wondered if the driver of the truck had been following us, and what that could mean. It was a big Dodge Ram, coal black. It stopped some twenty feet away, and the driver killed the engine and lights. I could see him now, a Black man in a straw cowboy hat. The woman with him was white and platinum blond, and already I could see she was pretty.

"Maybe they're going fishing," Jackie said.

"In a cowboy hat, I doubt it. Let's get out of here."

"What the hell, Peter. We have a right to be here."

I shrugged. "All right. Fuck it."

"You better straighten out your attitude. We're going to sit here till you talk to me."

The truck door opened and the driver got out, glanced at us and stretched, silvered in moonlight. He wore a red-and-gray Western flannel shirt, tight jeans, and cowboy boots, and he was rangy and loose-limbed and looked like a roper, a bronco rider. He nodded to us, tipped his hat, then went around to the front of the truck and stood with his hands on his hips and his forward knee bent gracefully, gazing out over the water, studying it.

"The Marlboro Man," Jackie said.

The woman had gotten out on the far side. She came around to the front of the truck beside the cowboy and leaned back against the hood with her arms folded. She wore yellow slacks, and her yellow hair was gathered above her neck, which was slender and ivory-white.

"I'm going to say hello," I said.

"Why?"

"Why not?"

"We didn't come out here to socialize."

"There's no reason to be unfriendly," I said.

"*Or* friendly, damn it," Jackie said.

The man and woman turned when they heard me get out. They watched me come around the front of the car. I moved halfway to the truck and turned and looked out to sea.

"Beautiful evening," I said.

"Can't argue with that, sir," the cowboy said.

Sir. After years of it, it still felt like somebody else, a mistaken identity.

"I just love the ocean," the woman said. She spoke softly, with a sugary southern accent.

"I'm afraid we're intruding on you," said the cowboy.

"We're too old to be intruded on," I said.

He looked at me and smiled. "Use it or lose it," he said.

"Tommy," said the woman. "Your manners."

"It's good advice," I said.

The blonde turned and came around beside the truck and stood facing me. A salt breeze blew in off the water. The waves splashed the beach, drew slowly back, came on again.

"We only came here to talk, ourselves," the woman said. She smiled. "Like we couldn't do that anywhere, right?"

"That's what we came for," Jackie said from the window. "To talk."

"We must all be getting old," the cowboy said.

"You folks don't look old to me," the woman said.

"Moonlight is forgiving," I said.

"Peter, why don't you get in the car and stop bothering these people," Jackie said.

"He's no bother," the woman said. "I like havin' y'all here. I feel like you're sympathetic. We got all night. I'm Lottie, by the way. This here's Tom."

Tom turned and tipped his hat again.

"Pete," I said. "Jackie riding shotgun."

"Hey, Pete. Hey, Jackie."

Lottie turned toward her cowboy. "Tommy, whyn't you come join us, not stand there with your back turned."

Tom swung around slowly and moved to Lottie's side, his gait a rolling, long-legged amble. She took his hand.

"It's real pretty here, isn't it," Lottie said.

"Been here before?" I said.

"Lord, no."

"I thought you might have followed us."

"We never. We were drivin' around and saw the dirt road and took it. We're here on vacation. We drove all the way from Denver, Colorado. We always wanted to see Cape Cod. Well, I did, anyway."

"I used to bring Jackie here when we were kids," I said. "Did some serious necking, right, Jack?"

She was looking out at the water. "Sure," she said.

"My lord. High school sweethearts, right here in this town. Think of that, Tommy."

"It happens often, or so they say," Tom said. "Marry the girl next door."

"Y'all been married a long time, then," Lottie said.

"We sure have."

"That's so unusual in this day and age."

"Where are you from, Lottie?" I said. I wanted to keep this going, give Jackie time to think things over, maybe cool down.

"Little city called Auburn, Georgia. Tommy's from Billings, Montana, originally. Now he travels all over. We do, I should say. Tommy's a rodeo rider, in case y'all didn't guess that already."

"We thought he might be a model," I said.

"Well, he could be, for sure."

"Are you having a good vacation?" I said.

"We're getting our minds straight, aren't we, Tom."

"You are," Tom said. "Mine's straight as a West Texas highway."

"I'm sure it's going to work out, whatever it is," I said.

"I think so too," Lottie said. "Tommy, whyn't we take a walk down the beach? Walk and talk."

"Why not?" Tom said.

Lottie gave me a parting smile and nod, took his arm, and walked with him down the short path worn through the beach grass. She looked very small, doll-like beside him. They stopped, Lottie holding on to his arm while she leaned sideways and removed a shoe. She removed the other shoe and dropped them at the foot of the path. I watched them move away down the beach, Lottie still on his arm, slow, shrinking smaller and smaller in the silver-blue light of the full moon.

"Are you going to stand there all night?" Jackie said from her window.

I went around to the driver's door and got in, and we sat in the car, a dark pocket in this firmament of moonlight.

"I wonder what they have to work out," I said.

"He wants to get married, and she's holding back. Her family's probably against it."

The waves plashed down, receded, and the south wind chased a distended cottony cloud past the moon.

"Maybe it's the other way around," I said. "Maybe she's the one wants to get married."

"So I'm a racist for thinking she's saying no."

"You're not a racist, Jack. You never were."

"You thought so."

"No. I thought your father was."

A boat was passing some miles out, probably a trawler out of New Bedford, its yellow lights moving steadily, sedately, from right to left.

"What were you doing that night?" Jackie said.

"What night?"

"Stop it, Peter."

"We've been through this a million times," I said.

"That's one million lies. Now you're going to tell me the truth, before it's too late."

"I never lied to you."

"You didn't tell me everything."

"That's not lying."

"I'll be the judge of that," Jackie said.

thirty

"So I'm the only one in the world who knows," Jackie said.

"Unless Aunt Jessica and Uncle Maurice told their kids, which I doubt."

"Are the kids in Switzerland?"

"As far as I know. I haven't seen them in years."

We'd gotten out of the car and gone down the cut through the beach grass and were sitting on a creosoted timber that had been storm-wrenched from some dock or wharf and had floated here and there on the shifting tides until another storm had flung it halfway up this beach, where it would rest till the ocean took it back again. Jackie had taken off her shoes. The moon shone so bright we could see Lottie and Tom in the distance, standing side by side, looking out over the bay, maybe talking, you couldn't tell.

"I wonder if you'd have done something like that for me," Jackie said. "Take me to get an illegal abortion."

"Sure I would have," I said.

"But you wouldn't cut me a break for staying home that day. For not hurting my father." She turned, looked at me. "That's the hard stuff, Peter. Racing off into the night on an adventure with a pretty girl is easy. You weren't going to get into any trouble. You knew that."

"I didn't think about it, one way or the other."

"Exactly my point. Why would you?"

Lottie and Tom were coming back, walking side by side, no longer holding hands.

"An open bottle in the car," Jackie said. "The cops must have loved that. You're underage. You're speeding. How'd you get off?"

"It was a small town then. The cops knew who I was, knew my father, and I guess they figured I'd suffered enough. I always wondered if my father intervened somehow. Maybe Chief Baker owed him a favor. The bottle disappeared. Maybe it broke, I don't know. Maybe one of the cops took it home."

"Ironic, huh? The privileged liberal. If you'd been some poor Black kid from East Dunstable, they'd have thrown the book at you."

"You think I haven't thought of that?"

Lottie and Tom were within earshot now. Jackie and I watched them, wondering what had happened. Tom dropped us a nod and tipped his hat, then went on up toward his pickup. Lottie watched him a moment, then turned. She'd let her hair down. It fell to her shoulders, and I thought she looked even prettier.

"Y'all mind if I join you a minute?" she said.

"Sure, the more, the merrier," Jackie said.

It was her idea to move over, inviting Lottie to sit between us. Lottie sat down and folded her arms, huddling, as if this balmy wind had a chill in it. She gazed out over the water. The trawler had disappeared, but I couldn't have said when.

"Y'all don't seem too merry, if you don't mind me saying so," Lottie said.

"It hasn't been a great evening," Jackie said.

"Well, you aren't the Lone Ranger, as they say. Tommy and me's talk didn't go as good as I thought it would."

I turned, looked up toward the clearing. Tom was standing in front of his truck, smoking a cigarette.

"I'm sure it'll work out," I said.

"The thing is"—Lottie looked at Jackie, at me—"y'all don't mind me telling you?"

"Tommy might mind," Jackie said.

"Too bad if he does. I want to get married, is the thing, and Tommy doesn't. 'Why fix what ain't broke?' he says. He doesn't want to have children, you see. He says he doesn't want to bring children into such a world as this."

"Sounds like our daughter," Jackie said.

"She must be a pessimist, like Tommy."

"She's a lesbian," I said.

"Oh."

"You wouldn't know it, to look at her," I said.

"What the hell does that mean?" Jackie said.

"I don't have anything against lesbians," Lottie said.

"I don't, either," Jackie said, "except when they're a pain in the ass about it, complaining about sexism every time you say 'girl' instead of 'woman.'"

"Y'all have any others?" Lottie said.

"We couldn't," Jackie said. "*I* couldn't, I should say."

"I'm sorry."

"Don't be," Jackie said. "She's a full-time job by herself."

"Bein' a lesbian I guess she doesn't want kids," Lottie said.

"Nothing would surprise me," Jackie said, "but I don't think so."

"Well I sure do," Lottie said. "It's a little bit of immortality, don't you think?"

"In their memory of us," I said.

"And in their genes," Lottie said.

"Jennifer has Jackie's good looks," I said.

"See?"

"You and Tom would have beautiful kids," I said.

"I told him that, and he didn't argue. But y'all have been real nice to listen to me. I know you have your own worries to talk about. I guess all marriages, you got to work at it."

"I guess so too," Jackie said.

Behind us, sudden in the whispery stillness of the wind and waves, the dancy, playful horn prelude to "In the Mood" came swelling out of the open door of the pickup truck. We all turned. Tom stood with his thumbs hooked in his belt at his hollow belly. He was smiling.

"Glenn Miller," I said. "Tom's too young."

"He loves all that old stuff," Lottie said. "Glenn Miller. Benny Goodman. Fats Waller. I do too, now I've gotten to know it. I better; we listened to it all the way from Denver."

"He's going to bring the police down on us," Jackie said.

Lottie turned. "Turn it *down*, Tommy."

Smiling, Tom leaned into the truck and cut the sound a few decibels.

"He's tryin' to soften me up," Lottie said.

"Don't let him," Jackie said.

"You wait. He'll ask me to dance."

"Don't do it."

"I'm a fool for him, is my problem."

"He seems like a good guy," I said.

"Oh, he's a total sweetheart. My whole family loves him, it doesn't matter he's Black."

"In the Mood" romped to its tag, finished, and it was quiet again.

"Here it comes," Lottie said.

"Lot," Tom said. "Come on up here."

Now it was "Moonlight Serenade," slow, yearning, as sweet and sad as love itself.

"Don't go," Jackie said.

"Come on, Lot."

"I'm just a fool," Lottie said, and stood up.

I watched her go up the short path, still barefoot, and step into Tom's embrace. He wrapped both long arms around her, pulled her up against himself, nearly lifting her, and she looped her arms around his waist.

"She forgot her shoes," Jackie said.

"I don't think so," I said.

We turned, watched them. They danced as if they were asleep, a dreamy shuffle, swaying languorously. Jackie and I turned back finally, looked out at the glimmering, wind-stirred water. Their dance ended, and we heard Tom and Lottie get into the truck. Glenn Miller still played, but softly now. The truck sat there, dark, Tom and Lottie conversing quietly.

Jackie looked down between her knees.

"I just can't get around the fact you never told me any of it," she said. "The abortion. That the accident was your fault. That you loved the girl. Especially that."

"What good would it have done?"

"It would have made you honest."

"I was trying to bury it."

"From me."

"From myself."

The moon still hung well above the horizon. It laid a fine silvery sheen over the water, and the wind had come down and the waves fell more gently. I'd always wondered about the two doctors, Norton and Sutton, whether they'd blamed themselves in any way or had spoken of it to each other. Sutton, at any rate, must have wondered why we were on our way back to Dover. Or maybe not. On our way back, speeding.

"No one could tell she was bleeding?" Jackie said. "Her uterus was probably perforated, no one noticed that?"

"Her neck was broken, Jack. They weren't doing a damn autopsy."

"And then you ran away to Switzerland."

"You could put it that way. I couldn't sleep. I'd get the shakes at night, sometimes I'd cry. I refused to go to school, said I couldn't. My mother wanted me to see a psychiatrist. Switzerland was my father's idea. It probably saved my life."

We sat awhile, watching the bay, the lights of a distant boat. "Tuxedo Junction," sly, sultry, issued from the open window of the pickup.

"For a long time I thought I'd see Denton again, and then I stopped thinking it," I said. "I forgot about him. I used to think her brothers might look me up, beat the hell out of me. Or her father, the cop. But they never did."

Jackie again bowed her head and put both hands to her face. As if to blot the world out. I thought about touching her, a hand on her leg or the small of her back, but I knew it wouldn't do any good. A weariness had come over me, mind and body, an overpowering lassitude. Jackie leaned down, dug up a handful of sand, and sifted it from her closed fist, as through an hourglass, over her bare foot.

"I'll tell you something my aunt Joanie said to me one time," she said. "She was a pretty wise lady, but not always. She said to me, 'You seldom regret the things you do, but you always regret the things you *don't* do.' According to Aunt Joan's theory, I'd have regretted it if I hadn't married you."

"Would you have?"

"Oh, yeah. I'd have wondered about it forever. The good times we'd have had, the places we'd go. I'd have thought about all I was missing."

"And now you regret marrying me. Regret, either way."

"Or not. Barry, the guy I lived with, wanted to marry me. But I wanted more than he could ever give me. More excitement. More laughter. Better sex. 'You're never going to be happy,' he told me. 'You want the world on a platter, and you're never going to get it. No one does.' But Aunt Joanie was wrong. I never regretted not marrying him."

"And you thought I could give all these things to you."

"No. I knew better by then."

"Then why'd you marry me?"

"I just told you. Because I knew better."

Jackie sat back, braced herself with both hands behind her on the edge of the timber. I could see her crow's-feet in the moonlight.

"What I finally realized," she said, "this idea of doing something, as opposed to not doing something, is specious. Is that the word?"

"It could be."

"We make choices, that's all. To do one thing or to do another. Someone says, 'Come to Europe with me' and you say no, you're choosing to do something else. Your job. Going to your kid's Little League game. Staying home with your wife."

"So?" I said.

"You made a choice," Jackie said.

"I know that."

"No you don't. Not really. In your mind, it wasn't a choice, at all. You were like my aunt Joanie. You figured you'd always regret not hitting on Corinna, and the hell with everything else."

"I regret it now."

"You regret it because she's dead. If you *do* regret it, and I'm not so sure of that. I *loved* you, you son of a bitch."

"Jack . . ."

"Don't say anything. Just don't." She closed her eyes, opened them. "*God* why can't we be happy," she said.

"We can be. We were happy today. We made love. We were happy in Italy. We were happy in Santa Fe."

"Were we?"

"You know we were."

"Maybe we should have taken more trips."

"We can. It isn't too late."

"A forty percent chance, Peter. Remember?"

"I don't believe that," I said. "I never will."

Jackie drew herself up and looked out over the water as if I hadn't spoken.

"Let's just please go back to the motel," I said.

She looked at her watch, holding it up to catch the moonlight. "Whatever," she said.

Tom swung himself down out of his truck as we came up the path. He tipped his hat. Grinned.

"You know what that damn girl just did?" he said.

"Told you to take a hike, I hope," Jackie said.

"Whoa, girl. What's your problem?"

"Men are my problem," Jackie said.

Tom looked at me, unoffended but puzzled, and I answered with a shrug.

"Are you going to tell us what that damn girl just did?" I said.

"Nothing, only talked me into marrying her," Tom said.

Lottie was out of the truck now, smiling. "Y'all should come to the wedding," she said. "It was because of you I think Tommy changed his mind. We were watching you, sittin' there talkin'. You looked so *familiar* with each other. I said, 'You know how long they've been together, Tommy? Years and years. That's what it's all about,' I said. 'Through thick and thin.' I said, 'Do you have the gumption for that, Tommy? Do you love me that much? Or are you gonna pick up and go first time some pretty young thing winks at you, or when my face wrinkles up, or my figure isn't what it was? Put up or shut up,' I said."

"What could I say?" Tom said.

"I can think of a few things," Jackie said.

"Well, I couldn't come up with any but yes," Tom said.

"Congratulations," I said, and gave him my hand. His was muscular, roughened. "Congratulations, Lottie."

"You're sweet," she said, and stepped quickly forward, bobbed up and pecked my cheek. She hugged me hard and stepped back.

"Jackie, honey," she said, "y'all are going to be just fine. Isn't anything you can't straighten out, I can see that just by lookin' at you."

Jackie looked away and nodded. Lottie went to her and they held each other in a long, still embrace.

"You got one of those for me, Jackie?" Tom said.

Jackie turned, and he enfolded her in his long arms, and I thought—Jackie was just that much taller than Lottie—what a beautiful couple they'd make if Jackie were twenty years younger. She stepped back and managed a half smile.

"Sorry I was a bitch," she said.

"Bitch? Nah. Not even close."

"Tommy, go in the truck and get something to write on," Lottie said. "I want y'all's address for the wedding invitation. It'll be pretty soon. In the fall, probably."

"We'd love to come," I said.

"It'll be out west somewhere," Lottie said, "maybe Montana. Auburn might not approve, Tommy bein' Black and all. Other than my own folks, that is. But you'll love Montana, it's so unspoiled. You can imagine buffalo running around, and Indians."

Tom came back with a tourist map of the Cape and a ballpoint pen.

"You got room to write on that?" Lottie said.

"Sure," I said, and laid the folded map on the hood of the truck and bent to it.

"We'd be pleased to have you there," Tom said.

Jackie's apology to Tom told me she was softening, conceding the sadness that was her life and mine and everybody's of a certain age, just part of the deal, let's move on. But I was wrong about that. We left Tom and Lottie—there would be some amorous doings in the roomy cab of the pickup, I imagined—and drove slowly back down the dark passageway of the dirt road.

"Nice people," I said.

"Yeah," she said.

She was sitting with her arms folded, looking out the open window.

"Might be fun to go to their wedding," I said.

"Sure. Maybe Buffalo Bill will be there."

"We could go to the Custer Battlefield," I said. "I've always wanted to do that."

"The Custer Battlefield. Just what I need."

"It'll be fun. A new part of the country. All that history. Something we can share, Jack."

She watched the trees and lighted houses scroll by on the Quick's Hole Road. The open windows pulled the night air in, warm and summer fragrant.

"I've always wondered why you married me," she said.

I looked at her, her averted face, the smooth plane of her cheek.

"I don't believe that," I said.

"Well, I'm wondering it now."

"It makes no sense, Jack."

"Think about it."

"How did this start?" I said. "What the hell happened tonight?"

She sat as before, erect, her face to the window, and did not answer, and we drove the rest of the way in silence. Past the Green and the two churches, down Main, past the bookstore, the library, then over to the motel.

"Leave the key in the ignition," Jackie said. "I'm going to take a drive."

"To where?" I said.

"I don't know. Anywhere." She was softly visible and quite lovely in the light from the big motel, the floodlit parking lot.

"Jack," I said. "Don't do this."

"Go on to bed. I'll be back in a while."

"I'm not going to beg you," I said.

"It wouldn't do any good," she said.

thirty-one

The notice on the glass door of the hotel fitness center said OPEN SIX A.M. TO EIGHT P.M., but I tried my key card and the lock light winked green and I swung the door open. The big shadowy room was so preternaturally silent it seemed in the thrall of long abandonment, unvisited and forgotten. The pool whispered and tinkled, its smooth surface shifting restlessly. I stripped to my bathing suit and let myself down into the tepid chlorine-smelling water and set out, swimming easily, measuredly, a sexagenarian's unhurried crawl but dogged, still some muscle in it. I would swim for a long, long time.

You find a pace that your arms and lungs can handle, and as you settle into it your mind slips free of trouble and worry and whatever memories are nagging at you, and you know only the water and your slide through it, down the length of the pool and back again, a stroke at a time, stroke upon stroke upon stroke, down and back, down and back. I hadn't looked at my watch and I didn't count laps, so I didn't know how far I'd swum or how long I'd been at it when I began to tire. Your arms weaken and you feel your weight, the downward suck of gravity. I kept swimming, kept swimming, and then I'd had enough, and I coasted onto the steps at the shallow end, pushed myself to my feet, and climbed out with water streaming off me. My arms felt light and shaky, and there was a good tightness in my shoulders, and I figured if I popped an Ambien and took a very hot shower, I might sleep now.

The call on the hotel phone woke me at two-fourteen by the digital bedside clock, glowing ruby-red in the darkness. I felt beside me, pretty sure I wouldn't find Jackie but hoping, then rolled the other way and stretched for the phone. I'd been sleeping deeply, double-drugged by muscle fatigue and Ambien.

"Are you Mr. Hatch?" A young woman's voice. A girl's.

"Who is this?" I said.

"Morgan Edwards, sir. Is your wife Jacqueline Hatch?"

"What the hell's going on?" I said.

"Just listen, okay? I'm with Jacqueline Hatch. Me and two friends. We found her in the water between Shawmut and Quick's Hole."

"This is a joke, right?"

"No, sir."

"Found her in the water doing what?"

"Swimming. With her clothes on, like she'd fallen off a boat, but there wasn't any boat around. We were coming back from a party on Shawmut and we picked her up."

"If this is a joke you guys are going to pay worse than you know. You aren't going to know what hit you."

"It's not a joke, sir. I think your wife's depressed."

I swung my legs over and sat up. I turned on the bedside lamp. It cast a sour amber pool out over the gray carpet, the composite-wood dresser.

"What are you saying?"

"Well, I don't know what would make someone try to swim from Quick's to Shawmut in the middle of the night."

The world had stopped turning, time stood still. It would end like this, I would sit on this bed, gripping this plastic receiver, forever.

"Are you there?" said the girl, Morgan.

I lifted the phone. "Where are you?" I said.

"Quick's. We brought her in and helped her to her car. She wants us to leave her alone, but we don't feel right about that. We want to know what to do."

"Put her on," I said.

Morgan lowered the phone and spoke softly, indistinctly. Someone spoke, a boy, and Morgan lifted the phone again.

"She's upset. She might be in some kind of shock, I don't know. She doesn't want to talk."

"Is she cold? Shivering?"

"Just wet."

"Talking funny, acting strange?"

"She's just upset."

"You said she was in shock."

"Maybe not. She doesn't want to talk, is the main thing. What do you want us to do?"

"Bring her here. In our car. Do you have the key?"

"We have the key, but I don't know if she'll let us."

"Force her, for Christ sake. There are three of you."

"Two. Owen can't leave his boat."

"Do whatever you have to. The Holiday Inn, you know where it is?"

"Yes, sir."

"If Mrs. Hatch gets cold or acts funny on the way, take her to the hospital, no matter what she says, and call me."

"I think she's okay physically."

"Drive carefully. Did you get drunk at that party?"

"A little, but it's worn off."

"Drive carefully."

"You said that," Morgan said.

thirty-two

She takes the back road to Quick's Hole because it is winding and slow and she has no desire to speed, only to drive, to keep moving, stay out ahead of her troubles while she tries to take hold of what is left of her life. She comes out of the woods with the sound in front of her, still moonlit, though the moon has fallen lower over the course of this long night. The road bends, climbs the steep headland where the lighthouse flaunts itself against the sky, rotund and bone-white in the moonlight. She lets the Subaru coast down the other side, then cruises on past a crescent of white beach and into the woods again.

She passes the Coast Guard station and comes into Quick's Hole, cars parked along both sides of Water Street but the street itself untrafficked at this hour, lying grayish in the moon- and lamplight. The Topside is still open, and a sudden notion takes her, radical and immense, and she continues slowly down Water Street until she finds a parking space. She backs in skillfully—she is a better driver than Peter, more attuned to the car's needs, more alert to the road and its surprises, though she would never tell him—and gets out, bringing her purse.

It is warm still, the air here moist and pungent with sea salt and kelp and the tidal mud of the Oyster Pond. Across the street is a patch of pale stunted lawn with a couple of park benches facing the water, and below it a narrow beach and the long plank Marine Lab pier with a couple of Boston Whalers and a bass boat tied up alongside. The low islands in the middle distance are dark except for Shawmut, where lights indicate a pair of houses that nestle close to the shore.

She walks, high heels clicking smartly. There has always been a part of him she couldn't reach, a place in his consciousness that is closed to her. As if she owned only half of him, or only half knew him. She does not know the reason for this but has always blamed herself. Some failure in her, some incapacity to understand certain things, which—the incapacity—he has long since accepted as part of the agreement, the compromise he made when he married her. She thinks sometimes that Senator Powell knows Peter in a way she, Jackie, never can. And now that fucking girl from the long ago, dead all these years but never dead to Peter, following him, a mirage, a dream, a lie. She has never entered a restaurant alone, much less a bar, and it will be, she thinks, like stepping into another life, another role, another self. Fatigue has made her light-headed, but her body, notwithstanding her cancerous breast, has come wonderfully awake and alive.

The Topside is a murky, beer-redolent room standing half on stilts over the stagnant inlet that is the Oyster Pond. Tables are large and round, like overturned capstans, which perhaps they are, and the bar runs nearly the length of the room. There's a retro jukebox that you can play for free. Up front, to the left of the door as you come in, are several booths, where couples can isolate themselves somewhat from the clamor of voices and sixties and seventies nostalgia like "Brown Eyed Girl" and "Hey Jude."

It has the look and ambience of a dive, a haven for toughs and gum-smacking floozies and motorcycle queens, but this is Quick's

Hole, not the New Bedford waterfront, and the clientele is benign and mannerly, though loud: unmarried oceanographers, male and female Ph.D. candidates doing summer internships at the Marine Lab, hippie fishermen and carpenters, writers, artists, elderly drunks whose wives have left them. Jackie knows the place, has been here a couple of times with Peter over the years, or she would not have come in. The truth is, this bold act isn't in any way dangerous or risky, is hardly bold at all. But it's a start, she thinks, and who knows? Who knows what might happen, you walk into a bar looking pretty good in earrings and sandal heels? She leaves her wedding ring on, as if to remove it would be cheating.

"Lay Lady Lay" on the jukebox, a hubbub of voices, highlights of the Red Sox game on the silent TV above the bar. The young bartender watches her come in and smiles. A few heads turn. Jackie stands there, wonders what, exactly, to do, now she's here. The booths are occupied. There's one empty table, where she'd look unduly conspicuous sitting by herself. The other tables are surrounded by noisy young people, men and women, drinking beer out of bottles, carousing. The bar, then, is the only option. She comes on, the bartender watching her, chooses a stool down near the end, sits down, and crosses her legs. She unslings her purse and sets it on the shiny mahogany, as if she means to be here awhile.

She has attracted some notice—for her age, if not for her looks. There is a man at least her age four stools away from her, sitting thoughtfully over his drink, watching the TV fitfully and with only casual interest.

"What'll it be?" says the bartender, smiling still.

"I don't know," Jackie says, and wonders what the hell is so funny.

"I could suggest something."

He is, maybe, in his midforties. Not so young, then. He wears a bushy mustache and sideburns, and his hair is parted and combed down flat and she can imagine him singing in a barbershop quartet or tending bar in a Wild West saloon, setting down foaming mugs of beer for cowpokes and card players.

"Like what?" she says.

"A cosmopolitan."

Jackie snorts a laugh. "That'd be like ordering filet mignon at McDonald's," she says. She's on her game now, feeling good.

The bartender doesn't miss a beat. "The place went up, stylewise, when you came in. We're the Four Seasons now."

Jackie cocks her head over, gives him a look of mock curiosity and suspicion.

"Do you have any idea how old I am?" she says.

"Forty-five?"

"You're full of it. You know that, right?"

"Fifty-five, then."

The man perched four stools away has been listening, his eyes on the ball game.

"Hey, Dylan," the bartender says. "This lady won't tell me her age. What's your guess?"

Dylan turns, nods hello to Jackie. "I wouldn't tread there, Russ. You guess wrong, you're in trouble."

"If you guess right, you're in trouble," Jackie says.

"Point taken," Dylan says.

"I still say fifty-five," says Russ, the bartender.

Dylan smiles but doesn't join the game. He's drinking a highball gone pale with icemelt. He lifts the glass with his left hand, takes a meditative sip. No wedding ring.

"Are you going to drink," Russ says to Jackie, "or just sit here?"

"Maker's on the rocks," she says. "Better put some water in it."

"My pleasure," Russ says.

She wonders if he's getting ideas and dismisses the thought as absurd. He's only having fun, and why not?

"Are you expecting somebody?" Dylan says.

Jackie turns, appraises him. Blue workshirt, faded jeans, docksiders. He has a wiry body, iron-gray hair trimmed short. His lean face with its deep lines is worldly wise, knowing, hardened against surprise. He has seen more with those sea-gray eyes than most.

"Why do you ask?" she says.

"I was wondering if you wanted company."

She thinks about it, or pretends to.

"Sure, why not."

He dismounts, brings his drink. He swings a leg over the stool next to her. The jukebox has gone silent.

"You a baseball fan?" Dylan says.

"Not particularly," Jackie says.

"Me neither."

Russ brings her drink.

"First one's on the house," he says.

"Jesus," Jackie says.

"You've made my evening, why not?" Russ says.

Jackie takes a gingerly sip of Maker's. "I thought you were going to put some water in this," she says.

"I did," Russ says. He drops her a wink and moves halfway down the bar, where the sole waitress, a black-haired girl in a black shirt and slacks, is unloading her tray of empty glasses.

"Another round," the waitress tells him, "table over in the corner."

Jackie watches him dump the cubes, scoop new ones, and pivot for the bottle, moving in the quick seamless way of a good bartender. He pours the whiskey with deft twists of his wrist, and she thinks of a magician's sleight of hand.

"What's your name?" Dylan says.

Jackie drinks some bourbon, considering her answer, eyeing the bottles arrayed along the shelf across from her. Amber whiskeys, clear gins, mint-green crème de menthe.

Russ has come back.

"I'm Dylan," Dylan is saying, to prompt her. "Dylan Thomas. Named for the poet. Your turn."

"Peggy," Jackie says, snatching it out of the air.

"Peggy?" Russ says. "Peggy Sue?"

"If you want," Jackie says.

"I do," Russ says. "I love that song."

"Yeah, like you really remember Buddy Holly," Jackie says.

"Gone from the charts but not from the hearts," Russ says.

"He died in 'fifty-nine as I recall," Dylan says. "Do you have a last name, Peggy Sue?"

"Smith," Jackie says.

"Smith," Dylan says. "Prosaic name for an orchid."

"Is he always this full of shit?" Jackie asks Russ.

"Depends on the girl," Russ says.

A customer has materialized beside her, a young guy, bringing three empty beer bottles.

"Last call in twenty minutes, Eric," Russ tells him.

He opens the cooler under the bar and brings up three wet bottles of Budweiser, gathering them by their necks. He turns to open them. Eric gives Jackie a nod, a nice smile.

"Evening," he says.

"Evening," she answers.

He's wearing a Stanford sweatshirt, and she thinks of Sonny Jenerette, and now a wave of sadness rolls through her, a cognizance of all she's lost in the years gone by, and is losing in this funky barroom, minute by minute. She even misses her time with Sonny, who chose SMU, not Stanford, left after his junior year to play for the Eagles and was gone from the pros three years later. Jackie wonders where he is now. She wonders what he looks like. She sits up straighter, sips her drink, focuses on the TV, the post-game show, several guys talking, Jackie fighting thinking about Sonny Jenerette, fighting thinking, period. She swallows more sweet bourbon, wonders where this is going and why she is still here.

Russ sets the three open beer bottles down, and the Stanford kid, Eric, lays a ten on the bar, collects the beers and is gone. Russ wanders away to see about a customer at the other end of the bar.

"A nightcap, Peggy Sue?" Dylan says.

"Better not," she says.

The juke wakes, "Hey! Baby," sixties gold, that good blues harmonica weaving and hopping along under Bruce Channel's reedy vocal. The seven or so patrons around a nearby table begin to sing along, belting it out. Jackie wonders how they know the song, ancient history to them. Gone from the charts but not from the hearts, she wonders where Russ picked that up. On the TV a replay of a home run by somebody or other, the ball a tiny gleaming marble as it soars off into the night above the left field wall at Fenway.

Dylan is watching her. "Hey," he says. "What's the matter?"

"Nothing," she says.

"Something is," he says.

"Oh Christ," she says, and the feeling swells inside her, bursts, and she looks down and shuts her eyes against the tears, which roll down anyway.

"It's okay," Dylan says, and places a gentle hand on her shoulder. "It's okay, it's okay."

The young oceanographers and hippies are still caroling "Hey! Baby."

"I'm not Peggy," Jackie says.

"I was wondering about that. It doesn't fit you. Want to get out of here, take a walk?"

She nods, wipes her tears with the back of her hand. She leaves her drink half finished, takes up her purse.

"Last call," Russ says, coming toward them, drying his big hands with a dish towel. He sees Jackie, stops, peers at her.

"Ma'am?" he says.

"She'll be all right," Dylan says.

"What happened?"

"Nothing," Dylan says.

"If you need a lift home or anything . . ." Russ says.

"I got it, Russ," Dylan says.

"Joanie could take her home. She's about to get off anyway."

"I *got* it," Dylan says.

"Good night, then," Russ says. "Thanks for coming in."

"Good night," Jackie says, and slides down off the barstool.

The song has ended, and around the room the drinkers have turned quiet too, watching her. She walks erect, chin high, let them stare at her wet face and think what they will. Dylan is close behind her, she knows, moving sure and catlike on her heels. She pushes through the door, out into the moist sea air, the suspended swirls of mist, the peace, of Water Street.

"Where's your car?" Dylan says.

"Just down there."

He is hardly taller than she, but there's a rangy grace about him, an air of agility and athleticism. He looks like he could still play center field.

"Come over, have a nightcap," Dylan says. "Or coffee. It's a five-minute walk. You don't want to be alone now."

Jackie looks down the faintly lamplit street, past the auxiliary fire station, the big Marine Lab, the shops. So empty, so stark, at this lonely hour.

"Coming?" he says, and half turns, as if to leave without her.

Jackie nods and falls in beside him.

thirty-three

He's a freelance photographer: *Life* magazine, *Newsweek*, the AP, Reuters. He tells her this, unsolicited, as they walk, speaking in a casual conversational way that has nothing of boastfulness in it, just stating facts. But still, a photographer, a freelancer. Photographers go where the action is—wars, presidential campaigns, urban riots, shootings, coronations.

"I'll retire one of these years," he says. "Go sailing. Fishing. Sleep late."

"Sounds nice."

"I'll hate it."

His house is a big shingled Victorian with gray trim and an ell, perched among trees above the Oyster Pond, and she wonders why he would live alone in a place so rambling, so spacious. The door isn't locked, and he opens it for her and turns on lights in the living room. She sits down on the taupe sofa and crosses her legs.

"Wait here," Dylan says.

The house is neat and kempt, and its stillness seems to have taken possession, so longstanding as to be impervious to voices, laughter, music. Dylan, she figures, spends most of his life on assignment. *Time* and *Newsweek* on the coffee table, today's *Wall Street Journal* and *New York Times*. On the papered wall is a large framed photograph in black and white of an American infantryman sitting on a broken slab of concrete on some ruined city street, a collapsed highrise behind him, a fire-bombed van. He sits slumped and listless and stares dully down at nothing—the very portrait of battle fatigue. There is also a large acrylic of a zaftig nude sitting on a straightbacked chair with her legs crossed, hugging herself, her head bowed sideways in an attitude of penitence or sorrow.

Dylan comes in with a bottle of Heineken and a short bourbon on the rocks. He sets the whiskey on one of the magazines and sits down beside Jackie with his beer.

"Knob Creek," he says. "See what you think."

She leans forward, takes up the cold glass. She takes the smallest of sips and puts the glass down. The bourbon is sharper than Maker's, but smoky and rich. Expensive. She sits back and looks again at the poor soldier.

"Did you take that?"

"Baghdad."

"You do wars, then."

"Iraq. I was in Somalia a while. Terrible place, I'll never go back." He tilts the bottle up and drinks. Sets it down on *Time*.

"What's your real name, Peggy Sue?"

"Jacqueline."

"Pretty. Jacqueline what? Not Smith, surely."

"Does it matter?"

"Depends where this is going."

"I'm not sure," Jackie says.

"Me neither. Where's your husband?"

"He won't come looking for me, if that's what you're asking."

"It isn't," he says. He tilts up his bottle, swallows. He looks at the shell-shocked soldier. "Is he cheating on you?" he says.

Jackie looks at the nude, dark hair spilling across the averted face, half hiding it. "Not in the normal way," she says.

"I didn't know there was an abnormal way."

"It's what's in his heart," Jackie says. "I don't know if he loves me. I don't think he does. He may never have, in thirty years."

"Something must be wrong with him."

"Or me."

Dylan moves closer. Lifts his arm, wraps it around her slumped shoulders.

"Nothing's wrong with you," he says. "You're smart and you're beautiful."

"I'm an old lady. I made a fool of myself in the bar, all those kids staring at me."

"Hardly. You stole the show."

"Fools steal shows."

"So do classy women."

He turns her face to his very gently with two fingers. Kisses her lightly, lingeringly.

"Want to go upstairs?" he says.

She stares past the coffee table at the beige carpet. There's no going back. There never is. She wonders if life becomes fated at some point, an unalterable future we set for ourselves. She bends over, removes her heels, and rises without speaking.

She uses the bathroom, looks at herself, her pale tear-stained face, in the bright unforgiving mirror. The face looks soft to her, puffy, its once-fine planes beginning to sag inward. There are creases in her neck, the flesh under her chin is loosening, and she wonders why

Dylan Thomas wants her in his bed. *Old hag*, she says to the mirror, but she knows it isn't true, not yet; can see in the wreckage a remnant of the woman who turned heads, was propositioned times beyond counting, into her fifties. Her *late* fifties.

She washes her hands and goes down the narrow hallway to Dylan's bedroom. His clothes have been tossed on a chair and he is propped up in his big bed with the sheet over his lap. He watches her come in. His body is whippet lean. There's a book on the bedside table, *The Sun Also Rises*, by Ernest Hemingway, and she thinks of Peter and has to stop, draw breath, calm herself.

"You okay?" Dylan says.

She nods, sits down on the bed, sideways to him. There's a big flat-screen TV on the opposite wall, a single window looking out over the Oyster Pond.

"You've never done this," Dylan says.

She shakes her head, eyes downcast. He watches her.

"Why not?" he says.

"I never wanted to."

"Everyone wants to."

"Which is why I didn't."

"Didn't do it, or didn't want to?"

"Both."

"I admire that," he says.

"But here I am."

"I admire that, too."

"Liar."

"No I'm not. Would you like to get in bed?"

"Turn off the light," she says.

She has lain beside no one but Peter all these years, and the fact seems to have gathered itself in the darkness as something sentient, a witness, curious, wondering, as she is wondering, what will happen. Because even now, with his little body enfolding her, she cannot imagine it. He eases a leg between her two and explores her with a light practiced hand—breast, hip, leg.

"You're wonderful," he says.

He rises over her, comes down slowly and kisses her.

"Relax," he says.

His face is inches above hers. Beer on his breath, a stale yeasty smell but not unpleasant.

"I've got a sailboat," he says. "A beautiful Alden cutter. I'll take you sailing."

He kisses her again, tongue between her lips, then in her mouth, probing tentatively, gently. He's good, but she isn't feeling anything. She reaches down and touches him, thinking it might turn her on. She caresses his solid shoulder, his arm. She returns the kiss but her mind isn't on the kiss, even as she gives it; she's thinking how strange it is, how unreal, to be doing this with anyone but Peter. It is another woman, a stranger, in this bed with this man.

"Relax," he says again.

"I don't want to talk anymore, okay?"

"Understood," he says.

This was her choice, made when she left the barroom with him, if not sooner, and the torment of admitting this is upon her even before he finishes. He collapses back and works an arm under her neck, cradling her in its sinewy crook. It hurt—her breath caught, she almost cried out—but she knew it would, and went on anyway, to finish what she'd begun, to get it over with. Because then she could move on, put it behind her.

But it will never be behind her, she was so wrong about that. It is built in, inescapable. Adulterer. Cheater. She has always despised a cheater.

"Where are you?" Dylan says.

"Here."

He brings his other arm over, taps the tip of her nose. "I don't think so."

She turns her head away from him, looks out at the starry sky above Quick's Hole.

"I have to leave," she says.

"Do you." He pulls his arm out from under her.

"I can't see you again," she says.

"Why not?"

"I just can't."

"That's no answer."

"There are things I haven't told you."

"That's still no answer."

"I'm sorry," Jackie says.

"I am too. You sure about this?"

"Very."

"Can I walk you to your car?"

"No thanks."

"I'd like to."

"No."

She rolls away from him, gets up.

"Don't be hard on yourself," he says behind her. "Whatever your husband did, I'm sure he was asking for it."

But she isn't sure, not anymore, and anyway that isn't the point. She dresses with her back to Dylan Thomas, looking out at the scattered shadowy motorboats on the Oyster Pond, asleep at their moorings. Dylan watches her, risen with his head propped on his elbow.

"I was married once," he says. "A journalism major at Columbia. She graduated, got a job at the *Wall Street Journal*'s Washington bureau. I was taking pictures at that point for the *Post*."

Her purse. Where did she leave it?

"I come home one night, she tells me she's leaving me. For a Broadway composer, you'd have heard of the guy."

Downstairs. She must have left it there. And her shoes.

"I got drunk for a week, lost my job at the *Post*. I've never loved a woman since, and never been drunk again. I wish I could do both. I'm not proud of myself, Peggy Sue."

"Good-bye, Dylan."

"Good-bye, Jacqueline. Good luck to you."

thirty-four

The lights still burn in the living room, the soldier stares benumbed at nothing, the nude tucks her head over sorrowfully. On the coffee table are Jackie's drink and Dylan's half-drunk bottle of beer. She steps into her heels. Her purse is on an end table. She shoulders it and lets herself out into the clean blessed night.

She walks quickly back toward Water Street, more alone than she has ever been. She tries to think why she went to his home with Dylan and can find no tolerable explanation. She cannot now remember what impulse sent her into the bar, it is a blur. She turns the corner onto Water Street, passes the gabled house acquired recently by the Marine Lab, a dormitory for interns in the summertime, dark now, the kids all finally asleep. She crosses the drawbridge, hears the water chuckling down below the grille. The Topside is dark, everything is. She clicks on past Jaskin's Market, the Peterson Art Gallery, Laurie's Gifts and Souvenirs. She unlocks the car and gets in. She does not know what to do.

He'll wake up and frown in that sleepy puzzled way he has, squinting in the sudden lamplight.

Where the hell have you been?

Nowhere.

Nowhere? Do you know what time it is?

Or maybe, just maybe: God, Jack. I've been so worried.

But when he's fully awake and looks at her, he'll know. He'll see it in her eyes. He'll smell it on her. *And I'll smell it on myself.*

She has never lied to him, and anyway he'll know, he'll see it on her, he'll sense it.

Peter, I'm so sorry.

It would sound cheap, pathetic, even to her. Especially to her.

Nothing is inevitable, fated. To think so is a coward's way out.

Okay, then.

She looks out over the water. To her right, Gosnold Point, with its low flattened hills and mansions, creeps darkly out toward the islands. Straight across the water, lights twinkle in one of the two seaside dwellings on Shawmut Island, and she knows now what she is going to do, the perfect solution. The best one, at least. Call it Russian roulette. Let God or chance decide it; she loses, either way. Or wins, depending on how you look at it.

She places her purse on the passenger seat, drops the car key into it, strips her watch and stashes it. She gets out of the car. The door closes with a soft final blink of sound, and she leaves it unlocked. How silent it is. The world is asleep, the stars burn unwatched. The streetlamps cast their pale halos on sidewalks that look as clean as if they'd been scrubbed. The full moon floats over the westernmost rooftops of the village of Quick's Hole.

She looks both ways, absurdly, and crosses Water Street to the strip of sea-stunted park lawn with its two benches. She sits down and thinks about this. Shawmut is a mile away, not impossible. Fatigue, chronic these days, seems to have released its grip. She feels wide awake, limber. There are currents in these waters, but she has no idea of their strength, or which way the tide is running. The water appears calm. There is the question of undressing, but she refuses to arrive on Shawmut, or be found floating facedown, in her underwear. She kicks off her heels, tugs off her nylon anklets. She places the sandals side by side under the bench and tucks the nylons under the straps of one and rises.

Really, it's not so crazy. She's a strong swimmer, as strong almost as Peter, and a mile isn't anything. She will travel at a leisurely pace, alternating crawl with sidestroke, stop and rest at intervals, you can swim forever that way. There's a dock on Shawmut where boats come and go, with a ladder, surely; she sees herself rising from the water and sitting on the dock with her legs dangling, looking across the water at the lights of Quick's Hole. Rest awhile, then let herself back down into the water and swim *back*, why not?

Well, you'll never guess what I just did.

How'd you get all wet?

Oh, I just swam to Shawmut and back, that's all.

Did WHAT?

Swam to Shawmut and back.

Baloney.

Honest to God. It isn't so hard, it turns out.

You really did, didn't you.

Would I make that up?

He springs up from the bed and holds her, hugs her desperately. God, you could have drowned.

It was because I did something awful, Peter. I didn't care if I died.

Don't talk like that. You're alive, and nothing else matters.

She goes down the several wooden steps to the little private beach where scientists and their families sun themselves and swim on summer afternoons. The sand is soft, bunching in her arches. She goes to the water's edge, slow, and wades in. Ankles. Calves. Knees. The water is warmer than the air, as the ocean always seems to be on a summer night. It is pasting her slacks to her legs, but that can't be helped. She stands waist-deep and looks at those distant lights. They glitter playfully, coyly, calling to her across a mile of saltwater, tendering some sweet nameless promise.

I'm coming.

She dives, slicing in noiselessly, breaks clear and swims. It is easy at first, a glide, her arms loose and strong, legs supple, even with the slacks gripping them. Some minutes go by. Quick's Hole falls away behind her. She pauses to look back, treads water, and swims on, into the crosswise rip stirred by the flood tide.

The fact that she isn't going to make it through the rip, that it is going to kill her, merely saddens her. It's a disappointment, and that is all. She had so wanted to surprise Peter, to see his face when she told him what she'd done, to be hugged by him and breathe the clean dry smell of his skin.

She has fought the rip for some time now. Fifteen minutes? Twenty? She has no idea. It has pulled her off course, but she can still see the lights on Shawmut, nearer now but not near enough. She sidestrokes diagonally toward them, refusing to quit till she has to. Her blouse weights her arms, her slacks seem to constrict her legs, tighter and tighter. She thinks of stripping them, but she is too weary, too weak, to tread water with one arm and peel the sodden clinging slacks with the other—she would sink if she did. She strokes, kicks feebly, strokes, kicks. She feels more sleepy now than bone-tired. You can't know what drowning is like until it happens to you. Maybe you just go to sleep. Yes, she will go to sleep any minute now and sink painlessly, and she almost smiles and maybe does at how easy this is.

Then the snarl of an outboard, coming fast, the Whaler passing maybe sixty yards wide of her, skimming, planing, its flat bottom slamming the water, jouncing, slamming down again. Jackie turns herself, treading water, and cries out uselessly and swallows saltwater.

She tries again, a stifled half shriek, drinks more seawater, but they've seen her in the moon-glazed water, and the snarl cuts suddenly to a growl, and the Whaler slows abruptly and circles toward her. It comes on at a creep, wary, and she hears the three kids, their voices carrying on the water.

"What the *hell*?"

"It's a person."

"No shit."

The outboard sputters in neutral and the Whaler floats close to her, bobbing lazily on the quiet swell.

"Ma'am?"

"Ma'am, what are you *doing*?"

"She must have fallen off a boat."

"*What* boat, you moron?" A girl's voice.

She hears them as if from far away, and recognizes, indifferently, that they sound a little drunk. She closes her eyes, chooses life, and lunges with the last of her strength and grips the gunwale with her right hand and hangs there.

"Grab her, Owen." The girl again.

The boy Owen takes Jackie's right arm and hauls on it until the second boy can hook an arm under her left shoulder and lift. The Whaler has heeled over, nearly shipping water. The two boys pull clumsily, and Jackie slithers up and up, limp and dripping, the boys dragging her over the gunwale, then turning her and lowering her to the floor as the Whaler drops back level, rocks, is still.

"Are you okay?" Owen says.

"No," says the girl, "she isn't."

The three of them crouch around her. Jackie is sitting with her back against a seat, facing the grumbling outboard motor, which is coal black and looks huge.

"Ma'am?"

"She's in shock," the girl says.

THE SWEETEST DAYS   267

She has a generous mouth, good cheekbones, pale-brown hair bunched in a ponytail. A charcoal sweatshirt, *Mocha Mott's, Every damn day*, whatever that means. She's wearing baggy khaki shorts, they all are, the boys in T-shirts.

"We should call the cops," the second boy says.

"No," Jackie says.

The kids look at each other.

"No cops," Jackie says. "Just take me back."

"Back where?"

"Quick's."

"We aren't going that way," the second boy says.

Owen and the girl look at him.

"You're pathetic, Michael," the girl says.

"I'm just saying . . ."

"Shut up."

"Where in Quick's?" Owen says.

"My car's on Water Street. You know where the Marine Lab beach is?"

"We'll take you there," the girl says.

Owen nods, rises, and steps over the seat, catches a foot, stumbles and nearly trips, says *Shit*. Michael bleats a giggle, then gets up and follows him forward.

"Sit up," the girl says. She laces her hands under Jackie's shoulder and lifts while Jackie pries herself up onto the seat. The girl sits down beside her and takes her arm.

"Are you cold?" she says.

Jackie shakes her head.

The slumbering outboard wakes with a deafening gnarl, startling her, and the boat springs forward with its blunt bow in the air. It yaws briefly then rockets ahead, flying, skimming, bouncing. This Owen is a rich kid, he has to be, with a boat like this. He will go out in it drunk some night and hit a wave too fast and flip the Whaler over. Jackie hugs herself, *Who cares?* and watches the snowy plume of their wake fan out over the black water.

"I'M MORGAN," the girl says, shouting it against the din of the motor.

Jackie nods, watching the beautiful wake.

"I GUESS YOU DON'T WANT TO TALK ABOUT IT," Morgan says.

"No," Jackie says.

"I'M COOL WITH THAT," Morgan says.

She is barefoot and her legs are a luminous bronze in the moonlight. Jackie wonders if she knows how sexy she is and guesses she does, by the way she talks to the two boys. *Enjoy it while you can,* Jackie thinks.

They ride in silence for perhaps five minutes, then Owen throttles down and the Whaler skids, slowing, its bow dropping, and crawls on. Jackie turns and is amazed to see that they are twenty yards from the lab beach. Morgan stands up. Michael, who seems to function as first mate, steps over the seat past Jackie to the outboard. Owen shuts it down and Michael reaches behind it and pulls it forward, tilting it out of the water. The Whaler rides its momentum, scrapes gently onto the beach.

"All ashore who's going ashore," Owen says.

"Thank you," Jackie says.

She rises, finds she is able to stand. She takes hold of the gunwale and gingerly lifts a leg over. She lifts the other leg out and stands on dry land, testing her legs. They seem okay, but her wet clothes encase, encumber her. She moves, stiff, to the wooden steps, climbs them slowly.

"You guys just hold it a minute," Morgan says behind her.

"Hold it for what?" Michael says.

Jackie's sandal heels and anklets are beneath the park bench, as she left them. She sits down.

"We can't just leave her," Morgan says.

"She seems okay," Owen says.

"Owen Brady, you get your ass away from that boat. You too, Michael."

Jackie stuffs her nylons into her wet, tight hip pocket. She brushes the sand from her feet with the palm of her hand and pulls on the sandals. The kids have come up the steps.

"We're not leaving you," Morgan says.

"I'm all right," Jackie says.

"We just want to be sure you get home."

Jackie rises without answering and begins the walk to her car, wobbly on her heels. She steps down off the curb onto Water Street and crosses it with the kids surrounding her, like bodyguards. The Subaru sits alone in the melancholy lamplight. Jackie opens the driver's door. She gets in and pulls the door after her, but that damn Morgan, quick as a cat, is around the other side and in the passenger seat before Jackie can lock her out. The boys clamber into the back seat. Jackie gives up. She will simply wait for whatever is going to happen.

"Where do you live?" Morgan says.

Jackie looks at Gosnold Point and remembers now that that is where Peter and the girl Corinna got the money for her abortion. Years ago he'd told her about the rich playboy and his sexy wife and how salacious and outrageous they were, but he had allowed her to believe they'd donated food, not money.

"A long way off," she says.

"Where?" Morgan says.

"Northampton."

Morgan sighs. "All right. Where are you *staying*?"

"Please," Jackie says. "I'm okay."

"Yeah, Morgan, cool out," Michael says. "She says she's okay, she's okay."

"He's right, Morgan," Owen says.

Morgan turns and looks at them back there. She seems to be considering whether to speak to them at all, whether they are worth it. She nods, deciding they are, but just barely.

"I think she was trying to kill herself," she says. "Are you two dumb fucks okay with that?"

Silence.

"I didn't think so," Morgan says. Then, to Jackie, "Ma'am, where's the car key?"

Jackie doesn't answer her. Doesn't look at her.

"Try her purse," Owen says.

"Ma'am," Morgan says, " I'm going to look in your purse, and you can sit there and not say a thing."

Jackie shrugs. "Whatever," she says.

thirty-five

The girl and boy brought Jackie into the lobby, one on either side of her, each of them holding an arm with both hands. As if she might stumble and fall, or her knees buckle. Propping her up, lifting her along. There was no one behind the desk. I was drowsing on the sofa by the stone fireplace, feeling the drag of the Ambien in my blood. Jackie's clothes were sopping and her hair snarled and matted. Her face was chalk white and drawn, and she seemed to have shrunk, grown thinner, in her wet clothes. The kids saw me and stopped, still holding on to Jackie. Jackie looked at me sadly, and I saw her swallow.

"Jack," I said, and heaved myself up.

She looked away, past the girl, Morgan. Morgan and the boy let go of her.

"You kids go on," she said, and she moved to the sofa on her sandal heels and landed heavily. She turned, looked into the darkened restaurant, then back at the boy and girl.

"Go on," she said.

Morgan and the boy looked at each other, and Morgan shook her head, *Not yet*. She was a tall good-looking girl, and she fixed on me now, eyeing me boldly and critically, as if this were my fault. The boy folded his arms and stared back out the window.

"Go on, Morgan," Jackie said. "I'm okay. I just need to rest now."

"Wait," I said. "I want to make this up to you."

"You better look to your wife," Morgan said.

"I intend to."

"You don't need to worry about us." She turned, and the boy glanced at me and followed her.

"At least let me pay for a cab," I said to her back. "Please, Morgan."

She stopped, seemed to consider, then turned, and looked at me with a pretty tilt of her head, a half smile, a change of heart. "There were three of us, remember? Kid who owns the boat's coming for us. It's fine, Mr. Hatch."

"One other thing," I said.

Again that winsome tilt of her head.

"I was hoping you could keep this to yourselves," I said.

"We can do that," Morgan said.

"The boys?" I said.

Morgan gave me a half smile. It was a woman's smile—wry, self-knowing. "Leave the boys to me, Mr. Hatch."

"I appreciate it," I said. "And I'd really like to give you something for your trouble."

"It wasn't any trouble," Morgan said, and turned to the boy. "Right, Michael?"

"Not really," Michael said. He couldn't look at me or Jackie, and I wondered what Morgan was doing with a boy so feckless.

"Thank you," I said.

"You take care," Morgan said.

"She isn't his girlfriend," Jackie said, as if it mattered, as if the girl needed defending on my account. Her voice had gone hoarse, whispery. Fatigue, I thought. Exhaustion. "The other one, either," she said. "They're dopes. She just went to the party with them."

"They brought you back, Jack."

"The girl brought me back. Morgan. It's an odd name, isn't it."

We were moving slowly down the carpeted hallway, Jackie carrying her sandal heels, her other hand in mine, her purse hooked in my other arm. She'd felt for my hand, and I'd given it.

"I'm cold," Jackie said, as I unlocked the door.

"Are you hungry? The 7-Eleven's open all night, I could—"

"Just cold."

I locked the door and chained it.

"Get your clothes off."

"I wanted to die, Peter. Or at least I didn't care if I died."

"Get them off."

She sat down on the bed and dropped her sandals to the floor. Gazing unseeing ahead, she felt for the top button of her blouse.

"It's the strangest thing. You feel like you've died already and it's just a matter of making it official." She worked her way down to the next button, and the next. I stood watching her.

"So it's not so hard," she said. "I never knew that."

"You're shivering," I said.

"Am I? The water was so warm. It was warmer than the air. It was so easy, being in it."

She peeled her blouse back, and I moved to her and pulled it from her arms and tossed it to the floor. I unhooked her bra and it fell into her lap. She was stark white in the lamplight, as if the ocean had bleached away what tan she had. She unzipped her slacks.

"Lie back," I said.

The wet slacks clung to her legs, and I yanked them down, yanked them clear and dropped them in a wet heap on the carpet.

"Into the shower," I said.

Jackie sat up and hugged herself.

"You're going to leave me when you hear," she said.

"Get in the shower, Jack."

"I'll be okay, you know. I won't kill myself, it didn't work, so fuck it. Let the cancer do it."

I took her hand and drew her, light and unresisting, to her feet. I led her into the bathroom and turned on the shower. Jackie stepped out of her underpants. I held my palm to the water, dialing it hotter and hotter.

"I knew I couldn't lie to you," Jackie said. She stood there hugging herself. "That you'd *know*. I thought that was the problem, that I couldn't get away with it, but turns out it wasn't."

"I guess I'd have known if you'd drowned yourself."

"The problem is, I don't *want* to lie to you. I never have. Did you know that?"

"Of course I did. You're not making sense. Get in."

Jackie looked down at herself. "I'm a mess, aren't I. Old, skinny. God, we just don't know what's going to happen to us, do we? We have no idea."

"Get in the damn shower," I said.

Then she curled up on her side, naked under the blankets, no longer shivering but round-eyed, as at some wonderment she couldn't fathom, and I wondered if she'd suffered some mental trauma, a kind of shell shock, and I knew I wouldn't sleep. The bedside lamp was on; I wanted to keep an eye on her until she slept. It would be daylight soon.

"I don't feel tired," Jackie said, "I don't know why. I just feel sad. I feel swamped with sadness, isn't that a good way to put it? Very literary. Like I weighed two hundred pounds because of all this sadness in me."

"It's over now."

"It isn't over. I need to tell you what I did. The reason I went in the water."

"I know the reason."

"Peter, listen to me. I had sex with a guy tonight."

Hallucination, I thought. *She's confused.* Then I looked at her in the lamplight and knew it was true.

"I felt so alone. So desperate. I wanted to hurt you. At least I think that's what it was."

I rolled away from her and turned off the light. The window curtains were drawn, and we were shut in pitch darkness. Jackie now a huddled black shape.

"I don't suppose it was Ballard," I said.

She moved, gave a jerk. "*Mike?*"

"He's been eyeing you for years."

"Oh, Peter. Oh, God."

"No?"

"He's married to my sister. And he's a moron."

"It would have been a good way to hurt me."

"I'd die first."

She lay still, and I could hear the slow rise and fall of her breathing. A car passed on the road out front, hurrying on some pre-dawn errand, whispering away into the night and gone.

"Who was he?" I said.

"What difference does it make?"

"Who was he?"

"A stranger. I met him in the Topside and went home with him."

"You picked him up."

"Or he picked me up. What's the difference?"

"None, I guess."

"It wasn't any good, Peter. He didn't turn me on. Good-looking guy, but I felt nothing."

"Is that supposed to make it all right?"

"I'm sorry, Peter. I'm so goddamn sorry. Oh God . . ."

She was weeping now, and she slid in close and tucked her head down and clung to me like a child, and I gathered her in. She was shaking, and I pulled her in tight.

"I wanted to die, Peter."

"It's over," I said.

"It won't ever be."

"Go to sleep."

"You won't go anywhere?"

"Of course not. Go to sleep."

She rolled away, extended her top leg, shifted onto her stomach, facing away from me. I raised myself on my elbow and looked at her in the dark. I could just make out her thin shoulder, the wet blanched-yellow tangle of her hair.

"I'm glad you didn't die, Jack," I said, and that much was true.

thirty-six

I slept after all, finally entering a dream of long ago, my parents alive, Jackie young and beautiful, the four of us seated in a jet plane, the ether a lucent indigo beyond the little window, fleecy shreds of cloud slipping by. We were going . . . where? Switzerland! Switzerland, that was it, we were going to spend a year with Aunt Jessica and Uncle Maurice, we were going to learn French and explore Geneva and . . . "Jacqueline," said my father, sounding like Lovey Lawrence, "you'll have to help me, I'm no good at foreign languages." "Well, sure," she said, "I'm great at them." And I knew it was true, and wondered why she'd never mentioned it to me. The dream collapsed, fell apart, then came back, and the four of us were in Santa Fe, in the great plaza, where the Navajo vend their crafts, displayed on blankets in the arcade of the stucco Palace of the Governors, their silver rings and bracelets, their gemstone earrings, the famous handwoven blankets. We were walking there, browsing. "Jacqueline," my father said, "wouldn't you like one of these rings? I'd like to buy one for you. Or something else. Whatever you'd like." Jackie smiling, oh she was beautiful. "But can you afford it, Mr. Hatch? Peter's rich now, he writes speeches for the president, did you know that?"

I woke to daylight, to Jackie's naked back. The slow rise and fall of her shoulder. The bedside clock read eight eighteen. Voices passed in the hallway, receded quickly. I remembered it was Sunday and felt the day's laxity in the air, its permissiveness. Sit around all morning reading the Sunday paper. Watch a ball game. Do nothing. I left the bed and dressed without waking her.

A group of Japanese tourists was spilling noisily out of a bus and into the lobby, crowding the desk, and I sat down on the sofa, where Jackie had sat not many hours ago. She'd left a damp stain on the cushion, and I wondered if anyone had noticed. The dining room was bustling, and there was the good smell of coffee. The bus that had brought the tourists growled lazily and moved out from under the portico. The tourists began percolating into the hallway in twos and threes, carrying their bags, their suitcases. A final couple departed, the woman chattering at her husband, berating him, it seemed. I stood up, moved to the desk. The girl looked at me brightly. I asked her for another night.

"Sir, we're full tonight. Every room booked."

"On Sunday?" I said.

"July, you know? A tour group coming in at nine in the morning, who ever heard of that? But listen, I could call the Nautilus Inn, see if they have a room."

I turned, looked across the road at the pond. The morning sun had put a waxy gloss on it. The day would be hot.

"I guess we'll head home," I said.

"You sure I can't help you?"

"When's checkout time?" I said.

She slept on her side, as I'd left her, snoring gently now. She denied she ever snored and I did too, but we laughed about it, a game. I pocketed my wallet and car key and scribbled a note on the hotel pad

and stole out as before. The sun was above the treeline and the summer morning seemed hopeful in its radiance, its sticky fragrant air. I
drove to the intersection, waited for the light, and sped on to Bagel
Heaven, which fronted the main road into town.

The cop stopped me on the way back, just short of the intersection. He'd come up a side street in time to see me go by doing fifty
without knowing it, and I heard the screech of his tires as he floored
it around the corner, saw the pulsing blue lights in my rearview coming up behind me, fast. I swore and pulled over and got out of the car,
which my father had taught me to do long ago. Stand up and speak to
them man to man, he said. Tell them you screwed up and you're sorry.
They don't like to approach a car, they never know if the driver has a
gun in his lap.

The cop got out slowly, as cops do, and gave his belt a hitch.
He was in his twenties, with sandy hair and broad shoulders, and I
guessed football. The cruiser lights still throbbed back and forth, and
drivers going by slowed and looked to see what was happening.

"Where's the fire?" the cop said. The tag on his shirt pocket said
Robert Canning.

"No fire," I said, "just me screwing up. My wife's at the motel, and
I wanted to get back with her breakfast before she woke up. She had
kind of a bad time last night."

"Did she. See your license?"

I pulled my wallet, opened it. Canning took it, looked at the
photograph, looked at me, smiled, and returned it to me.

"You're Jill Russell's brother," he said.

He hadn't quite lost the smile, and I knew I wasn't going to get a
ticket. "My baby sister," I said.

"I went to school with her son," Canning said. "Whit. Whit used
to talk about you. How you worked for Senator Powell."

"I'm sorry I was speeding."

"I'm not going to cite you. You probably figured that out already."

"I appreciate it," I said, "and I'll try to smarten up."

"I would. You kill somebody, it doesn't matter whose brother you are."

I looked across the street. A small office building, white cinder-block. MARK LISKA, M.D., DUNSTABLE DERMATOLOGY.

"No," I said, "it doesn't matter, at all."

Canning looked at me, catching something in my voice.

"You better get back to your wife."

I'd opened the car door when Canning called to me from the door of the cruiser. "Whit used to call her his pretty aunt," he said.

"She still is," I said, and saw Jackie in bed with another man, and now I had to know who the thief was.

She was sitting up in bed shirtless, watching CNN. I sat down beside her with the brown bag in my lap. Jackie aimed the remote and killed the broadcast. She pulled the sheet up over her breasts.

"I just got stopped for speeding," I said.

"That was smart of you."

"The cop let me off. He went to school with Whit Russell. He said Whit called you his pretty aunt."

"When was this, thirty years ago?"

"Whit's in his twenties. And you did all right last night, it sounds like."

She glanced at me, considered speaking but did not. I brought out the two tall Styrofoam cups of coffee, set one down and pried the lid off the other and presented it to her. She set it on her lap, cradling it between her hands. I began extracting the wrapped sandwiches, laying them on the bed beside her.

"Ham and cheese," I said. "Hummus wrap. Lox and cream cheese. Fruit cup. Yogurt. More fruit cup."

"I don't know what I want."

"Start with the yogurt."

I opened the cup and planted the plastic spoon in it. Jackie transferred her coffee to the bedside table and took the yogurt. She scooped a small bite, swallowed it, and stared at the blank TV.

"Who was he, Jack?" I said.

She closed her eyes, sighed, opened them.

"Does it matter?" she said.

"Who was he?"

"All right. He was a photographer. Freelance. *Life* magazine, things like that. Divorced. Lives by himself in a big empty house. Like I said, I didn't feel anything."

"But you went through with it."

"Is that a question?"

"It's an answer," I said. I was unwrapping the lox-and-cream-cheese bagel, not looking at her, and I didn't look now. I crumpled the wax paper and pushed it into the brown bag.

Jackie dug some yogurt, spooned it up, thinking. "Once it started, I didn't see any way out," she said.

"Get up and leave, that would have been a way out."

"It seemed like I had to finish what I'd begun," she said.

"Finish hurting me."

"No. Finish my mistake. Own it. I'd stopped wanting to hurt you."

The AC kicked on, blew. I bit into my sandwich, and we ate awhile in silence. Jackie finished her yogurt and put the cup aside and took up her coffee. I got up, brought my coffee to the high window, pulled over a vinyl motel chair, and sat down facing the window. Summer-blue sky above the summer-green trees. I thought of Jackie in dangerous water a half mile from shore in the middle of the night and saw that I'd taken her rescue for granted, as if a boat had been bound to come along sooner or later, even at that hour. I saw that only a fluke, a near miracle, had saved whatever was left of Jackie's life, had preserved, by a hair's breadth, the weeks or months or maybe even years we had in which to wake up next to each other, see our reflections in each other's eyes, come home to each other at day's end, tell each other our stories.

"Peter?" she said.

I rose, went back, and sat down beside her as before. I took up her hand, felt the warmth in it. I leaned and brushed her soft shapely cheek with the back of my hand.

"Jack, listen. I'm as guilty as you are. Guiltier."

"A girl fifty years ago you didn't sleep with. I'm rethinking that."

"A girl I *did* sleep with."

Jackie's blue gaze came up and fastened on me.

"And who would that be," she said.

She found the ham-and-cheese bagel in the carton beside her and carefully unwrapped it, waiting. I lifted my coffee, drank. The AC hummed. A car door slammed in the parking lot below.

"Remember Sue Cook?" I said.

"Senator Powell's office manager. Looked like Bette Davis."

"I had sex with her a few times."

Jackie leaned forward as if she hadn't heard me, and took a bite of her sandwich. She chewed, thoughtful, swallowed.

"And when was this?" she said.

"I don't know. Late eighties."

"Late eighties."

"Maybe 'eighty-eight."

"Tough to pin down, huh?"

"I'm sure it was eighty-eight."

And just how long did it go on?"

"A few weeks."

"Where?"

"Her place. An apartment in Georgetown. I'd come home afterwards across the Key Bridge."

"Why would you do that, Peter, when you had me?"

"Good question."

"I thought that was the one thing I gave you. Good sex."

"You gave me more than that."

"Then why?"

"Curious, I guess."

"Curious about banging Sue Cook, or cheating on your wife?"

"I knew what cheating on you would feel like. Or thought I did."

"But you went ahead."

"Not for long. I'm sorry, Jack," I said.

"Not sorry enough to try to kill yourself."

"No. Not that sorry."

"She was the only one?"

"Afterwards, I said never again."

"But you wanted to."

"No more than anyone does. Less, probably."

Voices passed in the hallway, a gaggle of children.

"Does this make us even?" Jackie said.

"I thought it might," I said.

Jackie's half-eaten sandwich lay on the sheet over her waist. She felt for it, took a bite and chewed and swallowed slowly and mechanically, while I watched her.

"I suppose those three kids'll spread it all over town, me trying to kill myself," she said.

"I doubt it. That Morgan's someone to be reckoned with. Those boys won't cross her."

"They might. They're dopes, like I said."

"They won't cross her. I sure wouldn't."

A faint smile. Jackie thought some more. "Are we going to tell Jennifer?" she said.

"No reason to."

"She'd be furious. She'd hate me."

"She'd love you. As much as ever. More, maybe."

"Would she?"

"Guarantee it."

"But we won't tell her."

"No."

Jackie had returned her sandwich to its carton. She looked out at the empty, vivid sky. "It was crazy, what I did," she said.

"A little."

"Do we just forget everything and go on?"

"We forgive each other. If you forget, there's nothing to forgive."

"It's a nice word, *forgive*."

"It's a beautiful word," I said.

"How was the Devil's Foot?" Jennifer said.

"Same as it used to be."

"Romantic?"

"Sure."

"I hope so. Mom was tense last night. Something was wrong, I know that. Is she right there?"

"She's in the shower."

"Then tell me."

"There's nothing to tell. What are you and Allison doing today?"

"Going to the Phillies game. Allie's firm has season tickets, remember?"

The shower had stopped running. The bathroom door opened and Jackie came out wrapped in a towel.

"Got to go, sweetheart," I said.

"You sure you're okay?"

"Yes."

"And the signing went well?"

"Sure."

"Literary lion," Jen said. "It's a great read, Dad. Allison agrees."

"Allison actually read it?"

"Big surprise, huh? You sound like Mom."

"Thank Allie for me," I said.

thirty-seven

We paid Mr. Lawrence a visit on our way out, the old man in faded urine-smelling pajamas watching *Meet the Press* with the volume off and subtitles scrolling across the bottom of the screen. He wore a look of vacant wonderment, as if television were new to him, a marvel he couldn't quite make sense of. Jackie kissed her father's papery cheek, and we sat down on the sofa, and I took her hand. She wore a cool pale-blue summer dress. Bare legs, sandal heels. The smell of bacon from the kitchen, the daytime aide frying up Lovey's breakfast.

"We came to say good-bye," Jackie said. "We're going back to Northampton, Daddy."

"Yes, that's fine," he said, watching David Gregory.

The aide had come through the dining room and stood in the doorway. Anita Pires, another old Cape Verdean family. Jackie had met her but I had not.

"How are you all?" she said.

"You don't want to know," Jackie said.

Anita smiled. "Probably don't," she said. "Want some breakfast?"

"We have to be going," I said.

"Got plenty if you change your mind," Anita said, and left us.

Jackie leaned forward, and her grip tightened around my hand. "Daddy, I won't be seeing you for a while," she said.

"You're Pete," Mr. Lawrence said, eyeing me through his glasses. "You were the football player."

"Oh, Jesus," Jackie said. "Oh God. *Daddy.* He's my *husband.*"

"Yes. I thought so."

"We have to go, Daddy. Back to Northampton. I won't see you for a while, do you understand?"

"I understand."

Jackie let go of my hand and stood up. She went to him, placed a hand on the back of his neck. He was watching the TV again. Jackie leaned and kissed the top of his head, her hand still on his pale skinny neck. Anita had come to the doorway again.

"He'll get his shower after he eats," she said.

Jackie nodded. She didn't look at Anita, only at her father.

"We'll take good care of him for you, Mrs. Hatch," she said.

"She knows that," I said.

"Good-bye, Daddy."

He looked up at his daughter, and in his watery eyes I saw a sudden lucidity, comprehension, fright. Jackie saw it and leaned again and embraced him, her cheek to his. Her eyes were closed.

"I love you, Daddy," she said.

She was still dry-eyed when she straightened, but the eyes had narrowed, hardened against whatever god or other agency had let this happen to her father.

She slept most of the way home while I listened to classical music on NPR and then, at low volume, the first couple of innings of the Red Sox game. The summer air blew in through the windows, commingling its fragrance with Brahms and Haydn, and I thought about my wife and the myriad times I'd wronged her, the small things, not just my fling with Sue Cook, omission after omission committed blindly down the years. *She knows how to keep her mouth shut and she's smart as a whip,* Alan Keating had told Pauline; when had I said as much to anyone, or to Jackie, above all?

She woke up in Northampton as I parallel parked in the shade in front of the record and CD store on Pleasant Street. Late afternoon, Sunday, people wandering in and out of the nearly subterranean shop. Jackie removed her shades and rubbed her eyes.

"What's going on?" she said.

"One of my silly ideas," I said.

The sales girl's hair was dyed flamingo pink but she knew whom I was asking about. "Look in the jazz section," she said.

The rows of CDs were in alphabetical order, and I found what I wanted, paid for it with my card, and asked for a paper bag.

"Let me see," Jackie said, reaching, but I held the CD away from her and pushed it down into the pocket on the driver's door.

"What is this, keep-away?" she said. She was smiling now, a smile that chased the wrinkles back and beautified her, the first real smile since we'd left this town nearly forty-eight hours ago.

"You owe me a dance," I said, and started the car.

"That's your silly idea?"

"The music. Maybe not the dance."

"That's how it all started," Jackie said. "A dance in a high school gym. Who'd have thought?"

"The Fleetwoods," I said. "'Mr. Blue.'"

"Was it?"

"You don't remember?"

"Yeah. Yeah, I do. A sad song. Is that a Fleetwoods CD?"

"It's the dance we *didn't* have."

"I don't know what you're talking about."

"You will."

"That first dance," she said. "I remember how you smelled. Like the outdoors. Like earth and grass and woods all warm in the sun."

"Sounds like I needed a bath," I said.

"It was *your* smell. It was nice."

"So was yours."

"It doesn't seem so long ago, does it."

"It wasn't," I said.

thirty-eight

We danced to it, "Moonlight Serenade," each of the three nights before her surgery. For luck, we said. Drinks and dinner on the screen porch as twilight fell on the neighborhood and the swallows hunted above the backyard, flitting, darting, tracing erratic loops in the dimming air. On the other side of the chain-link fence, beyond some woods, kids played soccer beside an elementary school, their cries shrill and musical and far-carrying at this hour. Together we washed the dishes, and then a nightcap in the near dark on the porch as the waning moon emerged, talking quietly of this and that. And then the dance.

Just the one. The Bose was on the kitchen counter, and I would cue "Moonlight Serenade" and Jackie would douse the overhead light. We would meet in the middle of the room, as if it were so scripted, and Jackie would step into my embrace, holding herself erect and formal, my two arms wrapping her, discarding the formality, pulling her in tight but very gently.

The song played out and she sank onto her heels, let her hands linger a moment on my shoulders, eyeing me with an arch half smile, the girl she once was, the teen beauty. The feeling held, the abandonment to the music and each other, until "My Blue Heaven" cut in, a raucous intruder. Jackie stepped back from me and I turned and stopped the music.

I took her hand, and we climbed the stairs, both of us more tired in those three nights than we could remember. *Don't call us after nine*, we told Jennifer. We had always read till sleep overcame us, but these nights Jackie said she wanted to be close and talk, there'd be time enough to read after her surgery. Northampton is hot in summer, and we slept in the airstream of an electric fan.

"Like Cambridge," I said.

"With the Red Sox game going. I never understood that."

"Ambience," I said.

"I thought it was kind of cute at the time."

"Maybe that's why I did it."

"I doubt it."

"Remember how lumpy the pullout sofa was?" I said.

"How would you know? I'm the one who was on my back."

"Not always," I said.

"No, not always."

We did not make love on Sunday night, and I suspected Jackie wouldn't for a long time after what had happened, but on Monday night she touched me and offered herself to be kissed. We threw the sheet back and the fan's steady airflow caressed us, and I thought again of Cambridge, the shade trees and warping brick sidewalk on Inman Street, the quiet darkness out there. There was a marble fireplace in the studio, dating to the 1800s, with a marble mantel shelf. I remembered it now, and remembered Jackie's body in the faint light falling through the window, and her gamine smile when we talked afterward.

"Where are you?" she said.

"I was thinking about Cambridge."

"Think about right here. About me."

"I *was* thinking about you."

Afterward I lay on my back, with Jackie snuggled sideways against me, her arm lightly draping my chest. The ceiling was a soft dingy white in the creep of light from the residential street below, the moon and stars.

"Peter."

"What."

"Is there anything you want to ask me?"

"About what?"

"Anything."

"The other night, you mean."

"Not just that. Anything, going all the way back."

"I can't think of anything. Why?"

Jackie rose on her elbow to face me. "Peter, listen to me. Day after tomorrow, everything changes. We have a chance—you and me— to put things behind us. This could be the sweetest time we've had. Maybe it's good I got cancer."

"It's changed already," I said.

"It has, hasn't it."

"Was there anything you wanted to ask *me*?" I said.

"Not anymore."

"Me, either."

"Then maybe you want to make love again."

I touched her cheek, stroked her hair. She watched me.

"Only to you," I said.

We did not make love on the last night, only held each other and hardly slept, as on the night we'd gotten the news at Dana-Farber. Jackie had wept that night, but she was dry-eyed now, and talkative. Jennifer had called, and Jackie had spoken cheerfully to her and told her not to worry. Jen had told her how some women have beautiful tattoos in rainbow shades on their chest where the breast had been, and Jackie had looked at me and rolled her eyes and said what an interesting idea, she'd think about it.

"I wish I liked Allison better," Jackie said. It was cooler; we'd left the fan off, and the quiet seemed right for tonight.

"She's a pain in the ass," I said.

"Jennifer thinks you at least like her."

"I'm nice to her for Jen's sake."

"Daddy's little girl. You and Jen. I've been fighting with her for thirty-three years."

"Two strong women, that's what happens."

Jackie lay awhile with her eyes closed, breathing evenly, and I thought she'd gone to sleep. Then I felt her move, and she opened her eyes.

"I love Jen," she said.

"I know you do, and so does she."

"I drive her crazy."

"She drives *you* crazy."

"Love can be like that, can't it."

"It's a good kind of love. It's caring."

We talked about what we would do after this next year at Smith, when our savings, we thought, would enable us to live wherever we wished. I said we could move to Dunstable if she still wanted to, but she didn't, not anymore. So we commenced a game, *If you could live anywhere, where would it be?*

"I liked Santa Fe," Jackie said. "The light there was so beautiful."

"San Francisco," I said. "I've always wanted to see it."

"What about Boston?" Jackie said. "That's kind of our city."

"Greenwich Village," I said. "I could write, hang out with writers like Pete Hamill. You could take acting lessons at NYU. I always thought you'd make a good actress."

"A writer's life, you'd go to Paris, like Hemingway and all those others. Except what would I do?"

"Type my manuscripts. I'd be writing longhand at cafes. You'd type them up for me on the computer every night."

"Type them yourself."

"William Styron's wife did his typing."

"Some guys have all the luck, don't they."

She was quiet again. She lay so close I could feel her breath on my chest.

"Jack."

"What."

"Let's go to Tom and Lottie's wedding."

"If we're invited."

"We will be. Then we'll go to the Custer Battlefield."

"What is it with you and the Custer Battlefield?"

"The drama of it. The hubris of Custer. Shakespeare could have written him. The two cultures colliding, the life-and-death struggle. And then that moment when Custer and the others all knew they were going to die. You imagine it—the smoke, the noise, bedlam— and it's as if you were there."

"Why would you want to be?"

"I don't know. Some primal fascination, I guess."

Jackie lay still, thinking. "Okay," she said. "*If* I have the strength."

"Of course you will," I said.

"It better be worth it," she said, and from her voice I knew she was smiling.

We lay awhile. Jackie squirmed, made herself more comfortable.

"You should sleep," I said.

"I'll sleep all day on the operating table."

"You need your strength."

"I feel like there's more we should say to each other."

"You could tell me you love me," I said.

"Well, I do," she said. "What about you?"

"What do you think?"

"I think I'd like to hear it."

"Okay. How do I love thee? Let me count the ways."

"Shakespeare?"

"Elizabeth Barrett Browning."

"What are the ways?"

"I've forgotten the poem."

"*Your* ways, dummy."

A car passed out front, slow, prowling the sleeping town like some curious outlier who'd taken a wrong turn off the highway.

"I love your courage. Your honesty. I love your wisdom."

"What wisdom? You're the wise one."

"Knowing who wrote a poem doesn't make you wise."

I looked at her in our private darkness. She was watching me. "Is that enough?" I said.

"For now."

"Go to sleep, angel."

She moved back to look at me, surprised by the word, curious, then slid in close again. I bundled her in both my arms, as I'd often held Jennifer, and after a while she slept.

thirty-nine

The surgeon's name was Kent Stevens. I'll always remember that, and remember how young and fit he was, and that he was balding nonetheless, with his head fashionably shaved so that you couldn't tell where the bristles left off and the baldness began. The naked sculpted head of a young man of action, an athlete, a warrior. He still wore his green scrubs, with the surgeon's mask dangling down his chest.

I stood up. The waiting room was large, and its few occupants sat widely scattered, as if we all wished to be alone with our worries. As if any remark or salutation or query would be an intrusion.

"Sit down, Mr. Hatch," the young doctor said, and looked at the floor, silent for the moment, and I knew this would be bad and wasn't surprised. As if I'd known all along, after all, the bright optimism a dodge I'd devised, looking at the world in a trick mirror. Dr. Stevens sat down beside me and leaned forward with his wrists on his knees. Weary.

I'd kissed Jackie good-bye four hours ago and left the hospital. I'd walked down Brookline Avenue to Fenway Park. The Red Sox were on the road and the old brick ballpark was gated and quiet and would be all day, but you could feel the thousands of ghosts from seasons long past thronging through the archways and turnstiles, and the individual Olympian ghosts hidden within, in the clubhouse and dugout, Williams and Doerr and the more recent demigod, Yastrzemski. Yaz, with that quick sweet cut from the left side. I walked around the park, then up onto the bridge over the Mass Pike and stood looking down at the traffic, toy cars and trucks flying up and down the wide white highway as in some boy's battery-powered game. I walked on into Kenmore Square and ate some pasta and drank a draft beer at Uno Pizzeria, then watched the traffic again from the Mass Pike bridge. Then I went back to the hospital.

"She's in recovery," Dr. Stevens said quietly. "You can see her in a little while."

"She's okay," I said.

"Right now, yes."

"Right *now*," I said.

A man over against the wall heard me and looked up from his iPhone, his video game or rerun of *The Sopranos*.

"You'd better tell me what's going on," I said.

Stevens was still looking down between his knees. "There's more lymph node involvement than we thought," he said.

I didn't say anything. I knew what it meant. The surgeon looked at me and understood this.

"How much more?" I said.

"I can't say, exactly. Dr. Shapiro will look at the report and talk to you and Mrs. Hatch about your options."

"When?" I said.

"Tomorrow. I'm sorry, Mr. Hatch."

"It isn't your fault," I said.

"It's not the end. There are treatments."

"Of course," I said.

Dr. Stevens stood up. "The nurse'll be down soon. She'll take you to Mrs. Hatch."

I nodded and sat hunched as he had sat, staring at the red-brown carpet, its coarse nap. The man by the wall was watching me, but I didn't look his way. *Jackie*, I thought. *Oh, my sweet brave Jackie.*

part four

forty

"Montana," Jennifer said.

"Why not?" I said.

"Why?"

"Because I'll regret it if I don't go."

"I hate weddings."

"I do too."

Silence, and I wondered if she was in bed with Allison, and if they were reading, or doing something else. Their condominium was spacious, a suite of rooms on the eleventh floor of a former luxury hotel. A domicile appropriate to a pair of lawyers, though both young women litigated on the side of the angels. Beyond the panoramic windows the glittering cityscape spreading toward a vague distant wall of darkness, the quiet suburbs of the Main Line, my Quaker alma mater out there, a twenty-minute ride on the Paoli Local.

"This is about Mom, isn't it," Jennifer said.

"I think so."

"It'll just make you sad."

"I'm already sad. Your mother told me to go without her if I had to. It'll be like taking her with us."

"Do we want that?"

"She does."

"You're not getting religious on me, are you?"

"I don't think so. Jen, please."

Another silence, while Jen thought. I knew she'd say yes. "All right, then. Sure."

"Allison could come if she wanted to," I said. A gesture, as Jennifer well knew.

"Right. Dance with her at the reception, that'd get everybody's attention."

"Maybe not. The groom's Black, remember. The bride's white."

"We'll leave Allie out of this."

"There's one other thing. Since we'll be out there, I thought we'd go see the Custer Battlefield. It's right near Billings."

"You want to go see *what?*"

"The Custer Battlefield. The Little Bighorn."

"You're kidding."

"I've always wanted to see it."

"Why?"

"I just have."

"Take Uncle Joe. It's a guy thing, and he loves history."

"Take him when? I'll never be out there again."

"You know how I feel about General Custer and what he did to the Native Americans."

"He didn't do much to them that day."

"It was a Pyrrhic victory."

"I wonder if Custer saw it that way."

"I hope not."

"I need you, Jen. The wedding. The battlefield."

I could hear her sigh, picture her looking out over the light-spangled city as she got used to the fact that she was going to spend a day, maybe two, traipsing around the Little Bighorn Battlefield.

Maybe she was already thinking about how she'd explain it to Allison.

"You'll do it, won't you, sweetheart," I said.

"You knew that when you called," she said.

Maybe you'll meet somebody, Jackie said. People hook up at weddings all the time.

I don't want to hook up with anybody, I said.

If I'm not around, why not? I want you to.

You're going to be around.

No I'm not, she said, and I knew she was right.

She was sitting on the screen porch in her bathrobe, huddled as if the summer night were chill. Her bald head was wrapped quite stylishly in a red scarf. We did not know then how little time we had, and I believe now that it's good we didn't.

At least I won't have to go to that battlefield, she said. There's always a bright side, isn't there.

That isn't funny, I said.

Yes it was. Lighten up, Peter. Everything's going to be fine. I'm not minding this. I'm really not.

I couldn't answer her, couldn't think how to.

Maybe Jennifer will go with you, she said.

A cowboy wedding in Montana?

A Black cowboy, Jackie said. That'll get her.

I'm not going without you, I said.

It's the only way I'll get there, she said.

By some genetic caprice Jennifer's hair was a vivid ginger. It fell fine and soft, almost shimmering, to her shoulders. She had her mother's blue eyes, another caprice, unusual for one with her hair color. She'd played sports in high school and was tall and slim, and men looked at her in airports, I was noticing. Jen knew they were looking but didn't look back at them, just smiled a faint private smile that told me she took some satisfaction in their interest, though it was of little use to her. She carried herself erect and sat that way, like her mother.

She met me at Logan Airport bringing a Travel Scrabble set, a miniature board with plastic tiles that snapped into place in case the plane pitched or rolled. She disliked flying, though she flew quite often in her job, and Scrabble distracted her, she said. She and Allison played when they flew together, and Jen, alone, would invite the stranger next to her to play. The men usually said yes.

She fetched the game out of her purse and opened it on her lap while our 747 was lumbering to the runway. October, a gray midmorning, very warm. Indian summer.

"Draw," Jennifer said, offering me the cloth bag of tiles.

"Already?" I said.

"Draw."

She was on the aisle, sitting with her legs swung toward me. A towheaded boy of about thirteen owned the window seat and was watching us with open curiosity. I groped around in the bag, selected a tile. C. Jen drew an E. I would play first. The plane had reached the top of the runway. It swung itself around and sat idling. I dug my tiles out of the bag, Jen dug hers.

"How does this game work?" the boy said.

"It's anagrams on steroids," Jen said, arranging her tiles on the little plastic rack.

"What's she talking about?" the boy asked me.

"Intensity," I said. "Scrabble players don't like to lose."

The first time Jackie beat me she smiled and kept on smiling as we gathered and bagged the tiles. We'd taken up the game in Northampton, where her workday ended at five and mine sooner, granting us the leisurely cocktail hour we'd never had in Boston or Washington. She won

again a few nights later, and again, and now she was winning one of
every three games, sometimes two or three in a row.

You hate losing, she said after her fourth win.

Not when it's close.

You always hate it. But isn't it more fun, now I can give you some
competition?

It was, and after the sting of losing wore off—bourbon did the trick—
I was proud of her.

The plane revved and went into its sprint, the world rushing past
our porthole. It grew lighter on its wheels, sliding, yawing, then leap-
ing smoothly into the thin lightless air. Boston tilted crazily and fell
away beneath us, the brown-and-mustard triple-deckers of Dorches-
ter and South Boston, cars scurrying insect-like on the expressway, the dun-blue harbor, and everywhere the trees flaunting their
autumn reds and yellows. We climbed into the overcast and tunneled
through it into sunlight and blue sky. The boy turned from the porthole, nodded at the two of us, as if the takeoff had gone according to
his expectations.

I asked him where he was going.

"Visit my grandparents in Denver."

"We're going on to Billings, Montana," I said. "To a wedding."

The boy looked out the porthole, then at me. "Who's getting
married?" he said.

"A cowboy," I said.

"Cool."

I snapped *hence* onto the board, the H on a double-letter square,
the word doubled because I was playing first.

"Shit," said Jennifer.

"She doesn't like to lose," I told the kid.

"She seems to like to swear," he said.

"It runs in the family," I said.

"What's your name?" Jen said.

"Ethan."

"I apologize, Ethan."

"I don't mind," Ethan said.

I beat her twice, and she called me "obnoxious" the second time and unsnapped the tiles and bagged them. She asked Ethan if he wanted to try.

"You just want to beat me," Ethan said.

"I don't know," Jen said, "you seem pretty smart to me."

"I'm not as smart as your father."

"You're about twice as smart. You're just not as old."

She watched me out of the tail of her eye, saw me smile, and smiled too, already over being twice beaten. We traded places and I sat on the aisle and read *A Terrible Glory: Custer and the Little Bighorn—the Last Great Battle of the American West* while Jennifer coached Ethan through his first game of Scrabble.

"You don't want to play there," she said. "Do you see why?"

Ethan considered the word he'd put down, *thug*. "Oh. Yeah."

"Dangerous," Jen said. "I could play off it and get a triple-word score."

"Can I take it back?"

"Sure."

Another time Ethan asked, "Would you use an S here?"

"For twelve points? Never."

"Twelve is good."

"You just got fourteen *without* an S. Save an S for a big score."

"How big?"

"Thirty points."

"I can't even get twenty."

"Sure you can. Watch for your chance."

I read my book and listened to the soporific drone of the plane while the Scrabble game went on. After a while Jennifer snapped her last tiles into place, and the game was over. I came up out of *A Terrible Glory*.

"Good *game*, Ethan," she said. She was gathering up the tiles and Ethan was holding the drawstring bag for her.

"Who won?" I said.

"She did," Ethan said.

"Not by much," Jen said.

"Yeah, right," Ethan said. "Fifty points."

"If you hadn't set me up for that triple-word score . . ." Jen said.

"Yeah. I should have seen that."

"You will next time," Jen said.

We took turns getting up and making our way down the aisle to the coffin-sized bathroom. Ethan went last.

"Nice kid," Jen said.

"I was thinking what a great mother you'd make."

"I probably would."

"Ever think about it?"

"No, but Mom sure did. Did she put you up to this posthumously?"

"Jennifer Grace *Hatch*," I said.

"All right, all right. It's just that she nagged me about it. And she didn't like Allison."

"Allison didn't like her."

"No wonder."

"Maybe," I said, "you need to think about your mother while we're out here."

"Is that why you brought me?"

I looked away from her, out the porthole. Pale-blue sky, racing fragments of cloud. After a moment Jen took my hand.

"I miss her too, Dad. It makes me bitchy sometimes."

Standing in the aisle, Ethan saw me pat Jennifer's hand, the hand that held mine, and saw my tears when I looked at my lovely daughter.

*   *   *

The small plane from Denver to Billings was assailed the entire time by a manic wind that buffeted and threw us about, and Jennifer gripped my hand through most of those torturous ninety minutes while a comely flight attendant strolled up and down the narrow aisle bestowing smiles, touching shoulders, inquiring after our needs, like some angelic guarantor of God's mercy.

"Want to play Scrabble?" I said.

"Shut up," Jen said.

The late sunlight through which we bucked and slewed belied the wild wind, tincturing the air with a fine, diffuse gold.

"You have to admit, it's pretty," I said.

"I'm not looking," Jen said, and squeezed my hand tighter.

The wind kept up, yanking and shoving even as the pilot brought us down, the plane landing hard and bouncing, bouncing again and careering on till the thrust reversal kicked in, the pilot in control again, moving us to the gate. Only then did Jennifer open her eyes and let go of my hand.

"This better not be a harbinger of things to come," she said, "this hurricane we just flew through."

"That's redundant. Harbinger of things to come."

"Oh shut up."

The high airport seemed enveloped in blue air. The distant sun was below us, suspended above the darkening horizon.

"Montana," I said.

"I hope you don't regret this," Jen said.

"I'd regret not going, so what does it matter?"

forty-one

The wedding took place in a red sandstone quasi-chateau built in 1903 by a banker named Preston Moss. The mansion was sumptuously appointed, a pristine survivor of the Gilded Age. The drapes were drawn, and the lighting was a golden oily lambency that seemed somehow of another time, as if the air were as old as the rooms themselves.

In spite of this genteel and vintage setting, and perhaps because of it, Tom's family and guests went cowboy, including, of course, the kids. Cowboy hats, Western shirts, cowboy boots, the men in bolo ties and blue jeans, the women in short skirts and embroidered boots. Several little boys wore six-shooters on their hips. Tom's father wore a frock coat and white shirt with ruffles, à la Wild Bill Hickok; his mother an embroidered white blouse and full skirt, like Miss Kitty on *Gunsmoke*.

"I didn't know I was coming to a costume party," Jennifer whispered.

"I didn't, either," I said.

"They should have told you."

"I like the surprise," I said.

"I have a feeling there'll be more," Jen said. We were waiting for the groom and bride to come down the aisle between the folding chairs. The room a central hall with oak paneling and blue velvet wallpaper, Edith Wharton's New York. Jen wore a rose-pink dress and heels, and was drawing looks.

"Mom would have loved this," she said.

"I was thinking the same thing," I said.

Tom came down the aisle with the man who would do the officiating, and the room got quiet. Tom of course in a black Stetson, white shirt, bolo tie, jeans, and cowboy boots. The officiant was a rawboned young white man in a raspberry shirt and white hat and white bolo. They turned and waited for Lottie, and here she came, on the arm of her father, in a traditional snow-white wedding dress, and everyone smiled just seeing her in that dress, seeing her radiant face and eyes. Tom was taller than I remembered, Lottie about as short.

Her father was a short stocky man with iron-gray hair and a smile so broad and unguarded you thought he might break out laughing at any moment. He delivered his daughter to Tom, and they joined hands and turned to face the Stetson-hatted officiant. The officiant dug a pair of glasses from his shirt pocket and opened a black leatherbound prayer book. He looked at Tom and Lottie.

"You ready?" he said.

Laughter sputtered across the congregation.

"Not too late, Tommy," said a man near the front.

Laughter again.

"Y'all quit that," Lottie said over her shoulder.

"Then," said the officiant, "let's get her done."

They found us in the conservatory, where the bar was. The genial young bartender splashed me a Maker's on the rocks and poured Jennifer a tall glass of sauvignon blanc, and we turned, wondering where we might find companionship among all these strangers, and there they were, the bride and groom, who had come looking for us.

"Oh sweetie," Lottie said. "Oh lord."

I held my drink up out of the way as she hugged me. I could smell clean white silk, perfume.

Tom shook my hand, his face sober under the brim of his Stetson.

"You'd be Jennifer," he said, offering his hand.

Jen took it, smiling, and dropped a half curtsy.

"Welcome, sweetie," Lottie told her, and wrapped her up in a hug.

"Let's get away a minute," Tom said.

They led us through a sitting room and out oak-paneled French doors to a corner veranda with wide steps to the lawn. It was nearly full dark, the air warm and scented with the burnt-leaf smell of autumns everywhere. Hedges walled the lawn, and beyond them to the east rose an enormous ancient spruce. To the south, a row of cottonwoods, golden and faintly visible. You couldn't see the city from here but you could hear it, a steady hurried drone of rush-hour traffic, the bleat of a horn. A siren screeched somewhere, diminished and died away.

"You got my note," Lottie said.

"It was lovely," I said.

"We had no idea last summer, else we wouldn't have presumed."

"You didn't presume," I said.

Jennifer took a sip of her wine, watching us. Tom hooked his hands in his hip pockets and looked down, standing loose-limbed and athletic and somber. My drink was cold in my hand, and I tasted the good bourbon and wondered, *Now what?* Wondered for the first time why I'd come.

"Oh lord," Lottie told Jennifer, "I'm sittin' there practically tellin' 'em my life *story*. I just rattled on like a fool, and your mom with cancer."

Tom took her hand. He seemed to find it without looking.

"It wasn't like that," Jen said. "Even I know that."

She watched me, worried now. I drank off half my bourbon.

"Tom didn't marry a fool," I said.

Jennifer took my arm. "My father's been singing your praises for weeks," she said. "And it was so nice of you to let me come."

"Well, honey, we wanted to *meet* you. And you don't look like what we expected at all, does she, Tommy?"

"Oh?" Jen looked at me, and I figured there'd be hell to pay, but she turned mildly to Lottie.

"You expected a shaved head," she said. "Tattoos."

"Well, we don't *know* many of y'all and . . ."

"Lot," Tom said, "better quit before you bring the ACLU down on us."

"No offense taken," Jen said. "I like your honesty."

"Gets me in trouble, is what it does. I always say that, but I never learn."

"You aren't the one in trouble," Jen said, and her eyes cut to me.

"Shouldn't anybody be in trouble, not today," Lottie said.

"I'll try to keep that in mind," Jen said.

"Lot, we should get back to our other guests," Tom said.

"I know, hon. But Pete, I can't help askin' . . ."

"Lot," Tom said, "not now."

"It's okay," I said.

"She just didn't seem that sick," Lottie said.

"It went very fast after her surgery," I said. "And then the chemo—chemotherapy—went wrong somehow."

"Dad," Jen said, and took my arm.

Tears had sprung to Lottie's eyes. "Oh hon," she said. "Oh lord sake."

"Hey," Tom said, and clapped his big hands. "Going to be food soon. And dancing. We got a kick-ass band. Do you dance, Jennifer?"

"Depends who asks me," she said.

"It might be me," Tom said.

"Then I might say yes," Jen said.

"A writer?" Lottie's father said. "Lottie didn't tell me that. That's great."

"Just one book, and it . . ."

"One book, hell, how many people write one book? What's it about?"

"It's a political thriller," Jennifer said. "Order it at your local bookstore."

"I sure will. What's it called?"

We drifted around with our drinks, room to room, inspecting the artwork and curiosities—a Crow warrior's blouse under glass, a copper samovar.

"Going to the battlefield, are you?" An older man, Ray, in a maroon shirt, black bolo tie, no hat. "Watch out for rattlers and bull snakes," he said.

"Good God," Jennifer said.

"Yeah, the big old ones are out lookin' for them last rodents before they den up for the winter."

"I think I'll skip the battlefield, Dad," Jen said.

"No need for that, young lady. Just don't step on 'em, you'll be okay."

An attractive cowgirl of some indeterminate middle age, café au lait skin, black eyes, shoulder-length black hair with some silver gray in it, introduced herself as Katie. She was drinking red wine.

"The sunsets out there at Little Bighorn are plain gorgeous," she said. "Grab you some pictures."

"What about rattlesnakes?" Jen said.

"Honey, I've been out there dozens of times, and I never saw one."

"I've always wanted to go," I said. "Been reading about it all my life."

"You'll like it," Katie said. "It's hardly changed. You'll see what Custer saw."

"And Sitting Bull," Jen said.

Katie smiled. Pink lipstick. "Sitting Bull, Gall, Crazy Horse. They got to enjoy it a little longer than Custer."

The dinner was buffet, served in the kitchen, and the reception in a large parlor with pocket doors that looked more like the Palace of Versailles than Edith Wharton—rococo, white columns and cornices, red velvet wallpaper. There were tables and chairs for maybe fifty people, and the remaining guests ate at high cocktail tables along the walls, seated on three-legged stools, or in other rooms of their choosing, wandering about with their plates and drinks. The kids were helling around from room to room with their six-shooters, but no one seemed to mind.

Jen and I chose a cocktail table and pretty soon two of the Georgians sat down with us, an insurance salesman and his wife, who said she was a personal trainer, whatever that was. Sam and Holly Whistler. We all fell to eating.

"We heard about y'all's loss," Holly said, "and we sure are sorry."

"Heard about it where?" Jennifer said.

"Lottie, of course. She feels real bad. She said your wife was real beautiful."

"They might not want to talk about it, Holly," said her husband.

"We don't mind," I said.

"Well, if this doesn't cheer you up, nothing will," said Sam. "Look at all those gals in their cowboy skirts. We should have put you in one, Holly."

"They're kind of tacky, you ask me," Holly said.

"What sort of training do you do, Mrs. Whistler?" Jennifer said.

"Please. Call me Holly."

"Call her anything, just don't call her a Democrat," Sam said.

"Why, Sam," Holly said, "they might *be* Democrats, they're from Massachusetts. Y'all don't pay him any attention."

"Actually," Jen said, to amuse herself and plumb the Whistlers' gullibility, "we're Republicans."

"Well, there you go," Sam said.

"I don't know about Tom and Lottie, though," Jen said.

"Oh, I shouldn't wonder they're Democrats," Holly said. "Lottie's parents, though, Joe and Rhonda, they're just wild for Tom, doesn't matter what he thinks."

"Or what color he is," Jen said.

"That's exactly right. Once they got to know Tom, they didn't think a thing about it."

"Hell, we've got a Black president, don't we?" Sam said. "Who would have thought?"

"Is the bar still open?" I said.

"Go see," Jen said.

"We'll save your seat," Sam said.

I looked at Jennifer and she nodded. *Go ahead, I'll take care of this.* I didn't much want another drink but got one anyway and took it out into the cool night on the veranda. There was an oak bench against the wall, and I sat down on it in the dark. Despite the city's milky glow the stars blazed hard and bright as jewels in the black sky.

I drank, and the smooth bourbon went down burnless and brought a pleasant sad repose. A lightness. Somewhere to the south a train rumbled by, a mile-long freight, ponderous, a patient, lonesome sound. An occasional distant screech of steel on steel. I had thought that coming here would in some way bring Jackie back from wherever she'd gone, but it had not. The train drew slowly away, click-clack, click-clack, diminishing to rumor, gone.

*   *   *

"Why would you tell strangers on a beach that your daughter was a lesbian?" Jennifer said.

"It was just Lottie. Tom didn't hear it."

"He's heard it now."

"So what? They obviously love you."

"Good thing for you," Jen said.

The caterers had taken away our plates, and Sam and Holly Whistler had departed for the bar and not come back.

"We were talking about children," I said. "Lottie wanted them, Tom didn't."

"Children again. And Mom told Lottie I couldn't have any because I was a lesbian."

"I told her. It wasn't a complaint, just a fact."

"Mom wished I was straight. I always knew that."

"You're wrong, Jen. Dead wrong."

Jennifer shifted on her stool, thinking, and looked out over the portable parquet dance floor, where now the musicians were assembling. There were three of them, and they looked like stagecoach robbers who'd checked their guns at the door, pulled the bandannas down from their faces, and come in to play music and generally have a good time.

"The James Gang," Jen said.

"I expected a swing band," I said. "Tom loves the big bands."

"Get out."

"He does. He was listening to Glenn Miller that night."

"A Montana cowboy listening to Glenn Miller. Will wonders never cease."

"Your mother used to say that."

"I know."

"She'd be saying it now," I said.

"I keep saying dumb things about her, don't I."

"She loved you, Jen."

"I know," Jen said.

*   *   *

They called themselves the Miles City Cowboys—guitar, fiddle, keyboard. The guitarist was the lead singer, and he had a surprisingly deep smooth voice, almost Johnny Cash. The fiddler had a gentle touch with his bow, and the keyboard man played just behind the vocalist, never in front of him, so Tom had been right about the band. They opened with "Always Wanting You," and Tom led Lottie onto the floor by the hand and they danced alone, clinging to each other and shuffling dreamily about, and I remembered them slow-dancing to "Moonlight Serenade" under the full moon at the Devil's Foot, the precipitant of all of this. They danced for several minutes, then Lottie's father rose, proffering his hand to her mother. Another couple got up, and another, till the dance floor was full, and the Miles City Cowboys drew the song out, kept it going, making time stand still awhile for this flock of lovebirds.

"Put up or shut up" was Tom's invitation to Jennifer to dance.

Jen looked at me, smirked, then locked eyes with Tom. "You might get more than you bargained for," she said.

"You lookin' at a dancin' fool," Tom said. "I don't think so."

Smiling, Jen dropped from her stool and gave Tom her hand, and I watched them dance to the old Elvis number, "I'm Left, You're Right, She's Gone," Tom twirling her, drawing her in again, then a twirl the other way. He dipped her, scooped her upright, spun her again, other dancers watching by now, smiling in pure enjoyment. He dipped her as the song finished, pulled her erect, stepped back, and bowed with a sweep of his Stetson.

A youngish man in a coat and tie asked Jen to dance as she was leaving the floor, and she looked at me and I nodded, and she turned and followed him back onto the parquet.

"Mind if I join you?"

318 JOHN HOUGH JR.

It was the cowgirl with the black eyes. She wore a white straw cowboy hat, white cowboy boots, tan suede skirt, fringed, showing some leg. She'd brought a half-full glass of red wine. She wriggled up onto Jen's stool and set her wine glass down. The caterers had cleared and wiped down the table.

"It's Katie, right?" I said.

"And you were Pete."

"I still am."

It got the requisite smile. "Your daughter has some moves," Katie said.

"She didn't learn them from me."

Jen was dancing more sedately with the staid white boy, "Your Cheatin' Heart."

"Don't tell me you don't dance," Katie said.

"Not tonight," I said.

"Right. I'm sorry for your loss."

"Appreciate the thought. How come you aren't out there?"

"Isn't anyone asking me. I think it's because I just broke up with my husband. They don't want to jump the gun, so to speak. Either that, or I'm an old lady and I haven't caught on to it yet."

"You'll be dancing soon enough," I said.

"I don't mind waiting. It needs a rest sometimes." She sipped her wine, watching me. "Shoot. I think I just said the wrong thing."

"My wife, you mean."

"Like I said, I'm real sorry."

"It seems everyone is."

"It's Lottie, you know. She's got the biggest heart. You came so far, she wanted you to enjoy yourself. Wanted people to make you feel at home."

"I do."

"My impression is, you'd rather be someplace else."

She sipped, looked at me. Tilted her head. "You miss her," she said.

"There's a saying in French," I said. "*Partir, c'est mourir un peu.*"

"My French is a little rusty. To leave . . ."

"To part. To part is to die a little."

"Well, death is a parting, isn't it."

"Depends what you believe. Did Lottie send you over here?"

Katie looked toward the dancers. "She suggested it."

Jennifer was dancing with the rangy cowboy who'd married Tom and Lottie, swinging to "I Wouldn't Change You If I Could." Jen showing her moves again.

"You don't have to do this, Katie. Keep me company."

"I know I don't. Whyn't you get yourself another drink? Looks like your daughter's going to be out there awhile. Get me a refill while you're at it."

She was there when I got back, perched with her legs crossed, watching Jennifer dance, Jen still partnered with the officiant, doing a two-step to "I Fall to Pieces."

"Good-looking couple," Katie said.

"He better not get his hopes up," I said. "She's got someone back in Philadelphia."

"I'm guessing a woman," Katie said.

I looked at her, her face quiet, giving me time, if I needed it.

"How'd you know?" I said.

"A hunch. She's enjoying the dancing, but not caring about the guys so much. The way she looks at them, or doesn't. Plus she doesn't wear makeup, that's often a clue."

"How do you feel about that?"

"Honey, I've got a lot of things to worry about, but that isn't one of them. What does she do, your daughter? Something important, I bet."

"Lawyer."

"I wish you hadn't told me that."

"She's one of the good ones. Works at a place called the Juvenile Law Center, trying to keep kids out of jail, get them justice, get them turned around."

"Then you're proud of her."

"Very."

"Well, seeing as how we're boasting, my girl's all A's at the university in Missoula. She's a senior now. History major. You got any others?"

"We couldn't."

"Me neither, after Susanna. Good thing, the way Hal turned out. That was husband number one. Husband number two wasn't any better. I guess I'm a slow learner."

"Did you love them?"

Katie drank, regarded the dancers. "You know what? I don't know what love is anymore. Maybe I never did know."

"You will," I said.

"Why don't you tell me, save me some time."

I took a sip of bourbon and set the glass down. "It's choice," I said.

"Say again?"

"Love's a choice we make."

"Like choosing a job, a place to live? Doesn't sound very romantic."

"It can be. It's still love."

"What about love at first sight?"

"I don't think that's love. Not yet."

"Well, my choices didn't work out, for sure."

"Maybe it wasn't love you chose."

"I'll think on that. Think about what I did choose."

"It might be obvious."

She smiled, dimpling her cheeks. "Yeah, and that only goes so far, doesn't it."

"Only so far."

Katie looked into her glass, gave it a jiggle, watched the dark wine stir and slop against the thin glass. "After you go to the battlefield, then what?"

"Home."

"And I guess you won't be back here."

"I doubt it."

"Well . . ."

"But you never know," I said.

"That's right, you don't."

The set was over, the dancers dispersing, the Miles City Cowboys setting down their instruments and heading, I guessed, for the bar. I saw Jennifer put her hand on the cowboy officiant's shoulder and say something. He nodded, shrugged, and watched her walk away with the wistful half smile of the graceful loser.

Katie dropped neatly to the floor.

"No need to leave," I said.

"It's best I do. Doesn't look like anybody's going to dance with me, and I don't need any more wine. I don't guess you'll be here much longer, either."

"Probably not," I said.

"Well, then." She offered her slender pale-brown hand, and I reached across the table and I held it a moment.

"I enjoyed talking," I said.

"Me too. You're ever back this way, give a holler. I'm Katie Jackson, but I'll be Katie McBride time you get back, if you ever do. My maiden name. I'm going to start all over again."

"McBride," I said. "When Irish eyes are smiling."

She smiled, the lyric on display. "My momma was a full-blooded Cheyenne," she said. "Left the Tongue River Reservation, got her degree, became a schoolteacher. Then my Irish daddy came along. You might run into Momma's great-great-grandfather tomorrow."

"I'll look for him," I said.

"Was she hitting on you?"

"I wonder what Hawthorne or Melville would say about that expression," I said. "Sounds like something a mobster would do."

"Was she?"

"The Reverend Dimmesdale hit on Hester Prynne," I said. "There aren't any women in *Moby-Dick*, of course. Or in *Billy Budd*."

"Dad, cut the crap."

"She was being kind," I said. "Lottie sent her over to cheer me up."

"Lottie's rushing things, seems to me."

"Lottie's a sweetheart and you know it. Let's go back to the hotel. Big day tomorrow."

"It's polite to wait till they cut the cake."

"I don't even know if there's going to be a cake. Katie wasn't worried about it."

I'd watched her walk away in her suede skirt, her gait the graceful prowl of her Cheyenne ancestors. I thought she might pause in the doorway and look back, but she did not.

"Katie?" Jen said. "I took her for a Native American."

"Half," I said. "Katie McBride. Half Irish, half Cheyenne Indian."

"So she's a drinker and a warrior."

"I thought the Cheyenne part would please you."

"I just don't want anyone to take advantage of you, Dad."

I picked up my glass and drained it. "Are we going to walk or take a taxi?"

forty-two

Toward the end of the afternoon we sat on a bench on the museum terrace looking out at the high knob of grassland, the northern terminus of a ridge, where the last of them had died. They were crouched low, fighting hopelessly from behind a breastwork of dead horses, shot by their riders for this purpose. Small marble headstones, so white they seemed to glimmer in the fading afternoon, marked where each man had been found, the thin erect slabs cluttering the summit in seeming random and trickling downhill toward the distant river, whose meandering course a mile away was traced by golden cottonwoods and aspens. To the south, ahead of us, were the faraway Wolf Mountains, veiled in a faintly aureate autumnal haze.

"They were making a run for it, looks like," Jennifer said, meaning the downhill scatter of gravestones.

They had not gotten far. A hundred, a hundred fifty yards. They had fled in disarray into a broad basin, angling toward a ravine that cut slantwise downhill. Men had died on the lip of that ravine earlier, sent to clear the basin of Indians, who instead engulfed them, stampeding their horses and slaughtering them as they sought shelter in the ravine. On a ridge shrugging up beyond the ravine, a solitary slab. Who was he? How did he come to be so far from his comrades?

"I'm thinking how far from home they were," Jennifer said. "How empty and desolate this must have seemed."

It was as infinite-seeming and as trackless as any ocean, an endless heaving ravine- and gully-cleft sea of prairie grasses paling to yellow and clotted with wispy teal-blue sagebrush. In the broad valley across the river a highway ran roughly parallel to it, with tiny semis moving intermittent and silent up and down it, but trucks and roadway seemed incidental, a trifling anachronism in that vast, stark, prairie wilderness.

"Some of them were just kids, I imagine," Jen said.

"A lot of them," I said. "Right off the boat from Ireland and Germany. You starting to feel sorry for the invaders?"

"It's just sad, the whole thing."

We had been here since ten, had driven everywhere there was to drive—Reno Hill, Medicine Tail Coulee, Calhoun Hill, Last Stand Hill—and walked till our legs ached. The tourists were dispersing slowly as the day waned. There were a dozen or so on the hilltop, several strolling down the asphalt path toward the river. Browsers lingered in the small museum and its bookstore. Jen and I were alone on the terrace, where a Park Service ranger had delivered a lecture this morning.

"Are we coming back tomorrow?" Jennifer said.

"I don't think so."

"We can. We saw everything in a rush today. I know there are places you want to study."

"I kept thinking of your mother. Everything we saw, I was trying to think what she'd have made of it."

"I think you knew."

"I guess I did."

Jen gave it a moment, then: "Tell me about that woman yesterday. Katie. Divorced?"

"Twice."

"You got her life story, it sounds like."

"A fragment of it."

I thought about her now, Katie McBride, wondered what she did for a living. A teacher, like her mother, maybe. Businesswoman. Proprietress of a shop that sold Native crafts, a smart businesswoman.

"What else did you talk about beside her divorces?" Jen said.

"Our daughters. I bragged about you."

"Lesbian, you tell her that?"

"She spotted it, watching you dance."

"Maybe she's gay herself."

"I doubt it."

"I'm being a bitch again, aren't I."

"You're thinking of your mother. I'm glad, Jen."

We were silent awhile, gazing at the rugged prairie ridges and ravines with their myriad gleaming marble slabs. At the faraway mountains.

"Katie said a funny thing," I said. "She was talking about her exhusbands, said she didn't know what love is anymore."

"I'm sure you enlightened her."

"Why not?"

"No reason. What did you say?"

"I told her what I knew. Or thought I knew."

She died at home. I was at the Stop & Shop, buying coffee and paper towels and deli sandwiches, when it happened. Jennifer and I. I had sat with her since dawn, and at noon Jen said I needed a break. She said the air and sunshine would do me good, and that we would not be gone long.

Jackie loved Patsy Cline and Dolly Parton, and we played them on CD all morning, softly, thinking she was listening in some way as she lay with her eyes closed, breathing raspily and shallowly. She loved the Beatles too, in a different way, and we mixed in the Let It Be *album, and* Sgt. Pepper's Lonely Hearts Club Band. *I held her hand and tried to work* New York Times *crossword puzzles on my lap out of a book I'd bought just for this. I did not want to remember her looking this way and was afraid I would.*

Her sister sat with her while Jen and I ran our errand. Margie. Linda Jean was coming tomorrow, or so she'd said. And so it was Margie, whom I'd always liked, who saw Jackie out of this world. Jackie sat up, Margie said, and opened her eyes. Margie said she saw something out ahead, and that the slackness and torpor vanished from her face as she stared at it. Her eyes were wide, surprised, but unafraid. Then she sank back and closed them.

It stopped me in my tracks when Jen and I walked in with our purchases, Margie in the doorway to the living room with the tears streaming down, her fair, still-girlish face, stricken, tragic, Dolly Parton trilling "Sweet Summer Lovin'" to nobody. We'd been gone twenty, twenty-five minutes, at most, and it did not seem accidental, the timing of my wife's departure.

Jennifer said it was an act of love, she said Jackie waited for me to be gone, to spare me. I thought this might be true, and sometimes was sure of it. But in bed at night, sleepless, I wondered if there was repudiation in it—if she was saying she could do even this without me, and that I'd been with her all along on sufferance, and would be in time to come.

"You know what love is, Dad," Jennifer said.

"Do I?"

"I know you and Mom were different. But you adored her. Anyone could see it."

"I could have done better."

"So could she."

"No," I said, "I don't think so."

Jen rested her chin on her fist and looked up at Last Stand Hill. The last tourists were straggling down the walk that ribboned up over the hill. The sun was getting low, suspended fat and molten gold over the broad valley where the highway ran and where the Sioux and Cheyenne had encamped. The village was three miles long, witnesses said. There was a moment when Custer and several others, including his brother, crested a rise and looked down upon this immensity of white tipis for the first time and knew, with a stab of recognition that must have stopped their hearts, that they could never prevail here.

"Dad?"

"What."

"What are we doing out here?"

"Keeping a promise."

"On a battlefield? Where men got scalped, shot with arrows?"

And worse. I hadn't told her how the Indians had stripped and disfigured the soldiers' bodies. Braves and women too, coming up afterward bringing knives and hatchets and stone clubs.

I smiled. It seemed funny suddenly, a miscalculation so deluded as to be joke material. "Your mother would have hated it," I said.

"It's a guy thing, like I said."

"I told her it was Shakespearean. The hubris of Custer. The Indians combining forces for one last great effort to save themselves. A few days before the battle Sitting Bull did a sun dance and had a vision of hundreds of soldiers falling from the sky. Beware the Ides of March."

Jen looked west over the valley. The sky was now a brilliant gold behind the lowering white-gold sun. "She'd have liked that. She listened to everything you said, Dad. She learned from you, even if she didn't always admit it."

She took my hand, lifted my knuckles to her lips. Placed the hand in her lap and held it there. "She loved you, Dad. She died loving you."

Maybe it didn't happen the way I remember it, I said. Maybe I imagined everything but the accident.

The Sierra Grille on a quiet weeknight, Jackie looking good in her headscarf, the weight loss just beginning to show, a faint hollowing of her cheeks, an unremarkable thinness to her neck and arms. She would gain it back, I thought. We were sipping Manhattans, the drink of our long-ago days in Boston and Cambridge. There had been no postsurgery prohibition of alcohol and I think she'd have refused to comply with one.

The accident and the abortion, I said. I didn't imagine them. The rest, I don't know anymore.

You know what, Peter? How many wives are there, their husbands fall in love with someone else? Thousands. And you never did, except in your memory. Remembering someone who didn't exist anymore. Who may never have existed. I was lucky, the way I see it now.

I was too, Jack.

Even if you didn't always know it.

I knew it.

You do now. She reached across and touched my cheek. She smiled.

The western sky had caught fire, a swirl of yellow and carmine behind purple tatters of cloud and the reddening sun.

"Your girlfriend told you to get a picture," Jen said.

"She told *us*," I said, "and my phone's in the car."

"Figures," Jen said.

She stood up, pulled her phone from the left front pocket of her jeans, went to the west edge of the terrace. She sighted, snapped. And again. And again.

You didn't kill her, Peter. It was an accident. Everyone has them. Some moron left his car in the middle of the road, it wasn't your fault. Put it behind you, for the Lord's sake. You should have, years ago. She would want you to.

Jen had moved over and was photographing Last Stand Hill and the gravestones fleeing downhill toward the ravine. She took a final shot, stored it, and slid the phone into her pocket.

"What are we going to do with these pictures?" I said.

"Put them in our memory book."

"You want to remember gravestones? Guys shot with arrows?"

"The sunset. The mountains. And you know what else? Sitting here with you."

"Giving me hell about Katie McBride."

"Talking about love. About Mom."

"Worth the trip," I said.

"Definitely."

I got up, and Jen came beside me and took my arm. We stood like that, looking at the distant purple blur of the mountains.

"Thanks for coming," I said.

"Thanks for asking me," she said.

forty-three

She got on the train in New York, wheeling her suitcase up the aisle, looking from side to side for a seat, finally choosing the one opposite me. She had flaxen hair, wore a tight-fitting russet dress, and looked to be in her early thirties. She placed her purse and tote bag on the aisle seat then hoisted the suitcase, paused with it shoulder-high as if reconsidering, then heaved it up onto the rack. She sat down next to the window and pulled her laptop from the tote. She crossed her legs and opened the computer.

We were rolling now, through the pitch-dark catacomb beneath the city, lit feebly at intervals, the coach windows throwing our reflections back at us. Then out into the spring sunshine, the gay diffuse light of Memorial Day weekend, with its sudden warmth, its promissory taste of summer. We scurried north, into Connecticut. I took another look at the young woman, busy now at her keyboard, and reopened *All the King's Men*, which I was studying for pointers, instruction, in the art of political fiction. *The Minutes of This Night* had sold something under five thousand copies and had failed to earn back the advance, but Jennifer was at me to try again.

"But no more thrillers," I said.

"I agree," Jen said. "Stretch yourself. The human condition, Dad. The verities."

"The verities. That's what I get for sending you to Swarthmore."

The woman across the aisle was gazing out the window with two fingers tapping her chin. Thoughtful. She was on the left side of the car and would not have the view of the Connecticut shore, the seaside cottages, the shining ocean, the inlets and estuaries where now boats were moored or tied alongside plank docks, fresh out of winter storage, their hulls glossy in new bone-white paint.

I'd been in Philadelphia for my daughter's wedding to Allison Rebecca Dinsmore, whose parents were biting the bullet in acquiescing in this. George Dinsmore was an executive at Procter & Gamble, Meredith a board member of the Junior League of Philadelphia, a thin and timid woman with the fragile prettiness of a pressed flower. She called her husband "Dinsy," which afforded Jennifer no end of private amusement. The reception took place at the Merion Cricket Club, where Allison had come out as a debutante, and I think her parents knew how thoroughly Allie and Jen scorned the place, knew even that they had consented to the venue in the spirit of a lark, a costume ball or Halloween party. Their friends, gay and straight both, went along with the game, dressing up and conducting themselves with elaborate country club decorum, while Allison's parents, aunts, uncles, and Main Line friends— I'll say this—saw it through with admirable civility. I left early, and one of Jen's law partners, an earnest young man who plied me with questions about Senator Pauline Powell, drove me to my hotel. I'd begun rather to respect Allison, who had looked quite lovely in her mint-green wedding dress.

This morning Jennifer had come to the hotel at seven, having hardly slept, and driven me to 30th Street Station for an eight-ten departure.

"You should have stuck around," she said. "Allie's parents, aunts,

and uncles and their friends left soon after you did. Then the fun
began."

"I'm an old man, I need my sleep."

"Oh *please*." Jen looked at me. She'd braked for a red light she
could have run, the suburban streets Sunday-morning empty. "I was
thinking you might meet somebody."

"I didn't know you wanted that."

"It's time, Dad."

The traffic light went green, and we drove on.

"It's been almost nine months," Jen said. "Mom talked to me
about it a few days after her operation. We were having drinks on the
screen porch, you were late, at a meeting. She said I should give you six
months and then make you get on with your life. With a woman, she
meant. I didn't want to hear it, and we had another of our arguments.
I realized she was dying, is what happened, and I was mad at her for
it. For dying, and handing you off to another woman. I kept telling her
she was being morbid. What the hell was wrong with me?"

"Nothing."

"Shit," she said, and wiped her eyes with the back of her sun-
tanned wrist.

"Cheer up," I said. "You just got married."

We were on City Avenue now, traffic still thin. The road
had hardly changed since my college days. Malls sprawled out
on either side, the leafy campus of the Philadelphia College of
Osteopathic Medicine. Channel 6. The Hilton towered, somnolent,
on the morning-blue sky.

"You like Allie now, don't you," Jen said.

"I love her," I said.

We swung onto the empty expressway.

"I wonder," Jen said, watching the road, "what happened to that
woman in Montana."

"I wonder, too."

"You could find out."

"I could."

"Don't let me stop you," Jen said.

The blonde was typing again. She would stop and think, considering the scenery scrolling by, then type some more, tapping rapidly. Meanwhile Willie Stark was addressing the crowd at the Sunday barbeque, transfixing them with the revelation that he, and they, were being suckered by the bigshots in Baton Rouge, "those fellows in the striped pants."

I looked out at the new leaves and thought again of time to come. Smith had asked me to give them another year, or should I sell the house in Northampton and move on? There'd been a call from Pauline.

"Too old, hell," she said. "I'm old, too."

She was calling from her office in the Russell Building, seven thirty at night, the suites of rooms and marble halls empty and sepulchral around her.

"I've needed a writer," she said, "ever since Hannify left."

"You've done fine, as far I can see."

"Writing my own stuff, or Jane Marcus writing it. I need you, boy. I'm up next year, in case you haven't noticed."

"Who's going to beat you?"

"You never know."

"Yes you do."

"Think about it. There's plenty of time yet. And Pete?"

"What."

"Life goes on, buddy."

Outside of Old Saybrook the young beauty stood up and made her way, with queenly deliberation, to the restroom at the front of the car. Then she reappeared, pausing to slide the bathroom door shut behind her, heaving it over with both hands. I sank my attention in Robert Penn Warren's masterpiece, not wanting to embarrass myself with more looking. I did not see her till she spoke to me.

"Wendell?"

She had leaned in across the aisle seat, and at this close distance I saw she was no kid, no recent university homecoming queen, but a woman who had crossed into her forties, at least. Crow's feet spoked her summer-blue eyes. A comely line slanted downward to either side of her nose. She was peering at me, quite certain I was Wendell.

Wendell?

No, but I wish I were.

Wendell?

No, but if I were, what would you say to me?

Wendell?

No, but can I pretend to be?

Wendell?

I sure am. And you are . . . ?

These replies occurred to me later; meanwhile I sat speechless and only cocked my head inquiringly, within kissing distance of the lovely oval of her face.

"No," I said. "Sorry."

"Oh." Her smile contracted, was gone. She straightened. "You look like him," she said.

"I figured," I said.

"Yes. Of course."

"Who is he?" I said.

"A business associate." And with that evasive and slightly chilly answer—she was embarrassed, I think—she turned, leaving me to Robert Penn Warren and the greenery and bloom flashing past my window.

She got off in Providence. I looked up from *All the King's Men*

and watched her lift her suitcase down and draw out the handle. The
train slowed, slowed, braked with that lurch that springs from car
to car like an echo. The woman shouldered her purse and tote bag,
dropped me a smile that seemed at once forgiving and conspirato-
rial, as if her faux pas had in the end endeared me to her, and went
down the aisle, the suitcase skittering along behind her. In another
moment the coach doors hissed open, and she was gone, out onto the
bustling sunlit platform, the opportunity lost forever.

Wendell?

No, but if I were, could I buy you lunch?

The train gave a jerk, began to move.

Remember me?

Well, yeah. Sure.

My brother-in-law is hot to see the Custer Battlefield, so I guess I'll
come out there with him.

Really.

You said I should give you a holler.

I did say that, didn't I. When are you coming?

In a couple of weeks. Look, if you're busy . . .

Did I say I was busy?

I mean, have you started dancing again?

When are you coming?

The train racketed along, running late, highballing to make up
lost time.

forty-four

We had gone once more to the Devil's Foot.

We'd driven home to Dunstable for several days between chemo treatments, and stayed, at Jackie's insistence, at the Holiday Inn. The chemo had weakened her, but she was able to eat a bit, and drink alcohol. We called on Jill and Joe, on Linda Jean. Margie drove over from Yarmouth the second afternoon and took Jackie to visit their father, recently installed in the Royal Sconsett Nursing Home. It was on the third and final night that Jackie asked me to drive her to the Devil's Foot. I was surprised, but there was a reason for everything she did now, life too precious to squander a minute of it, so I said okay.

The moon hung over the bay that night, as it seemed bound to. A half-moon this time, the perfect cloven half of a white coin. Stars glittering down the sky. I parked and we left the music off and sat there.

"We had fun here," I said.

"I was shameless," Jackie said.

"You liked to enjoy your young body. Why not?"

"I was a predator."

"I didn't feel like a victim," I said.

"You weren't. I just didn't know it at first."

"We had good times here, Jack. Bottom line."

"Okay, but that's not why I wanted to come. Well, maybe part of why. But the night we met Tom and Lottie and then I tried to kill myself . . ."

"If that's what you were doing."

"It was. I see that now. But something happened afterwards. We were different together. It started here, when you told me about the abortion, and seeing Tom and Lottie so happy. It was bad, but it was the turning point. I wouldn't trade any of it. I wanted to come one more time, as a kind of acknowledgment. I'm glad there's a moon."

"It doesn't have to be the last time," I said.

"It isn't. You're going to put my ashes here."

I looked at her. So pale in the soft moonlight. We hadn't talked about where, her ashes or mine.

"You sure?" I said.

"This place is special to us. And I want to go to the ocean. Exist in it as long as it's there."

"We won't be together. We'll be spread from Central America to Maine."

"We'll be together, even so."

"Jennifer hears that, she'll ask if you're going religious on her."

"Depends on what you mean, *religious*."

"God. An afterlife."

"Maybe not that, but other possibilities. Mysteries. When you're dying, you begin to see them. The shape of them, anyway. There's a new knowledge sets in."

"You aren't dying, Jack. Not yet."

"Of course I am. We all are. Now are you going to kiss me, or what?"

*   *   *

It never rains on the summer solstice, is always fair, as if that long, long day must have the sun's full cooperation to display its bewitching length. We drove into town without telling anyone, even Joe and Jill, Jennifer my front-seat passenger, Allison in back with the box and my old Heritage Press edition of *Huckleberry Finn* with the Norman Rockwell illustrations that had entranced me as a kid. The newlyweds had flown up from Philly and we'd driven down from Logan Airport listening to Jackie's CDs. The Beatles, Patsy Cline, Lyle Lovett. Jennifer drew the line at Dolly Parton, I'm not sure why.

There was no one at the Devil's Foot at this hour just before supper, and I parked in the sandy clearing where Tom and Lottie had danced. The sun was still high, and a hazy southwest wind romped on the bay.

"I'll stay here," Allison said. She had a sweet rich voice, milky. She was wearing black jeans, matching her hair, and a silver-gray blouse. Jen had on a pale-blue T-shirt dress.

"No you won't," Jen said.

"I don't want to be in the way," Allison said.

"Dad?" Jen said.

"Come with us," I said. "Jackie would want you to."

"That's debatable," Allison said.

"She *does* want you to," I said.

Jen looked at me. "Does?"

"Mysteries, Jen," I said. "Who knows? Bring the book, Allison."

We got out of the car in the slow, cautious way of arrivals in an unfamiliar and curious place. I led them down the short path through the long pale-green blades of beach grass to the water's edge with the box under my arm. Waves foamed up over the flat shelving sand at our feet.

I set the cardboard box down and opened the lid. I untied the plastic bag and scooped a handful of the bluish-white grains and nuggets that were Jackie. Allison stood back of Jen and me with her arms wrapping *Huckleberry Finn*. Jen nodded to me, and I flung the ashes out and watched them scatter on the wind and disappear, peppering the rolling waves. Jennifer leaned and dug a handful and let it fly with an overhand toss, my athletic daughter. We each threw again, and it was done.

Allison stepped forward and handed me *Huckleberry Finn*. I'd read Huck's paean to Mary Jane Wilks from this same volume at the funeral, and twice lost my voice, stopped to recover while the congregants waited in patient forgiving silence. The fine thin sunlight of November in the high windows of the college chapel, a warm afternoon, a full house. Eddie McDermott, second oldest member of the US House of Representatives, and a couple of his staff. Alan Keating, graying and gimpy, and his wife. Smith professors, secretaries, President Christ herself. *See, Jack? They loved you.*

We stood facing the bay with the sweet salt wind in our faces, and I opened the book. I did not break down this time.

Pray for me! I reckoned if she knowed me she'd take a job that was more nearer her size. But I bet she done it, just the same—she was just that kind. She had the grit to pray for Judus if she took the notion—there warn't no back-down to her, I judge. You may say what you want to, but in my opinion she had more sand in her than any girl I ever see; in my opinion she was just full of sand. It sounds like flattery, but it ain't no flattery. And when it comes to beauty—and goodness, too—she lays over them all.

I closed the book, and Jen took it from me and took my right hand, while Allison found and held my left. We stood like that, hand in hand, silent, looking out over the water in the yellowish haze of the southwest wind, the wind whipping Jen's long fine hair, tossing Allison's black curls. A gull swooped down, skimmed the whitecaps, then climbed, up and up, onto the back of the wind, the boisterous southwester, and rode it away into the far high distance, the limitless golden distance where youth and dreams reside.

acknowledgments

I am indebted to tech whiz Derek Fairchild-Coppoletti, midwife Pamela Putney, Sergeant Skipper Manter of the West Tisbury Police Department, and Corinna Sinclair, Operations Manager of the Moss Mansion in Billings, Montana.

My niece, Jessica Hough Russell, sharpened my rusty French. Historian James Donovan, who doubles as a musicologist, provided help I didn't think I needed with sixties gold. Jay Russell refreshed my memory of Northampton and provided other assistance.

My editor, Jackie Cantor, has been nothing short of perfect, both as editor and friend. Assistant editor Molly Gregory provided a prompt and patient helping hand whenever I asked. Gratitude also to my agent, BJ Robbins, still tireless on my behalf after all these years, and my wife, Kate, who sustains me.

Heartfelt thanks to all of you.